THE COLONY

D1490511

THE COLONY

A Rasper Novel Book One

KATHLEEN GROGER

Leaf & Thorn Press, LLC

The unauthorized reproduction or distribution of this copyrighted work is a crime punishable by law. No part of this book may be scanned, uploaded to or downloaded from file sharing sites, or distributed in any other way via the Internet or any other means, electronic or print, without the publisher's permission. Criminal copyright infringement, including infringement without monetary gain, is investigated by the FBI and is punishable by up to 5 years in federal prison and a fine of $250,000 (http://www.fbi.gov/ipr/).

This book is a work of fiction. The names, characters, places, and incidents are fictitious or have been used fictitiously, and are not to be construed as real in any way. Any resemblance to persons, living or dead, actual events, locales, or organizations is entirely coincidental.

Published by Leaf & Thorn Press, LLC
Edited by Donna Alward and Nancy Cassidy of www.redpencoach.com
Book cover designed by Deranged Doctor Design

All rights reserved. Copyright © 2016 by Kathleen Groger
First print publication: April 2016
Print ISBN: 978-1-945040-01-6
Digital ISBN: 978-1-945040-00-9

For my mom. Thank you for showing me how to be a butterfly and letting me soar. I wish you were still here to read my book.

ALSO BY KATHLEEN GROGER

Seam Stalker Series
The Shattered Seam, A Seam Stalker Novel Book One
Silencing The Seam, A Seam Stalker Novel Book Two

1

It'd been 118 days of suffering and suckage.

Today was just supposed to be a food-gathering day, but everything about it felt *wrong*. My nerves twitched and my skin seemed a size too small. I inched my way along the concrete side of the Walmart, my gun leading the way. When I reached the corner, I poked my head around.

All clear.

I tied a scarf over my mouth and nose, then darted into the abandoned store, trying to avoid the broken glass, but shards crunched under my boots, the noise echoing in the silence. The blue-vested grandmother type wasn't around to greet me. That all ended when the world went to hell.

Now I received a very different kind of welcome. Flies swarmed above my ponytail, dive-bombing my head in an endless stream. I swatted at the insects and clicked on a flashlight, checking for wild animals. The stench of rotting food seeped through my scarf and boiled in my stomach. I breathed through my mouth and worked my way to the first aid supplies. I stuffed the last box of bandages in my bag. If I tried really hard, I could still picture the way the store, and my life, used to be. I wanted to erase the mess they were now. Wanted things to go back to normal. Wanted to forget the *Great Discovery* was ever discovered.

The creepy sensation of someone—or something—watching me raised all the hairs on the back of my neck. I whipped around and checked out the aisle. Empty. There couldn't be Raspers in the store. I would've heard their erratic breathing.

I backed up and slammed into the shelving. Bottles of vitamins showered to the floor, adding to the vandalized chaos. The shadow of a small animal scampered across a shelf. Oh, God. Rodents. I ran to the clothing section to get the essentials. I glanced over my shoulder every few seconds as I stuffed socks and underwear into my backpack. I could wear other people's clothes, but using their socks and undies grossed me out.

A scratching sound carried over the buzzing of the flies and I ducked behind the closest shelf of shirts. More scratching.

Rats? Raccoons? Raspers?

I couldn't control the shudder that rippled down my body. Rats might be worse than finding a Rasper. Rats were fast and could run up my legs before I could shoot them. Raspers, at least, provided much bigger targets.

I had to stop freaking out.

I slipped my backpack off my shoulders, pulled out the pepper spray Dad had given me last year, and tucked it into my front pocket. At the time, I'd told him he was being paranoid. Now, I was glad for his over-protectiveness. I raised my first two fingers to my lips and blew a kiss to the air, wanting to yell, "Thanks, Dad," but settled for whispering it instead. I missed him—and Mom—so much it physically hurt when I thought about life *before*.

With my bag back in place, I continued to the canned food aisles. The vermin invasion made anything that wasn't in an airtight container off limits. I moved past an end display stocked with cereal and my flashlight illuminated at least five beady-eyed rats feasting from the boxes. Nausea swirled in my gut. The store's stench and the sight of the rats overwhelmed my stomach until it revolted. I moved, pulled away my scarf, and got sick. After wiping my mouth, I shuffled back a few steps, keeping the vile critters in my sights. A fat one waddled off the cereal stack and scuttled over. The rat's nose twitched back and forth, then it dove into the remains of my granola bar lunch. I covered the fleabag with pepper spray and it squealed at such a high pitch that my teeth rattled. So gross.

I gagged, then rewrapped the scarf. I had to eat, but I didn't know if I could handle the store a millisecond longer. The stench, the flies, the maggots. And oh, man, the rats. I heaved and chills hijacked my body. I needed to grab the basics and get the hell out.

I raced through the aisles and snagged bottled water, canned Spaghetti O's, beans, and tuna. The scratching intensified and I dumped my stash in a plastic bag. The image of hundreds of rats following me sent me sprinting out of the store.

Outside, I leaned against the wall, pulled the scarf off my face, and sucked in fresh air. There was no way I could do that again. The store had finally crossed the line between food source and garbage dump. I tried to calm my breathing.

I ducked into the alley between Dollar World and Vincent's Pizza.

Then I heard it. No. Not possible. It was still light out.

I tightened the straps on my backpack, set the bag of supplies on the ground next to a pile of fallen bricks, and flattened myself against the wall.

A scratchy, asthmatic-like breathing filled my eardrums. The sound came closer and closer. My breaths came faster and faster.

I ducked behind an overflowing nasty dumpster and waited.

Any time now. Any. Time.

I pulled out my Glock and set my grip. It couldn't end now, not after all I'd done to survive—the running, the hiding, the stealing...

The killing.

A guy wearing sunglasses and dressed in a brown deliveryman-style uniform turned the corner and entered my alley. I squinted, staring at his skin. It was tinged yellow. A Rasper. Crap. I glanced back, making sure the bastards weren't cutting off my escape.

He sniffed the air, then broke into a run straight toward me.

Shit. He moved fast. Faster than I'd seen them move before. I darted out from behind the dumpster.

Aimed.

Fired.

A burst of crimson blossomed across his arm. The brass casing blew back into my shoulder, the burn slicing through my shirt. My focus zeroed in on the Rasper's right hand. Instead of a fingernail, his index finger ended in a pearl-white stinger. And he had the finger-weapon pointed right at me.

I jumped out of the way and fired again.

A direct hit to his chest. The creature went down, landing on his face. My heart plummeted. Not only had I killed another one, but the other Raspers had to have heard the gunshots—and could probably hear the booming of my heart.

I made myself approach the body and kept the gun aimed at his head. I couldn't afford to have him spring back up like the first one I'd shot. With the toe of my boot, I rolled him over. Blood stained his filthy shirt, but his chest remained motionless. His broken sunglasses dangled over a goatee that reminded me of my dad's. Dad was the one who'd taught me how to shoot. If it wasn't for him, I'd be dead.

Pushing the memory away, I jogged to the end of the alley. Nothing moved. A popping sound echoed behind me. What the hell? I turned back.

The Rasper's jaw broke open with a crack, his lips ripped apart, and skin detached from his facial bones. All of his front teeth shot out of his mouth like darts. My mind shouted for me to run while I still had a chance, but my feet carried me back to the body.

A silver, bug-like creature the size of a golf ball crawled out of the dead Rasper's mouth. It scuttled down his chin on six long steel legs and slipped onto the ground, avoiding the still expanding pool of blood. Holy shit.

It took all my focus to keep from screaming.

I stumbled back, watching the thing, but it turned as if it heard me move. Its front legs rubbed together in a scissoring motion and the squealing noise of metal on metal filled the air.

This couldn't be real. Maybe I'd hit my head during one of

the recent aftershocks. Maybe I'd imagined the thing. Maybe it was a frickin' hallucination resulting from me not sleeping more than a few minutes at a time.

I closed my eyes for a second, hoping the creepy thing had disappeared. Nope. The damn bug still sawed its limbs together, the metallic song grating down my spine.

The creature shifted in my direction and I fired, my aim dead on. It flew into the air, exploded above my head, and shards of metal rained down. One sliced my right hand, and warm blood seeped across my skin.

I bolted and snagged the bag of supplies. At the end of the alley, I jumped a chasm in the road and ran until I reached the shopping center parking lot across the street. The buildings here were burnt-out shells in shades of black and gray, while the stores in the next lot over remained relatively intact. All were devoid of human life.

Carcasses of vehicles filled the ruined parking lot. The nose of a red sports car rested buried in a gaping hole in the asphalt, as if it had tried to hide from the surrounding decimation. I ducked behind a minivan with its side door open, then raised my head and peered through the windows.

Nothing in the lot.

My gaze fell on the empty car seat in the van and a shiver crawled up my back. I tried not to picture the angelic face of my two-year-old neighbor, who I used to babysit. What had happened to her?

I checked through the windows again, then sprinted toward the closest store. Matt's Sporting Goods had once been lit up in red neon, but now it read *Mat Spo Go* in broken, unlit letters. I cleared the pile of glass filling the doorway, dove behind the busted checkout counter, and landed on my stomach. My backpack crashed into my head, snagging my ponytail while the bag of food shot across the floor. Swallowing a groan, I shoved the backpack into place, scrambled to a crouching position, and retrieved the food.

Quiet. I needed to be quiet. Quiet and calm.

I checked out the window. Nothing yet. They would be coming

soon though. It didn't matter if the body was human or not, the Raspers always came to collect the dead.

Two deep breaths later, I looked at my hand. Blood blanketed the back and streams of red snaked down the inside of my arm. Crimson spots decorated my favorite tee, my Alberdine High Volleyball shirt with 'Val' stenciled on the back. I'd practiced forever to make the team, but never got to play a game. Now the shirt was ruined. Just like the world. Just like my life. Spectacular.

I grabbed a bottle of water from my backpack and rinsed away the blood. The words, which filled my arm from wrist to elbow, reappeared.

My Rules.

I'd written them in permanent marker to remind myself of the code for my survival:

Trust no one.
Never go out in the dark.
Always carry a weapon.

Minutes ticked away. I needed to get out of here and get back to the house. Back to safety. I pulled a bandage from my backpack, covered the gash, then bee-lined for the hunting section and swiped the last few boxes of 9mm bullets, wiping out the inventory. I shoved the bullets in my bag and surveyed the parking lot from the busted front window. Nothing moved. Time to go.

I slipped outside and made my way across the cracked, weed-covered pavement, stopping and hiding behind a grouping of dead cars. I raced to where I'd left the mountain bike my parents had given me four years ago for my twelfth birthday. It had only survived when the garage collapsed because I never put it away. I hadn't appreciated it then, but now the bike, my bag, and the Glock were all I had.

Everything else was gone.

As I tied the bag of supplies onto the handle bar, the bottom ripped out. Everything I'd swiped littered the ground. No time left. I had to leave it or risk them catching me. I slammed my foot onto the pedal and took off toward safety, all the while shooting glances at the sun sinking low in the horizon. If one Rasper had been out while it was light, others would be out when the sun set. They were like roaches. For every one I saw, dozens lurked in the darkness.

I had to make it. Had to. I pushed harder until my thigh muscles burned.

Within a few minutes, the trail opened up to the street. I white-knuckled the handlebars and eased onto the road. The openness of the street made me a target—exposed—with nowhere to hide, but it was the fastest way.

I maneuvered the bike closer to the woods to avoid a bigger-than-a-car hole in the asphalt. The earthquakes had almost destroyed this section of the street. The overgrown grass on the berm slapped my thighs and cars littered the broken road. The "Alberdine, MO Pop. 15,500" sign came into view. I swerved off the road, onto the gravel, and went around it. The 15,500 had been crossed out with a black marker and the number one written next to it. My once cute artwork now screamed, "Hey, come get me."

I should have just skipped searching for more food. If I had, I would be inside now. Hidden. Safe.

A tall evergreen tree marked the entrance to my shortcut. I turned the bike down the trail into the park where the playground swings drifted in the breeze, as if pushed by an invisible hand. The creaking of the unoiled chains sent goose bumps down my arms and the prickly sensation of someone watching me returned. I glanced around, but didn't spot anyone.

The sun sat too low. I needed to get inside and end the freaked-out feeling of being tracked like prey.

I pedaled faster. Harder.

A warm breeze tickled my face and dried the moisture clinging to my back. It was winter and it should be freezing, but after all the destruction, it seemed like the seasons had shifted. Today felt like a summer day instead of the middle of February.

The trail through the park ended and I turned down my worn path to the development. I stayed on the broken sidewalks until I reached a two-story brick house still decorated with plastic pumpkins, even though Halloween had passed months ago. The once-manicured lawn had grown uncontrolled, but a quick check confirmed the grass hadn't been disturbed.

I hopped off the bike and wiped the sweat from my face. The sun retreated and shadows crept across the ground toward the house.

I'd done it. I'd beaten the dark. I'd made it home. What I was calling home, anyway. I'd been living there for the last two months, but it wasn't mine, or my family's. I reached for the door handle, then stopped. The eerie feeling of being stalked pierced my skin. I drew the Glock and turned, ready to fire.

There wasn't anyone—or anything—there.

I opened the door, went in, and slammed the dead bolt to lock. I holstered the gun, leaned the bike against the olive-colored wall, and shoved a folding chair under the knob. Not that it would hold the door, but it made me feel better.

Pictures of the once happy—and alive—family covered the walls of the house. The photos never failed to remind me of my home. I wanted to go back there, but that wasn't possible.

Not after what had happened.

"Hide in the basement and don't come out until I get back..." I shook my head to clear away my dad's last words to me. Otherwise, the hurt would rip open the still-scabbing sore.

I walked into the granite and oak kitchen where I dropped my bag on the table, blew out a deep breath, and collapsed into a wooden chair. "Why does everything suck?"

Today should have been the same as every other day. Instead, it had turned into a scene from an old horror movie like the ones I used to stay awake to watch, even though my parents told me not to.

Images of the metallic bug crawling from the dead guy's mouth took over my thoughts. What was it? Did every Rasper have one inside them? Did the other two I'd shot have them and I missed it?

I needed a name for the nasty little things. Mom always said if I put a name to my fears, they would seem less scary. It worked when I was six, but not so much now. Still, I racked my brain for something, anything. Maybe just Bugs.

"Bugs." Not great, but it would work until I came up with something better.

I reached for my worn backpack. It used to hold my schoolbooks, but now it carried the essentials for survival. My index finger traced the faded red heart on the front. I pictured my mom drawing it, her blonde hair tucked into a messy ponytail and paint splattering her shirt. A tear pooled in the corner of my eye and slid down my cheek. I wished my parents were still here to hold me and tell me everything would be okay. My gaze fell on the calendar I'd drawn on the wall. I'd marked today with a heart. It wasn't just my birthday, but also the holiday my parents named me after, Valentine's Day. No birthday presents or roses for me though. Just killing a guy and a crazy creature.

Happy stinking birthday.

Exhaustion stabbed behind my eyes. I rested my elbows on the table and buried my face in my palms. I couldn't stop the graphic images looping through my mind. Bugs. Raspers. Dead bodies.

The media had called it the Great Discovery. Yeah, it was *great* all right. But I had no clue what the finding of a huge-ass cache of oil in the Gulf of Mexico had to do with what happened. The TV anchor had said man's greatest question had finally been answered. He'd promised to tell me the breaking news at five, but Mom had texted me—*be home soon*—from her art class and...and everything had gone dark. Then came the days of earthquakes, the sounds of people dying, no more electricity.

And then the Raspers invaded.

More like the Sucky Discovery.

I still didn't know what made some people turn into Raspers while others died. They weren't zombies or vampires—not that I believed either existed—and there was no way for me to get any answers.

Night descended, plunging the world into darkness. I lit a candle and cleaned up with baby wipes. God, how I wished I could take a shower and wash my hair. But the water had dried up, at least around here. I wasn't sure about everywhere else.

I dressed in my standard uniform—jeans, tee, gray hoodie,

gun belt, and hiking boots. I was ready. I had to move on. The Raspers were closing in. First thing in the morning, I would take off on my bike to somewhere new. Somewhere with fresh water, and Rasper-free.

I grabbed a soft, cotton blanket and wrapped it around my shoulders, then dropped onto the couch. I set my gun on the cushion and stared at the flat screen TV. It didn't work anymore. Nothing did.

My eyelids drooped. Maybe I could sleep, just for ten minutes. I stopped fighting and let exhaustion win the battle. Dreams of my parents, friends, school, and normal life swirled into a jumbled mosaic.

A crash echoed outside the house, jarring me from sleep. I leapt from the couch, my mind racing as my body went on full alert.

The next few seconds blurred together. I grabbed my gun. Blew out the candle. Slung my bag over my shoulder. Dashed to the living room wall and, keeping my back against it, forced myself to take deep breaths.

Fully awake, I crept along the wall toward the window. I slid the blinds aside with the muzzle of the gun and peered out, but the darkness made it impossible to see anything.

The Raspers had to be out there. Every other time I'd spotted them, they'd traveled in groups of two or three. The guy today had been an anomaly in more ways than one. The others had tracked me somehow. I shouldn't have stayed here, but it was too late now.

I eased my way up the wooden stairs, hugging the wall, making sure not to touch the cooking oil I'd poured down the middle. At the top, I went into the young boy's bedroom. His laughing face smiled at me from pictures all around the house. The construction truck mural that covered one wall of his room gave me an idea.

I crossed the carpet, placing the dump trucks and other vehicles the kid had owned all over the floor. If the Raspers made it this far, the truck obstacle course might trip them. At the very least, it would give me a warning they were close.

Another thud resonated outside. If the buzz of everyday life still existed, I probably wouldn't have heard it, but since silence consumed me, noises were easier to detect.

I opened the door to the full-sized stairs that led to the attic, and stopped. A wave of stale air choked me. Without giving in to the urge to cough, I closed the door and made my way up the stairs.

Winding my way through the maze of boxes and old furniture, I moved to the far corner by the full-sized window. I peeked out. Nothing. I doubted they'd left. Somehow, they knew I was here. I'd been an idiot to think I was safe.

A pounding filled the air like they were outside, banging on the first floor windows. I tensed, afraid they'd break into the house any second. I crouched against the wall, my spine aligned with the corner.

Sweat beaded along my skin. I yanked off my hoodie, tucked it in the bag, and removed an extra gun, setting it in front of my boots. My Glock weighed down my left hand.

Silence once again blanketed the night. I yearned to know what they were doing. Why hadn't they broken the glass and busted in? Maybe they had. Crap.

My knees ached so I shifted my weight to the right. I counted backward from sixty over and over. A few minutes of absolute quiet ticked by, then my patience detonated.

The Raspers wouldn't have left. Not if they knew I was here. What the hell were they doing?

The adrenaline started to fade and my eyelids grew heavy. I tapped the muzzle of the gun against my cheek. The metal reminded me what I had to do: survive.

Time seemed to stand still, but only a few more counts of sixty slipped by. I was fighting a losing battle with exhaustion when the crash of glass broke the stillness. Blood roared in my ears. What had they broken? A window? The storm door?

I checked my arsenal and readied myself.

Random images flew through my mind. My mother's face as she painted one of her pictures. My father's SWAT uniform when he shoved his service Glock in my hands, then screamed at me to get in the basement. The ground shaking. Flashes of light accompanied by terror-filled screams. Days and days and days of darkness.

There was no way I was ever hiding in a basement again. No more playing the victim.

A thud brought me back to the current problem: Raspers coming for me.

Seconds turned to minutes. I waited, the gun shaking in my hand. I rested my arm on my knee to steady my aim and patted the knife strapped to my calf.

A crash and a muffled groan told me the toy obstacle course had tripped them. Shit, that meant they'd made it past the oil on the stairs. The moan of the attic door grabbed my heart and catapulted it into my throat.

I moved to one knee, gun ready to fire.

Two more steps then they would be visible. A sliver of light from the moon cut through the window, illuminating the target area. I wanted to scream and run, but it would just attract more Raspers. My bladder threatened to release.

A shadow reached the top of the stairs.

I brought up my right hand and steadied my left.

A figure stepped onto the attic floor.

I bit my lip, then squeezed the trigger.

2

My ears rang from the shot, and a pain-laced shout filled the room.

"Son of a..."

I heard the words, but they didn't process. The Rasper should be dead. How had I missed? A male figure took a few steps forward. I raised my gun.

"For God's sake, don't shoot me again." The guy clutched his left hand to his upper right arm. "I'm not one of them." He continued his slow shuffle.

"Stop." I pressed my back tight to the wall and aimed the gun at his chest. "You'd better stop if you don't want to die. I won't miss a second time."

"Please listen to me. Listen to my breathing. It's different from them. We don't wheeze like they do. I know you've heard them."

I did know the wretched sound, but he gasped in pain and it was difficult to be sure.

He took another step closer. My weapon wavered. Everything I knew told me to shoot again and not take the risk. Raspers were tricky. But damn it, he was right. He didn't sound like the bastards. Their breathing resembled a death rattle, like any minute they would take their last gasp. Not that I'd ever been lucky enough to have one of them stop because they ran out of air.

"Who are you?" I needed to see the color of his skin to be sure. I reached into my bag and pulled out the flashlight, but I kept the gun trained on him. Deep down I wanted him to be a normal guy. The last human I'd seen was my dad and that had been four months ago.

The guy sighed. "Adam. My name is Adam Solomon. Yours?" His words were forced and clipped.

I shined the light on his face and he shielded his eyes with his hand. He looked to be about my age. And his skin didn't look yellow. He seemed normal. Well, except for the blood oozing down his arm. Had I just shot—*grazed hopefully*—another human? No. I couldn't have. Wouldn't have.

"I'm Val." That sounded so stupid. *I know I just shot you, but let me introduce myself as you bleed out.*

"Please, Val. Help me." He slumped to the floor, knocking into cardboard boxes.

I lowered the gun, but tightened my grip on the flashlight. Before all this happened, I trusted everyone and would be the first to help someone with a problem. That's how my parents raised me, but the last few months changed me. Toughened me. Hardened me. I've done things I never thought I'd ever do. Rule Number One—Trust No One. It was the key to my survival. Since the Raspers seemed to be developing, this could still be a trap. If I were smart, I would finish him off now. It was the safest option. It could be the difference between living and dying.

But could I kill a wounded guy? I could if it was me or him, but I didn't know if I could do it in cold blood.

"Uh, hello, don't worry about me. I'm doing great." The sarcasm didn't cover the pain in his voice.

Sarcasm. Raspers didn't use sarcasm. Their speech pattern came across more staccato, almost formal, like English wasn't their native language. With every passing second, I doubted he was my enemy more and more.

And I'd shot him. Great.

"Answer this first. Why are you here? What do you want?" I pointed the gun at him just in case he was playing me.

"I. Followed. You."

I *hadn't* imagined someone watching me earlier. A small comfort, but I should have seen him. "Why?"

"Because...you're not one of them."

My heart skipped a beat. My rational side told me to hug him. But the side that had become less and less rational wanted me to run. Now.

Adam sat bathed in a shaft of light from the window, his shirt stained crimson. I lowered the gun again and shoved it into the holster. Before I could stop it, a crazy sounding giggle escaped from my lips. I was probably stupid for putting my gun away.

"Can you stand?"

He nodded. "I think so." His voice seemed forced and blood soaked his arm.

I pulled a T-shirt out of my bag. "Let go of your arm for a second."

He stared at me and then lifted his hand, allowing me time to press the shirt onto his wound. It looked nasty in the faint light. He needed a doctor and I was anything but.

"Hold it there."

I helped him stand and then directed him down the stairs to the kitchen, where I pulled out a chair. "Here, sit." I lit three candles to provide enough light, but not so much as to draw the attention of a Rasper, and double-checked his skin. No yellow tinge. "How did you get in?"

"Back door. I broke the little window, unlocked the door, and tripped over the wire." He wobbled to the right and I hoped he wouldn't fall off the chair.

"Why did you make so much noise breaking in? You could've just knocked."

"The damn things were after me."

"They're out there? Right now?" I ran to the door, relocked it, and stared, but couldn't make out anything in the darkness. I brushed my palm across the butt of the Glock.

"I think I lost them. I knew you were here. I thought I'd be safe, not get shot."

"Your own damn fault. You shouldn't have broken in."

He glared at me like he wanted to scream about how much it hurt, but was too much of a dude to do it.

I took out my first aid supplies. The bullet had grazed the top of his arm above his bicep, destroying the sleeve of his black T-shirt in the process. Blood oozed from the wound and stained his skin. My first thought was to stitch it up, but there wasn't anything to pull together, and besides, I didn't have a sewing kit.

His gaze shifted from the calendar on the wall to the bottle of saline in my hand. "What are you going to do with that?" Droplets of sweat ran down his face.

"I'm going to clean your wound so you don't get an infection. I'm sure this will sting like hell, though."

"What?" He shielded his bloody upper arm with the palm of his hand.

"It's got to be cleaned before I bandage it."

Adam's eyes widened. In the flickering light, I caught how green they were and how his dark brown hair grazed the top of his shoulders. Despite his pasty skin—thanks to my bullet wound—he was more attractive than I'd first thought.

I set the saline down and removed gauze from my kit. He tracked my movements as I took out a pair of stainless steel scissors. "Do you have another shirt?"

"Why?"

"Because I'm going to cut this one off you." I opened and closed the scissors. I could do this. Or so I hoped.

"Yeah, okay." He said the words, but the blank look on his face told me otherwise.

Why didn't he have any supplies?

I stepped closer to him. So close, only inches separated our bodies. He could have a knife. He still might want to hurt me. I brought the scissors to his faded cotton T-shirt and my hand trembled. I was too close. I backed up, thrust my hand behind my back, and shook my fingers a few times, but I couldn't get the nervousness to release its grip on my hand.

"What's wrong?" His breathing was even shallower than minutes ago.

"Nothing." He was the first human I'd seen in forever, but

I couldn't trust him and I was more freaked out than I'd ever been. I wasn't telling him that.

I stepped forward, slipped the scissors into the fabric, and sliced it apart. The material fell away, revealing a super toned chest. Adam had definitely hit the gym *before*. God. He needed a doctor and I was checking out his muscles. What was wrong with me? Licking my lips, I stepped back from him again, grabbed the saline, and pulled the blood-soaked shirt away from his arm with a sickening rip. Yikes.

My rules flashed repeatedly in my brain. Careful to keep a small distance so my legs didn't touch his, I stepped closer and tipped the bottle toward his wound.

"Okay, well, here we go." I could do this. I chewed on my lower lip and poured the saline onto his bloody skin.

Adam grimaced and grabbed the side of the chair. His face paled to the chalky whiteness of a corpse.

I blew a wayward strand of hair out of my face and kept pouring. He looked on the verge of passing out. Leaning closer, I tried to see if I had cleaned it enough. More blood seeped out of the angry bullet track and onto my hand.

"Hang on. I almost have it cleaned." At least I hoped I did. A little more, then I dabbed the wound with gauze until the bleeding stopped. Heat flared from his skin. It was hot. Too hot. He couldn't have an infection yet. Could he?

Adam's eyes glazed over. He was going to pass out. I lightly slapped his cheek.

His head lolled to the side, but he straightened. "Damn, that hurt."

After setting the saline back down on the table, I held up a tube of ointment. "This might burn like a bitch."

I spread the cream on his jagged wound, making him wince and close his eyes. I bandaged him with gauze and wrapped surgical tape around his arm. When I was done, I eyed my handiwork. Not bad for my first time playing doctor.

"All right. I'm done. Hopefully, you won't get an infection." I took a step toward my stash of bottled water to rinse his blood from my hands.

Adam looked at the bandage.

"If you want, you can sleep on the couch in there. It will be daylight in about an hour. Once you rest, you can head out."

"Val?"

I stopped and faced him. Our eyes met. Pain—and something else—flashed across his face.

"What?"

"Thanks."

"For what? Shooting you?" Maybe being alone had made him a little crazy too.

He blinked back at me. Had he gone into shock? What had Mr. Cheeves said in health class about the signs of shock? Clammy hands? I couldn't remember.

He stood and teetered as if he was trying to walk a tightrope. I stepped forward, but he held up his hand. "What I meant to say was, thanks for not killing me." He stared at my arm.

I stuck my hand over my stomach. "Are you feeling okay?"

He tilted his head to read my rules. "Why did you write that on your arm?"

I rubbed my hand across my arm. A smear of his blood marred the words. I cringed. I *had* to wash my hands. "Why?"

He shrugged. When he winced, I could tell pain had shot through his arm. "You have to trust some people."

"No, I don't. Until you stalked me, I didn't even know anyone normal still existed. I mean I hoped, but..." I clamped my mouth shut and glanced away from his talk-to-me-I'm-a-good-listener face. I grabbed a package of wipes and scrubbed until my skin was raw, but clean.

"You're not alone. There are more of us who have survived." He took a step closer.

"Then what are you doing here? Why aren't you with them? Where are they?" I fired the questions at him, but my brain lobbed conflicting messages when he didn't answer right away.

It made me dizzy to process what he said. Other people lived. Normal people. Not just Raspers. No.

I'd been alone for months. Yet, he stood in front of me telling me everything I believed true was false. Maybe it was all a trick. Trust no one. The rule was Number One for a reason. Maybe I'd seen too many scary shows—that is, when television had worked—but I didn't take chances. Not anymore. A part of me wanted to believe him. Part of me wanted to fall into his strong arms and cry. I wanted to trust him, but my brain resisted the idea. Had I really and truly thought I was the only one? Maybe my mom might still be alive...

"I'm telling you. Others survived."

I tugged at my hair. "How do you know?"

"Because I've seen them."

"Where? Where have you seen others?" I slid down onto the floor, my back leaning against the kitchen island.

He licked his lips and locked his gaze with mine. "Have you really not seen anyone else since that day?"

I pulled my knees into my chest and wrapped my arms around them. Not the best offensive position, but I could reach my gun quick enough. "No. No one human."

"Others are out there."

"Well, if you've seen them, why are you on your own?" I unclasped my hands.

Any remaining color drained from his face. He eased himself back into the chair and stared at the floor. "They got them."

"The Raspers?"

"The what?"

I stood and ran a hand across my jeans brushing them off. "It's what I call the yellow-skinned shallow breathers." I leaned my elbows on the island counter.

He nodded. "It fits."

Great, he liked the name. But I needed answers from him. "What happened?" I took a step toward him, and then froze. I chanted Rule Number One in my head. He had followed me. Stalked me. Broke into my hideout. I couldn't trust him.

He stood, looking rather dazed. "You know, I think getting shot is catching up to me."

His words were tense. I did feel bad for causing him pain, but *come on*, he had to know something. Why wasn't he answering my questions? Was he lying? I entertained the idea of holding my gun to his head and demand he tell me what was going on, but it'd be a bluff. I wouldn't be able to kill him without a reason. I knew that for sure.

"I'm going to grab that couch and rest for a few minutes." He walked out of the kitchen.

"Okay then, be that way," I whispered to myself. I didn't need him or his full-of-shit lies. Lies of fictitious survivors. Yeah, he'd made it, but really how many others had?

I used to be safe during the day. Today, I'd lost my last form of protection. The Raspers wouldn't stop. And now Adam had found my hideout. Who—or what—else would?

I gathered all the bloody gauze pads and tossed them in a plastic bag, then put it by the door. With cardboard and duct tape, I patched the broken window. Not great, but it didn't matter. I was leaving.

I stowed my first aid supplies, then double-checked my bag, making sure I had everything. I'd used one of my shirts on Adam's wound. It wouldn't hurt to get a few more. While clothes were easy to come by, I wanted ones that fit. I took out my flashlight, slung the bag on my shoulder, and walked into the living room. He slept on the couch, his chest rising and falling with soft snores. I shook my head. I had a hard enough time sleeping alone. There was no way I'd sleep if I was with a total stranger.

I went past him, crept up the stairs, and entered the master bedroom, my light casting a shadowy path. The woman who lived here once upon a time had worn my new starved-for-real-food size. The plush, carpeted floor cushioned my steps when I entered the closet. After searching the woman's vast collection, more T-shirts, jeans, and an extra hoodie went into my already-stuffed bag.

I shifted to the guy's side of the closet, shoved aside the numerous suits, and found his small stash of comfortable clothes. I swiped a couple of T-shirts and sweatshirts, piling them into my arms, then lifted the hefty bag onto my back as the first ray of light peeked in the window.

Adam was still asleep when I got downstairs and I stood next to the couch, staring at him. A lock of hair had fallen onto his stubbly jaw. I deposited the clothes at his feet and for the briefest of seconds, contemplated waking him. It would be nice to have some company on my trek to—*wherever*. I had no idea where I was going or if I'd ever see another human again. No, keep the status quo. I shook my head and walked into the kitchen.

I inhaled a granola bar and slugged down a bottle of water for breakfast. It was time, but I had to do one thing first.

My Rules.

I retraced the words, capped the marker, and slid it back in my bag. I ran my finger over Number One. Trust no one.

The conversation with Adam replayed through my mind. Why hadn't he told me what happened to the people he was with? What did he want from me? And why didn't he have any supplies? Questions about him swirled around my brain with the force of a hurricane.

I closed my eyes, released a long breath, then moved to the door and unhooked the trip wire. My legs ached to start running and leave him behind, to continue this existence on my own.

Screw him.

I slipped on my sunglasses. Walked outside. Didn't look back.

3

Well, crap. In my show of bravery—or stupidity—I'd left the bike in the house. I scuffed my boot across the ground, grinding pebbles to dust. If I went back, Adam might wake up. Damn it. I was supposed to be planning prom with my best friend, Sofie, and worrying about exams, not creatures that wanted me dead. Sofie had said Evan was going to ask me to the dance *that* weekend, but the damned Great Discovery had come first. Now they were both gone.

Visions of Mom, Dad, Sofie, and Evan flashed in my mind. I couldn't take it anymore. My life had gone to hell and there was no hope I'd get back what I'd lost.

I took off running, tears clouding my vision. Where to, I didn't know. Just away from here. It took two miles—maybe three—but the waterworks dried up and my insides unclenched. I reduced my pace to a fast walk and surveyed my surroundings.

A hazy mist of fog rolled over the Harden River that undulated to my left and right. An iron girder bridge that had survived the destruction spanned out beneath my feet. Bands of metal crisscrossed up the sides, and a mesh-like support flanked the edges of the paved part.

Wind spiraled through the girders and blew loose strands of my hair into my face. I inhaled the crisp, almost citrus scent of rain. Damn. Another storm. My throat spasmed in short fast hits. I couldn't hyperventilate. I just needed to breathe. Inhale. Exhale. It was only a storm.

Rainstorms were different than they were before. What had once been mild showers now erupted in explosive thunderstorms. I only had a few minutes before the storm consumed me. A few minutes to get off this massive lightning rod.

I broke into a run and reached the middle of the bridge when a new sound drowned out the storm. The rumble grew louder and louder. Vibrations zipped up my legs. Another earthquake?

My chest burned and my heart skipped a beat. I had to get off this bridge. I ran. Metal pounded under my feet. Faster. Faster. Lightning zapped. A tree cracked. Smoke curled around me. The storm was close. Too close.

The vibrating rumble turned into a metallic grinding noise. I stopped, my feet frozen to the ground. No. Not that noise... But it was the *same.*

The whistling wind ripped across my ears, whipping my ponytail around behind me. I tried to swallow, but my throat refused to work.

Bugs. Lots of them. I pulled out the Glock.

Rain pelted my face. Just what I needed. A killer combo. Thunderstorms and Bugs.

Where were they? I looked around, but nothing was behind me, so I closed my eyes and focused on the hellacious noise.

They were under the bridge. My feet felt heavy, as if they were stuck in hardening cement, and every step was a chore. I walked to the side of the bridge and looked down.

Hundreds. No, thousands of the creepy Bugs crawled from the river. Some swarmed the white rocks and scuttled up the grass. Others stood still and rubbed their legs together. Fog spun cryptically around them.

Did they know I was here? I took a step back from the edge.

Thunder cracked. Marble-sized pellets of water pummeled my face. Then another noise added to the chaos. This one sounded mechanical. Almost like an engine.

I spun around. I couldn't see what it was through the frickin' rain. My stomach burned as if a swarm of hornets were fighting their way out. I swiped the water from my face and ran as fast as I could. But it didn't seem fast enough. The machine noise gained on me from behind and the Bugs crawled up both sides of the bridge's girders. They were so close.

I aimed my gun and started shooting. For every Bug I hit, three more took its place. They dropped from the girders and landed on the pavement. My gun clicked empty. I pulled another clip from my bag and slammed it home.

I stumbled back. Bugs swarmed before me, the machine noise roared behind me, and thunder boomed above me.

Trapped. On a damn bridge. This was not how I wanted it to end.

"Val! Val! Val!" It took me a second to realize someone was yelling.

Time shifted into slow motion. I spun around. A dirt bike zoomed out of the gray fog and squealed to a stop.

"Get on."

I clutched Adam's outstretched arm and swung myself onto the bike behind him. He gunned the engine and directed the bike right at the Bugs. "What are you doing?"

He didn't answer.

Bugs filled the road. I aimed the Glock and shot off another round while we tore through them. The bike's back tire kicked out and we leaned to the right. Adam jerked to the left and kept the bike vertical. I held on to him with one hand and turned back.

The horde of Bugs kept coming, filling the road behind us like a tiny mutant army. I kept shooting. Adam kept driving.

The Glock clicked empty and I couldn't see any more. I stopped watching behind us and buried my face in Adam's back. Water dripped into my eyes, my mouth, my clothes, while heat radiated from Adam. His warmth seeped into my chilled core.

Adam cut off the paved road and drove through overgrown fields, the grass slapping at the tires of the bike. He wove a crazy path in what I could only guess was a ploy to lose the Bugs.

I lost track of how long we drove. Adam slowed the bike when we reached an old gas station, so old that the pumps had been removed way before the Great Discovery. But the old sign proclaiming the place as *Joe's* stood in all its faded blue-and-red glory.

Adam cut the engine and I hopped off. Spirals of pain shot through my butt and a shiver spread across my skin. Without Adam's body heat, the wind and rain slashed through my hair and clothes.

He climbed off the bike and before I knew what I was doing, I wrapped my arms around him. My cheeks burst into a swirl of heat. I'd almost died back there. There was no way I could have gotten away from all those Bugs if Adam hadn't showed up. If he hadn't saved me.

"Thanks." I mumbled the word and dropped my arms. I turned and sprinted to the door of Joe's once-gas-station-turned-body shop, praying it was unlocked. I pushed on the handle and it opened. Hallelujah. I held the door open and Adam walked the dirt bike inside.

His gaze met mine and my body went numb, but not from the cold. I waited for him to say something sarcastic. Instead, he spoke in a voice that made my legs wobbly. "Glad I found you when I did."

I nodded and swallowed the lump that had wedged itself in my throat. "Me too. Where did you get the bike?"

"Found it in a shed along the way."

I had to look away from him. Guilt and another feeling—one that warmed my insides—dug at my senses. I turned, shrugged off my backpack, and thanked my stars that I'd convinced Mom to buy me a semi-waterproof one. I set the bag on the grungy, blue-stained counter and looked around.

Besides the counter, the small area held two cracked plastic chairs. A waist-high paneled wall partitioned the space from the work bays where a green car hung suspended on the hoist. A scarred door led out back. Next to the door, a vending machine stood across from what must have passed as the worker's restroom. It didn't have a door. Nice.

"Well, it'll do until the rain lets up. Think they followed us?"

"With the way you were weaving, I hope not. Did you see how many there were?"

Adam shook his head. "Where did they come from?"

"They were crawling out of the river." I tried to keep my voice out of shrill-worthy decibels, but failed.

Full body shakes hijacked my muscles. I walked back to the counter, and with water-withered fingers, removed a small towel from my bag. After I wiped my face, I offered it to Adam. "Here. I need to change before I freeze to death." I picked up the bag and went to the doorless bathroom. "Can you turn around?"

A strange look flickered across Adam's face, but he didn't say anything. He rubbed the damp towel across his forehead, then turned his back.

I ducked into the tight space. A stained toilet and a blackened sink took up most of the area. I hung my bag on one of the hooks on the wall. A work shirt and a leather jacket hung on the other hooks.

It took me a minute to get my boots off, but I changed as quickly as possible. Here I was changing in front of a virtual stranger when no guy had even seen me in my bra before. When I got to my underwear, I moved as if my life depended on it. Jeans, tee, hoodie. Check. "Okay, I'm ready."

I zipped up my hoodie and left the confines of the dingy bathroom. Adam turned; his wet clothes clung to him like a second skin. The faint light streaming in through the garage windows highlighted his broad shoulders.

I had to remind myself to breathe. "You didn't bring the other shirts I gave you? You'll freeze if you don't change."

"No. I kind of forgot them in my hurry to make sure you didn't ditch me."

"About that—"

"Don't worry about it." He touched his bandage. "I could use another bandage though. This one's soaked through."

I nodded and pulled out my first aid kit. "Take your shirt off."

"You're not going to cut it off this time?"

When our eyes met, my heartbeat thundered in my ears. "No. But there's a work shirt in there." I hooked my finger to the bathroom.

I averted my gaze to the window while he removed his shirt. Rivulets of rain ran down the glass and I tracked the water until a crack of thunder made me jump.

I turned back to Adam. Shirtless Adam.

I closed my gaping mouth and focused. I pulled off his wet bandage. His skin radiated heat, but the wound didn't look infected. In fact, it looked like it had healed more than it should have. Maybe the original wound hadn't been that bad. No. I didn't buy it. I had seen it. Cleaned it. Bandaged it.

I shifted my focus to the dull-but-once-sparkling, emerald-colored car. It was the same shade as Adam's eyes. That line of thought wasn't helping to clear my mind. "You're hot."

Adam winked and grinned. "Thanks for noticing."

Heat flared across my face and neck. Had I really said that? Dumb. "I meant, do you have a fever?"

"I don't think so."

Moving much slower than I wanted to, I put on a new bandage. A loud clap of thunder shook the building. I jumped and almost landed in his arms.

"Are you okay?"

"Yeah. Fine." I wasn't. I didn't like thunderstorms. Hadn't since I'd been stuck alone in the basement for three weeks.

"If you say so." He went into the small restroom and came out buttoning the faded blue shirt with the name *Dale* embroidered on the pocket. He had the leather jacket draped over his shoulder.

I tried not to stare at how Dale's shirt defined Adam's shoulders.

Adam opened the back door. A chain link fence surrounded a dozen rusty vehicles. "After it stops raining, we need to check out these cars."

The rain blew sideways in the door and he slammed it shut.

"Too bad we can't get this one down." I ran my fingers across the lever buttons.

"Since we can't bring it down, maybe we can go up to it."

"How? There's no ladder."

"Come here. I'll lift you up."

What? "No. No way."

He bent down, grabbed me by my thighs, and lifted me up. And I forgot all about the Raspers and the Bugs. Holy crap, my butt was in front of his face. I knew I was blushing, but thankfully he couldn't see it. He shifted me so I sat on his shoulders, his head in front of my... Oh. My. God.

"See if the door's unlocked."

I tugged on the driver's door handle and it clicked open.

"Anything?"

The car was immaculate. Not even a speck of trash. "No. I'm going to pop the trunk." I flicked the lever and truck unlatched with a whoosh.

Adam tightened his grip on my legs and walked to the back of the car.

I so needed to get down off his shoulders. I held onto the edge and looked in. A flashlight, rope, and a backpack. I took it all.

"Let me down." I tapped his head.

"What did you get?" He bent down and I crawled off, tugging at my jeans.

"A flashlight, bag, and rope. Here, take the light. I have a couple."

"Can you hold it for me? I don't have anywhere to put it." He held his hands out, palms up.

"Take the bag too." I gave him the blue backpack.

He unzipped it and dumped the contents. Sheets of paper fluttered to the floor. "Thanks."

"Are you even armed?"

"No."

And I had shot him. He had saved my life. Maybe he deserved a chance. An out-of-body-like feeling overcame me. I grabbed my bag, shoved the rope inside, pulled out one of my extra guns, and held it out to him, grip first.

"Thanks." He took it and tucked it into the back of his jeans.

"Make sure you don't blow your ass off. I'm so not bandaging that."

"Good to know." His face lit up.

I was such a dork. Why had I said something so incredibly stupid?

"Stand back. I'm going to see if I can break into the vending machine." Adam hit the plexiglass with a hammer-type tool he'd found. It took him a few swings, but he cracked it open. "Here." He tossed me a bag of peanuts.

I tore it open and inhaled them.

We polished off the chips and candy bars. I stuffed all the crackers in my bag, then pulled out two bottles of water and handed one to Adam. He chugged it down in one gulp, staring at me the entire time. I broke the connection.

Silence surrounded us. I stole another glance out the window.

Adam tossed the water bottle back and forth between his hands as if it was a football. "Where are we going?"

I crushed my bottle. "Where?" I was so tired. My temples throbbed and I rubbed them to ease the pain. "Away from here."

"Obviously, but what's your plan? I mean, when you left me this morning, where were you going? The next town or someplace distant, like New York?" He slipped on the leather jacket.

"Why does it matter? There isn't anything anywhere." I threw the crumpled bottle at the green car.

"How do you know?" He raised the tone of his voice. "I told you. We're not the only survivors. There are others like us out there. We need to try to find them." He paced back and forth, gesturing with his hands. "Maybe then we can get answers to why so many people died, why the others want to kill us, and what the hell those metal things are that are chasing us."

With the amount of waving he'd just displayed—not to mention lifting me up—his arm was healing faster than I expected. And he was determined to believe others survived.

"Where are they then?" I got in his face. "Why haven't I seen anyone?" I all but spit the words at him. Anger boiled in my veins. I couldn't explain why I was so mad.

He stared at me, his green eyes intense. In a calm, flat voice he said, "You've seen me."

I backed off, walked to the wall, and slid down until I sat on the cold concrete floor. Rain pounded on the windows, matching the rhythm of my heartbeat. I tucked a strand of hair behind my ear. "I'm sorry. I've been on my own for so long. How do you know for sure? I mean *really know* there are others?"

Adam grabbed a nearby bucket, flipped it over, and sat on it. "The government was sending people to safe havens."

I sprang to my feet. "What—where—how do you know?"

He stared at the floor. "Because I was supposed to be going to one. But that was before..."

He raised his head. His eyes seemed too shiny. But after I blinked, his eyes were clear.

I walked the few steps separating us and touched his shoulder. Heat radiated through my palm. I knelt next to him. "What?"

Silence hung in the air until he finally spoke. "My dad worked for Pearan Chemicals. Right after they found the oil, he told my mom and me to pack a bag with food and supplies. He put us on the safety vehicle heading north from Houston. I think the final destination was a safe house up north, but we only made it to just south of Tulsa." He paused and stared out the window.

The silence dragged on and I wanted to fill it, but I refused to be the one to break it. Yet the look on his face tugged at my heart. He continued to gaze outside. What was he seeing in his mind? I couldn't keep quiet any longer. "What happened?" It came out as a whisper.

Adam ran his hands through his hair, and it left his waves wilder. Untamed. "We ran out of gas. When the vehicle stopped, everyone got off. The area we were in already looked like a ghost town. Some buildings were destroyed. Empty cars sat in the streets. I walked away from the group to see if any of the buildings had food, while everyone else stood around talking trying to come up with a plan when a... Rasper..." He glanced at me. "That's what you call them, right?"

I nodded. Maybe trapped alone in a basement hadn't been so bad.

"A Rasper came up to them and everyone thought it was cool because he was dressed like a cop. He seemed normal, seemed to be there to help. Seconds later, more Raspers surrounded the group. Everyone screamed and dropped to the ground in what looked like seizures. Mom yelled at me to run..."

He closed his eyes and clenched his fists. "She collapsed to the ground, legs twitching. I tried to help her..." He squared his shoulders and jumped up. "I don't know what the Raspers are, but I want them dead. They killed my mom. Most likely my dad, too."

His story paralleled mine in a number of ways, and I had acted like a nasty witch. Visions of my dad slapping the Glock in my palm played on a continuous loop in my head. I blinked back tears.

"Where were you going before you found me?" I couldn't meet his eyes.

"My dad said if anything happened to the first safe haven, I should go to Pennsylvania. He said there's an underground bunker there. Site R. Ever heard of it?"

"No, I don't think so. Is it like Area 51?"

"No. No aliens. It's supposed to be a shelter or something. Dad said the government would move there in an emergency. It might be a safe place for us." He ran his hands across his face and through his hair.

"You think a safe place exists some—"

"Ssh." Adam raced to the garage door, pulled out the gun, swung his left hand up faster than a rocket, and took aim at the front of the building.

Stunned for a split second by his speed, I regained my focus and yanked out my Glock, following his aim. "What is it?"

"We're not alone."

4

Adam crouched below the garage door windows. I crawled forward and flanked the other side. I couldn't hear anything but the rain pellets dancing on the roof.

I counted the minutes off in my head. The waiting dragged on and on. After three more counts of sixty, I couldn't stand it anymore.

"What is it? I don't hear anything." I tried to speak in a hushed whisper, but it sounded more like I was using a bullhorn.

Adam gave me a will-you-keep-it-down look, then whispered, "You don't hear it?"

"No. What?"

"Metal scraping the asphalt."

Bugs. They had caught up with us. Probably had us surrounded. The garage floor seemed to disappear. I swore I spiraled down ten feet, but my body remained rooted in place. I touched the cool metal of the door to center myself. I wasn't going to die hiding from the enemy. No more hiding.

"I need to see what's out there. We need to know how many we're up against." I counted to three, then stood, squishing myself into the corner. I glanced out the windows. Didn't see any Bugs. I rose onto my tiptoes to check the ground.

"Well?" Adam's voice held a note of anxiety.

"Nothing. Do you still hear—"

A clanking of metal stopped me cold. But it didn't sound like the Bugs rubbing their legs together. It was different.

"I hear it." I leaned forward until my forehead pressed against the damp glass. Black fur slammed against the other side. My heartbeat shot to warp speed and I screamed, then fell back on my ass.

Cracks splintered across the glass, like ice breaking.

"What the hell was that?" Adam aimed the gun at the window. "Are you all right?"

"Yeah." I scrambled to my feet.

Then the barking started. Dogs. It was just dogs.

"How many are there?"

I went back to the corner of the cracked window. "There's a pack of at least ten. A Pit Bull, maybe a Rottweiler, a couple black ones. They might be Labs. I don't know. Nothing that looks cute and cuddly."

I stared out the window. "They must smell us." The dogs weaved back and forth in front of the windows, their bones protruding under their tight, wet fur.

"They look hungry."

"Uh huh. The Pit Bull must have broken free. There's part of a chain attached to his collar."

As if he knew we were talking about him, the dog cocked his head to the side and bared his teeth. The fur on his back rose as he ran, and slammed into the door. The chain clanged against the pavement. The other dogs barked in a hideous chorus.

"They'll draw Raspers to us. We have to get out of here or shut them up." I tried to keep my voice even, but it sounded little-girlish.

"We could shoot them." He said it more calmly than I expected.

My chest burned. I loved dogs. And even though these were starving savages, they had once been someone's pet. Like Barney, my beagle. I missed running my hands over his silky, floppy ears. It was my fault he was gone. I hadn't held him tight enough when the earthquakes started...

We backed away from the windows.

"What about the back door?"

"Let's go." Adam grabbed the bike and pushed it while I opened the door. The rain had reduced to a foggy mist.

"There's an eight-foot high chain link fence out here. We won't be able to get the bike over it."

One of the black dogs slammed into the cracked front window.

"There has to be a gate to get the cars in and out."

"I doubt any of those cars have moved in years. And even if we can find the gate and open it, the dogs will hear us." I had to yell over the barking.

Adam slammed the door shut, blocking some of the canine choir.

"Now what?" I glanced back at the wall of windows. The dogs still circled. The Pit Bull launched himself at the glass. His chain clanked off the window. More cracks zigzagged across the glass.

"We get gas for the bike. Then we get the hell out of here before we become dog food."

"Or the Raspers show up."

"That too."

"But we found the only gas station without gas. Think we can get some out of the cars out back?"

"No." Adam eyed the suspended car. "But I think we can get some from this one."

"How?" Had he lost his mind?

He picked up the bucket he'd used for a seat and set it on the floor below the car's gas tank. He snatched a crowbar, a hammer, and a screwdriver from the tools hanging on the wall. "Can you grab one of the plastic chairs?"

Another dog crashed against the glass.

I handed him the orange one. He stood on it and stretched his left hand up, gauging the distance.

"Stop! What are you doing?" I couldn't keep the squeak out of my voice. "Won't it explode?"

"No. There's no spark. At least I don't think it will. If we don't get some gas, we're going to die. Then again, if it explodes, we die. How would you rather go? Explosion, ripped apart by starving dogs, or Raspers?"

"God, none of them. I want to live."

"Well, this is the only way I see us having a chance."

I blew out a long breath. It was logical. Another dog pounded against the strained glass. "Okay. Hurry up."

Adam positioned the screwdriver into the car's metal. "Here goes nothing."

Then he hit it. Again, and again, and again.

He pulled out the screwdriver and inserted the crowbar, then yanked down. A waterfall of gas whooshed into the bucket, but it didn't mask the constant dog howl.

"You did it." Guess it hadn't been such a crazy plan after all.

He climbed off the chair, searched the tool counter, and came back brandishing a black plastic funnel. He glanced at the dog pawing the glass. "We've got to go. Can you roll the bike over?"

Adam had me hold the funnel in the bike's gas tank while he poured the gas. It wasn't a ton, but it was better than nothing. I tossed the funnel into the empty bucket.

"Let's grab the rest of the snacks from the vending machine. We can distract the dogs with the Twinkies."

I loaded my arms with junk food.

One of the black dogs slammed into the shattered glass. A small hole opened.

"They're breaking it." I shoved a bag of popcorn out the hole. The dogs jumped on it. Growls replaced the barking.

Adam straddled the bike. "Hurry. We'll toss the food and get the hell out of here."

"What if that doesn't work?"

"Then it's back to the original plan. We shoot them."

Ah, hell. I hoped it worked. My heart seized thinking about committing dog murder. "All right. Let's do this." I cracked the front door open and launched some of the food at the dogs. They tore at it in a frenzy of fur and fangs.

"Now!"

Adam gunned the throttle. I tossed the rest of the food at the dogs, ran, and climbed on behind him.

The Pit Bull raised its head and growled low enough to break my skin out in goose bumps.

"Go! Go! Go!"

***

We rode for what seemed like forever, but was probably only an hour or two. Plenty of time for me to figure out why death was snapping at my heels. I'd broken one of my rules and was now running on luck. Luck that might not hold.

I finally braved the wind, lifted my head from Adam's back, and checked out our surroundings. We cruised down a two-lane road flanked by woods and an occasional piece of farmland. A charred church loomed to our left and a cemetery filled the ground beside the church. Some of the gravestones remained upright, while others were broken or ripped from the ground.

Gravestones. The sight of the gray headstones pierced my heart. At least the people buried here had funerals. Mom and Dad had nothing. No service. No marker. No plaque. I was the only thing left to prove they had even existed.

My eyes burned. I should have searched for them. Should have left the basement. Should have... I inhaled and blinked back the moisture. I had begged Dad not to go, but his boss had ordered him to work. He'd promised to come back. I hadn't told them goodbye. That I loved them. Tears slid down my cheeks, despite my refusal to cry.

I tapped on Adam's back. He stopped the bike. "Are you okay?"

I knuckle-rubbed the corners of my eyes. "Yeah. Fine. I just need a break."

"Okay. We can check out the house up on the hill." He pointed to the structure next to the church.

We rode up the gravel driveway and stopped the bike next to a two-story red brick house. It probably had been the preacher's—pastor's—whoever's. Overgrown grass covered the lawn and a fallen tree blanketed the driveway, which split and curved toward both sides of the house.

Adam tilted his chin at a three-sided girder antennae towering over the trees. "What's that for?"

"No clue. Maybe a TV on steroids?" I hopped off the dirt bike and handed Adam his bag. The loss of his body heat made me shiver. I massaged my backside. "Man. My butt's numb."

A slow smile spread across Adam's lips. "Yeah. Happens to everyone. Helps if you rub it like you're doing."

A flush of heat shot through my body, all the way to my toes. At least he didn't offer to rub it for me. "I'm going to check the back."

"Okay. I'll keep guard here."

I pulled out my gun and walked around the house, pushing a jungle of weeds out of the way as I went. I almost needed a machete to hack my way through the growth.

The back yard grew wild and more overgrown than the front. Nothing tamped down. No person, large animal, or Rasper had been anywhere near this place. A pool, complete with green algae and dead leaves, filled a portion of the yard. Huge trees dominated the far side of the house, blocking my view of the other side of the driveway.

I fought my way back to the front where Adam waited. "Looks good."

He pushed the bike toward the steps.

Saying a prayer, I turned the handle. The door swung open without even a creak. No rancid smells hit me.

We went into the old, but well-kept house. Adam pushed the bike inside and parked it in the hallway. A staircase rose to the left and the foyer opened to a green-colored living room decorated with floral print couches. Crosses and other religious artifacts decorated the walls. Down the hallway, I got a glimpse of a yellow-countered 1970's-style kitchen. The stale air gave every indication the place was empty. I wanted to push aside the heavy cream-colored drapes and open the windows to let in fresh air, but the price of freshness wasn't something I could afford.

I turned back, one foot poised on the bottom step. "I'm going to check out the upstairs."

"Does this place seem creepy to you?" He looked around.

"Creepy, how?"

He shook his head. "I don't know. It just feels weird. Like someone's watching us."

"God, I hope it's not more dogs."

"We got lucky back there. I didn't want to have to shoot those dogs. No, this feels different, but I don't know. I'm not sure..."

Listening to my own instincts had saved my butt a couple of times these last four months. But could I listen to his too? "You think someone's in the house?"

He shrugged. "No. Forget it."

I stepped off the stairs. "No, I'm not going to forget it and you shouldn't either. More times than not, your gut's right. Follow me upstairs, but come up backward so you can see if someone sneaks up on us. Okay?"

"Yeah."

We worked our way up the stairs and checked the four rooms. No one anywhere, just empty bedrooms filled with antiques and more religious pieces. I didn't know what Adam was picking up on, but the house gave me vibes of abandonment. The fact that I was listening to *his* instincts violated Rule Number One. I pushed the thought aside. I'd tossed Rule Number One away when I jumped on the bike with him the first time.

"Still feel it?" I leaned over the banister. Empty.

"Not as much as when we first walked in. But yeah, it's still there. I'm sure it's nothing." Adam led the way back down. "Come on, you need to rest."

I did need to rest, but I couldn't doze off while he was all weirded out and there was still more house to search. "Can you check the basement? If it's clear, I'll take a short nap."

"Sure." He opened the door next to the kitchen and glanced back at me, his face still red from the wind. "You coming?"

"No, I'll stay here and be a look out." No way was I voluntarily going in a basement again.

Adam nodded and disappeared down the steps. I shoved my right hand under my left arm and tapped the gun into the air, counting the seconds.

He thundered up the stairs carrying a case of bottled water. "This is all I found."

"Nice find. We needed more."

We entered the kitchen and he dropped the water on the lace-covered table. "Where's that door go?" Adam walked to a wooden door tucked in a nook of the kitchen, opened it, and went inside. "Holy shit."

I had no idea if it was a good holy shit or a bad holy shit. His voice held a note of excitement, but, just in case, I tightened my grip on the Glock. "What?" I followed him into the room and my breath caught.

Adam waved his hand to the right. "Look at all this stuff."

The room was what my grandparents would have called a den. The walls were paneled in faux-wood. Electrical equipment, computers, and papers covered a dark desk. An old-time microphone sat in front of speakers and boxes with more dials than I could count.

"It's a ham radio." Adam lifted up the microphone.

"A radio made of ham? Really? You need to sleep more than me." I sat on a scarred coffee table in front of a black leather couch.

"No. My grandfather had one. You can talk to people all over the world with it."

I jumped up. "Can you work it?" If he was right and other people lived, maybe we could contact them.

"No. You need electricity. That tower outside is for this radio. I should have realized what it was."

Hope whizzed away like an untied helium balloon. I shouldn't even have considered the possibility of contacting anyone. I turned. A map of the United States filled with colored push pins hung on the wall. "Whoa. Look at this map. What is it? One of those put-a-pin-where-you've-been deals?"

"Maybe places the guy talked to on the radio?" Adam picked up a pile of papers from the desk and flipped through them.

The map shifted out of focus. It felt like needles poked my eyes from the inside. I blinked, but it didn't help. I was going to have to let him watch my back while I rested or I would collapse. "Do you care if I lie down for a minute?"

"No. Go ahead."

"Can you wake me in an hour?" I stifled a yawn and glanced at my watch.

"You can sleep longer if you need to. I'm going to go through these pages. Seems like some strange stuff."

"Thanks. An hour should be good. Besides, it's going to get dark soon."

Adam shuffled the papers. "We should probably stay here for the night. Who knows where the next house will be."

"Maybe. Wake me if you find anything important in there."

He nodded.

It was only an hour. One measly hour wouldn't get me killed. At least that's what I chanted in my head. I reclined on the leather couch and set my gun on the table. My eyelids closed and I gave in to my exhaustion. Sleep wrapped me in its embrace.

A bang vibrated through my head. Heart racing, I opened my eyes, grabbed my gun, and bolted up from the couch. Another bang like the closing of a cabinet door rang out. That had to be what woke me. I glanced around, searching for Adam.

I checked my watch. I'd slept two hours instead of just one. I peered into the kitchen. Adam stood at the counter fiddling with something I couldn't see. I lowered the gun and counted to ten, concentrating on slowing my heart rate.

"How was your nap?" He asked with his back to me.

I didn't think I'd made any noise, yet he'd sensed my presence. Maybe I was still groggy and had made a shuffling sound without realizing it. I tried to convince myself, but... I ran a hand across my forearm and the rules written there.

"You should have gotten me up." I holstered the Glock and walked into the kitchen. The flowery wallpaper and yellow counters reminded me of my grandma's house. "What are you doing?"

He turned and presented two plates and water in two mugs. "Making us a snack. I even poured the bottled water into a mug. Like civilized folk. Here."

The plate of crackers and peanut butter spoke to my stomach. "Thanks." I sat on one of the counter's vinyl bar stools and inhaled the food. I sipped the water from the black mug with a white Z logo.

Adam devoured his food even faster than I did. "Wish they had some soda. Do you know how long it's been since I had a Mountain Dew?"

"Coke was the best. You know, stores probably have some left on their shelves. The Walmart by my old place did."

"Yeah, but it'd be warm and that would be gross. Know what else I miss?"

"Red meat, fresh fruit, bread? I could list them alphabetically, but I'm guessing you have something particular in mind. Burgers?"

"Pizza."

I sighed. "Oh. My. God. Yes, pizza. Pepperoni pizza."

He rubbed his belly. "French fries."

"Stop. No more. I can't take it." I laughed, but was serious. I'd lived on granola bars, nuts, and dry cereal, and my stomach rumbled its annoyance at me not feeding it pizza or fries.

"Sorry. Hey, while you were sleeping, I went through the papers." He grabbed the stack from the counter.

"Anything useful?"

"Maybe. Most of these were printed from websites and blogs on the internet. This one mentions the Great Discovery."

I snatched the sheet he held.

Pearan Chemicals found deposits of mineral–rich oil in the Gulf. While analysis continues, energy proponents have stated the cache of oil is large enough to end the United States' dependence on foreign oil...

I scanned to the end of the article.

This is a game-changing find for the United States. Some have heralded it the Great Discovery.

"Didn't you say your dad worked for Pearan Chemicals?" I handed him the paper.

Oil. This whole disaster was set into motion because of oil. Dad had always said the war over oil would kill us, but he'd meant if the Middle East got nuclear weapons. Boom. World War III. Not eradication by earthquakes and mutant creatures. And I still didn't see the oil/Rasper connection.

"Yeah. He did." He ran a hand through his hair. "Hey, I used the map to figure out the route we need to take." He grabbed my hand and dragged me back into the room full of gadgets.

I didn't blame him for not wanting to talk about his dad. I know I didn't want to talk about mine.

"Look." He had pulled out all the map's pins from the Midwest to New Jersey.

"So, we're in Missouri." I dragged my index fingernail over the map. "South of St. Louis. We need to get to where?"

Adam tapped the map at the spot he had starred where Pennsylvania and Maryland touched. "Here. It looks like we'll have to go about 750 miles."

"We're gonna need to find a car with keys *and* gas."

"We have the bike."

"Yeah, but I won't have an ass left if we travel that far on that vibrating motor. Besides, if we hit rain, the bike will suck." Part of me wanted to keep riding the dirt bike. I hated to admit it, but I liked wrapping my arms around him—a sacrifice I was going to have to make until we found a car. Then I realized something. Something I should have thought about before. I bit my lip.

"What's wrong?"

"Shouldn't this house have a garage? God, what if Raspers are out there?" The crackers fought their way up my throat. I swallowed hard.

Adam dragged his hand across his chin, and then pulled out the gun I had given him. "It doesn't have an attached one, but we never investigated the other side of the trees, did we? How did we miss that?"

I wanted to believe it happened because I was so exhausted, but it had been simple carelessness. A foolish mistake. Total stupidity. I drew my gun and nodded to him.

We left the kitchen single file, past a laundry room, and found the side door. A breezeway led from the house to a brick garage no more than twenty feet away. Trees lined one side. I should have checked what the trees blocked.

We stopped on opposite sides of the garage door with our guns held up as if we were cops making a bust. Adrenaline spiked my heart rate. I raised one finger at a time. At three, I slammed the door open. Both of us pointed our guns into the darkness. An overpowering stench almost knocked me backward.

"Chlorine?" I coughed and pulled my shirt up over my nose.

Adam covered his face too. "I think so. We need a light."

"I'll get one." I coughed again. I kept my eyes on the open door as I retreated. When I reached the house I ran to the kitchen, grabbed the flashlight out of my bag, and made it back, gasping for breath. I flicked on the light and shined it into the garage. I stepped forward and scanned the space.

What the beam illuminated tore a scream from my throat.

5

The flashlight fell from my hand and rolled across the floor, spotlighting the object commanding center stage. The chlorine fumes burned my throat.

"Holy shit." Adam coughed and tucked the gun at his back.

My stomach dropped. The light illuminated the macabre display of a human skeleton next to a dark-colored, ancient-looking, sedan-style car. The bones were twisted in an unnatural pose, as if the person had died in severe pain. The jaw hung open, locked in a permanent scream. I covered my mouth to keep from throwing up.

An industrial-sized tool chest, which once stood as tall as me and twice my width, now lay on top of the leg bones, trapping the body in place.

Adam bent over, picked up the light, and jumped over a twelve-inch-wide crack in the garage floor behind the car. "The tool cabinet must have fallen during an earthquake and pinned the guy. Sucky way to go."

"He probably suffered for a long time." I swallowed, fighting another wave of nausea. He had probably screamed and screamed for help that never arrived.

Adam turned from the skeleton to me and cocked his head. "How long does it take for a body to decompose?"

"I don't know. Why?"

"Well, for some reason, I think I saw on TV that it's a couple of months or so."

"What difference does it make?" My voice cracked and I backed into the breezeway. I needed air before the chlorine choked me to death.

"Why didn't the Raspers take this body like they took all the others? Most people died either from natural disasters or Rasper attacks four months ago, and those that didn't turned into Raspers. And they took the dead bodies. Why not this one?"

"Maybe they didn't know it was here?"

"I doubt it. It's like they can smell a body from miles away. Maybe the chlorine somehow blocked the scent?"

"I don't know. Maybe." I walked to the doorframe and leaned against it, still holding my gun.

Adam pulled his shirt over his nose, crouched next to the bones, and shined the flashlight all around. "Check that out."

His light shined on white granules—most likely chlorine—spread across the garage floor and pushed up against the walls.

"I thought chlorine only came in the disc things."

Adam shrugged. "I think it comes in a powder, too."

"Weird. They should have put it in their green pool instead of the garage."

"What do you think it's for?"

"No idea."

Adam stood up and rubbed his arm. His white bandage reflected in the dim light like a beacon.

"See anything else?" I needed to get out of here. Something wasn't right. "Hurry up."

"He has his right fist clenched. I think he's holding something."

An invisible army of ants marched across my skin. I took a step forward.

"Think we should open the hand?"

"If you do it. I'm not touching dead-guy bones."

"I didn't picture you as the type to be freaked out by some bones."

"It's not just bones. Look, there's still some hair on the skull.

45

Creepy." I shuddered and crossed my arms, gun out front. Why hadn't the Raspers claimed this guy? What made him different?

"Fine. I'll do it. Hold the light."

I stepped over the gaping chasm in the floor and took the flashlight. "Faster. The smell's killing me." I coughed again, the chlorine burning my throat.

Adam pried open the fist. With a slight tug, the bones fell apart and clattered to the cement.

"Eeww."

"Didn't expect that." He pushed away the pieces and picked something from the mess.

My mouth went dry. Oh, God. He touched the pile. "What is it?" The words came out in a hoarse whisper.

Adam stood. "Looks like the type of map you get at a rest stop. Do you want it?" He pushed it at me with a Joker-worthy grin.

"No." I stepped back. My foot slipped on the edge of the gap. I almost fell, but caught myself. "Let's get out of here."

Once we got back inside the house, I stuck the flashlight into my back pocket.

"Can you pour a bottle of water on my hands? I gotta get this skeleton ash crap off." He put the map on the counter and held his hands out over the sink.

I got a bottle from the case and poured it into his palms.

He wiped them and then rubbed them almost raw on a towel hanging on the handle of the stove. "Okay, let's see what's so important that the guy held onto it when he died."

Adam blew bone dust off the paper and an icy shiver sliced through me. He unfolded it and blinked at the map.

"What?"

He didn't answer.

"Well?" I resisted the urge to tear the sheet from his grip. I *so* didn't want to touch it.

He held it out to me. My skin crawled with more imaginary insects. I rubbed my arms to stop the heebie-jeebie sensation. I bit my lip, then, with the tips of my fingers, took it by the top left corner and set it on the table. Someone had drawn a picture of an anchor and scrawled the words *300 Seed Plot* across the top of a map of Missouri.

"What does it mean?" I leaned over the map and rubbed my hands down my jeans—to the point my palms turned fire-engine red.

"Not sure." He shrugged. "What's up with the—" He cocked his head as if he heard something, stuffed the map in his pocket, and pulled out his gun.

"What's wrong?" I raised my gun.

"I—"

Glass exploded in the front room.

Adrenaline shot through my veins, screaming for every muscle to assume battle stations. I sprinted to the wall and looked down the hallway toward the front door. The crunch of broken glass and the wheezy breath of Raspers filled the air. "Oh, God. They're inside."

Two Raspers came around the corner.

I fired and fired. My gun clicked empty.

"There are more—" Adam stepped in front of me.

I loaded the extra magazine I had in my pocket.

"The bike." Ears ringing from the shots, I waved him back and fired again.

"It's a goner. We've got to get the hell out of here." Adam grabbed my arm and yanked me into the hall that led back to the breezeway and the garage.

I jerked away. "I need my bag." There was no way I was leaving my backpack. It had everything.

He said something, but I didn't hear what. I couldn't think. I had to get my bag. It was my life.

I raced back to the kitchen and came face to face with a Rasper. Two rapid shots later, he went down. I dove, slid, and snagged our bags.

An explosion ripped through the air. The kitchen filled with broken glass. I turned. A Rasper was halfway through the kitchen window. I fired and she dropped onto the counter.

Wheezing sounded behind me. I spun. Another yellow-skinned Rasper blocked my way to the breezeway. He brought his hand up and pointed his index finger stinger at me.

I pulled the trigger. Nothing happened. I pulled again. No. I was empty.

The Rasper cackled a throaty laugh. Oh, God. I backed up and fumbled with my bag's zipper. He sauntered toward me. Got closer with each passing nanosecond. I had to get my other gun. Not enough time.

I reached for my knife.

The Rasper's head exploded.

Blood sprayed the walls and splattered my jeans. Holy hell. I jumped back, hit the counter, and brushed against the other dead Rasper's arm.

Adam stood over the Rasper he'd shot in the head. "Come on. We have to go. Now!"

Heart beating quadruple time, I ran, leaping over the body. I wasn't going to wait to see if he vomited a Bug. We raced back to the garage. Adam pushed me through the door and slammed it shut. I whipped out the flashlight and flicked it on. The smell of the chlorine made me cough.

Adam grabbed one of the large-wheeled, industrial tool chests and rolled it against the door.

I dug in my bag for more bullets. Inserted them, pushed them down. Got three in, dropped four.

The tool chest rattled.

I shoved in two more bullets, then pounded the magazine home.

Adam said something.

"What?" I shook my head and tugged my ear. He spun me around and pointed. I wrinkled my forehead. What did he mean? The body? He pointed again. Not at the skeleton, but at the car behind it.

I nodded and raced to the passenger side, remembering at the last second to leap the gaping crack in the floor. We climbed in and I tossed Adam's bag in the back, but there was no way I'd let mine go.

Adam touched the empty key hole.

"Try the visor." I yelled.

Adam gave me a blank look. With a silent plea, I pulled his visor down. Nothing. I opened the glove compartment. Bingo. I handed the keys to Adam. He dropped them in his lap. As he fumbled with the keys, a sense of despair blanketed my heart.

The Raspers had tracked us. Found us. Almost killed us. We had to go.

Adam got the car started. He grabbed his seat belt and I clipped mine, too. I shined the light back at the door. The toolbox slid to the side and the door opened. "Go!"

Adam turned on the headlights, dropped the car into drive, and jammed his foot on the gas. The car jumped, then caught. The vehicle crashed into the garage door. I pitched forward, and then the seat belt slammed me back.

The door had broken enough to let light in, but hadn't shattered. We were still trapped.

Adam threw it in reverse and revved the engine. The car was the size of a tank. We had to get out. I turned and caught the faces of two Raspers coming up behind the car. Their mouths were open, like they were screaming. My breath caught. "They're behind us."

Adam glanced up at the rearview mirror and his eyes widened. He shoved the car into drive and hit gas with what sounded like a yell.

I shut my eyes.

The car crashed through the door. The seat belt stole my oxygen and dug into my chest. I tried to scream, but couldn't. The car pushed forward, then jerked to a stop. A Rasper stumbled and stopped at the wrecked garage door. "They're still coming."

"There're more coming around the house. Hold on." Adam stomped on the gas pedal. The car shot forward and he twisted the wheel. With a spin of tires, we roared out of the driveway, spraying gravel in every direction.

Thwamp. A loud thud reverberated through the car.

"What was that?" I spun in my seat, but couldn't tell where the noise came from.

"Hold on." He jerked the wheel to the left, then the right. Something shifted on top of the car.

A burning, anvil-like weight crushed my chest. There was a Rasper on the roof. Could I shoot through metal? Or would the bullet ricochet?

Adam pushed down on the gas and turned the wheel. I grabbed the handle above the door.

A sallow-skinned hand reached down my window and a whimper tore from my throat. I went for my gun, but it wasn't in the holster. No. No. No. Where was it?

The hand slid further down. Instead of a fingernail, the Rasper's index finger ended in a long, pearl-white stinger and he dragged it across the glass.

My chest burned. I couldn't breathe. Couldn't move. Couldn't think. I tore my gaze from his stinger and looked at Adam.

He spun the wheel and my Glock skidded across the floor mat. I bent down and reached for it.

"Val, stay down!"

A gunshot rang out above me and glass exploded. I lifted my head. Adam had shot out my window.

"Missed." He jerked the wheel again.

This time the Rasper's body slipped off the roof, but he caught himself on the window frame and pulled himself up, his stinger aimed right at me. His face loomed a foot from mine, his eyes shaded by sunglasses. He opened his mouth and released a foul stench, like dead vegetation and dog crap. My throat spasmed. I wanted to throw up, or scream—or both. I pulled back, but the seat belt locked.

"Val! Shoot!"

I raised my gun. The Rasper exposed gray-tinged teeth and grinned using only the left side of his face. He let go of the car. Disappeared.

My breaths came in fast gasps, teetering toward hyperventilation. I unclipped the belt and leaned out the window, searching for him. What the hell? The Rasper rolled across the road and into the ditch. Son of a bitch. He had smiled at me. That was the second one to smile as if they knew something I didn't.

"Why did he let go?" I brushed away the shards of glass, and then had to shove my hands under my legs to stop the trembling.

"Did he sting you?" Adam glanced at me, then quickly focused on the crumbling road.

"No."

He exhaled visibly and bobbed his head. "Thank God. Are you okay?"

"Yeah." No. Not really. "You?"

"Yeah." He swerved, just missing a series of cracks big enough to swallow a motorcycle.

I turned back expecting to see more yellow-skinned Raspers giving chase, but the road remained mutant-free. After a few minutes, I faced forward. "That was shitballs intense."

"You're telling me." Sweat dripped down Adam's brow and he clenched the wheel as if he was afraid to loosen his grip.

I spread my thumb and index finger across my forehead to erase the craziness. The terror. The pain. It didn't help. "Where did you learn to drive like a race car driver?"

"Video games."

I didn't have the energy to laugh. I clutched the handle above the door again, bracing myself to ask the question I didn't want to ask. Wind whipped through my hair. "How much gas do we have?"

"About half a tank."

My grip loosened. "Better than fumes. How far can we get?"

"I'm not sure." Adam checked the rearview mirror and smacked his palms on the wheel. "Damn."

I spun around searching for Raspers. "What?"

"I left the papers from the gadget room on the table."

"Well, at least you have the map. Right?" Weary jitters replaced the adrenaline jolt of the crash.

He pulled the map from his pocket and tossed it at me. "Here. See if you can figure out where we are."

I tried not to think about why the man had clutched it when he died.

Adam drove down the two-lane, pot-holed road and I watched out the window for any sign of a major interstate. Trees flashed by my busted window and the wind howled in my ears. I couldn't think straight. My mind churned with thoughts of Raspers—Bugs—Adam.

"Any clue where we are?"

His question pulled me from my highway hypnosis. "No. Find me a sign and I'll see if I can spot it on the map."

Adam nodded then pointed to his left. "There. Interstate 70."

I consulted the map. "Take it and keep going."

Before long, we were speeding down the highway, dodging abandoned car after abandoned car. Barren landscape slipped past the windshield, a surreal scenic blur.

I caught movement in my peripheral vision. I turned my head just in time to see a deer run into my side of the car. The car jerked left and ran over the animal. Adam yelled. I screamed.

The tires squealed, followed by a metallic groan. Adam gripped the wheel harder, but the car spun 360 degrees and skidded toward a bathtub-sized hole in the road.

I couldn't stop screaming. My head slammed against the window frame and a kaleidoscope of pain and color burst in my eyes. I groaned and tried to focus.

The car refused to cooperate with Adam's attempt to steer. It didn't want to go any farther. It shuddered, jerked, died.

Adam faced me. "Holy crap. You're bleeding."

I touched my forehead and my fingers came away smeared with blood. "How bad is it?"

"Can't tell. There's too much blood." The tone of his voice told me it was bad. Real bad.

I reached in my bag for anything I could use to stop the blood. The first thing my fingers snagged was a clean sock. I pressed it against the cut, then rolled my neck. I pulled my makeshift bandage away and checked out the damage. "Crap, it's really bleeding."

Adam rested his forehead against the steering wheel. "This blows."

I unclipped my seatbelt, got out, and hoisted my bag on my shoulder.

Blood and deer pieces covered the road surrounding the animal carcass. The car was equally dead. The front driver's-side tire had landed in the hole and it spun in the air. The front end was crumpled halfway up the hood and the metal twisted into the front passenger tire. I looked around. Massive trees flanked the road and climbed up the hills on either side. The deer had stranded us in a remote area. Perfect. Droplets of blood dripped down my cheek. I pressed harder.

"How far do you think we are from the next town?"

I jumped and squealed like a little girl. "Don't do that." I hadn't heard Adam get out of the car. "Damned if I know. Stupid deer. We finally get a car and the animal totaled it. Idiot thing couldn't have waited ten seconds before it bolted? This sucks ass."

"Glad to see you're remaining positive. Maybe we can cook the meat over a fire."

"Sounds disgusting." I shook my head. My vision exploded with spirals of white and my stomach churned. I closed my eyes and counted to ten, then walked back to the car. Why was I being such a bitch? My head pounded an out-of-tune rhythm. I wanted to crawl into a ball and sleep for days. Maybe then, the pressure in my head would release. The sock was almost saturated and I folded it. I leaned in the broken window. The car seemed to swim beneath me. I picked up Adam's bag and tossed it at him.

Adam swung his bag onto his injured shoulder. "We need to keep moving. Do you think we should stay on the road or move into the trees?"

"Doesn't that hurt your arm?"

Adam glanced at his arm and shrugged. "It's okay. What do you think? Road or trees?"

Whatever. If he wasn't worried about his wound, I wouldn't either. I had my own problems. I scanned the area. Trees of all sizes and species filled the landscape. "To find a town, the road would be better. But it leaves us totally open to a Rasper ambush. The trees provide some cover, but who knows what's lurking inside." I took a deep breath and exhaled. "I don't like either option. Damned effing deer. I'm thinking trees."

"Me too. Hang on." He crossed back to the car and popped the latch for the trunk. "I want to see if there's anything useful." He bent inside. "Yes."

"What is it?"

"A blanket and an umbrella."

"Leave the umbrella." I dabbed the sock on my cut, pulled it away. "Has it stopped bleeding?"

"No. It's a small gash, but head wounds bleed forever. You want me to put a bandage on it?"

Shots of pain seared through my scalp. "No, thanks. We need to keep moving."

I tossed the bloody sock into the wrecked car. I prayed the Raspers couldn't track us by following the scent of blood. I grabbed a fresh sock and held it against my head.

Adam stuffed the blanket in his bag. "You sure you're okay to go?"

"Positive." There was no way I was staying here, a bleeding beacon to the creatures. We had to keep going.

We walked to the guardrail, climbed over, and cut our way through the forest. While the woods grew wild and untouched, they seemed more orderly than the chaos of the lawns neglected when everyone died.

With every step I took, my eyelids grew heavier and my veins felt filled with lead. Every cell in my body screamed for me to rest, yet I kept walking. No stopping. Not here. Not now.

I pulled out a bottle of water, had one sip, and then the trees spun. The bottle slipped from my hand and blackness clouded my vision. The world tilted. I could still hear, but I'd lost the ability to see. Panic choked my lungs, but I couldn't scream.

"Val. Val." Adam chanting my name was the last thing I heard before I slipped into darkness.

6

When I opened my eyes, shades of blue and gray undulated like jellyfish. I tried to sit up, but nausea swirled through my belly.

"Stay put." Adam pushed me down until I was staring at the jellyfish again. My vision cleared. Wait, not jellyfish. Blue sky and clouds.

"What happened?" Stabbing heat poked behind my eyes. My whole body hurt and my head throbbed. I wanted to curl up and sleep to numb the pain.

Adam bent over me. His dark hair fell forward, framing his face. Stubble covered his strong jaw line. "You passed out. Almost cracked your head on a rock. I just managed to catch you. I think you might have a concussion."

My vision swam and for a moment, I saw two Adams. I blinked repeatedly until only one remained. "Can you get me some water?"

God, what was wrong with me? I didn't think I hit my head that hard, but my body screamed otherwise. I touched the cut. At least the bleeding had stopped.

Adam nodded, then disappeared. He came back, sat, and lifted my shoulders up onto his legs. Heat seeped through the denim and warmed my head. He gave me a bottle. "Sip it."

"Thanks." I took a drink and the nausea went away. Thank God.

"Let me see your eyes." He leaned over and I stared into his green irises. They stayed in focus. He fumbled in his bag for something.

When he flashed a light into my eyes, my head screamed, *asshole*. "Stop, that hurts."

"Sorry. I think you'll be okay, your pupils seem to be dilating correctly. My mom always checked my eyes whenever I hit my head. We need to find shelter. The sun is just about down. Can you move?"

Strange noises only found in the wild raised the hairs on my arms. "Is that an owl? A bobcat?" My thoughts spun out of control.

"I don't know."

I pushed myself away from the comfort of Adam's legs. He helped me stand, but I tilted to the side. He reached out and caught me around the waist.

"Thanks again." Rule Number One, trust no one, flashed like a fritzing neon sign before my eyes. To hell with Rule Number One. I had absolutely, completely, totally violated it. There was no going back now. Not when Adam seemed in the habit of saving my butt.

A howl tore through the air. "Oh my God. More dogs." My chest burned and panic squeezed the air from my lungs.

"It's okay. They're probably a long way away."

The woods closed in, smothering me in a blanket of green. Visions of predatory animals circled around my mind. My head still pounded enough for my eyes to lock in a semi-squint.

"We have to go." Adam took my bag.

"I can carry it."

"No. I'm good. You need to keep your strength."

I didn't like it, but I let him carry my bag; my life wrapped in canvas.

There wasn't a path to guide us. We weaved around tree after tree. I took a deep breath of the clean air. The scent of leaves and dirt had replaced the stench of rot and decay. We walked on. There was nothing but woods and more woods. With each passing moment, what little confidence I had in our plan slipped away.

"What were we thinking? We should have stayed on the road, Raspers or not."

Adam didn't answer for a minute, but he finally said, "Look up there."

I stopped and tried to make out what he pointed at, but trees littered the hill. "What? I don't see anything."

He inched closer, lifted my left arm, and extended it out and up. His touch made my cheeks feel like hot coals.

"Look where your hand is pointing. I think it's a cave."

I still didn't see anything, but met his gaze. "Maybe."

Adam maintained the eye contact a few seconds too long—long enough for my heart to stop beating—then released my hand, and turned. Oxygen seized in my lungs. I tried not to think about how it took all my effort to stop staring at him and focus on our dilemma.

A cave. We were going to spend the night in a cave. Most likely with bats. I shivered, but bats were better than wild animals—or Raspers.

It took us awhile to climb the hill and navigate around the trees. When we reached the top, more pain exploded into my head, like firecrackers. Maybe it was the lingering effects of a concussion. I hoped not. I needed a clear, focused brain, not a muddled mess. That would get me killed.

We stepped inside the cave, which extended back about twenty feet into the rocks. Packed dirt covered the ground. We searched every inch of the place, making sure there was no sign of any animal living there. The cave would protect us and provided a birds-eye view of anything approaching.

"Go ahead and get some sleep. I'll take first watch." Adam tossed me the blanket then sat down with his back to the rock wall.

"Okay, I will in a few minutes." I wanted to sleep. Needed to sleep. But my mind spun at cyclone speed. Adam... My parents... Raspers... Bugs...

I sat on the blanket and pulled out my Glock. I took a cloth out of my bag and worked on cleaning the gun. I had to keep it clean, in perfect condition. My dad's last gift was keeping me alive. I ran my finger over the small chip in the gun's handle. When I was done, I glanced up to find Adam watching me. "What?"

"Nothing. Are you going to sleep or polish your gun all night?"

"Sleep." The task had quieted my brain enough that exhaustion threatened to force me to sleep. A quick rest, then Adam could take his turn. He had to be tired too. I pulled an extra sweatshirt out of my bag, balled it into a makeshift pillow, and tried to get comfortable. It didn't work, but I drifted off.

A crack of thunder woke me. Darkness blanketed the cave. Damn, I'd done it again. I'd slept longer than I planned. I pulled my flashlight out of my bag and flicked it on. Adam's backpack rested on the ground, but he wasn't in the cave. The light stung my eyes and I clicked it off.

"Adam?"

No answer.

I scrambled to my feet and grabbed the Glock. I aimed my gun and made my way to the mouth of the cave. It was too damn dark out there to see anything.

"Adam?" I wanted to scream his name, but kept my voice to a whisper.

Again, no answer.

Where was he? What had happened? I pushed the light on the watch I had swiped from the sporting goods store when I first ventured out after *that* day. The green light blinked 7:15.

I tried to make out anything in the blackness, but couldn't see. Minutes ticked by while I stood there waiting. Thinking. Figuring out my options. I couldn't go wandering around in the dark. I had to stay put, at least until dawn. My eyes adjusted to the dark while my stomach twisted from a combination of nerves and hunger. I turned to grab a candy bar from my bag.

A wheezing sound came from outside the cave. Raspers.

I strained, trying to hear it again.

Wheeze. Rattle.

Son of a bitch.

Adrenaline slammed my heart into overdrive. Did they have Adam? I wiped a hand across my hairline to clear away the sweat, grabbed my bag, and moved to the back of the cave. I crouched down, pulled out another gun, and set it on the ground. I double-gripped the Glock.

Branches crunched. Someone was close.

I tried to calm my racing heart with deep breaths, but instead of slowing down, it jumped into hyper-drive. I pulled out the flashlight and held it in my right hand, crossed under the gun like Dad had taught me. Maybe it was Adam and not a Rasper. But if a Rasper came that close... Oh, God. It could be a pack of Raspers. They traveled in groups. Ready to attack.

A shape crossed the front of the cave. I hit the button on the flashlight, hoping to temporarily blind the Rasper.

A crash thundered through the cave. "Goddammit."

I turned off the light and jumped up. "I almost shot you! Don't you know I'm always armed? There are Raspers out there."

"How do you know?"

"I heard the wheezing. Now be quiet." My words were harsh.

We stood there. The thumping of my heart roared in my ears.

"I don't hear anything." Adam whispered.

"Where were you?" At least the Raspers hadn't gotten him. I felt like smiling, but didn't. Something about the whole situation still seemed off.

"I went to get some sticks to start a fire. Maybe you heard me huffing as I came back. Or it could have been an animal. I didn't hear anything."

His answer made sense, yet I wasn't entirely convinced. "How did you see where you were going?"

"My eyes were adjusted to the dark until you blinded me."

"Damn lucky I didn't shoot you again. You have to stop sneaking up on me."

"Might as well turn the light back on so I can start the fire."

"You think that's a good idea? A fire might draw the Raspers."

"It might, but it's getting really cold out and I don't want to freeze."

Adam had a point, but it went against my better judgment to build a fire and take a chance of announcing *here we are, come get us*. A shot of icy air blasted my skin and set my teeth chattering. "Well, we have our guns."

I gave in and flicked the light back on. Adam grabbed the wood he'd dropped. When he was ready to light the fire, he conducted a weird patting of his pockets.

"Need a lighter?"

"Yeah, got one?"

I walked back to my bag and pulled one out. "Catch."

His kindling caught instantly and soon we had a roaring fire in the opening of our small cave. I put the flashlight away, holstered the Glock, and shoved my extra gun in the back of my jeans. We sat next to each other, sharing the blanket.

I stared into the flames. "What's our plan for the morning?"

Adam pulled out the skeleton's map. "This guy knew more about what happened and the creatures than we do. He obviously talked or communicated with others. And he survived. Well, until he lost the battle with the tool box."

I shrugged. "So what?"

"I think this might be an address and if so, it has to be important. Why else would the guy have written it on the map and held it as he died?"

"Even if it is an address, there's no way to know where it is."

Adam shoved the paper back in his pocket. "Maybe it's in the next big city. I mean, it's like the dead guy knew where it was."

"That's a big assumption. It could be anywhere. Maybe it's not even in Missouri."

"I say we look for the next town and see if we can find this place."

I didn't care. We just needed to survive. Where we tried to survive didn't matter. "Okay. But how do the Raspers keep finding us? It's like we have trackers on us or something."

"Maybe they're like Bloodhounds. Once they've got our scent, they can track us."

Fear crashed into my chest and squeezed my heart. "I hope not. That means they'll keep coming."

"But we won't be waiting around to find out."

The scent of the burning wood and the flicker of the flames lulled us into a comfortable silence for a few minutes until I blurted out, "Where do you think the Raspers came from?"

"Had to be something related to Pearan's Great Discovery of the oil. Everything was normal before then."

I shot a glance in his direction. His face filled with a faraway look I couldn't decipher. Thunder boomed. I shivered and scooted closer to him. "What about the Bug creatures?"

"They're evil." He juiced the words with venom. The wood popped in the fire.

I swallowed the baseball-sized lump in my throat. "You know more than you're telling me."

He licked his lips. "The Raspers surrounded us after we got out of the transport vehicle." He paused and cracked his knuckles. "They came after us with their stingers and took out about half of the people. The Bugs got the rest. It was like a war zone."

"God." I shivered.

"The Bugs...they shot long metal pokers into people's legs. The person would fall and twitch as if they were having a seizure. And when they stopped moving, the creatures moved on to their next victim."

He stopped again and a wave of goose bumps sizzled across my skin. Holy crap. The Bugs stung people too. I couldn't imagine what would have happened to me if Adam hadn't shown up with the bike. I shuddered and hugged my knees to my chest. Heat radiated from the dancing flames, but it didn't block the cold wrapping around my body.

"Then the unthinkable happened." He traced the creases in his right palm. "A couple of people opened their eyes and got up, but they'd changed. They were Raspers."

"What about the rest of the people?" I said the words so softly, I wasn't sure he heard me.

"The rest didn't get up. I think they died. It was the most messed up thing I've ever seen. It's like they can only transform some people. Not everyone."

He balled his fingers into a tight fist. His mouth scrunched together and he shook his head and released his grip. He turned and faced me. "They took over my mother and she tried to get me." His voice wavered and Adam stared at his hands.

I wanted to hug him. I leaned closer so my shoulder brushed his. "How did you avoid being stung?"

His eyes clouded over and the light from the fire bathed them in an eerie glow.

"I didn't."

7

My throat closed, choking back my disbelief. My heart sped up and I gasped. The cave walls spun.

He'd been stung.

Goddammit. Now I knew how he survived without a weapon. How he could see in the dark. How he heard things I couldn't. I scrambled to my feet and pulled my extra gun out of the back of my jeans.

"You're a Rasper?" My hand shook so bad I almost dropped the gun. I couldn't trust him. I'd been such a fool. And I had given him a weapon.

"Put your gun away."

"No way in hell. You might kill me. Or send a Bug after me."

Adam stood and straightened his shoulders. "No, I won't."

"Get out." I waved the gun at the mouth of the cave. Lightning flashed, followed by thunder.

He held his hands up. "Val, listen to me."

"The hell with that, you son of a bitch." I stepped toward him. "I said leave."

"No." He came toward me.

I aimed the gun at his chest. *Shoot him. Shoot him. Shoot him.* I hesitated.

He dove for me.

I twisted away and ran out of the cave. And kept running. How could I have been so dumb? That's what I got for breaking my rules. I'd thought he was my friend. I hated him. Hated myself. Was he planning on killing me or making me one of *them*? Fear made my feet go faster.

"Val, wait!"

The stupid idiot was yelling at me, probably to draw more Raspers. It was so dark out, I couldn't see where I was going. The tree limbs tore my skin as if they were trying to take a souvenir.

Lightning lit the sky. Thunder rumbled seconds later. Fear clutched my lungs and squeezed.

Rain pelted my face. I kept running, dodging trees. The ground turned to mud. I slipped and fell on my butt. I scrambled back up and kept running. My legs ached and my lungs burned. I needed to stop, but I couldn't. I had to keep going. I had to outrun the Raspers.

The intensity of the storm drowned out any other sound. I couldn't tell if Adam had followed me or if he'd stayed in the cave. Thinking of the cave drove a knife through my gut. I had left my bag there. I was so stupid. I had really blown it. I'd violated Rules One and Two and was probably going to die tonight.

Tears welled in my eyes, but I blinked them back. I would not cry over his stupid, lying ass.

My hair plastered to my head and I pushed it out of my eyes. My fingers slipped on the handle of the gun and I almost dropped it. Tightening my grip, I calculated how many bullets I had. Two in this gun and a full round in the Glock.

Sharp pains in my side made me stop and bend over for just a second. The wheezy breathing of Raspers filled the air. Adam *had* been out rounding up the mutants. A shadow moved on my right. I aimed and fired. The shadow went down. Was it Adam? Had I shot him? It didn't matter. Score one for me.

Adrenaline coursed through my muscles. I took off again and tried to quiet my thoughts. How many more Raspers were there?

A flash of lightning illuminated the area ahead. My heart stopped. There was nothing there, just yawning blackness. I willed my body to stop, but I was going too fast. It was too late.

I left solid ground and the sensation of flying overtook my senses. Then I dropped. I was going to die. I slammed into the ground, landing on my right knee. The gun flew out of my hand. Damn it all to hell. I reached out for it, but I had fallen down about ten feet into a stream. A cry tore from my throat. Not only were Raspers after me, but Mother Nature was screwing with me. I needed to find a place to hide. I needed to survive.

When I stood, my knee popped and crackled like the twisting of bubble wrap. I tried to ignore its protests, but daggers of pain skewered down my leg. I stumbled along the rocky streambed, trying to stay vertical.

I reached for the Glock. At least I still had Dad's gun.

Lightning flashed, highlighting an alcove under a fallen tree and a ledge of branches above it. Heart hammering, I worked my way there through the shallow water. The wind whipped, shooting shivers down my body and into my toes.

The earthy smell of dirt filled my nose. I crawled into the cavity under the tree. I had to calm down. I recited the alphabet in my head. Had to keep quiet. It was so cold, the gun shook from my shivers, but at least I was out of the water.

A branch snapped above me. All my muscles tensed. Were Raspers up there? Had Adam found me? Was he even looking for me? Probably not, the jerk. Then again, I could have shot him. *Again.*

I breathed through my nose to stay silent. Tingles zipped over my skin. Oh, God. Something crawled across my arm. I bit my lip to keep from moving. What was it? Lightning streaked, lighting up the night. I risked a quick glance at my arm. I shouldn't have.

Two spiders crept over my upper arm. Spiders. I hated spiders more than rats. My chest heaved and I fought not to scream. Tears ran down my face, but I didn't dare move to wipe them away.

Another branch crunched above me.

"Vvvaaalll."

The gravelly voice filled my ears and pierced my heart with its lack of inflection. How the hell did the Rasper know my name?

"Vvvaaalll."

It was dark. I had spiders on my arm. Raspers were stalking

me. Talking to me. I was going to die. Rocks dropped from the ledge and I brought the gun up close to my ear. If I shot the gun from this position, I might or might not get the Rasper.

Another flash of lightning.

Two Raspers stood on the other side of the stream, not twenty feet away. I was surrounded.

"Vvvaaalll. Time to join us." The wheezy words seemed to be coming from right next to me.

This was it. Time to react. I needed to move, but my muscles froze as if they were concrete. A pounding of feet then a thud sounded above. My finger twitched on the trigger.

Splash. Something landed in the water. Someone. I pointed the gun at the body in the water, but hesitated. Something wasn't right.

Another flash of light.

The Rasper wasn't standing, but lying on its side in the stream. In the brief instant of light, I recognized the face. It was one of the Raspers that had been at the church house. It had stalked me here. Crap.

The ground above me moved again. How many were there? All my brain cells screamed *run*. I needed to get away. I pointed the gun at the Rasper in the stream and fired.

Lightning zapped across the sky and thunder roared. The Rasper's mouth opened. Then it was dark again. I wasn't waiting for the next flash of light to see another Bug crawl from the Rasper's mouth.

I swatted the spiders off my arm and struggled to my feet. A shadow danced to my left. I fired. There was at least one more still hunting me. Where was he?

Raspy breathing sizzled down my spine. I glanced back. Couldn't see anything. My knee threatened to drop me, but I pushed on. If I was going to die, I was going out fighting. Mom would have wanted it that way. Dad would have expected it. Tears streamed down my face, mixing with the rain. Pain seared through my leg as if a hot poker had been driven into my kneecap.

With another flash of light, I caught movement to my right. But before I could fire, pain exploded in my calf. I went down, my knee striking the ground again. My vision burst with fireworks of white light. I dropped my gun.

I reached for the weapon, but it was too far. I crawled forward. Pain sliced my leg, burning as it tore through my system.

I'd been shot.

My head became too heavy for my neck to support. The ground twisted. I couldn't move anymore and collapsed on my stomach. Coldness wrapped my body like a blanket. This was it. I was dying. Visions of my parents flashed before my eyes.

Then nothing.

***

Someone—something—was moving. Raspers. I kept my eyes shut and tried to figure out how many there were. It sounded like only one. I opened my eyes and my body cried with pain. What had happened? Where was I?

I was on top of a blanket in the dirt. The ceiling above me was rock. I had to be in a cave. I struggled to sit up, but couldn't. Stabbing sensations shot through my legs. Was I paralyzed?

I tried to swallow, but gagged on something wedged in my mouth. Oh, God, there was something in my mouth. I pictured the Bug ripping the Rasper's face open. No. Please no. Not a Bug.

I thrust my tongue at the object. It was soft, not metallic. Cloth, not creature. My heart resumed beating. Until I glanced up and came face to face with a gun. The bastard Adam stood over me, pointing a gun at my head.

I tried to curse him out, but the gag silenced me. My arms were bound with rope. I shifted my legs, but pain shot through my calves. He was so going to die.

"Stop moving."

I narrowed my eyes and tried to give him my meanest look, but since I was bound and gagged, I don't think I pulled it off.

"I'll take the gag off. If you scream or attempt to kill me, I will shoot you. Do you understand?"

I nodded.

He reached down and pulled off the gag. I spit, then

swallowed, and ran my tongue around my teeth. They were fuzzy, as if I hadn't brushed them in years.

"Tell me your name." He moved the gun closer to my face.

My throat closed and it felt as if I'd swallowed sand paper. I stared into the gun barrel. Any second a bullet could rip through the metal and end my life. It was the first time I had been on this side of a gun. I didn't like it.

"You know my name." I choked the words out despite the desert in my mouth. What game was he playing?

"Tell me your name or I pull the trigger."

I exhaled. "Val, you asshole."

He smiled in an I-missed-you way and pointed the gun at the floor. "You're okay."

He'd gone insane. Nuts. Crazy. He tucked the gun in the back of his jeans and bent down. I didn't move. He untied my legs first, then my arms.

I sat up and boiling pain radiated from my toes to my butt. "Who shot me?"

"You weren't shot."

"Like hell." I twisted my leg and tried to see the wound. My jeans were rolled up to my knee and my calf was a purplish black, with tendrils of color radiating out of a pea-sized hole. But it wasn't a bullet hole. What the hell?

"Hurts, doesn't it?"

"Shut up, Rasper." I needed a plan. I didn't have any guns and my knives were gone. Bastard probably took the knives. I plotted his painful death.

"I'm as much a Rasper as you are."

I ignored him and struggled to stand.

"I wouldn't stand. You'll just fall back down."

I got vertical. Took a step. My leg gave out and I collapsed.

"Told you."

I wished I had a weapon. "What's wrong with my leg then, Genius?"

He sat on the ground next to me and rolled the rope into a ball. "You were stung."

8

My vision and thoughts spiraled with the speed of a tornado. It had all been for nothing. The hiding. The training. The running. The Rules. None of it mattered. Didn't make any difference. I'd been stung by a Rasper. Was I one now?

"Val?" Adam leaned forward and touched my arm. His touch wasn't warm like it had been before. The realization set off warning sirens in my head.

"This is hell, isn't it?"

Adam let go and laughed. The happy noise sounded wrong. "Not technically, but some days it sure feels like it."

"Am I dead?"

"No. I think you're like me."

"What?" I couldn't focus. The rocky cave walls spun with a kaleidoscope kind of dizziness. What was happening to me? Was I changing into one of the creatures? I glanced at my hands. No yellow.

"I didn't lie to you and I'm not a Rasper. You asked me before you stupidly ran away how I avoided being stung. I said I didn't." He bit his lip.

"But you said after the people got stung, they fell down and came back as freaks with a desire to kill everyone else." Would I want to kill Adam? I mean, more than I already did?

"That's not exactly what I said, but close enough. The thing is, I never collapsed and the damn things never took over my mind."

My skin itched and crawled. I hugged myself, trying not to picture myself as a Rasper. "Why not?"

"That's what I don't know. Everyone else collapsed. Even my mom. When she came back to and turned to me with that look in her eyes, I...I took off running. I wish I had the answers. But I do know the stinger poke hurt like hell." He rubbed his side.

"What happened after you got stung? Did they chase you? How long did it hurt? Why did he sting me in the leg? I collapsed, so how do you know I don't have a Bug in me? How do they know my name?" I fired the questions at him in rapid succession. Then pain like I'd never felt before seared through my muscles and I moaned. I rubbed my calf, but the pain burned more and more. I had to be morphing into one of them. But my skin stayed the same color and my fingernail didn't change into a stinger.

"I was there. I saw you fall and picked you up. I thought I was going to have to fight the Raspers while holding you. But they stopped their attack."

I stretched my leg, trying to make the pain disappear. "Why does it hurt so much? Why did the Raspers stop? Why did you save me?"

"I don't know why they stopped, and the pain will go away. I shouldn't have let you run out of the cave. It was my responsibility to make sure you stayed safe."

I half-snorted, half-groaned and the obscene sound echoed around the cave. "Kinda messed that one up, huh?"

"Yes and no. You're alive."

"Why did you tie me up and point a gun at my head?"

"Your gun."

"What?"

"I pointed your gun at you."

Relief flooded my senses and masked the pain for a minute. "You have my Glock? Can I have it back?" He had to give me the gun. One, it was my dad's. Two, I needed a weapon. And three, if I turned into a Rasper, I needed to be able to end it. I hoped I didn't have to.

Adam reached to his back, withdrew the gun, and handed it to me, grip first.

I snatched it from him and ran my finger over the notch. "Why did you tie me up if you were trying to keep me safe?"

"I had to make sure."

"Make sure of what?"

"That you hadn't turned into a Rasper. Your skin stayed the same color and you don't have a stinger."

I flexed my index fingers. Still the same. My stomach churned. I couldn't be a Rasper. "How can you know for sure?"

He grinned. "I knew when you called me an asshole."

"You are an asshole, but how did that tell you I was Bug-free and not a damn mutant?" I tapped the muzzle of the gun on my thigh. I wanted to shoot something. Not him anymore, but something. Anything to release the energy threatening to explode.

"Your breathing, and Raspers don't use emotion in their voices. They're all monotone. Your words were full of anger."

"You're sure I'm good?" I hoped he was right. I'd rather be dead than a Rasper. I didn't feel like a Rasper. But then again, I didn't know what being a Rasper felt like. I clutched the Glock tighter.

"You're not a Rasper. In an hour or so, the pain should stop and we can test out your skills."

"Skills? What are you talking about?" He was so damn calm while I teetered on the edge of freaking out.

He pulled a bottle of water out of his bag and took a long drink. "The actual sting hurt worse than you shooting me. After the sting, it seemed like heat burned through my veins, but it stopped after a few hours. Like the venom, poison, or whatever it was, shot through my body, but didn't work." He took another drink. "The Bugs made an ear-piercing sound and looking back, I think maybe they were communicating."

"What happened then?"

"Mom reached for me...as did the other two who got back up, but...I still had pain in my side. I took off running. I used to run track at school, so I was faster than them. But the funny thing was, I was much faster. Beyond my normal faster. Heightened somehow. Eventually, the rest of my senses got stronger, too."

"You're like superhuman now?" My head spun and the cave rotated with it. I couldn't take it. His story was too much. It couldn't be real.

"I think maybe." He shrugged. "You might be, too."

"Can you hear better now?" I twisted my ponytail. I needed to focus, to process the information. To figure out what to do now.

"Hear more, see farther and in the dark, move faster than I should be able to, and lift heavier stuff than I could before. Not sure if my sense of taste is increased, because I haven't had any real food." He laughed without humor. "For me, the muscle strength was instantaneous. Then the hearing a few hours later, my vision the next day or so."

Well, that explained how he had heard me at the church house. But it didn't make me feel any better. "When you went out to get the wood, you could see where you were going?"

"Yes."

I couldn't comprehend what it all meant in the long run, like what would happen to me—or him—in a month or more. We could transform into Raspers at any time. "You're scaring me."

"Why?"

"I don't know. What if it kills us or something?"

"I hope not." He licked his lips. "You'll probably get some headaches. I did."

Shivers sliced across my skin. I might now have superhuman skills. While it sounded cool, it scared me shitless. The real question was if I could trust Adam or not. I'd given up on following Rule Number One. "Tell me why I should trust you."

He ran his index fingers under his eyes and pressed on his sinuses as if he was trying to relieve pressure. "I don't know. Maybe you shouldn't. You've been somewhat of a bitch. I mean, you did shoot me once already. Say the word and I'll leave, but I would like the company. Besides, we're stronger as a team than alone. Don't you think?"

Blood sizzled under my skin. Bitch? He had the nerve to call me a bitch? What an ass. I balled my fist. I so wanted to hit something. Or someone. But, damn him, he made too much sense. And if I was honest with myself, I had been a bitch.

My shoulders rounded and sagged under an invisible weight. "How about this? We can hang together, but if you betray me, or I even think you've betrayed me, I'll shoot you like the heartless bitch you think I am."

"Well, I guess I'll need to make sure I don't piss you off, then." Adam smiled an I-may-or-may-not-be-kidding smile.

I didn't know how to respond to that, so I turned away from him. The sun peeked through the trees. "Hey, it's daylight."

"I spotted a cabin in the woods. We need to check it out once your leg stops hurting."

My stomach rumbled an audible groan. "I need to eat first. I'm starving."

Adam had not only recovered my gun, but he'd brought me back to the cave. I pulled granola bars and water from my bag. I was so sick of granola bars.

"Here. You can have this back." He tossed me the rope ball and I stuffed it into the bag.

Once the pain in my leg subsided, we headed out and hiked along the hillside until we came to a clearing.

"You ready to test yourself?" Adam dropped his bag on the ground.

I shrugged. "I guess. What should I do?"

"Run to that tree." Adam pointed to a large oak about fifty yards away.

I set my bag next his and took off. I moved faster than I ever had. All without any pain in my knee or leg. I reached the tree in no time and my breathing remained normal. Wow. Cool! Freaky. Scary.

"Can you hear me?"

"Of course I can hear you if you yell," I called back.

"I'm not yelling. I'm whispering. Try it. I should be able to hear you."

Yeah, right. "Well, can you hear me, Hotness?"

"Hotness?" His voice had a teasing tone.

Shit. He *could* hear me. And I was making a total ass of myself. "Uh…"

Disbelief tap-danced through my brain. Holy crap. Maybe I was superhuman. Like a superhero or something. I ran back to Adam, moving faster than I had before. I flew past him, then backtracked. And tried to forget I'd called him hot. *Again.*

"What's going on? Why can I do this stuff?" I wasn't sure I really wanted the answer.

Adam turned and his arm brushed against mine. "I don't know. Must have something to do with what we were injected with."

"Why are we immune to the poison or whatever it is? What if we aren't immune? It could be slowly shifting through our veins before it kills us."

"I don't want to think about that. Truth is, I have all those questions too. Come on, I'll race you."

We picked up our bags and took off to the tree. I matched Adam stride for stride and we reached the oak at the same time.

"How long ago were you stung?"

Adam turned to me. "Maybe three and a half months ago. Why?"

"Just hoping we won't drop dead."

"Me too." He tugged on the bottom of his shirt. "You know, I never asked. Is Val short for something?" He tilted his head to the side and his hair framed his face.

My cheeks ignited. Damn, why did I have to blush? I clutched at my backpack strap and squeezed. "Valentine. My name's Valentine Moore. My mom named me after the day I was born. I mean how corny is that? I hated going to school and the teachers calling me Valentine." I clamped my mouth shut.

Adam inched closer to me. "If the calendar on the wall back at the house was right, then yesterday was your birthday."

I nodded.

"Well, happy birthday, Val. I'm sorry it was so awful for you."

"Yeah, it rates as the worst one so far." As much as I still distrusted him, I was beginning to think meeting him was the best part. There was no way I was telling him that, though.

"How old are you?"

"Sixteen. You?"

"The same." He grabbed a twig from a pile of branches. He drew something in the dirt with the stick.

"What are you doing?" I leaned closer, but couldn't make out his drawing.

"Hang on." He scratched the dirt more with his makeshift pen. "Okay, come see."

I walked to his side. He had drawn a cake with sixteen candles on it. My heart beat faster and twisted itself in a knot.

"Sorry, I wish it could have been a real cake."

Damn him for being so nice. My eyes stung with unshed tears. "Thanks. I wish it were a real cake, too. Jeez, doesn't that sound delicious?" I rubbed my stomach.

"Don't start talking about food again. It's too painful."

"You're right. No more talk of real food anymore. I swear." I held up my right hand.

Adam grabbed my hand. Heat radiated up my arm. "It's a deal then. No more discussing real food."

His eyes locked on mine. I couldn't think. He leaned toward me. I couldn't breathe. He was going to kiss me. Oh. My. God. I couldn't do it. I backed up, consumed with panic. I had never kissed anyone before. And I couldn't remember the last time I had used mouthwash. I cleared my throat. "So, this cabin? Where is it?"

Adam closed his eyes for a second, ran his hand across his face, then turned away. "This way."

I'd killed the mood for sure. Maybe I had misinterpreted his actions. There was no way he had planned to kiss me. Was there? The moment played on a never-ending loop through my brain as we hiked back into the wooded area and came to a stream. It had to be the stream from last night. In the light, it looked serene and calming, not the scene of my almost death. "What happened to the Rasper in the water?"

"The others took him away once I grabbed you."

"Was he dead?"

"I'm not sure."

I rubbed my throat. "What about the Rasper that stung me? What happened to it?"

"I don't know. I think he took off."

"Did they call you by name?"

"No."

"Well, they knew my name. Creeped me out."

"That's messed up."

"They stalked me. Why do you think they did that?" The vision of the Rasper's face shattered the replay of Adam's almost-kiss.

"I wish I knew. Seems like they're evolving, though—look, there's the cabin."

I tried to let Adam's comment about the Raspers evolving go, but it circled in my mind like a vulture looking for the dead. If they could get smarter than they already were, I doubted we'd reach seventeen. The sting had helped us. Made us stronger. Would we be able to use it against the damn creatures? I hoped we could. "Hopefully there's a car so we can get to your safe house. And have a doctor or something make sure we're not going to become Raspers."

"I think this will be our lucky day. We'll be able to check out the address and get to Site R soon."

I glanced at the cabin in an attempt to quiet my whirling thoughts. It wasn't just a shack, but an honest-to-goodness one-story log cabin with a large tower behind it. Black panels covered the roof. The grass in the front yard was wild and up to windows, but a concrete walk ran from the gravel driveway to the front door. A dirt road extended out from the driveway. Well, after the rain, it currently classified as a mud road. I wasn't sure it was going to bring us the luck Adam hoped for.

I pointed at the metal structure. "Isn't that a radio tower like the other house?"

"Yes."

"What's on the roof?"

"Looks like solar panels," Adam whispered. "Think anyone's inside?"

I drew my gun. "One way to find out."

We took up positions on opposite sides of the black-stained door. There wasn't a doorbell. Adam knocked.

We waited. I counted out thirty seconds in my head. "Hear anything?"

Adam shook his head and knocked again. Still no response.

I reached out, grabbed hold of the doorknob, and opened the door. We entered the cabin, trying to imitate the cops on old TV shows. The scent of lemon furniture polish filled my nose. The place was clean and decorated in a rustic style. We stood in the living room and surveyed the layout. The kitchen stretched out across the back wall, and three closed doors lined up along the left side. I tapped Adam on the shoulder and gestured at them with the Glock.

Adam walked to the first door and stood on the left side. I took the right. He held up three fingers and proceeded to drop them in a countdown. When he put down the final finger, I opened the door to a clean and empty bathroom. We repeated the procedure with next door. It opened to a small vacant bedroom. The final door revealed shelves of canned goods. Jackpot.

"Soups and veggies." Adam grabbed a couple cans from the shelves. "Want to eat?"

"You don't have to ask. Think this place has power and water?" I didn't wait for his response, but went to the kitchen and flicked the light switch.

The light above the small table and two chairs came on. I broke into a smile bigger than I had when I went into Disneyworld. The movement made my face feel funny. I couldn't remember the last time I'd smiled. I said a silent prayer at the faucet, then pushed the lever. Clear water flowed into my hands. I cupped the clean liquid in my palm. Sniffed it and didn't smell anything funky. I almost cried. I might be able to get a real shower.

"Does the stove work?" Adam came up behind me.

I turned the knob and the range roared to life.

Adam gave out a whoop sound and jumped up. "I need a pan to cook the soup. I'm so hungry." He bent down and searched the cupboards. I pulled open drawers, located a can opener, and opened the cans.

Within minutes, the tantalizing scent of tomato soup filled the small kitchen and my stomach gurgled. Adam reached into the pantry closet. "Tea bags." He held up a box. "Not coffee, but still awesome."

A teakettle sat on top of the range. "Bring them here." I filled the kettle and Adam found bowls, silverware, and mugs.

We sat at the table and devoured the food. When I got to the bottom of the bowl, I lifted it to my lips and slurped the rest. Adam grinned and did the same. I inhaled the steam from the tea and warmed my fingers on the mug. It was so good to have something hot.

"What now?" Adam leaned back in the chair.

"You could use a shower, but I'm taking one first." I rinsed off my dishes, then grabbed my bag. "You'll keep watch?"

Adam picked up his dishes. "Of course. Don't take too long. Who knows how long the water will stay warm."

I went into the bathroom and locked the door. I hadn't taken a shower in forever. Did I dare get naked long enough for a shower? Logic said no, but every inch of my skin screamed for me to get in. The fall in the stream had left a layer of imaginary grime all over and I itched to wash it off.

I turned on the water. The temperature was perfect. I put my gun on the ledge out of the way of the water, but close enough for me to reach it, if I needed to, then I stripped and got in.

It was heaven. I had missed the scent of shampoo and soap. I scrubbed every inch of my skin until it turned pink. And after about five minutes, I got out. Before I put my clothes on, I eyed my calf. The sting looked like a small bruise. I got dressed, wrapped a towel around my wet hair, and crossed to the mirror. I wiped the small amount of steam off.

My skin was more tanned than normal and it brought out the spatter of freckles across my nose. My eyes seemed browner than I remembered them, but that might be a result of no eyeliner. I pulled the towel off my head and rubbed my hair. I'd put it back in my standard ponytail once it was dry. I stuffed my dirty clothes in my bag and grabbed the Glock. When I came out of the bathroom, Adam turned and stared.

"What?" I holstered my gun then tugged on a damp strand of hair.

Adam shook his head. "Nothing, just your hair...looks good."

I tucked it behind my ears. Heat burned a trail from my cheeks to my feet. "Thanks. It's all yours." I waved at the door.

"Great." Adam nodded. He walked toward me and stopped. He reached out and touched a strand of my hair. "I really like your hair this way." Then he went into the bathroom.

I stood stunned. Maybe I hadn't imagined him almost kissing me. I put my bag on the table and sat in the wooden chair. The sound of running water filled the room. I strapped my knife to my leg and then finger combed my hair. I debated about saying something when he came out. I was probably reading him wrong, though, and I'd make a fool of myself if I said anything. He was just being nice.

The sensation of being watched crept across my skin. I drew my gun, stood, spun around.

There was no one there.

I walked over to the bathroom door and tapped the barrel of the gun on it. "Adam, get out."

The water shut off and the door opened. He clasped a towel around his waist. Water dripped from his hair. "What's wrong?"

I had to tear my eyes away. "Something feels off. Get dressed." I went back to the table, picked up my bag, and slid it onto my shoulders.

Adam came out of the bathroom, dressed and armed. "What happened?"

"Nothing, but I felt someone watching me."

"Let's do a search outside."

We went outside, circled the perimeter of the cabin, but came up empty.

"Guess it was nothing." But I couldn't shake the feeling. I opened the door to go back inside.

And stared into the barrel of a shotgun.

9

"Drop your weapons." A blonde girl, about my age and height, spit the words at us through clenched teeth.

So much for it being a lucky day. I raised my gun higher and Adam followed my lead. "No."

"I'll shoot."

"Yeah, so will we. And there are two of us. Even if you get one of us, the other will kill you. You lose." Brave words. But an iron vise clamped around my lungs. I couldn't breathe. It was a gamble. I hoped she wouldn't pull the trigger. She was close enough she might get us both.

"What are your names?" She didn't lower the shotgun, but it wavered.

The vise loosened its grip a fraction.

"I'm Adam. This is Val. What's yours?"

"Are you one of them?"

"Raspers? No."

She cocked her head to the side. Her straight hair fell past her shoulders. "Raspers?"

"It's what I call them because of the way they breathe." I tightened my grip on the gun.

She lowered the gun. Adam did too. I exhaled, but didn't drop mine. "Your turn."

The girl's brown eyes narrowed. "What?"

"I need proof you're not a Rasper before I put *my* gun down." I steadied my aim.

Adam raised his weapon again.

She kept her gun at her side, but shrugged and appeared more confident than she should. "Suit yourself."

The barrel of a gun jabbed me in the back. My insides clenched at the steel stabbing my spine. Son of a bitch. She wasn't alone. How the hell had they gotten behind us? So much for better hearing.

"I suggest you drop your weapon before I'm forced to kill you and your friend." The voice was deep and gruff.

I debated. I didn't want to leave myself vulnerable, but I didn't want a bullet to the back. I put the Glock in its holster and Adam jammed his gun in the back of his jeans. We then both raised our hands and turned.

A man who looked to be in his sixties, with a face lined from too many hours in the sun, aimed a shotgun at us. A younger, second guy who looked like he was in his mid-twenties pointed a pistol. He bore a slight resemblance to the girl. Maybe he was her older brother.

"All right, then." He lowered the gun and shut the door behind him. "I'm John. You met my niece, Megan. This is her brother, Lucas."

"I'm Adam."

I licked my cracked lips. "Val."

"Megan, please gather their guns from them." She moved closer to Adam and held out her hand. He locked his gaze with mine, withdrew his gun, and handed it to the girl.

She turned to me. I stared at her open palm. No way. I wasn't giving it up. Lucas jabbed his pistol into my arm. I took the Glock out of the holster and held it by the barrel. Megan snatched it from my grasp. It felt like my soul went with it.

Megan handed our guns to Lucas and he tucked them in the back of his jeans.

John inspected our skin and nodded. "Well, glad we got the pleasantries out of the way. Adam, Val, why don't you two tell me what you're doing here alive?"

Adam held his hands out, palms up, in front of his chest. "Sir, we apologize for entering your house, but we checked and thought the house was empty."

"Well, it ain't."

"We'll just go now." I backed up a step toward the door.

"No." Megan swung the shotgun back at me.

John ran his fingers across his stubbled chin. "Megan's right. You're not going anywhere. We need to know what y'all have seen. Come now, follow me." He went to the door housing the pantry and opened it.

I gave Adam a what's-the-guy-doing look. Was he counting his cans to see what we ate?

"Over here." Megan motioned with the gun.

We went over and stood by her.

John reached up and pulled something in the corner of the closet. A creaking noise preceded a slow groan. The shelves slid to the right side of the wall.

I took a step closer to see what secrets the shelves concealed. I gaped in shock. It was a tunnel.

"This way." John disappeared into the darkness.

I glanced at Adam. He returned my look, but followed John with Lucas on his heels. Once Adam entered the blackness, I turned to Megan. "If this is a trap, I'll kill you."

"Just go." She waved the gun again, but she didn't have a tight grip on it.

This was my chance. I could grab it from her. What if I missed? I had another gun in my bag, but not enough time to get it. What would they do to us? The consequences were too great. I bit my tongue instead and stepped into the blackness.

I stood in the dark waiting for my eyes to adjust and to my surprise, it took a lot less time than normal. Guess my vision skills accelerated faster than Adam's had.

When Megan came in behind me, she latched the shelves back into place, and a row of bare lights on a string lit up, revealing a descending staircase.

The soup turned to granite in my stomach. I didn't want to go down the stairs. Technically, it was a basement. My heart rate climber faster than a rocket leaving the atmosphere. A basement.

"Move." Megan tapped the muzzle of her gun into my back.

My internal radar screamed for me to run, but I forced my lead-filled muscles down the stairs, Megan and her gun a breath behind. With each step, my pulse accelerated. I was swimming in a pool of terror. Step. My legs turned cold and numb. Step. My chest constricted, cutting off my oxygen. Step. I gasped for air. I was drowning.

Weight clamped on my shoulder. I struggled to the surface. "Val. Are you okay?"

Adam's voice circled me like a life preserver, rescuing me from drowning in the nightmare of my memories. "Huh?"

He gave my shoulder a squeeze, then let go. "It's okay. Come on."

I focused. Breathed in for four seconds. Held my breath for seven. Exhaled for eight. Did it two more times. I calmed myself, but replaced the panic attack with the feeling of entering my grave.

John had led us into an underground bunker of sorts. Light shone from more bare bulbs on a string, and multi-colored rugs covered the dirt floors. Worn furniture lined the area in front of where we stood. Behind the couches, a table covered in mounds of radio equipment spanned the length of the back cement-block wall. A small kitchen filled the space to the right of the table and three doors stood closed on the left. It was an eerie resemblance of the floor plan upstairs.

"Please sit." John motioned to the couches.

Adam sat on the faux leather one and I took the brown suede. The bank of glowing color TV monitors lining the wall grabbed my attention. They didn't show programmed shows; the monitors showed the outside and inside of the cabin. My mouth went drier than a lizard's skin. I scanned the images. Exhaled. None of them showed the bathroom.

Megan crossed to the first closed door and tapped the barrel of the rifle on it three times. The door opened with a creak. A man carrying a gun and a blonde girl slightly older than me came out. My fingers ached to grab my gun. But it wasn't there.

Instead, I balled my hands into fists, my nails digging into my palms. I needed my gun back. We needed to get out of here. And pronto.

"What do we have here?" The man directed his question to John.

"This is Adam and Val. Adam is more cooperative, even if he's wearing someone else's shirt."

Adam touched the name on his shirt.

"Val is currently plotting an escape route." John chewed on the side of his thumbnail.

I glared at him. How did he know what I was thinking?

He spit something, I didn't want to know what, on the floor, and then said, "It's written on your face, darling."

"Don't call me darling." I tried to sound menacing, but I'm pretty sure I came off as bitchy. Oh, well, that worked too.

"My apologies." John nodded.

"I'm Frank. This is my niece Bethany. You've met my daughter and son? This is my brother John's place." He stepped into Adam's personal space and looked into his eyes. Adam didn't flinch. Frank turned to me and I narrowed my eyes at his soul-searching stare. He smacked his lips together and bobbed his head up and down. Then he set his gun on the table. "Give them their weapons back. They're good kids. I can tell."

I snatched the Glock back from Lucas's hand and suppressed my urge to kiss the barrel. I had it back. Dad's gun. My gun. My lifeline.

"Let's sit with our guests."

The others, except Bethany who leaned against the kitchen counter, joined Adam and I on the couches. Lucas sat next to me and smiled a how-you-doing smile. I cringed and forced a smile back, but my attention went to Megan sitting closer than she needed to Adam. Prickles of anger poked my brain.

"Where are you two from?" Frank turned from Adam then to me.

"I'm from Houston and Val's from..." Adam pulled at a loose thread on his shirt. "Alberdine."

He didn't know for sure where I was from, because I hadn't told him. But he was right. Alberdine was the only place I'd ever lived. Goose bumps rippled across my arms, but they had nothing to do with the temperature. Rule Number One—trust no one—came back to life and roared to the forefront of my brain. I pulled the sleeve of my hoodie down and traced the rules with my index finger. I needed to rewrite them again. The shower had removed some of the marker and I hadn't touched them up since just after I met Adam. A sure sign I *did* trust him, but the reality tasted acidic in my mouth. When I glanced up, I met Adam's stare.

"We're from Louisville, but when it all went bad, we moved up here to John's safe house. Thank God he's a paranoid SOB," Frank said.

"Have you seen any other survivors?" Adam leaned forward.

Frank shook his head. "No, just the damn night-walkers. But only two here in the woods."

"Night-walkers?" Did he mean the Raspers? Funny how we'd each come up with our own names for them.

"Val calls them Raspers," Adam offered.

"I like it. We haven't heard that one on the airwaves." John stood.

"Wait. Airwaves? You can communicate with others?" Adam bounced in his seat. "How many are there?"

John held up his hands, palms out. "Hang on there, son. Do you mean to say you haven't seen others between Houston, Texas and here?"

"I traveled with other people to just south of Tulsa, but the Raspers killed or took everyone over there. I made my way alone until I met Val."

Lucas sat up straight. "Adam, you said the Raspers took the others over. What do you mean?"

"Hold on. Hold on." Frank held up his hands and got to his feet. "We need to do this logically. The more we know about them, the better chance we have to survive."

We all nodded in agreement. But I wasn't spilling all my secrets if they didn't give me any useful information. I traced Rule Number One again, but this time I used my nail.

Frank pulled a white board from behind the one couch. Mathematical problems covered the board. He flipped it over to the clean side. He wrote *Great Discovery* and *four months ago* on the top in neon orange marker. "Okay. The Great Discovery."

Adam looked at me then turned back to Frank. "Something about oil."

"Yes. Supposedly enough oil to power the United States for over a hundred years." He added *oil* to his list. "The government kept it quiet until the day the deep sea rig was scheduled to puncture the ceiling of the oil chamber. All the major news networks were there on the platform. Video showed people cheering when the drill broke through."

I hadn't seen that on TV. "What does this have to do with the Raspers?"

"I'm not sure. Within minutes of the breach, the world lost contact with the platform. Then everything went to hell and Mother Nature unleashed her fury. The Raspers showed up while our friends and neighbors died." Frank wrote *Raspers* and *destruction* on the board.

Was he a teacher or something? I ran my tongue back and forth on the roof of my mouth. "What makes you think these things are related?"

"Well, the Navy sent a search helicopter to find out what happened, but the platform was gone. Do you know how big one of those things are? They don't just disappear. Then all we heard about were strange happenings all along the Gulf Coast. I don't believe in coincidence."

"Do either of you know why some people die and others turn into Raspers?" Megan inched a hair closer to Adam.

"No. Do you?"

"No. Seen anything else crazy?"

Adam's gaze connected with mine. Either they didn't know about the Bugs, or they were testing us. I nodded to him.

"The metal creatures."

"They really exist?"

Adam bobbed his head. "We've seen them in groups, by themselves, and with Raspers."

"One crawled out of a Rasper's mouth when I shot him." I worked hard at keeping my voice flat and not screechy.

"Holy..." Lucas slammed his fist against the arm of the couch. "Can they be killed?"

"Yes." I ran my hand over my lips. Could I have a Bug inside me?

John pointed his thumb at the equipment. "Back before you all had cellular phones, gadgets and gizmos galore, us old timers talked to one another using radios. Ham radios." He picked up a microphone that was attached to the radio equipment.

"My grandfather had one." Adam got up and walked to John's side.

John flipped some switches and spun a dial. "We only listen. No talking."

"John has this theory that the Raspers are able to pick up on the radio transmissions and can pinpoint the origin." Frank ran his palm across his retreating hairline. "In the beginning, we heard a lot of chatter. No so much anymore."

John hooked his thumbs in his belt loops. "Before all this happened, I used to be able to talk to people pretty much anywhere. Now I run on solar power and batteries. Sometimes the radio doesn't work, but it's a connection."

Adam moved closer, seemingly captivated by talking to others on the radio. He thumbed the button on the microphone.

"Stop! Let go of it." John ripped the mike from Adam's grip.

Adam backed up a step. "Sorry. My grandpa used to let me push the button. Sorry."

I didn't like the radio. There was no sure way to tell if the person on the other end was a Rasper or not. It wasn't a clear signal and they could hide their raspy breathing.

"Val, you've been on your own?" Frank seesawed the marker between his fingers.

I watched the marker bob up and down. "Yeah."

"Being by yourself for so long must have been hard on someone your age. What are you, sixteen or so?"

"Yeah." Manners dictated I should give the guy more than one word answers, but I couldn't bring myself to. And I wanted out of the basement.

"Megan's sixteen, too, and Bethany's seventeen."

I nodded. I didn't care. It wasn't as if we were going to have a slumber party or something. Adam checked out the radio and I stared at his back. He needed to get over here. He was better than I was at chitchat. And I hadn't been around this many people since my last day at school.

Lucas got up from the seat next to me and took Adam's vacated spot. "Where are you guys headed?"

I exhaled and figured I should share something. "Adam found an address of sorts. We were going to try to figure out what it meant."

Frank turned to Adam, who'd finally stopped salivating over the radio. "What do you mean, you found an address?"

Adam dug the map out of his pocket, walked over, and handed it to Frank. "Do you know what it means?"

Frank held the paper in his left hand and rubbed his right across his mouth. "Where did you get this?"

"At a house in the last town we were in. Why? What is it?" Adam leaned on the couch's arm.

Frank stood and paced the room. We all watched in silence. "How religious are you?"

"Not much, sir."

"Well, the anchor symbolizes hope. Hope in Christ, more specifically."

Adam frowned. "I think the guy was a church pastor or something."

"Makes sense. 300 Seed Plot."

"And that means what?" I tried to keep the edge out of my voice, but failed. Adam looked over, but I glanced away from him.

"Seed Plot means nursery."

Adam rubbed his temples. "As in babies?"

Frank stopped pacing. "It could also mean seminary."

"So it's not an address?" I knew it was nothing important.

"The Triad Theological Seminary isn't too far away. The radio said people were starting a safe community there."

"Why write it in a code?" Seemed to me like he was stretching.

"Well, now this is just a theory, but my thought is the Raspers are functioning off a collective computer-type mind."

I sat up straight. The walls closed in, inch by inch. I blinked and forced myself to breathe. "A collective mind? Are you serious?"

"I think whatever information one gains is somehow transmitted to some central thing and it gets sent back to all of them. Maybe your pastor was trying to keep the community's information from reaching their collective."

"That's beyond scary." I couldn't control my nerves and jumped up. I had to move. They shared information? I so didn't want them to be able to access my thoughts.

"Do you know where the seminary is?" Adam directed his question at Frank.

Frank nodded, walked to a map on the wall. "Yes, come here." He pointed to a spot on the map. "We're at the foot of Miller's Mountain. The seminary is here." He traced a line to the closest town to the east.

We stood on either side of Frank, looking at the spot he'd indicated. "We should go check it out. I bet they have resources." Adam bounced on the balls of his feet.

John slapped his palm on his outer thigh. "You're welcome to go, Sonny, but we're staying here. This place is safer than most. I built it to be."

"A lot of people went to other safe places. We haven't heard back from most of them." Frank turned his back to the map. "If you like, you can stay here for a few days."

I didn't want to stay. I didn't want to spend any more time down here. I wanted to go. The rules burned on my skin like a new tattoo. The Raspers shared a hive mind and knew my name. I wanted to get far away from here as possible. The sooner the better.

The room came alive with flashing red lights.

"What's happening?" I glanced up, then yanked the Glock out of its holster.

"Perimeter alarm," Frank said.

"Hey, Uncle John, look at the monitors. There are guys outside the cabin." Bethany pointed at the screens.

I had forgotten the monitors were there. "Who are they?"

John moved to the bank of screens and flipped a switch,

turning off the alarm. "Looks like military from their uniforms. Might be here to rescue us."

Or kill us. But I didn't say that aloud. The words wouldn't form. It felt like my windpipe had been crushed.

"Frank, Lucas, and I will go upstairs. You four stay down here until we call you up." John hoisted his rifle.

I wanted to argue—almost did—but I couldn't voice my suspicions.

The three guys went upstairs, weapons in hand. Adam and Megan held their guns at the ready. Bethany stood next to Megan. We all stared at the monitors.

Uniformed men carrying long-barreled guns surrounded the exterior of the cabin. I glanced at the screens that showed the interior. John led the way. He waved at the other two and they took up positions on the far side of the room, facing the door. A man in uniform stood just to the side so the camera wasn't focused on his face. I moved closer to the screen, trying to get a better look.

Damn it. They were in full assault gear with camo paint covering their faces. Gloves. Goggles. Every inch of their bodies covered. There was no way to tell if they were legit.

"Val, what is it?" Adam moved to my side.

Somewhere mixed in the chaos of panic and fear and horror, I found my voice. "This isn't right. These guys wouldn't just show up." I pointed at the screen. "Were you expecting the military?" I turned to Megan.

"Not that I know of. Do you think my family's in danger?" A scared look crossed her delicate features.

"Maybe. Oh, I don't know." I turned back to the screens. My ears buzzed like a cluster of hornets were circling me. Something was definitely wrong.

The military man closest to the door busted it open. A short stocky one entered next and stopped. He looked down at something.

"There." My finger bounced off the monitor with a thud. "His neck. There's no camo paint on his neck."

I searched the bank of monitors to get a better look. And found one. Camera 4. Its angle was perfect. I leaned closer.

"His neck is yellow."
They all looked at me as if I was crazy.
"Rasper yellow!"

10

"Raspers!" My heart seemed to stop. "They're friggin' Raspers."

"Where?" Adam ran toward me, his gun already drawn.

I jabbed my finger at the screen. "Right there. Look at his skin."

"No." Megan dropped to her knees, her body shaking with out-of-control sobs. Bethany scrambled across the floor and wrapped her arms around her cousin.

I fixed my gaze on the monitors. John fired his shotgun at the tall Rasper who'd broken the door. A crimson cloud of blood and flesh exploded from the Rasper's head. He collapsed, his jaw ripping apart from what was left of his face.

No. No. No. I couldn't watch, but I couldn't turn away.

Lucas fired at the Bug that crawled from the Rasper's mouth, but missed. More Raspers broke through the windows and crashed in the backdoor, opening fire.

Frank went down. Megan screamed.

"Ssh." Adam told her. Bethany caressed her hair.

I stared in horror. My heart went from stopped to slamming against my chest as the Raspers mowed down the rest of their family. Oh, God. Part of me wanted to go upstairs and fight, while part of me wanted to run.

The Raspers searched the cabin. We had to get out. I turned to

Megan. She'd brought her knees to her chest and tears streamed down her face. "Megan?"

Bethany just stared blankly at Adam. He touched Megan's shoulder. "I know you're hurting, but we need you."

His voice got through to her in a way mine didn't. She raised her head.

"Megan, is there another way out of here?"

There had to be. John was a planner. He would have an escape route.

Bethany nodded and pointed at the first door.

While Adam helped Megan up and supported her arm, I watched a Rasper open the door to the pantry.

"We have to move. Now." My nerves sprang to attention, hyper-alert and ready for action. I grabbed Bethany's arm and pulled her to the door.

We entered a bedroom complete with bunk beds. Bethany pulled away from me and sat on the lower bunk. I spun around, closed the door, and tried to shove the dresser in front of it. The dresser refused to budge.

"Just a second." Adam deposited a wide-eyed, gunless Megan on the lower bunk next to her cousin. He then helped me push the dresser.

"Where's the way out?" I looked around the room. Nothing.

"Megan?" Adam dashed back to her and shook her shoulder. "Where's the exit?"

Bethany pointed to the floor.

I rolled up the rug covering the dirt floor and revealed a wooden hatch. One swift yank on the handle and the trap door opened. Another staircase descended below me. "Come on. We gotta go." I grabbed two flashlights from my bag and tossed one to Adam. I held the light in my right hand. My left cradled the Glock.

Adam tucked his gun in the back of his jeans and pulled Megan to her feet.

A pounding thudded from upstairs. They had to be breaking the pantry shelves. "Adam, we need to leave. Now."

"I know." He dragged Megan to the hatch and helped her down the stairs. Bethany followed without a word.

I jumped down and repositioned the rug as best as I could before latching the overhead door. If they got in the room, it would be obvious someone had moved the rug, but I had no other choice. I clicked on the flashlight and followed the others down the stairs.

The stone steps were slick with moisture. My instincts said to hold on to my gun, but I holstered the Glock. I kept one hand wrapped tightly around the flashlight and the other touching the rough rock walls. Panic tightened its freezing grip on my lungs. I couldn't breathe. I was going deeper. Below the basement. Down. Down. Down. I didn't count the steps, but figured there were more than thirty. I kept swallowing. The panic kept wedging my throat shut.

I reached the bottom and sucked in a gulp of the cool earthy air.

"Where to next, Megan?" I pulled a spare gun from my bag. I needed to be armed, but didn't want to risk losing the Glock.

"Huh?" Megan still seemed spaced out.

I couldn't blame her. She'd just watched her family die. At least I never saw mine shot to death. I shined my flashlight around. A stone tunnel about six feet wide by eight feet high stretched out before us. The scent of mildew and rotten vegetation had me picturing all sorts of creepy insects lurking in the dark. "Where does this tunnel go?"

Megan inhaled and wrinkled her nose. "Other side of the mountain."

"We're wasting time. Let's go." Adam tugged Megan by her sleeve. Bethany followed him down the tunnel like a lost puppy.

The temperature dropped lower and lower. Chills ran up my spine and made me shiver. My freezing wasn't all due to the temperature. I was underground. Under the basement level. Under life itself. Not even snakes went this deep. I was in hell. A cold hell.

My gut told me to run, and run fast. To get the hell out. But with the wet ground, it wasn't possible. We rounded a curve and the walls closed in. I hunched forward and kept moving. The vise clamped back down on my lungs, and jagged stones tugged at my hair.

"Shit, the tunnel's getting smaller." Adam's voice echoed around the rocks.

"Does it open up again?" My voice was far too high-pitched.

"Hang on," Megan said.

My brain screamed panic, but I kept my breaths shallow to make it look like I was calm. I wasn't. I wanted—needed—to get the hell out of this rock tomb. I inhaled, held my breath, then exhaled.

"It's getting bigger." Adam called from the front of our line. Thank God.

The tunnel transformed into an enormous cavern with rock walls higher than a church steeple. Stalactites hung from the ceiling in long, pointed shapes. Dripping water sounded from all directions.

"Is this cavern man-made?" Adam's voice echoed.

Bethany shook her head. "The cave was always here. John just added to it."

Ten feet in front of us, the ground dropped away, leaving a gaping hole of blackness. I shined my light on a lone rope bridge spanning the void. It had to be over fifty feet long.

My breath caught in my throat. Green algae or mold covered the rope every few feet. Megan and Bethany expected us to walk across that rickety thing, over a hole who knew how deep? They were nuts.

"Is this the only way?" Adam turned to Megan.

She stood with her back against the stones. I shined the flashlight on her, careful to keep it out of her eyes. A look of terror spread across her face. Her eyes widened and her mouth hung open in an 'o' shape.

"Megan? Are you okay?" I stepped toward her. Had she freaked out and gone into shock?

As if moving in slow motion, she nodded. She glanced at me, then sought out Adam. He moved to her side and she grabbed his hand.

My gut burned when he tucked her head against his chest. It wasn't fear causing the sensation. Could it be jealousy? No way. It wasn't as if he was my boyfriend or anything.

Bethany whispered, "It should hold."

"Ready?"

Adam released Megan and she faced me. My flashlight flickered in her brown eyes. It didn't seem like she was behind the glazed gaze. "Megan?"

She didn't answer, just stared like a zombie fresh from the grave. We needed her functioning, or she was a liability. At least Bethany seemed to know what was going on. I felt like a total ass thinking that way. I glanced over Megan's head and caught Adam's questioning what-should-we-do look. I raised my eyebrows at him in an I-don't-know fashion.

"Megan? Can you hear me?" When she didn't respond, he took off his backpack, pulled out a bottle of water, and dumped it over her head.

She shrieked and spun around. "What was that for?"

"I'm sorry. I know you're upset, but we need you here with us."

Adam amazed me. I had thought about slapping Megan to get her to pay attention, but I never would have acted on my idea.

Megan turned to me. "They died. They're gone."

"I'm sorry about your family, but if you don't want to end up like them, we need to move." I hoped I didn't sound too harsh, but there was no way I was dying here in this death trap.

"We need to cross the bridge. It should be safe. Uncle John built it to withstand the climate down here." Megan walked to the edge of the bridge and stepped onto it. "Come on, Bethany."

"Hang on. Let me go first. I have a flashlight." Adam moved in front of Megan and led our parade onto the bridge. The width allowed them to hold onto both sides as they walked.

I brought up the rear of the expedition, one hand on the rope for balance and the other holding both my small LED flashlight and gun. The slick spots on the rope made me cringe, but there was no way I was letting go. About ten feet onto the bridge, a shrill siren ripped through my eardrums and echoed around the cavern.

"It's the alarm. They've entered the tunnel," Megan yelled.

"Son of a..." Adam picked up speed.

The contents of my stomach shifted. The Raspers had

followed us. I cursed my poor covering of the hatch. I'd made it too easy for the damned uber-tracking Raspers.

The alarm lasted a few seconds, then shut off. A new sound replaced it. The distinctive tear of something ripping.

"What's that?" Whatever it was, it wasn't good. It felt like all the blood drained from my head and pooled in my feet. The bridge swayed to the left and then the right. I gripped the rope tighter. Sharp pain rocketed up my arm as the material bit into my hand.

"Nooo..." Adam's flashlight tumbled into the dark abyss.

I couldn't stop looking as it dropped. And dropped. And dropped. Never hitting bottom.

The bridge listed to the right. "Hand me your light." Adam let go of the bridge and held out his right hand.

I didn't want to throw it to him. Didn't want to miss. Didn't want the light to chase the other one down the bottomless pit. "Bethany, here take it. Pass it up to Adam."

Bethany nodded, braced herself, and released one hand. I stretched and extended the light to her. We were too far apart. One of us had to move. I released the rope and took two steps forward. It was enough. She snatched the flashlight and handed it to Adam.

Another ripping sound. Shit. The bridge shuddered and I lost my balance. I reached out for the rope, but missed. The bridge's wooden slats rushed up to meet my face. I hit them hard then slid toward the edge. No. I had to get a hold of the rope. I had no choice. I opened my left hand. The gun tumbled out, hit the plank of the bridge, and slipped off. The bridge swung to the left. I lunged for the edge, caught the rope, and clutched it in a palm-burning grip. My breath came in rapid pants. I did it. I'd lost my gun, but I was still hanging on. Alive.

"Val, you okay?" Adam shined the light at me.

"Peachy." The bridge jerked to the side again. I pulled myself up. "We need to get off this damn thing."

While the bridge continued to sway, we worked our way across. When my feet touched solid rock, I wanted to get on my knees and kiss the ground. I added rope bridges to my list of things to never do again.

"That was messed up." Adam held out my flashlight.

"No, keep it, I have another one." I retrieved another flashlight and my last backup gun from my bag.

"Vvvaaalll."

The sound of my name resonated off the cavern walls. I turned. Three Raspers, a female and two males, stood at the start of the rope bridge.

Every one of my muscles turned to stone. How did these ones know my name too?

Bethany backed up until she was flat against the rock wall.

"Come on." Adam grabbed my arm and forced me back.

Megan rolled up her pant leg and whipped out a wicked looking knife from a holder on her calf. She hacked away at the rope bridge. "Guys, help me."

I unsheathed my knife from my right leg and took the other side of the bridge.

The Raspers ran at us. The one in the front brought his gun up to fire.

"Duck." Adam hollered. He fired at the Rasper. Missed.

I dove to the ground and went for my gun.

"Val, no. Don't stop cutting. I'll get them." Adam rolled onto the ground. Another bullet shot toward us. "Bethany, get down."

Adam fired into the female Rasper's chest. The bridge rocked. She catapulted off the side.

I kept cutting.

"Almost there." Megan whispered.

I gave one more hack and the rope's connection next to me snapped. The bridge weaved like a snake. The remaining two Raspers increased their speed. They were going to make it to our side. I pulled the Glock. Fired. Missed.

Adam sent another blast off. One of the Raspers stumbled and disappeared off the bridge.

"Got it." Megan cut through the final strand of rope. The last Rasper jumped. The bridge dropped away and the Rasper reached out, catching the edge of the rock cliff with his fingertips. What saliva I had left dried up, leaving my throat raw and sandpapery.

Megan raced over and stomped on his fingers. "That's for my family, you bastard."

The Rasper couldn't hold on. He fell without a sound into the dark unknown.

Adam and I stood. Bethany raced to Megan's side. The four of us stared down into the nothingness. All of our breathing came out in gasps. My heart slammed against my chest.

Seconds later, I heard a thud. The last Rasper hit the bottom. Adam flinched, but Megan and Bethany didn't react.

"Are there more damn bridges in here?" I asked Megan.

"I'm sorry. I thought it was secure. It's the only one. Come on, we're not far." Megan passed Adam and grabbed the flashlight out of his hand. She went down another rock tunnel with Bethany on her heels.

Adam tapped my shoulder. I shrugged.

We jogged, more than ran, down the slippery tunnel. More rocks jutted out, poking us as we passed. After about fifteen minutes, Megan stopped.

The tunnel opened up into a larger flat space about the size of a living room. Three towering stone walls mocked me, blocking any possibility of escape. Wet white-and-gray stalagmites reached up from the ground toward the smaller stalactites growing from the ceiling way above my head.

"Crap. It's a dead end."

"Hang on." Megan bent over to catch her breath. Bethany gasped and clutched her chest.

Thanks to the Rasper's sting, neither Adam nor I breathed any harder than normal. I didn't want to think about the costs. Was I going to turn into a monster? Would it kill me? The questions spun a tangled mess in my brain and thumped at my temples. I needed to stop. Thinking like that would only get me killed.

"Okay, over here." Megan walked to the far wall and climbed up the rocks.

I squinted to see what she'd stepped on. Tiny stone shelves, no wider than a child's shoe, littered the wall.

Bethany climbed up next.

"Are you kidding me?" Adam tucked his gun back in his pants and put his hands on the rock ledge.

It didn't seem like a very fast escape.

Megan stopped climbing and glanced down. "It's designed so only those who know how to get out can. Took Uncle John forever to get them all attached."

Thank goodness, she had snapped out of her funk. Otherwise, we'd never get out of this mountain of horrors.

I grabbed onto the ledge and hauled myself up. My boot slipped. I took three deep breaths and regained control. We worked our way up the rock face by following Megan's lead and placing our hands and feet where she did. She was about three stories up when she stopped and transitioned to what must have been a tiny ledge. She methodically slid to the left for a few car lengths before she turned her body and disappeared behind the rocks.

What the hell? She just vanished. Bethany followed Megan's movements and—poof—gone.

"Megan?" Adam turned to me. His foot slipped. Pebbles rained down. His back straightened. He held on. "Shit. That was close."

"Come on. It's okay." Megan's voice echoed.

Yeah. Sure it was.

Adam mumbled something, then disappeared.

My turn. Crap. My heartbeat thundered in my ears. I placed a boot on the itty-bitty ledge and inched my way along, praying my backpack wouldn't throw me off balance.

With precise and careful steps, I managed to not kill myself. I turned and sidestepped into a stone room about the size of a one-car garage. The air smelled stale and dusty, but not wet and musty. I exhaled a long breath, then pointed at the brown tarp covering something in the space. "What's under there?"

Megan grabbed a corner of the tarp and yanked. The plastic flew toward her, revealing two ATVs.

"Do they work?" Adam walked closer to inspect the black four-wheelers.

"They should, and we have extra gas for both." Megan patted a storage compartment on one ATV. She took a waist pack that was hanging on the wall and strapped it on.

"How do we get out of here?" I searched the rock walls, but couldn't make out an exit.

Megan walked to the far rock wall and pushed. The wall opened up and glaring sunlight stung my eyes. I slid my sunglasses on. Holy crap, John had been a true prepper. He'd thought of everything.

"Let's get the hell out of here before any more Raspers find us." I hopped on the closest four-wheeler. The fact that two different Raspers had called my name haunted my thoughts.

Adam ran a hand through his hair, making it stick up a little. "Do you know how one of these works?"

"No. How hard can it be? Gas, steer, brake." I turned the key and the engine roared to life.

"I know how to drive one." Megan straddled the other vehicle. "Bethany, hop on."

"I can drive it." Adam gave me a pleading look.

"I got it. Come on, get on." I patted the seat behind me. He had driven the dirt bike. It was my turn. I needed this. Needed to be in control.

He climbed on and growled low in his throat. "Give me your bag before it takes my head off."

I slipped my backpack off my shoulders and handed it to him.

"Don't worry. I won't lose it."

"You'd better not."

I revved the ATV. Adam slid in closer. His thighs wrapped around my butt, his arms around my waist. I couldn't breathe. It felt like hundreds of feathers swirled in my stomach. He inched nearer and tightened his grip. My heart stopped.

Megan hit the gas and shot forward. I followed behind, trying not to wreck the metal beast. It took a few minutes before I was comfortable handling the machine. Adam's strong presence behind me might have helped. But, damn, I couldn't focus on how close our bodies were when all I could think about was the Raspers.

A second one knew my name. They *were* a collective. But they didn't call to anyone else. Just me. How did it work? Did they only know stuff if they learned, or could they somehow absorb memories from humans? Fear wrapped my veins in a tourniquet of alarm. If they could do that, they would know how to get past the stone rock face. They would know about the ATVs. They would know we were alive.

We had to go faster.

11

The ATV bounced over the rocky terrain, and wind cut into my cheeks like shards of glass. I shivered despite Adam's extra heat warming my back. When had it gotten so damn cold? It was as if Jack Frost snapped his fingers and we were plunged into the dead of winter.

We cut through the woods, dodging the trees that flew past. I hoped Megan knew where she was going. Another gust whipped the tips of my hair across my face. The skin on my hands felt frozen to the handlebars.

My mind wandered back to the Raspers and how they knew my name. Why me? What did they want? Were they tracking me? Why not anyone else? Adam pounded on my shoulder. I stopped focusing on the damn mutants just in time—I'd nearly run into the back of the other ATV. Stupid. I cut the engine. Adam climbed off and the icy blast tore through my clothes.

"Why are we stopping?" I rubbed my hands across my arms in a pathetic attempt to warm myself.

"It's freezing. I need a jacket." Bethany jumped off and huddled into herself, dropping five years off how old she looked.

Megan dug in the side compartment of the ATV. She pulled out two brown camouflage jackets, two black hats, and two pairs of black ski-type gloves. "There should be another set in your left-side compartment." Megan and Bethany both slipped on their jackets, hats, and gloves.

I checked the side bin and pulled out a similar coat, two hats, and two pairs of gloves. We were a coat short. "Well, crap. There's only one coat." I held it up.

"Go ahead. You take it." Adam grabbed a hat and gloves.

"It's okay. I have an extra sweatshirt." I was being nice, but I really wanted the coat for myself.

"No, you take it. I have the leather jacket. Besides, I'm warmer than you. You block a lot of the wind."

My cheeks burned. I prayed he didn't see how red my face was. I shoved my arms into the too-big-for-me coat and zipped it up.

"Damn, it got cold." Bethany's teeth chattered and her body twitched with waves of shivers.

"Well, it *is* officially winter. The Not-So-Great Discovery threw the seasons out of whack. Hope this cold spell doesn't last, but it could be worse." Megan tugged her hat down over her eyebrows.

"How?"

"There's normally a few inches of snow on the ground in February."

Snow. Yeah, Megan was right. It could be worse. I hadn't even thought about snow. The temperatures had been so warm since that day. I yanked the band out of my hair, let my mop of hair fall, and then shoved the hat on my head.

"Where are we?" Adam ground up a ball of dirt with his well-worn sneakers.

"On the east side of Miller's Mountain, following the logging roads. The seminary is probably twenty miles or so away."

Twenty miles. "Do we have enough gas to get there on these?"

"Each machine started with a full tank of gas and they both have the extra tank. We'll make it there. But not before dark."

Adam and I both glanced up. Anxiety coiled in my stomach like a venomous python waiting to strike. There was no way to beat the darkness.

"We have to keep going until we find a spot to hide." I tugged on the gloves, then rubbed my hands back and forth.

"If we follow this road, we should be safe until we find a secure spot to camp for the night." Megan pointed forward.

"Are you serious?" She thought we should camp outside? "That's insane."

"Why don't we crash in a house?" Bethany channeled my thoughts.

Megan pinched the bridge of her freckled nose. "Uncle John told me there isn't a house on this side of the mountain until we hit the town of Little Creek, and that's right before the seminary."

Perfect. We were officially in the middle of nowhere. We all climbed back on the four-wheelers. Had the Raspers gotten out of the mountain? Were they tailing me?

We had ridden for about another hour when Megan stopped in a small clearing. I idled the ATV, careful not to glance at Adam's arms wrapped around my waist. But I wanted to.

"This should be a good spot." Megan said.

"A good spot for what?" I glanced around. The logging road continued out in front of us and trees surrounded the dirt clearing.

"To camp for the night."

She had lost her mind.

"We are so not spending the night out in the open. We need to find a cave or something." I cut the engine.

Adam let go of me and everyone got off the vehicles.

"There's a two-person tent in the right compartment of your ATV." Megan inclined her head toward my vehicle.

I rubbed my arms. Stay outside in the night. Exposed. "There's no protection from the Raspers here."

"There aren't any Raspers here." Megan rubbed her palms together and blew on her gloved hands.

No Raspers that you know of. "I don't like it."

"Val, I think we should be okay. It's only one night." Adam touched my shoulder for a fraction of a second, then let go.

It was a bad idea. And he was siding with Megan. I opened the other bin on the vehicle and pulled out the nylon pouch wedged in the space. A white fabric swatch proclaimed the package as the easiest two-person tent to set up. Two-person. The words cut into me. How convenient. Adam and I would have to split watch duty. I bet Megan would partner with Adam. A part of me wanted to check in the right compartment of her four-wheeler to see if there was another tent she purposely wasn't mentioning.

"Uncle John was paranoid, but he knew how to prepare. He was the ultimate prepper." Her eyes grew shiny and she looked around at the woods. "I need to find a private tree." Megan dashed off into the woods, wiping her face as she went.

"Here, I'll set up the tent." Adam took the bundle from my arms and handed me my bag.

"Do you *really* think this is safe?" I barely whispered the words.

"I don't think anything is safe anymore, but we should be okay tonight." He gave my arm another small squeeze.

Heat radiated from my arm to my cheeks. I turned to hide it and checked my water inventory. Six bottles left. I pulled one out. I wanted to gulp it down, but forced myself to take small sips.

"I'm going to check the perimeter." I left before anyone responded. I needed to clear my head, and make sure this wasn't the stupidest plan ever.

I walked into the woods surrounding the clearing. Dusk lit the sky in a combination of reds and pinks.

I still hadn't processed my enhanced abilities. I didn't feel any different physically, but who knew what was happening inside my body? I ran my gloved hand across my cheeks. My head throbbed and dragged my eyelids to half-mast. Exhaustion wrapped its tentacles around me.

Counting aloud to keep myself alert, I continued walking and found nothing out of the ordinary. No Raspers, Bugs, or rabid animals. The breeze kicked up a pile of leaves and swirled them around. I tracked the leaves until they blew away. When I got back to the clearing, Adam had set up the tent.

"That didn't take long." I came up beside him in front of the blue nylon tent. "Do you think Frank was right? That the address is a safe community?"

"I hope so. I'm not big on camping."

"My parents took me camping one summer in the Smoky Mountains. It was okay, but I liked having my TV and running water." I let out a laugh and surveyed the makeshift campsite, the ATVs, the survival gear. The emptiness of the woods. My world had imploded and changed in less time than a normal school day. "Maybe they should have taken me camping more."

"Hey, guys, can you help?" Megan called.

Adam and I turned. Bethany and Megan dragged tree branches into the clearing. We grabbed part of their load.

"We should start a fire. It's getting pretty cold." Megan rubbed her arms.

"Don't you think it will be a beacon, showing the Raspers where we are?"

"We'll freeze if we don't start one. And Raspers aren't the only things to worry about out here."

She did have a point. We'd escaped the dogs before. I didn't want a pack of wolves surrounding us. "Fine. I'll do it." I grabbed a pile of twigs and built a tepee-shaped tower.

Bethany handed me a pile of leaves that I shoved under my structure. I lit the leaves with my lighter.

"Here." Adam handed me a few branches.

Minutes later, I had a fire roaring. Dad would have been proud. He had spent forever teaching me how to start a fire on that one camping trip. If I had known, I would have listened to him more. Told him I loved him more. Said I was sorry.

My mother's face flashed before me like a video on fast forward. I choked down a ball of grief that threatened to release. Would I forget what she looked like? My heart broke into even smaller pieces. I hoped not. I didn't want my memories to become shadows of the past.

Darkness dropped around us, the shadows hiding the emotions overwhelming me. We sat on logs we had pulled from the woods and stared into the fire, no one saying a word. What were they thinking? Megan and Bethany were probably mourning the loss of their family. And Adam—I had no idea what he was thinking.

Then it hit me. John had been Megan's uncle. Bethany was her cousin. Oh, I had been an ass.

"Bethany?"

"Hmm?" Her gaze focused on the flames.

"Was John your dad?"

She gave a barely-there head shake. Her hair fell and hid her face. "No, he was my uncle too. My mom was Frank and John's sister."

She didn't say anymore. I really couldn't ask about her parents without being rude. I didn't want to talk about my parents, so asking about hers wasn't an option. I pulled out four granola bars. "Anyone want one?"

We ate our gourmet dinner in silence. When I was done, I tossed my wrapper into the flames and watched it curl and burn. The branches popped and sizzled. I pulled out one of my knives and dug the blade into the log.

"You're left-handed." Megan crumpled up her wrapper.

The fire lit her face. She was pretty, almost beautiful. Her blonde hair hung past her shoulders and the flames danced in her brown eyes.

"Yeah, so what?" I cut a chunk out of the log.

"Well, my dad noticed you both were left-handed when you were upstairs in the cabin."

"You mean when you were spying on us?" Another chunk.

"Yes, but you were in our house."

True.

"What's the big deal with being left-handed? I think like ten percent of the population is. Or was." I had no idea how many people survived. I dug out another hunk of bark. It had been stupid of me to think I was the only one.

Megan sighed and her shoulders sagged. "I'm not sure, but he commented on it and became very interested in you guys after that."

Adam sat up straighter. "Interested how?"

"He became animated like he does—did—when he was working on a project for the university. Like it was a big deal or something."

"He didn't mention anything." Adam said.

"No. No, he didn't to you." Megan rubbed her hands down her jeans. "He was like that."

"He was a teacher?" I stopped carving and twirled the knife in my hand.

"A professor of history at University of Louisville."

"What did he say?" Adam shot me a look then turned to Megan.

She seemed to shrink back from him. "Just that you were both lefties and my age."

"Are you left-handed too?"

"No."

I held up the knife. The flames reflected along the blade. Frank had to have had a point in noting Adam and I were both lefties, but I had no clue what it was.

"Well, we should probably try to sleep a little." Adam stood and stretched.

"I think three of us can fit into the tent if we squeeze," Megan said.

I stifled a yawn. "I can take first watch. I don't sleep much anyway."

"You sure?" Adam stretched his arms over his head and rolled his neck.

"Yeah, I'm good. I'll wake you when I get tired."

Megan and Bethany ducked into the tent, Adam right behind. Into the tent. The small tent.

My heart flipped over and buried itself deep inside.

***

Anger—okay, jealousy—burned in my chest like a severe case of indigestion. I walked around the edge of the clearing to get away from the tent. Images of Adam and Megan snuggling in the confined space had me wishing for antacids. I shouldn't be this upset. He wasn't my boyfriend. I didn't even like him. But the voice that belonged to my heart whispered, *Yes, you do.* I told my heart to shut up and focused on the woods.

Arctic air sliced through my jacket and broke up my thoughts of Adam. I looked around. With my new ability to see better in the dark, I could make out individual leaves on the trees. I couldn't do that before the sting. It was cool, but creepy. Did I have teeny tiny little Bugs zooming through my blood stream? The image was enough to make me want to vomit my granola bar.

I made my way over to the ATVs. I spared one glance at the tent. No movements. No voices. Hopefully, they were asleep. I pictured Adam stroking Megan's hair.

I slammed my butt on the four-wheeler, my back to the tent. An ache thrummed behind my eyes. Exhaustion threatened to knock me out, but I had to stay awake. Had to stay alert. The wind howled—or was it a coyote? Crap. I pulled my hat lower to cover my ears.

I was in the middle of nowhere violating Rules One and Two. Trusting people and being out in the open at night. What was I doing? I dropped my face into my gloved hand. Look what had happened after I trusted Adam. The damn Rasper stung me and now I had super powers that were most likely going to kill me.

I lifted my head. White particles dropped down all around. No. It couldn't be. I held out my hand. Snow.

Tiny flakes dotted the material of my glove. Great. We were so unprepared for snow. I pulled my legs up and hugged my knees, mesmerized by the falling flakes.

Crunch.

The sound brought me back to reality. Something—or someone—was out there, about thirty feet away. I dropped my legs, pulled out my gun, and sat straight up. All my senses were hyper-alert. Tight. Focused.

Nothing moved. It was as if whatever was out there had heard me move and was waiting for me to strike first. I relaxed my breathing. Where was it? I narrowed my eyes at the woods. Snowflakes danced in the wind, but nothing else moved.

Had the Raspers tracked me? Had they surrounded us? What if Megan had been right and it was something else? I tightened my grip on the Glock. I considered waking the others, but there wasn't time.

A shadow crossed by the large tree to my right. I tracked the movement, cursing my super vision for not being super enough. What was it? A Rasper? A bear? What?

More leaves crunched. The shadow darted closer.

I double-gripped the gun. My nerves tingled, making me aware of every muscle twitch and blink of my eyes.

The shadow engulfed me from behind. And something touched my shoulder.

12

My heart ripped out of my chest. I yelped, dove off the ATV and hit the frozen ground. I pointed the gun, searching for a target.

And locked Adam in my gun sight.

"Sorry. Jeez. You'll wake up the girls."

"Adam, you dumb ass. I could have shot you again. Damn it." I picked myself off the ground and waved the Glock toward the woods. "There's something out there."

He pulled out his gun. "What—"

"I don't know."

"Raspers?" Adam's eyes glowed in the dying embers of the fire.

"Hopefully just a deer. Now shut up and listen." We waited. And waited. But nothing happened.

"I don't hear it anymore. It must have been an animal. It probably got scared and bolted."

"Probably, considering how much noise you made." I slapped him on the upper arm. "Don't sneak up on me again. Got it?"

A grimace of pain crossed his face. Crap. I hit his injured arm.

"Got it," he said through clenched teeth.

Great. Now I felt like dog crap. Again. "You want the jacket?" I made a move to unzip it, but hoped he'd say no.

"No. You keep it. I'm good." He pulled the gloves out of his back pocket. "Get some sleep before you collapse."

I rolled my neck with a series of pops and nodded.

I hadn't realized how tired I was until I shuffled toward the tent. I wanted—needed—to sleep, but wasn't crazy about crashing next to strangers. I still didn't trust Megan, yet I didn't have a choice. I wasn't sleeping in the snow. I ducked into the tent and zipped it closed behind me.

Bethany lay squeezed into the side of the tent and Megan curled in a ball, her hat pulled over her eyes. The blanket Adam had pulled from the car rested over her legs. They looked innocent and fragile. Megan wasn't my enemy in the way the Raspers were, but there was something about her. I just didn't know what.

I put my head on an extra sweatshirt and placed the Glock inches from my fingers. The blanket called to me. I pulled a corner across my chest, careful to keep Megan covered.

In what seemed like just minutes, I opened my eyes, shocked to see sunlight streaming through the walls of the tent. I turned to Megan and Bethany, but they weren't there. I checked my watch. It was just after seven. Not good. I grabbed my gun and scrambled out of the tent.

Outside, the morning was crisp and a fine blanket of snow covered the ground. Megan crouched next to the fire's ashes, poking them with a stick. Bethany sat on one of the ATVs. Adam wasn't anywhere in sight.

"Where's Adam?" I walked up next to Megan.

She stood and brushed her hands on her jeans. Her face was swollen and her eyes red-rimmed.

"Hey, are you okay?" I tucked my hair behind my ears.

She sniffed. "They didn't deserve to die." She snapped the stick she held and threw it in the ashes. "It's not fair."

"I'm so—" A stomping of feet sounded behind me. I pivoted, gun at the ready.

"Damn girl, you're trigger happy aren't you?" Adam grinned. "I didn't sneak up on you this time."

I settled for scowling at him, slipped the gun back in the holster, and adjusted my hat. I turned back to Megan.

She faked a smile. "What's the plan?"

"I think we should head to the seminary and if it's a bust, continue on to Pennsylvania and Site R."

Megan sniffed and nodded. "I'll start on the tent." She walked away and began tearing down our camp.

"What if there's nothing but destruction at both places?" I rubbed the words on my right arm, reminding myself of my rules.

"I wish I had the answers, but I don't. What's our other choice? Sit around shooting Raspers for the rest of our lives?" Adam shook his head, his hair slipping over his eyes. "I hope there's more to it than that. I want to stay optimistic that there is a safe place, free of Raspers. Maybe even a place where they know how to get rid of them for good. There has to be a way." Sadness leaked into his hopeful words. With a shrug of his shoulders, he grabbed the tent from Megan.

My view of the world didn't match Adam's optimism. The world was shit and we were swirling inside, not improving.

I slipped on my sunglasses and turned to Bethany. "How are you holding up?"

"Great." She jumped up and gave me her back.

What was she so pissed about? She was the one who had barely spoken.

Adam brought the tent over and shoved it into the compartment.

"Do you know why Bethany's mad and Megan's crying?"

Adam shrugged. "They lost their family yesterday. I'm sure they're just upset."

"I guess. Do you want to drive?" I ran my tongue over my cracked to hell and back lips. I so needed to get more lip balm.

"I'm okay riding. It's probably better for my arm."

"Okay." My stomach dropped. Once for him riding behind me again. Twice for his subtle reminder of my gunshot. But with how fast he healed, my heart leapt at the thought he was making an excuse.

"Ready?" Megan joined us.

"Yeah."

The four of us climbed on the machines and drove off down

the logging trail. The light coating of snow made control tricky. The path wasn't as bumpy as yesterday and the wind had died down to barely a whisper. But my insides felt like they were in a popcorn popper when I hit the ruts in the dirt road.

I couldn't stop worrying about what we might find at the seminary. The feeling of impending doom wrapped its talon-grip around my chest. I searched for any excuse besides the truth to convince Adam not to go.

I just couldn't tell him it scared me. I was tough. I shouldn't be scared.

And I sure as hell wasn't admitting my fear.

***

We stopped once to refill the gas tanks and eat more granola bars. We had left the snow and cold back in the mountains, but woods still surrounded us. It struck me that if a person looked at the world from inside the forest, they would never know everything humans created had gone to hell, while nature prevailed and remained strong.

Megan came to a halt on the crest of a hill. I braked next to her and shut down the engine. We were perched on an over-look. Below us, red brick buildings dotted the overgrown landscape.

My skin prickled from something more than the wind.

"Is this the place?" Adam and I climbed off the four-wheeler.

"I think so."

"This is the seminary? The safe community? Doesn't look too welcoming." I pulled off the gloves and stuffed them in the jacket pockets. "It feels wrong."

Bethany swallowed a long drink from her water bottle. "Seems kinda creepy."

"Maybe this isn't the place. It looks empty." Megan faced Adam.

"Your house looked empty, too." Adam's voice went lower and deeper than normal.

"Good point." She gazed back at the seminary.

"What are we going to do? Waltz up there and knock on the

door of the biggest building?" I still couldn't shake my sense of dread, but chalked it up to being scared.

Bethany pointed. "What's that on the top of some of the buildings?"

I focused on the tower of what looked like a cathedral. It was crumbling. Part of the structure still stood, but bricks littered the shingles below it. Some sort of blackish dome covered parts of the roof, and extended to cover a few other structures, too. "I'm not liking this. Let's keep going."

"Maybe it's a tarp. Maybe they put them up after the earthquakes as a makeshift hospital or something." Adam turned to Megan. "Your uncle didn't happen to pack a pair of binoculars in the ATV by chance?"

"No. I wish he had though. I'm getting a little weirded out."

"Let's check the place. If it's abandoned, we move on. There might be supplies we can use." Adam adjusted the straps of his backpack.

Damn him. He was right. We needed supplies. I swallowed my doubt and choked on the bitter taste. "I think we should leave the ATVs here. If Raspers are there, they'll hear us coming. We need to sneak in." I checked my ammo.

"I guess we'll need weapons." Megan said it matter-of-factly.

"There's nowhere to get any now." Adam rubbed his hand across the barrel of the gun I gave him.

"There should be Sig Sauers on the ATVs."

Adam shot me an is-she-kidding look. I shrugged. Megan reached underneath the vehicle by the left wheel and brought out a pistol. I bent down and felt by the tire of my four-wheeler. My hand brushed against cold metal strapped into a type of harness. I unclipped the weapon and held up a black Sig Sauer.

The little voice in my head spoke before I could sensor myself. "Is there anything else you haven't mentioned?"

Megan narrowed her eyes as she checked how many bullets were in the gun. "No."

Adam glanced from each of us, his face betraying his worry we might shoot each other. "Bethany, can you shoot?"

"I don't like guns." Her voice cracked. "Don't want one."

I glanced at her. The big jacket swallowed up her tiny body.

She didn't look seventeen. More like fourteen. A tiny part of my heart wanted to cuddle her. I held the Sig out to Adam. "Here, take a backup. I still have another one."

Adam took it and tucked it in his bag.

Megan slammed the bullet clip home. "Should we move the vehicles back into the woods so they're not visible?"

"Good idea." Adam and I maneuvered the quads into the trees.

"Now we need to get to the seminary from up here. Any ideas?" Megan shoved her Sig into her waist pack and bunched her jacket over the top.

I prayed her life didn't depend on her reaching the gun quickly. Out of the four of us, only two could shoot at a moment's notice. Cripes. Not good odds.

If we were going to do this, I wanted to do it my way. "I say we try over there." I pointed to my left. "It looks like an easier way down the hill."

Everyone nodded and we began our descent. Adam leading, the girls in the middle and me in the rear. The hill was steeper than it looked, leaving me no choice but to holster the Glock or risk losing it. Damn. With both hands free, I grabbed onto the trees to keep from falling butt first.

Megan's foot slipped in a tangle of weeds. She slid about five feet before she caught a tree limb and regained control.

"You okay?" I whispered. No need for loud voices.

"Fine." She said it with much more emotion than necessary. What was her problem?

It took us about twenty minutes to slip and stumble down the hill, but we made it. To our left, an army of trees lined up behind a murky green pond, and on the right, a weed forest grew all the way up to the seminary campus. It showed no resemblance to the once-manicured lawn it probably had been.

"This didn't get us any closer. We still need to march up to the front to find out anything." Megan's voice held a whiney pitch.

"Not so loud. We don't want anyone to hear us." Adam tapped her arm. "What do you think, Val?"

"I don't know." My head screamed for me to run away, but my

heart and the hope of a better place pushed me forward. "We could sneak around the edge of the buildings."

Adam's gaze shifted to the left. "I have a crazy idea."

"What?"

"Look over by the pond. There's a drain there." Adam pointed toward the water.

Crazy? Yes. Doable? Probably. My pulse jumped into overdrive. "That might work."

Megan tore off her hat. "Are you two nuts? I'm so not climbing into a sewer drain." Her blonde hair stuck up at all angles and she smacked at the wayward hairs.

"It's not a sewer drain."

My excitement was mirrored in Adam's green eyes.

"I'm going. If you don't want to come you can stay here, or use the front door." It came across as harsh, and I didn't understand why I was pumped to go through a drainpipe. I should have been scared like I was before, but I wasn't. Energy surged through my veins, and my nerves were hypersensitive.

"I'll go," Bethany said in a faint voice.

Adam and Bethany walked toward the drain and I caught up with them. Without looking back, I heard Megan's footsteps fall in behind us. I wrinkled my nose at the stale water and mildew stench.

"How do you know it's not a sewer drain? Smells like one." Megan came up by my side.

Adam turned. His wide grin surprised me with its intensity. "Let's just say, I wasn't the most well behaved kid on my block. And they make great hiding places from angry parents."

To get to the pipe, we had to go through the pond first. The algae-tainted pond.

"Grab a stick so we can see how deep it is." I told Adam.

He broke off a branch from the closest tree and dropped it in the murky water. It measured about a foot deep.

"We'll get wet to our knees or so." I hoped the water wasn't cold, but knew it would be. I shivered in advance.

"It could be crawling with bacteria, even if it's not sewage," Megan said.

"Look, Megan, we need to find some more supplies and I

don't know about you, but I'm starving. I'm going in." Adam stepped into the water and gave a low growl when the green liquid soaked into his clothes.

"Come on, Meg. It'll be okay." Bethany held out her hand.

"This really sucks." Megan stomped to the edge of the water, shoved her hat back on, then stepped in. "Aaah. It's freezing." She clutched Bethany's hand.

My turn. I took a deep breath, rolled my lip under my teeth, and joined them in the pond. The cold sliced through my jeans and chilled me to the core. Maybe this wasn't such a good plan after all.

"Let's go," Adam said through chattering teeth. "Val, maybe you should go first. You're the best shot."

True. I was. But that would mean Megan would most likely cling to Adam through the whole pipe. Screw it. I wanted to find out what was inside and if I didn't move, I'd become a popsicle. "Okay." I pulled out a flashlight and my gun. Slogging through the water, I walked in front of Adam and stood at the pipe's mouth.

Behind me, three more beams lit up the oversized tube. "Ready?"

"Yeah. Let's stay together." He put a hand on my waist.

Heat shot through my veins, making me forget about the freezing water for a moment. The putrid scent of mold snapped me back to attention. It was so strong I almost gagged. I hunched over and led our single-file procession into the dank drain. The water lapped my ankles, sucking every bit of heat from my lower extremities.

A few minutes into our slow wade through the cylindrical trail to hell, a buzzing sound echoed through the concrete drain. I stopped, leaned back, and whispered to Adam, "What's that?"

"I don't know. Flies?"

Flies wouldn't be awful. That meant food might be nearby. It was better than rats. A shiver, not from the cold, snaked all the way down my body. I pictured huge beady-eyed suckers like the ones I saw in a TV show about the tunnels under New York City.

"What's wrong?" Adam's soft words hit the back of my neck and his breath wrapped around my ear.

A whole new type of shiver consumed me, temporarily ending my rat obsession.

"Nothing." I continued walking.

We trudged deeper and deeper into the drain. The buzzing grew louder and louder.

Adam tugged on my waist and I stopped again. "Man, that noise is driving me crazy." He dropped his head to one side then the other as if he was trying to shake water out of his ears.

"What noise?" Megan said, her words full of uncertainty.

"The damn buzzing. What is it?" Adam asked.

"I don't hear anything." Megan's whisper rose. "Why don't I hear it?"

"I don't hear it either." Bethany said.

"I don't know. Count yourself lucky. It's annoying as hell."

It was driving me crazy, too. Why couldn't the girls hear it? Were Adam and I only hearing it because of the Rasper's sting?

I concentrated on finding an end to the cement tunnel. My back ached and my legs and feet were numb. My heart rate spiked. The overwhelming rot of mold filled my nose, and the buzzing sound lacerated my eardrums. Maybe this wasn't such a good plan, but at least we were still alive. For now.

"Look up there." Adam directed his beam of light to the top of the pipe.

A manhole-type cover filled the space above my head.

"Hold this." Adam handed me his light.

I tucked it under my arm and pointed my light at the circle. He pushed up with both hands and a moan of pain escaped his lips. I cursed my trigger finger.

"It won't budge."

I handed him the flashlight and our eyes met in the beam of white. My pulse quickened.

"Can we please hurry before I freeze to death?" Megan said breaking the moment. "Let's keep going. We'll find another one."

I turned around and continued forward.

The longer we walked, the louder the buzzing became. It seemed as if an unseen force was fighting to hold time in place.

A minute felt like five. Five felt like an hour. Finally, we came upon another circular hatch in the ceiling.

I stopped and lit it with my flashlight. Adam handed his light to Megan. "Okay. Take two." He reached up to push on the manhole cover.

A groan echoed off the walls, but the cover moved. Adam pushed it half open then stuck his head through the opening.

"Gimme my flashlight." He sounded like he was talking in a bubble. He held his hand low and Megan handed him the light.

"What's up there?" My back ached to stand up straight.

"Stairs. Sort of." Adam ducked back down. "Val, you go first. I'll give you a boost, then I'll help Megan and Bethany. After that, you guys can pull me up."

It was a solid plan. I glanced at Megan and she nodded. Bethany gave a thumbs-up signal. I holstered the Glock and gave my light to Megan. I put my hands on the rim and eased my cramped muscles into a full stand. Once my head was past the lid, the air was clearer but still rank. I pushed down on my hands and lifted myself up. Then I stopped. Shit. My backpack was caught.

I shimmed and slid back down. Adam caught me around the waist and eased my feet back to solid cement. Warmth shot from my toes to my hair roots. I needed to stop reacting so much to his touch.

"What's wrong?" A look of fear crossed Megan's pale face.

"My backpack." I took it off and bit my lip, trying to cut off the panic surging through my veins. I didn't want to give it up, but I didn't have a choice. I had to trust these people. They were supposed to be my friends now. The words of Rule Number One seared my skin. My heart jackhammered in my chest and my pulse thumped in my neck. I tried not to hyperventilate as I held the bag out to Megan. She took it without a sound. I gave one last glance at the backpack, then hoisted myself up by my arms.

When my waist hit the circle, I struggled to get my legs to join the rest of my body. Without warning, Adam pushed up my legs. He gave me another shove and I was completely through the hole and crouching on a small platform. I shoved my arm back into the hole and a flashlight was slapped into my open palm.

I shined the light and checked out my surroundings. I was on a three-by-three cement platform with a set of metal rungs ascending another concrete pipe.

"Come on, Megan." I bent down and held out my hand. Megan shoved my backpack into the hole. I grabbed it as if it was a life preserver, and slipped it on.

Megan's blonde head popped up and out of the hole, then dropped down like a sick version of a whack-a-mole game. She burst back up and I held onto her shoulder, heaving her up as Adam shoved her legs.

There wasn't enough room on the ledge. I grabbed a hold of the rungs, balancing one foot on the rung and the other on the edge of the deck.

Bethany joined Megan on the platform, and then flattened herself against the wall to make room for Adam.

He pulled himself most of the way up. Megan and I grabbed him by his jean belt loops and helped him the rest of the way. I caught myself staring at the waistband of his boxers.

I focused, shifted my weight, and began climbing up the tight tube. On the third rung, my foot slipped. My stomach plunged as my fingers clenched around the rung. I tried to regain my footing. Something hit my legs and butt. I glanced down. Adam straddled the opening and supported me by holding my bottom. Another flush of heat zipped through my insides.

"Thanks," was all I could manage to say.

"No problem. Hey, Megan, can I get a little help here?"

Megan slipped her arm around Adam's waist. I couldn't—okay, didn't want to—watch. I climbed the crude stair rungs. The flashlight clanged against the metal handholds, jarring my nerves with every bang.

Megan's weight joined mine on the poor excuse for a ladder. About ten feet higher, I found another manhole cover. I pushed it to the right. I eased my head through and covered the flashlight's beam with my hand to muffle its glare. I turned as far as my body allowed, then pulled myself out of the concrete cave.

I climbed onto a cobblestone street next to a brick building. The buzzing seemed louder. There was no one around and nothing moved. The buzz was the only sign the place wasn't entirely empty. The noise sizzled through my nerve endings and tingled in the roots of my teeth. I worked my jaw back and forth, and put my hand on the Glock as my creep factor shot through the roof.

I bent down and waved my hand in an upward motion. Within a minute, the other three had joined me on the street.

"Where are we?" Bethany said, her voice barely audible.

"In the compound. Do you hear anything besides the buzzing?" Adam surveyed the area, his gun following the path of his gaze.

"What's that?" I wanted to yell the question, but managed to keep my voice monotone and quiet.

A black tar-like substance covered the side of the building, snaked its way up to the third floor, and went into the glassless window.

"I don't know." Adam stepped closer to the material.

"It looks like what we saw partly covering the roofs." I reached out my hand to touch the stuff, but when it moved, I stopped. It undulated like a giant snake inhaling. "Did you see that?" I dropped my hand, backed up, and swallowed the scream clawing its way up my throat.

"Can we get out of here *now*?" Megan tried to still her hand holding the Sig.

This wasn't right. We shouldn't have come here. What the hell had I been thinking?

"We made it this far. Let's see if we can find out where the buzzing is coming from." Adam turned his back to the shifting material.

A sense of wrongness wrapped around my brain. I didn't think any of us should turn our backs to the substance. It was moving. *Moving.*

"I don't care what it is. I can't hear it. I want to go." Megan stomped a foot.

Her stomp ground down on my last nerve. I didn't want to know what was making the noise. But I needed to. Bethany just seemed scared out of her mind and shook as if she'd never be warm again. I exhaled and rolled my lower lip under my teeth. Adam waited.

"Ten minutes, then we get out." The words slipped past my lips before I could stop them.

Adam nodded. "Okay, let's go."

We walked to the front of the structure. The biggest building that we had spied from the hill lay opposite our current position. I closed my eyes and tried to focus on where the noise was coming from.

I pointed my Glock. "I think it's coming from the main building."

"I really think we should leave."

I turned to Megan. She looked on the verge of tears and was shaking as much as Bethany.

"A few minutes then we're gone. I promise." I gave them a half-hearted smile. It was the best I could do under the circumstances.

"Come on, then." Adam grabbed Megan's wrist in a handcuff-style grip. Bethany trailed behind them.

They led the way to what I guessed was the administration building of the seminary. I followed, but peered back every thirty seconds or so to make sure no one snuck up behind us. And to make sure the black ooze stayed on the building.

The insistent buzzing grew with each step, and I wanted to plug my ears and run the other way. I caught Adam's gaze. He wore a look of pain, as if the buzzing was actually hurting him somehow.

We surrounded the massive front doors. Megan and Adam took the right side; I pushed Bethany behind me and covered the left. Adam held up his index finger. He raised a second finger. I nodded that I understood his plan.

When his third finger extended, we both yanked the doors open then moved into a shooting stance.

The roar was deafening. I covered my ears, seconds away from blood bursting out my eardrums. Pain shot through my head and I dropped to one knee. Adam had covered his ears as well, but Megan was unaffected and she walked forward. Bethany turned her head from Adam to me, as if she didn't understand our problem. I struggled to stand.

Megan stepped into the lobby of what had been an ornate building. Destruction surrounded us. The grand staircase was broken and full of gaps. The columns on either side of the room had broken in two, and colored paper littered the floor in a mosaic.

Then I saw it. A mass of ooze crept along the walls of the building. It was thick, black, and pulsating. The buzzing followed the wavy pattern of the slime.

The stuff was making the noise.

My lungs caught fire and terror tore my senses to shreds. What was it?

Megan moved toward the ooze, as if she was compelled to touch it. She extended her hand. No. Bad idea. Before I could warn her not to, she laid her palm on the stuff.

The noise stopped.

"It feels like rubber." Megan said it in a normal voice, then let go and turned to us.

My mouth dropped open. The black ooze moved and started to take a solid, human-like shape. A baseball-sized sphere of panic slammed around my insides. I aimed my gun and was about to fire when a face appeared in the shroud of blackness. Then hands pushed at the material, stretching it like plastic wrap.

"Megan, move." Adam whispered as he brought his gun into firing position.

Megan turned. "Wha—" Whatever else she was going to say was lost in her scream.

My throat closed, strangling my own scream. All around us, bodies pushed through the black substance.

13

"We need to go." Adam's eyes were wide. "Now."

Sanity evaporated from every cell on my body, taking my ability to move with it. I stood there, transfixed by the black ooze.

Faces pushed into it. Stretching it. Trying desperately to escape it. A small rip on the left grew, and a hand appeared. Then an arm.

Adam shined his light at the expanding hole. "Their skin is yellow."

The words hit me like a lightning bolt, reenergizing my muscles. "They're Raspers! Go. Go. Go!" No need to be quiet now.

Adam grabbed Megan by the arm and ran. Together, we sprinted back to the entrance. I slammed my weight into opening the massive oak door. It didn't budge.

"Damn it. Guys, help me." All four of us smacked into the wooden barrier. Nothing. "Again."

We all stepped back and this time took a running start, hitting the door at the exact same time. With a thud, the door surrendered and opened. After we cleared it, we stopped on the broken cement sidewalk. Megan doubled over gasping for breath.

"Are you okay, Meg?" Bethany ran a hand down Megan's back. At least ten Raspers piled out the door behind us.

"There's no time for this. We have to get out of here." Adam practically dragged Megan as we took off back toward the pipe.

I rounded the corner of the first building. The deathly Rasper breathing grew louder and louder. "They're gaining on us."

I spun around and fired off two shots. I didn't know if I hit anything; I turned back and continued to run.

Adam and Megan skidded to a stop by the pipe. Bethany crashed into them.

"Megan, Bethany, go." Adam yelled, then fired his own shot. "Val, you next."

I wanted to dive head first into the pipe, but resisted. "No, you go. I'll be right behind you." I was the best shot. I had to be the one to cover our escape.

Adam shook his head and fired until his gun clicked empty. "I'm out." He dropped into the pipe.

I squeezed off my last two rounds at the Raspers coming around the building. One went down. I jumped in after Adam, grabbed the rungs, and wrestled the manhole cover back into place.

I wished I had something to block the cover with, but I didn't, and I didn't have time to think. I scrambled down the rungs and almost kicked the top of Adam's head.

The three of them had cleared the landing and scooted into the original tunnel. When I reached the landing, daylight streamed down from above, stinging my eyes. Crap. The Raspers had moved the cover. They knew where we were. I jumped into the drainpipe and shoved the second cover back in place.

I hunched over and moved as fast as the pipe allowed. The rank odor in the pipe smelled worse. My heart rate pounded quadruple time. This was insane. If I hadn't seen Raspers pop out of the tar-like stuff, I wouldn't have believed it possible. But I had. And they did.

Light ringed the pipe. The exit was up ahead. I was about to say something to Adam when a splash echoed. The Raspers had entered the second pipe.

I scrambled out of the confining cement cylinder, blinded

by the brightness of the sun. "We have to get to the ATVs," I shouted. "They just entered the pipe!"

"Son of a..." Adam yelled, but didn't finish.

We dashed through the pond and clawed our way up the hill. Weeds tore at my jacket. My pulse thundered in my ears, deafening me. Adam pulled Megan with him and I kept hold of Bethany.

Another splash. I glanced back. Three Raspers jumped into the pond. "They're out. Climb faster," I screamed.

"I'm trying. It's so difficult." Megan sounded on the verge of tears again.

The Raspers climbed—faster than we did.

We made it to the top and raced for the four-wheelers. Adam shoved Megan on one. She clung to him as if super glue covered her arms.

"Bethany, come with me." I glanced down at the seminary campus. My mouth went dry, so dry my tonsils felt the size of shotgun shells. Hundreds of Raspers spilled out of buildings and moved toward our position. They were scarier, faster, and creepier than any horde of the undead in all of the zombie apocalypse movies combined.

"Hurry." Bethany's voice rang higher than a child's.

I fired the engine of the ATV. A Rasper's head poked into view. Bethany tightened her grip. I pulled out my spare gun and fired. The brown mop of hair disappeared in a shower of crimson. I gunned the motor, then took off after Adam and Megan.

I pushed the machine hard and hit fifty. The vehicle bucked, but I kept going, occasionally glancing over my shoulder. Soon, the Raspers faded into small specs instead of looming figures out to kill us. Beat by beat, my heart rate dropped, settled.

Bethany clung to my back with a vise grip, seemingly unconcerned with my backpack in her face.

Thoughts flew through my head like a digital photo frame on fast forward. This wasn't how I had planned to spend the days after my sixteenth birthday. Mom was supposed to take me shopping with my best friend, Sofie. Dad was going to take me for my driver's test. I wasn't supposed to be racing for my life on a four-wheeler with people I hardly knew. I wasn't supposed to be toting pepper spray, knives, guns. I was supposed to be studying for a biology exam or something. Sofie and my family weren't supposed to have gone missing and most likely dead. Tears threatened to slip from my eyes, but the cold wind dried them in the corners before they had a chance to drop.

A motion to my left dragged me from my thoughts. Adam ran his hand across his neck then pointed down at the gauges on his ATV.

Dread crept across my temples. I glanced down. The gas needle hovered on E.

Perfect. Just perfect.

***

We stopped the vehicles. Megan climbed off and retrieved the gas can from the back of her four-wheeler. Bethany yanked the one free from ours and handed it to me. It was light. Too light to get us to safety.

That is if safety even existed anymore. And I had my doubts it did.

"I think we lost them for a little while." Adam took the can from Megan and filled the other four-wheeler.

I tipped the remainder of the gas into mine and slid the can back into its compartment. "Now what?" I leaned against the machine.

Adam shrugged. "Guess we find more gas and keep heading to Site R."

"What if that's not a safe place either? Megan's dad said people thought the seminary was." I tugged on the ends of my hair. "Going there was a mistake."

Megan cleared her throat, but didn't utter the *I told you so* we deserved to hear.

"Yeah. No joke. We almost died because of a stupid note on a map." Adam pulled the map with the *300 Seed Plot* notation out of his pocket. He ripped it into little pieces and tossed them in the air.

We all watched the confettied map scatter in the breeze.

"If no one has any other ideas, I say we stay with the original plan. Find gas. Go to this Site R and see what's there." Bethany crossed her arms across her chest.

"Then let's get moving before the Raspers catch up." I jumped back on the four-wheeler and Bethany followed.

Adam and Megan climbed on the other machine. "Let's see how far this gas gets us." Megan hollered over her shoulder. She slipped her arms around Adam's waist.

"Ready?" Adam turned to me and I gave him a thumbs-up sign. Bethany bear-hugged my midsection. I revved the throttle, then we were off.

We passed miles of nothingness. Just wooded areas. Finally, we reached a paved road. It was cracked and filled with holes from the earthquakes, but at least it wasn't dirt. I pushed the engine harder.

We had to keep going; had to distance ourselves from the Raspers. I hoped they'd given up and hadn't followed us, but I knew that was wishful thinking. The wind knifed my face and a chill slithered down my spine. I shot a glance back. No Raspers. Just a ribbon of torn up asphalt.

The vise that had constricted my throat since the seminary eased up enough for me to suck down deep breaths of the icy air.

Adam slowed down his four-wheeler. I checked my gas gauge—not much left. I caught a splash of color in my peripheral vision. A billboard filled the field off to my right. A picture of kids laughing proclaimed Wild Waters was two miles ahead.

"Adam!" I yelled and gestured for his attention. When he looked over, I pointed at the board.

He checked his gauge. "Okay."

I prayed we had enough gas to make it to Wild Waters. Whatever it was.

The woods cleared and a large chain link fence stretched out on the left side of the road, protecting huge, empty parking lots. A wooden structure spanned the fence. *Wild Waters* fanned across the wood in garish orange letters. We maneuvered the ATVs down the rut-filled drive.

The two-story sized signs that had once hung above the main gate now lay smashed across the turnstile chutes blocking the entrance.

Adam idled the vehicle. "Look over there." He pointed to the far side, to two ticket stalls free of sign debris. "I think we can get in there if we move the metal stanchions."

"Bethany, help me." Megan and Bethany hopped off and moved the barrier. It was a tight squeeze, but in minutes, we were driving into the African Safari-themed park.

Adam cut his engine in a round plaza that held a damaged fountain. Large cracks split the structure like a half-eaten pizza, and pipes stuck out at odd angles.

I shut off the engine and stared at the signs. A walkway to the *Waters*, where I spied large waterslide structures, was on the left. A walkway on the right led to the *Wild* and my heart caught in my throat.

"Guys, that's a zoo." I waved my hand in the direction of the large African masks decorating either side of the entrance. "Wild animals."

"Then we go to the waterpark side. I'm sure if any animal got out of its cage it didn't stick around. Come on, we don't have a lot of time." Adam tapped the muzzle of his gun on his thigh.

I reloaded my guns and Adam handed me the Sig. "Can you reload this one too?"

Megan pointed to a hut-like structure advertising stroller and wheelchair rentals. "Why don't you guys tuck the ATVs in there while Bethany and I check out the admissions office?" She walked to a building with busted out windows.

I handed Adam the loaded gun and we wheeled the vehicles into the hut. It was a wreck. Strollers were spread all over the cement floor. In the center, a gaping hole consumed a double-wide blue stroller shaped in the form of an elephant head. We turned the ATVs around so they faced out, and exited back to the plaza.

Bethany and Megan walked out of one of the buildings, each carrying two black objects in their hands. "Look what I found. And they work." Megan handed us each a radio.

"Awesome job, Meg." Adam turned on his radio.

He'd called her Meg. Like they had been friends forever. *Stop it. Stop the insanity. Stop worrying about Adam and Megan. Focus on staying alive.*

"I think we should split up. We probably only have an hour or so lead on the Raspers. We need to find gas." Adam turned in a circle. "I'm going to see if I can find the maintenance shed. Most likely over there." He pointed off to the left.

"We'll go this way." Megan grabbed Bethany and jogged to the right.

That meant I went forward. Okay. I clicked on my radio. "Testing."

"Got ya." Megan said back.

Adam responded, "Loud and clear."

I took off running, hitching my bag back up on my shoulders. Colorful plastic tubes spread out in a maze-like pattern. Some were broken and smashed on the ground, while others remained intact, waiting for water and screaming kids. In front of me, a staircase spiraled toward the sky. It was the tallest structure in the park. From up there, I might be able to spot something.

I took a deep breath, then climbed.

The stairs were about five feet wide and continued on and on, spiraling around and around. It connected to a slide, which snaked through the park in a dizzying design. No way would I ever want to ride this for fun.

It took me a few minutes, but I finally made it to the top. I had to be about fifty feet in the air. I walked to the edge of the structure and looked over. My ears popped and I swore my stomach flipped. "Wow."

The pungent scent of rot and decay filled my nose. It had to be coming from the zoo. I mentally crossed my fingers that it meant all the animals were dead.

The park was larger than I had thought. A number of the smaller buildings had fallen apart, and blue and white lounge chairs filled the empty wave pool. I searched for anything that might contain gas.

On the left, a cement structure hid behind a building designed to look like a tiki bar. I thumbed the microphone on the radio. "Hey, Adam."

"Yeah?"

"I climbed the tallest slide. To the left of the wave pool and behind the tiki bar, there's a building that might have vehicles in it."

"I'll check it out."

I was about to climb down the stairs when Megan's voice broke the silence. "We found something."

"What?"

A rumbling filled the air. I leaned further over the edge to find the source of the noise. What I saw curdled my blood.

A horde of Raspers swarmed through the entrance to the Waters park. I couldn't breathe.

I thumbed the mike again. "They're here. Raspers. Hundreds of them."

"Shit," Adam said.

Megan and Bethany didn't reply.

"Where are you guys?" I tried to say it as quietly as possible, but I wanted to yell it at the top of my lungs. I pulled out the Glock and for the first time, I wished I had a rifle. One with a scope so I could pick off the bastards.

"I'm near the tiki bar." Adam's voice whispered out of my radio.

"Megan, Bethany?"

"We're here."

"Where are you?"

"In the restaurant."

I searched the landscape for the restaurant and found it only feet from the horde of Raspers. "Can you guys get to the roof?"

"We can try."

The Raspers surrounded the building. No. No. No.

"Hey, assholes, over here!" Adam screamed aloud, not over the radio. What the hell was he doing? He hung on the support structure of another slide. About ten Raspers separated from the group and moved toward him. He jumped from the supports and ran into the tiki bar.

I spun around, looking for something to throw. The only thing on the platform was a five-gallon bucket filled with nasty green water. I grabbed it, dumped the vile water, and yelled, "Over here!"

Taunting the Raspers was not a good idea. It felt as if a swarm of bees were shredding the lining of my stomach. I tossed the bucket. It landed on the concrete with a thump and bounced around like a giant ping-pong ball. A few more Raspers moved toward my stairs. Now what?

I caught movement on the roof of one of the buildings. Megan and Bethany.

"What do we do now?" Bethany whispered over the radio.

I hit the talk button, but a new rumble filled the air. The stair structure shook. I fell onto the deck, frantically searching for something to hold onto. The radio slipped from my grip. Megan screamed, then a metallic screech drowned out her cries. I pulled myself to the edge as the slide shifted back and forth. A hole ripped open below the chairs in the wave pool, sucking them down.

Another earthquake.

All the vertebrae in my spine tightened. No. Not now. Not when I was fifty feet in the air. Not with Raspers below.

The Raspers.

"Go away." I whispered my useless request.

They ran in every direction to avoid the gaping crack breaking open at their feet. A few fell in. Then all at once, they turned in a collective, almost choreographed, movement and ran out of the park. What the hell?

My ledge rocked back and forth. My insides mimicked the movement. I had to get off this thing before it collapsed and dropped me to my death. "Don't let me die. Don't let me die. Don't let me die." I didn't care who heard my prayer.

A sickening crash added to the chaos of noise. Another sway to the right. A metal groan. The platform shifted enough to pitch my fallen radio over the edge. If I didn't move, I was next.

I only had one option. I let go of the railing and scrambled to the waterless slide. Could I survive sliding down? I holstered my gun and jumped into the plastic flume just as the staircase and platform broke away.

I screamed and crab scooted down the slide. I pushed myself faster. I refused to die on a damn water slide in the middle of an earthquake. The staircase slammed back into my chute, sending me tumbling head over feet down the twisting ride. I jammed my hand outward to break my momentum and after a few moments came to a skidding halt, leaving the skin on my palms ripped and burned. I managed to right myself, but not before I had entered the enclosed portion of the ride. Darkness enveloped me.

I couldn't tell what was happening. I was trapped in a tube—a tube of horror. Another shockwave hit. I pictured the water slide as my coffin.

My breath caught and my head pounded. I had to get out of the confined space. I tugged the jacket under my butt and stuffed my bag in front of me. I rocked back and forth to gain momentum. A creaking sound filled the tube, and panic squirmed under my skin, searching for release. The tube rocked to the right, and then I shot forward. I closed my eyes and prayed I wouldn't feel any pain when I died.

I flew through the ride as if I was sliding on water instead of nylon. I squeezed my eyes as tight as I could. Then a horrible thought hit me. At the end of water slides, riders were dumped into a pool of water. There wasn't any water in the park. If I survived the ride, I would crash into an empty concrete basin.

I pictured my mom and dad. Clutched my bag. Rocketed through the tube of death.

14

Light burned into my eyelids. The tube had opened back to the air. I couldn't look. Didn't want to see. I pitched forward and the tube dropped away. This was it. I hurtled through the air. My muscles tensed and I squeezed my eyes even tighter. I waited for the concrete. Waited to go splat. Waited to die.

My back smacked onto a hard surface that dipped with my weight. I skidded along, banging my tailbone, and slammed to a stop, sprawled like a turtle on its shell.

Was I dead? I didn't think so.

Bruised? Most definitely.

I opened my eyes one at a time. Blue sky met my gaze. My whole body ached and I couldn't get enough oxygen. I tried to sit up. Couldn't get traction. I rolled to my side and came face to face with a green canvas. The pool was covered. Water seeped up through the material.

I struggled to get upright when the sound of ripping sent alarm bells ringing in my head. I scrambled to my knees, frantically trying to get off the tarp, dragging my bag behind me.

The canvas pulled and shifted. I lunged forward onto the concrete just as the material gave way. The cement saved me, but took a few pieces of my hands and knees as payment. I didn't care. I was on solid ground.

The ground rumbled and forced me to my feet sooner than my body wanted. I slung my bag on my shoulder and searched for somewhere to go. Somewhere safe. It was as if the whole earth shuttered and moaned. Then everything went quiet.

Was it over?

My chest heaved as I gasped for air. The others. I had to find the others. Megan and Bethany were the closest. I turned to the restaurant. It still stood, but part of the staircase I had climbed was lying on the roof.

Oh. God. They'd been on the roof.

I stumbled toward the building and wished for my radio. My stomach rolled and lurched. Before I reached the door, I threw up some sort of greenish acid. I choked on the burning sensation and had to take a swig of water. I ran a scraped hand across my mouth, and braced myself for what I might find inside.

"Megan? Bethany? Where are you?" I entered the sad excuse of a restaurant.

While the outside of the building had remained solid, the inside was a mess of tables, chairs, and stuff I couldn't figure out. I needed access to the roof. I climbed over a pile of shattered wood and glass that might have been a cool bar at one time.

After clearing a mountain of broken tables, I made it into what used to be the kitchen and thanked God the park had removed the food after they closed for the winter. Even though it didn't smell, the kitchen was a wreck. Pots, pans, plates, and glasses had fallen from cabinets and shelves.

I waded through the debris to the far right side, where I'd spotted an open door and stairs. Putting both hands on the doorframe, I hauled myself from the pile of junk and onto the stairs.

With more energy than I thought I still possessed, and most likely due to the sting, I raced up the staircase. Whimpers of pain and muffled words floated down the stairwell. I let go of the breath trapped in my lungs. They were alive. I hurtled up the last few stairs two at a time and busted through the hatch to the roof.

I raised my head. A strangled cry escaped from the back of my throat.

Megan was on her hands and knees whispering to Bethany. Her ankle was stuck under the twisted metal and wood that minutes ago had been the waterslide staircase.

"Are you guys okay?" I rushed over and dropped next to Megan.

"Oh, thank God. I've been calling on the radio but no one answered." Megan looked at me with tear-filled eyes.

"I'm sorry. I lost my radio in the quake." I glanced down at Bethany.

She clenched her jaw, scrunched her nose, and closed her eyes. "Can you get it off?"

"We will. Just hang in there." I had no idea how.

"It's too heavy. I couldn't move it." Tears slid down Megan's face.

She might not have been able to move it, but I hoped that my little extra strength, compliments of the sting, would be enough. "Maybe we can do it together."

Megan wiped her eyes with the back of her hands and nodded.

"Okay. On three let's try to shove it off." I counted down then we both pushed, but couldn't free Bethany's foot. I rocked back on my heels. We had to figure out another way.

"Bethany, can you sit up?" I pushed on her shoulders.

With a guttural groan, she shifted into a sitting position.

"Good. Now when we lift, I need you to pull your foot out as fast as you can, because we will only be able to hold it up for a second. Can you do that?" I searched her blue eyes.

She blinked and nodded.

"Megan, you ready?"

"Yeah. Let's do this."

"All right. One. Two. Three..." I lifted with every ounce of strength I had. It moved a few inches. I was losing my grip.

With an, "Aaaahh," Bethany yanked her foot free.

I released the section of the stairs, as well as the breath I had bottled up.

"We did it." Megan cried and wrapped her arms around her cousin.

"Can you walk?" I stood and bounced on the balls of my feet. "We need to find Adam." I said a silent plea for him to be all right.

"I think I can." Bethany struggled to stand. When she got vertical, she almost collapsed, but Megan caught her.

"Megan, where's your radio?" I searched the ground for it, but didn't spot it among the busted plastic and wood.

"It's on the back of my pants. Can you grab it?" Megan had both of her arms wrapped around Bethany.

I unclipped the radio from her jeans and pushed the talk button. "Adam, are you there?"

No answer. I tried again, my voice pitched higher than before. Silence. Dead silence. A lump lodged itself in my throat.

"He wouldn't answer me either."

I glanced at Megan and saw she was fighting tears.

"We need to find him." I looked at Bethany. "Will you be okay?"

Her face was pale and her eyes glistened. "It hurts like hell, but I don't think it's broken."

Megan locked her gaze with mine. "What about the Raspers?"

"They ran when the earthquake started. Hopefully they all fell into a large hole and died." All the Raspers being killed by an earthquake would solve so many problems. But there was no way we'd be that lucky.

"You don't know for sure?"

I rubbed the stress knot forming at the back of my neck. "No. Not for sure. Just wishful thinking. Let's go."

It took us longer than I would have liked, but we finally made it to the front of the restaurant. I drew my gun and stepped outside. Not that a few bullets would do me much good against the mob of Raspers.

No Raspers. Just massive destruction. We worked our way to the wave pool, avoiding all sorts of debris and cracks in the earth. We reached the tiki bar where Adam had been. It was still in one piece. I hoped he was too.

I rubbed the muzzle of the Glock across my right arm. My chest burned like I had a severe case of indigestion. It startled me how much I wanted him to be all right. How much I cared. I was so going to need a new Rule Number One.

Megan righted a wayward lounge chair and deposited Bethany in it. "Here."

"Sorry. I need to rest for a minute."

Bethany's injury was going to slow us down, but what could we do? We couldn't leave her. I jammed the Glock in its holster, shoved the radio in my bag, and picked my way through the branches, metal scraps, and plastic chunks barring the door to the bar.

"Adam?"

He still didn't answer. Where was he? I cleared the pile of junk and entered the bar.

An overwhelming scent of whiskey assaulted my nose. All the bottles that once rested behind the bar had smashed, their contents mixing and running across the floor. The spillage leaked into my boots as I picked through the disaster zone of barstools, piles of chairs, and busted tables.

"Adam, can you hear me?" Megan called out from her position by the door.

He wasn't here. Crap. There had to be another room, a storeroom or something. I spun in a circle and searched for another door. There. Behind a garish totem pole. I billy-goated my way over a pile of chairs, landing with a thud on the tile floor, the shockwave zipping through my legs. I made it to the closed door and yanked the handle. Nothing happened. I pounded on it. "Adam, are you in there?"

No response.

I had to get the door open. But how? Another bang. "Adam. Answer me."

Megan crashed to a landing behind me.

"You okay?"

Megan stood. "Yeah. Is he in there?"

"I don't know. The door won't open."

Megan turned, walked to the corner, and came up with a piece of a wooden table. "What if we try to pry it open with this?"

"Might work."

She handed me the thin shank of wood. I jammed it in the

door by the handle and smashed the wood with a metal chair seat.

The wood shattered and the door groaned. I threw the seat back into the rubbish pile and pulled on the door again. It moved a crack.

"Come help me get this open."

Megan stood to my right and we both braced ourselves. "On three. One. Two. Three." We pulled with everything we had. The door moaned louder than before, but it still didn't move.

"Harder."

I put one foot on the wall and pushed out, trying to gain more leverage. It worked. The door surrendered and flew open, knocking both of us on our butts. I slammed onto my back, then rolled to my side.

"Damn." Megan rubbed her hip.

I stood and checked out what was behind the door, but it was too dark to see anything. I whipped out my flashlight and shined it inside.

Megan's cry rang through my ears. Adam lay sprawled on his back covered in boxes and a shelving unit. Terror sliced through my chest.

"Adam!" I fought my way into the closet-sized storage room. He didn't move.

Oh, God. Please. Please. Please don't let him be dead.

"Is he alive?" Megan cried.

"I hope so. Here, hold the light." I tossed her the flashlight and set to work moving the shelving unit. Once I had it upright, I threw the boxes off Adam.

Megan slid to her knees next to him.

I bent down and put my hand to his throat. A pulse. I swallowed the walnut-sized lump lodged in my throat, exhaled, and rocked back on my feet.

"He's alive?" Megan touched Adam's forehead brushing his hair back with trembling fingers.

"Yeah. Adam, wake up." I slapped his face just enough to try to jar him awake. How long had he been unconscious? "Come on. Wake up."

When he didn't respond, tears pooled in my eyes. Why wasn't he waking up?

"Is he in a coma?" Megan's voice cracked.

"I don't know. We need smelling salts or something." I had no idea what to do. I had no medical knowledge. I had surprised myself by patching up his arm and not killing him in the process.

"Can we use the liquor combo out there?" Megan tilted her head.

"It's worth a shot. Stay here with him." I jumped up, scrambled back over the pile of chairs and tables, all the while trying to quiet the voice in my head screaming *don't let him die*. I took out my almost-empty water bottle. I swigged the last drops, then bent down and scooped the whiskey and bourbon into the bottle. The stench made me gag. It had better wake him up.

When the bottle was a third full, I capped it and fought my way back to Adam. He was still out cold and Megan was holding his hand. I choked on a pang of jealousy and bent down on his other side. "Megan, can you lift up his head?"

She moved behind him and lifted him onto her legs, cradling his head in her lap.

I opened the bottle. The pungent aroma filled my nostrils and made me cough. I waved it under Adam's nose, praying for it to work.

He jerked and coughed. His eyelids fluttered, then closed. I waved the bottle again. His eyes flew open and he coughed again. "What the...?"

"Oh, thank God, you're awake." Megan laid her hand on his forehead.

Adam pushed himself off her lap and into a sitting position. "Damn. My head hurts. What happened?"

I capped the noxious vapors. "A shelving unit fell on you. You must have hit your head and passed out. How do you feel?"

"Like a freight train plowed through my brain."

"You didn't answer on the radio."

"It's in my bag. Where's Bethany?" He turned, but winced and squeezed Megan's thigh.

My chest burned as if it had been stabbed with a metal pole.

"Easy. We don't know how hard you hit your head or how long you were out. Bethany's outside. She hurt her ankle."

"By herself? What about the Raspers?"

Oh, crap. When he put it that way, it sounded so dumb. How could we have left her alone?

"You think she's in danger?" Megan sprang to her feet. A look of panic crossed her delicate features.

I stood and held my hand out to Adam. "I'm sure she's fine, but let's get moving."

"She won't carry a gun. Not after... Oh, how could I have left her?" Megan tucked her hair behind her ears. "I'm going back out." She slapped the flashlight into my hand and sprinted out the door.

"What do you think she meant about that?"

"About what?"

"About what made Bethany afraid of guns?" I hoped whatever it was didn't get her killed.

"I don't know." Adam swayed to the right.

"Can you walk?" I supported him by wrapping his arm over my shoulder.

"Maybe." He let go of me and took a few steps. He wobbled a little at first, and then gained his balance. "I think I'm good."

He might have been seriously hurt if he was just—just what? Normal? Human? The words seeped into my bones. What was he now? What was I? I shook my head. I couldn't think about it now. We had to get back to Bethany.

We crawled over the debris pile. I got over first and waited for him. Megan was already out the door.

"Bethany!"

Megan's scream had us vaulting for the outside.

"What's wrong?" Adam gripped Megan by the shoulder.

"She's not here." Megan waved at the empty lounge chair and then clutched at her hair like she wanted to pull it out by the roots.

I tucked the flashlight back in my bag and drew my gun. "Where is she? She could barely walk."

"Maybe she's going to the bathroom or something." Adam tried to sound light-hearted, but I could tell he was worried.

Megan sank onto the chair and dropped her head in her palms. Her sobs grated down my spine. I was responsible. I shouldn't have let her stay out here alone. The walnut-sized lump lodged itself back into position in my windpipe.

Adam sat next to Megan and put his arm around her. "We'll find her. Come on, crying won't help. We need to search for her."

She lifted her tear-streaked face. "Okay." She sniffed and wiped her cheeks.

"Where would she have gone?"

I closed my eyes and strained to hear anything that might give a clue as to her whereabouts. I caught a faint huffing noise and opened my eyes. "Adam, do you hear a strange noise?"

He let go of Megan and stood. He pivoted slowly in a tight circle.

"What is it?" Megan jumped up.

Adam held up his index finger. "Ssh. Let me listen."

I heard it again. It wasn't Raspers, but I couldn't place it. "I hear it. A faint, almost coughing noise?"

"Yes. Like someone puffing on a cigarette or something."

Megan latched onto Adam's bicep in an iron grip. "Where's it coming from?"

"Over there, I think." Adam walked forward.

When we reached the exit to the Waters, my stomach coiled into a ball of despair.

The sound was coming from the Wild side of the park.

***

"Oh God. No." Megan crashed to her knees.

Adam reached down and brought her back to her feet. I aimed the Glock. Images of hungry and desperate animals filled my overtired brain.

"Do you still hear it?" Adam whispered.

I tilted my head and tried to focus on the sound. It took a few seconds, but I heard it. "It sounds like it's moving away from us."

"I don't hear anything." Megan whined. "Guys, please. We need to find Bethany."

"We will."

We walked through the African-themed archway decorated with wooden tribal carvings. The ball of despair uncoiled and slithered up my throat. We were now in the Wilds. I'd been right. It had been a zoo. Bad, bad idea. She couldn't be here.

"Does she still have a radio?" Adam clicked his talk button. "Bethany, can you hear us?"

She didn't answer. A low rumble echoed in my ears.

"What's that?" Adam shoved the radio in his pocket.

I didn't know. Didn't want to know. But I did know that no matter what it was, it wouldn't be good. The rumble grew louder and louder. Closer and closer. "Another earthquake?"

"I don't think so."

Megan's eyes went wide. "We should move. Look." She pointed to the left.

I followed her line of sight and my stomach curdled. A cloud of dust billowed toward us and the rumble grew more intense. It reminded me of the horde of Bugs, but the sound was much deeper. We needed a place to hide.

"Come on. Over here." Adam ran to a line of trees.

Megan stood frozen in the path, staring at the swirling dust cloud. I looped my arm through hers and dragged her to where Adam hid. When we reached him, he forced Megan to take cover behind his back. He took one side of the tree trunk and I pointed my gun from the other side. It sucked as far as hiding spots went, but we didn't have any other option.

The noise thundered in my ears. Then they came down the path. Three emaciated zebras shot past us without even turning their heads in our direction. More bad news.

"Why are they only leaving now?"

"The earthquake probably knocked their gate or fence open. They looked starved," Adam said.

"If the zebras got loose, what else do you think is lurking around?" I whispered the question, not really wanting the answer. Thoughts of bears and wolves raced through my brain. We were so screwed.

"We need to find Bethany and get out of here." Adam left the cover of the tree.

"She couldn't have gone far with her hurt ankle," Megan wailed.

"I don't think she went by herself." Megan's already terrified eyes widened at the comment I should have kept to myself.

"Everybody quiet. I hear something." Adam held up his hand.

I strained to hear what he meant. There. The same huffing sound. I searched my memory for what animal made a sound like it, but came up empty.

Adam tugged on my sleeve and I met his gaze. He pointed to the trees and made a circle gesture. I nodded and brought up the Glock. He dragged Megan with him.

I took the lead. Dealing with Megan would slow down his reaction time, and we were running out of time. We had to find Bethany and get the hell out of here. We cut through the trees and up a small hill. The closer we got to whatever we were tracking, the louder the sounds became.

A small spot of color caught my attention. A piece of fabric was caught on a rock to my left. I stared at it, but kept moving so not to draw Megan's attention.

The swatch matched the jackets we wore. The jacket Bethany wore.

I wanted to point the offending piece out to Adam, but I couldn't risk having Megan see it. She was already a basket case, and thinking what I did would unhinge her. I kept walking, alert for more pieces.

A few more yards along, another scrap. My heart twisted in my chest. Something bad had happened to Bethany, I just knew it. I considered turning back and telling Megan we couldn't go any farther, but I knew she wouldn't accept it. She would have to see it with her own eyes, no matter how horrible.

More huffing. A ripping sound raised goose bumps across my skin. I exhaled and pushed on. When I crested the top of the hill, any remaining air in my lungs escaped and I froze, paralyzed with horror.

The containment fence below the hill had shifted enough in the earthquake to create a hole. My brain screamed for me to turn and run, to cover Megan's eyes, but I couldn't get my body to move. As if locked in slow motion, I turned and raised my hand to stop Megan from coming any closer. Adam tried to draw her to his chest.

But she knew. She tore out of his grasp and dodged my outstretched hand. She skidded to a halt and a cry, more animal than human, tore from her lips.

Another rip. This one the sound of flesh and bone.

I turned away from Megan. Locked my gaze on the bloody scene.

And watched a female lion devour its prey.

15

Megan moaned. Rocked back and forth. She needed to be quiet. Lions preferred living prey to dead, didn't they?

Adam raced to Megan's side and tried to cover her eyes. "Don't look."

I brought my gun level. My mouth went dry and rough as sandpaper. Would a bullet take down a full-grown lion or would she have time to get all three of us? I didn't know what to do. She had obviously escaped the fence. She could do it again. We weren't safe here.

The lioness tore at what remained of Bethany. Strands of her blonde hair danced in the breeze in a macabre fashion that churned my stomach. I was going to be sick. Again. I forced the bile southward. The rest of Bethany's body was spread across the dirt.

Megan vomited and rolled into the fetal position. The stench almost made me lose the little control I had over my intestines.

Adam's mouth simply hung open in shock.

I blinked to clear the fuzziness. Maybe it was better this way. Then I wouldn't see what was happening. But the horror scene came back into high definition focus.

"We should go." Adam backed up a few steps.

I couldn't tear my eyes from the lioness. Her ribs showed the depth of her starvation.

A low roar swirled through the trees, extracting a reply from the lioness. The hair on my arms poked into my sleeves as a male lion lumbered into view. Holy hell. My abdominal muscles contracted and spasmed.

He was smaller and didn't have a full mane. Was he her baby?

"Help me lift her." Adam said, jerking me from the brutal scene.

I tore my gaze from the lions as the juvenile sank his teeth into Bethany's left arm. The sound of her bones snapping echoed through my ears. The acid slithered back up my throat, demanding release. I managed to choke it back down, but just barely.

"Once they're done, they're going to come after us. They have to know we're here."

I agreed with him. Even if they hadn't heard us, our scent surely gave us away.

"Come on, Megan. We need to go." He reached down and gripped her hand.

She didn't respond. She'd retreated into herself. She rocked back and forth, both hands covering her face.

"Shit." Adam stuffed his gun in the back of his jeans, then hoisted Megan into his arms, holding her in a firefighter's carry.

Everything had gone to hell. Bethany mauled by starving lions, Megan traumatized, Adam unarmed. I might be able to shoot one lion, but there were two. There might even be more.

Adam shuffled down the hill, his balance off from Megan's dead weight. As sick as the thought was and as bad as it made me feel, I prayed Bethany would keep them satisfied long enough for us to get away.

We reached the path leading out of the Wild. When we got to the busted fountain in the center of the park, Adam set Megan down on the cement. Her face was an expressionless mask.

"Megan, say something." I bent down next to her. My hand brushed hers. Her skin was cool to the touch, and ashy looking.

She only blinked, slow and drawn-out.

I glanced back up the path, expecting to see a parade of lions coming for dinner. The trail was empty. No lions. Not yet at least.

"There's no time for this. We need to find gas and get the hell out of here." Adam seized Megan's hand and pulled her along. While she kept pace with him, she remained in the catatonic state.

"There's no way I'm going back into the Wild side of this park. We have to find something useful in the Waters. If there's anything to find." My words were rushed.

The three of us made quick time and within minutes, we made it to the building where we'd hid the four-wheelers. I groaned. I hadn't even given the ATVs a thought. Stupid. Stupid. Stupid.

The building was rubble, a ruin of bricks and wood. The vehicles were toast.

"Goddammit." Adam threw his bag into the hedge.

I bit my cracked lip until I tasted blood. This sucked beyond words. I wanted to join Megan in her numb state; just block all the uglies out and retreat into my own head. Escape all the destruction and death. But I didn't have that luxury unless I wanted to die. And dying wasn't on my to-do list for the day.

"Maybe there's a golf cart or something around here. The employees had to use something. We gotta get out of this place." Adam's words snapped me back to the here and now.

"Did you find the maintenance shed before?" I searched the collapsing landscape for any indication as to where the park kept their maintenance equipment.

"No." Adam hoisted his bag.

"Maybe over there?" I pointed in the direction behind the wave pool.

We all took off running and didn't stop until we rounded the destroyed wave pool that was now a cement slab.

"There." Adam tilted his head at a brick building off to our right.

It was—amazingly—still standing. I pushed on the door. It didn't budge. With a frustrated cry, I slammed my boot into the door. It relented and opened. "Yes."

A black pickup truck filled the small building.

"Please, please, please let there be gas." Adam let go of Megan, and she stood rigid and unmoving.

"And keys." I threw open the truck door. The ignition switch was empty. No keys. I tried not to cry. I had to keep it together. I ducked back out of the truck and slammed my hand against the hood. "Damn it."

"Maybe they're around here somewhere."

Not likely. We were doomed. If the lions didn't get us, I was sure the Raspers would be back any minute.

I glanced over at Megan. She stood ramrod straight, and with a zombiefied expression. An overwhelming urge to hug her overcame me. All her loss was my fault. I had brought death to her door. I pinched the bridge of my nose and scrunched up my face. I had given up my rules, and look where that got me. About to be killed—and probably sooner than later.

I walked to the corner next to Adam. "Find anything?"

"Just some tools."

My corner housed a workbench full of plastic pipes and wrenches. I picked up a baseball bat-sized pipe and banged it off the workbench. A jingling sound filled the building.

"What was that? Did you find keys?" Adam was by my side in a flash.

I searched the pegboard above the counter. Tons of wrenches hung on hooks, but about half way up the board, a set of keys dangled. I whipped the pipe onto the floor and snatched the keys. One was larger than the rest with black plastic on the end. It had to be for a vehicle.

I flew to the truck, plopped my backpack in the passenger seat, and said a small prayer before I shoved the key into the slot. It fit.

When I turned it, the truck roared to life. I zeroed in on the dashboard, willing the gas gauge to move toward F. *Come on. Come on.* It crept up to the three-quarters full mark. I yelled and jumped out of the truck.

Adam pulled down on a heavy-duty chain and the roll door that covered the one end of the building groaned. He let go of the chain and the door opened all the way. I grabbed Megan by the hand and hauled her into the cab of the truck, pushing her into the middle of the seat.

Adam walked to the hood of the truck. "Do you want to drive?"

"No, go ahead." I went to the passenger side. While I didn't have a problem driving the ATV, cars still scared me. I had gotten my learners permit and practiced a lot with Mom, but driving still made me nervous. And with the extreme craziness of the last few hours, I wasn't positive my nerves wouldn't implode. I jumped into the truck, sliding my bag by my feet.

Adam landed in the driver's seat and tossed his bag into the back. "Buckle Megan's seat belt."

The earthquake damage proved a challenge to Adam's driving skills, and after a narrow escape with the Turbo Swirl slide, we made it to the parking lot. I wrapped my fingers around the Glock in case the Raspers had stayed in the lot, but it was empty.

Adam hit the gas hard and the truck leapt forward, leaving the abomination of Wild Waters behind.

With every notch in increased speed, my heartbeat dropped. I slumped back in the seat and tried to formulate a plan of what to do next, but my eyes grew heavy. Exhaustion reared its ugly head. I pinched my cheeks to stay alert.

I glanced at Megan. She stared out the windshield. I was sure she wasn't seeing the landscape flying by, but remembering the horror of her family dying.

"Where are we going?" I yawned.

"Far away from here. I want to put some distance between us and the Rasper hive before we stop and figure where we are in relation to Site R." Adam's voice was part tired, part pissed off.

All I could picture was Bethany's demise. Guilt tore at my heart, shredding it piece by piece. We shouldn't have left her there alone. I needed to think about something else. I stole a glance at Adam. Megan's head blocked my view, but I caught sight of his wavy hair and the determined set of his jaw.

I shut my eyes and tried to burn his image into my memory; something to keep the bad visions away. I needed something to numb the terror threatening to push me over the edge. I slipped into a restless sleep.

A bumping of the truck sent me scrambling for my gun. I tried to process the scene before me, but I was too tired. "What's happening?"

"Hold on." Adam jerked the wheel to the right, then the left.

The road was broken open and filled with gaping holes. The earthquake had all but destroyed it.

"Over to the right. There's a clearing." I jabbed my finger toward the window.

Adam jerked the truck off the road and onto the shoulder. With a loud shudder, the truck shifted into the field. While not a smooth surface, the ground wasn't the roller coaster ride the road had been.

"Why didn't you wake me?"

"I didn't have a warning. The road was fine, then boom, it crumbled to hell and back. You woke up right when it started anyway." Adam opened and closed his hands around the steering wheel.

"Has Megan said anything?" I tapped her leg. She didn't change expressions or tell me to stop. I wished she would. I was scared she'd slipped so far away that we might not get her back.

"No. It's pretty creepy."

I opened the glove compartment of the truck and sifted through tools and papers. Nothing good. "Want a candy bar?" I extracted two out of my bag and waved them around like a flag of surrender.

"Break me off a piece. I'm starving." Adam maneuvered the truck back onto the road.

"Me too." I opened the chocolate bar and handed one to Adam, passing it right in front of Megan's nose on purpose. She didn't react.

"Thanks." He shoved the bar into his mouth in one bite.

I opened the other one and tapped Megan on the shoulder. "Come on, you need to eat. Here, have some chocolate." I shoved the food in front of her face a few times before giving up and eating it myself.

My stomach growled for more, but I tried my best to ignore it.

"Hey, there's a sign for Jenkinsburg." Adam pointed as the truck whipped by a sign I had no hope of reading.

"What's in Jenkinsburg?"

"Hopefully no Raspers or wild animals, but lots of food. Maybe a Walmart."

If there was a Walmart, I hoped it would be in better shape than the one in Alberdine. It took about fifteen minutes before we reached the outskirts of Jenkinsburg. It had been a typical small town before being destroyed by the earthquakes, and possibly tornadoes.

"This place is a war zone." Adam drove the truck along the right edge of the road to avoid a large crack.

"Think there's anyone here?"

Personally, I didn't want to find anyone else. Our little band of survivors was hard enough to handle. We didn't need to care for anyone else. Didn't need to lose anyone else. I couldn't handle any more scars on my heart. It made me sound like a total bitch, but I'd slipped so far out of the comfort zone of my rules, I didn't know what to do.

"Looks like the neighborhood store." Adam wheeled the truck into a parking lot full of abandoned cars. Some of their doors hung open. Others didn't have doors.

I unbuckled. Luckett's Market was still standing, but just barely. The roof, once a neat triangle, now resembled a squashed trapezoid. The glass windows were broken and a shopping cart hung on the frame of the broken door. I took a deep breath then opened the door of the truck, got out, and braced myself for the smell. It didn't reach my nose. Odd.

"Come on, Megan, get out." I didn't want to leave her alone. Not with how it had gone down with Bethany. "If she won't get out, what if we lock her in the truck? She should be okay then."

Adam looked from me to Megan. "Yeah, she should be fine in the truck." He got out, leaned back in to most likely tell Megan what our plan was, then locked her in.

"Did she answer?"

"No." Adam turned back to the truck. "What are we going to do about her? She obviously needs a doctor or something."

"I wish I knew."

We walked over the broken glass and Adam tossed the cart out of the way. Like outside, the smell inside the store wasn't bad—just a mild, musty scent. When we walked through the store, the reason for the lack of smell became apparent. The store was bare except for the fixtures.

"Where is everything?" Adam shoved a small display cabinet, smashing it to the floor.

"It's been totally cleaned out. Somebody must be living around here." It was the only reasonable explanation, but my mind wandered. For the first time in four months, I wondered if Raspers ate. They would need some sort of nutrition. Every living thing did. I learned that in kindergarten. So, did they eat normal food or is that why they took the dead? I had to think about something else.

I slid down the wall behind the checkout counter. I was exhausted, wiped out. I rested my head on my knees and willed myself not to cry. I lifted my head, and when I caught sight of the object attached to the bottom of the counter, I felt the long-unused turn of a smile cross my lips.

Adam snapped his fingers. "What are you thinking about?"

"There's a shotgun under here."

"What?" Adam came around the worn checkout stand and crouched down. "Hot damn."

I unlatched the gun and handed it to him.

He opened the barrel. "Two shells."

"Better than nothing."

"My thoughts exactly." Adam slung the gun's strap onto his shoulder and helped me up.

We went back outside. A yellow metal box by the building's edge caught my eye. I walked toward it, hoping it was what I thought it was.

"What are you doing?" Adam called.

"Hang on." My heart sped up. A newspaper box with papers. I tugged on the handle to open it, but it rattled in locked defiance. I spun around, searching for something, anything, to break the glass. The ground was as clear as the store. I went back to the truck and took the tire iron from the back. I smashed it against the plexiglass of the box. It took three whacks, but it finally broke open. I snatched a paper and glanced at the date. October 28. The day after the Great Discovery.

"Val, come on."

I folded the paper, stuffed it in my bag, and sprinted to the truck.

"What were you doing?" Adam asked when I slid into the seat.

"Got a paper."

"For what?"

"Information, hopefully."

"Where should we go?"

I put the tire iron behind the seat and set my bag on the floor. "Let's get out of this town and back on the interstate. We'll try the next town for food."

"Maybe we should check for other survivors first. Someone had to clear out the store." Adam tapped his fingertips on the dash.

"You know, I was thinking about something."

"What?"

I leaned forward in the seat to look around Megan so I could see his face. His stubble was even thicker today, but not in the beard range yet. "Well, it occurred to me that it might have been Raspers who cleared the store out."

There, I said it. I spoke the new fear aloud, but it didn't lessen its intensity like it should have. It didn't settle the candy bar churning in my stomach.

"Why would they clear it out?"

"Have you ever seen one eat anything?"

"No, but..." Adam wrinkled his forehead, which told me he was probably reaching the same thought pattern I had.

"Everything needs to eat. Do they eat normal food or something worse? I mean, are they like flesh-eating zombies?"

Megan whimpered, but remained glass-eyed.

"Sorry, Megan."

"Maybe we should talk about something else." Adam raised his eyebrows.

"Let's just go to the next town. It'll be easier that way." I gave Adam a glare, which hopefully pleaded my case strongly enough to move on. "Regardless of what Raspers eat, there isn't anything here for us."

Adam started the truck and I leaned back in my seat, lost

in my thoughts. Was it Adam's intention to find any and all survivors? While it was a compassionate gesture, my practical side balked at the idea. Right now, we didn't have much food and who knew what the state of other stores were. Maybe Alberdine's stores were the exception rather than the norm. It was becoming painfully obvious I had no idea what was really happening in the world.

I took out the newspaper and read the headline about the Great Discovery. Nothing new there. I flipped the paper over and below the creased middle, a picture of a group of people stared back at me.

Blood rushed away from my face and a chill sliced through my veins.

16

I read the caption below the picture.

Geo-scientists from Pearan Chemicals hailed after the discovery of a cache of oil in the Gulf of Mexico.

I couldn't swallow; my mouth felt like it was full of cotton balls. I'd seen the one scientist before. He was the Rasper from the car. The Rasper who freaked me out the most.

With shaking hands, I folded the paper in half again to block the penetrating stare. A scientist was a Rasper. Or was the Rasper a scientist? I couldn't process what it really meant. All I could think was, *why me?*

"Find anything?" Adam asked.

"No." I wanted to say yes, but decided to keep the information to myself right now. I shoved the paper deep into my bag, tried to focus on anything but his face, and failed. For hours, I kept seeing his yellow skin and smelling his retched breath.

I watched out the window. We were in the middle of farmland. For miles and miles there was nothing but fields of out of control grain and corn. There was nothing to distract me from the thoughts swirling in my brain. I'd survived for months.

Alone. Now the Raspers were tracking me. Why? I rubbed my hand down my throat. Maybe I was just being paranoid.

"How much ammo do we have left?" Adam's question broke into my thoughts.

I counted the bullets. "A full round in my Glock, and ten extras. You have about six and two in the shotgun. Not enough."

"Damn."

When the reds and oranges of evening crept into the sky, panic tightened my chest and climbed up my throat. We needed to stop somewhere. Driving at night with the Raspers out in groups would be downright idiotic. And I still couldn't shake the Rasper's image from my brain.

"We need to find a shelter." I leaned past Megan and glanced at Adam.

"I know. I've been looking, but it's all fields out there." He waved his hand at the windshield.

I gazed out of the truck, mesmerized by the muted colors of the sky behind the rolling clouds. It all seemed normal. The sky gave no indication that humans were all but dead and Raspers and Bugs covered the planet. The twilight display reminded me of one of my mom's paintings, and I couldn't stop the tears that leaked out of my eyes. I kept my face turned toward the window.

"Hey, there's something."

I ran my sleeve across my cheeks and turned to Adam.

He pointed to a collection of buildings where the one field ended. He turned the truck up a dirt driveway riddled with bumps and divots. I grabbed my bag with one hand and held onto the rollover bar with the other. Megan made no move to steady herself. She needed to snap out of the horrors in her mind and I had no idea how to bring her back. I had enough trouble keeping myself sane. I felt bad about Bethany. But Megan wouldn't survive much longer if she didn't rejoin reality. Maybe I was a monster for not having more compassion. Maybe it was because of the Rasper sting. Maybe I was just making excuses so I could cope.

Adam pulled the truck to a stop. There were three buildings, as well as the smashed remains of what once had been a house.

"Looks like a tornado ripped apart the house." Adam echoed my thoughts.

"And part of that building's roof. Think the place is secure?"

Adam shrugged, opened his door, and got out. "It's too late to search for anything else now." He reached in and latched onto Megan's hand. "Come on, Meg, we need to get out." He guided her from the truck and hoisted the shotgun onto his shoulder.

I got out, slung the bag on my shoulders, and reached for my Glock.

"Which building, do you think?" Adam whispered.

I took in the options. There was a grain silo, two large rectangular buildings, a barn, and I didn't know what the other was. "The barn looks the most intact," I whispered back.

The air here was clean and fresh smelling. No rotten or moldy scents, just the aroma of nature. Adam and I moved to opposite sides of the barn door. He shoved Megan behind him and nodded. I pushed it open with my right hand and pointed the gun. The only light in the building came from the opened door. It was difficult to make out the interior, but it seemed empty.

"Get your flashlight," Adam said, low enough that only I heard him.

I let go of the door, pulled out my light, and shined it into the cavernous space. Along the left side, five stalls that probably once housed horses stood empty. A loft filled with hay rimmed the top of the barn.

"This should work."

I was damned tired. Adam had to be tired too. At least I'd had a quick nap in the truck. How he and Megan were keeping their eyes open was beyond me.

Four saddle blankets sat on a shelf next to the horse stalls. Along with the hay, they would make a decent bed. I helped Megan lie down and stuffed a sweatshirt under her head. I lit a small jar candle I'd brought with me. The flicker of light threw shadows across her features.

"Are you hungry?" I got out some cans of tuna I still had. She didn't answer. I hadn't expected her to. She was really starting to freak me out.

Adam sat next to me and opened one can. The scent of the

tuna churned my stomach, but I was hungry enough to ignore my aversion to seafood. Dad had loved shrimp and lobster. Mom didn't really like the taste, but she told me she cooked it to make him happy. She always made me mac-n-cheese on seafood nights. I pulled out a fork and the two of us split the can. When I glanced at Megan, she had her eyes closed. I couldn't tell if she was asleep or not. I hoped she was. Her mind needed to rest and recharge.

"Think she'll be okay?"

"I hope so...I don't know. She probably needs a hospital or something."

Adam scooted closer to her and ran his hand over her hair. The candle's glow bathed his face in amber light.

A burning sensation flared through my stomach. When Adam kissed the top of her hair, I almost punched something. My reaction didn't make sense. He wasn't mine; I had no claim on him. Still, it tore me up to see his lips on her. I stood.

"What's up?" Adam stroked Megan's hair.

Nothing besides the fact I had a sudden urge to slap his face. Oh, my God. It was true. I was insanely jealous of him touching a girl who had just watched her family get shot to death and her cousin devoured by a lion. I couldn't believe myself. I was a total bitch. "I need some air."

"Be careful."

"Always." I was careful about everything. Except my heart.

I left the barn and went outside in the dark, violating my rules again. My skin prickled when I realized I hadn't retraced them lately. Leaning against the side of the barn, I ran my hand across the faded words.

I sank to the ground, pulled up my knees, and wrapped myself into a ball. I rocked back and forth for a while, then I raised my head. Stars shone bright in the sky. Were Mom and Dad up there somewhere watching me? What about dogs? Did they go to heaven? I missed my beagle, Barney. Missed his wet kisses. I dug my nails into the palms of my hands.

I couldn't change what happened, no matter how hard I tried. I needed to stop feeling sorry for myself. I stood and gave one last look up, then went back into the barn.

Megan was still asleep and Adam sat across from her, exhaustion obviously winning the battle no matter how hard he fought.

"Adam, you need to get some sleep." I plopped down next to him. He didn't answer me.

I turned and glanced at him. He had curled onto his right side and fallen asleep. Heat rolled off him and into the small gap between us. If he was on the side of his wound, it must have healed more. Good. It helped patch the hole of guilt in my gut.

I clicked on my flashlight, got up, and walked to the far side of the barn. What looked like the back seat from an old car sat on the floor. Various tools hung on pegs on the walls and metal parts in plastic jars littered the one workspace. I had no idea what they were for; farming wasn't something I knew anything about. The scent of oil hung thick in the air. I rummaged in a few of the boxes, but the only thing I found of use was a small flashlight. I tucked it in my pocket and moved to the opposite corner. Chains of various lengths and thickness hung from the wall. The rest of the barn turned up nothing of any help. Hadn't these people stashed food anywhere?

I walked back to where Megan and Adam still slept. My head hurt. It was as if a spear jabbed into my temples, sending a sharp pain radiating through my skull. I had a headache like this one last year, the night I tried to pull an all-nighter to study for my chemistry final. Sleep was trying to wrap itself around my body. I had to fight. I was the lookout. I sat down, stared at the lone candle, and counted to keep myself awake.

My eyes flew open and I scrambled to my feet, my gun already in firing position. I'd fallen asleep, and I was supposed to have been on guard duty. I turned so quickly that I knocked over the candle and it ignited the hay. I stomped on it over and over. Luckily, I put it out and relit the candle. What an idiot. Thank God, Adam and Megan still slept. I turned on my flashlight and searched the barn. Same stuff as before, but my heart refused to stop pounding. I took a few deep breaths willing myself to calm down. I must have had a dream or something.

My nerves only went further on alert. I walked to the door, tried to open it without waking the others, and slipped outside.

Darkness engulfed me. I leaned against the side of the barn next to the door and waited for my eyes to adjust.

The moon was almost full and cast eerie shadows around the crops. It had to be early in the morning, maybe three or four. A fog worthy of a good horror film rolled across the fields. It felt like the part in every cheesy movie where I'd scream at the dumb girl to go back with the others or she would die. I didn't take my advice and instead stared, transfixed, at the hypnotic waves of the fog.

Noises I hadn't noticed before filled the air. The corn stalks in the fields rustled and the leaves on the trees whispered. I caught the mournful gurgle of frogs in the distance.

A sudden chill raised the hairs on my arms. Something moved in the field. I squinted, seeing nothing. The vegetation crunched. Was it a threat or an animal? I raised the Glock and waited.

Then nothing. No more strange noises. Like whatever it was, stopped. I waited for what seemed like an eternity, then I slipped back into the barn.

"What were you doing outside?" Adam stood and put his hand on my shoulder. The heat of his skin seeped through the fabric of my jacket.

"I was right outside the door. I think there's something in the field."

"What?" He pulled out his gun, ready to go.

"I don't know. It stopped moving about ten minutes ago."

"Raspers?"

"I was thinking an animal, but it could have been anything. Should we wake up Megan?"

"No. Let her sleep. Come on, let's check it out."

"Maybe we should wait till it's light out." Even though my rules had pretty much gone to hell, I still couldn't completely abandon them.

"Probably. But I'm not taking a chance the bastards are surrounding us. Let's go up in the loft."

We climbed the ladder to the top, and went to the hatch in the wall at the front of the barn. It was bigger than a window and wider than a door. I unhooked and pulled back a latched wooden cover, revealing a large opening. The gap was big enough for me to climb through. Adam moved to the right side and I took the left. My boot slipped a fraction, and I grabbed a wooden beam to steady myself. The creepy fog was even worse than before.

We waited, with our guns aimed at the field. "We should have brought the shotgun." I said it so softly I wasn't sure I'd actually said the words aloud, but Adam nodded.

The frogs had gone quiet and the leaves barely whispered. It was as if nature paused because a predator waited in the mist. My stomach twisted as I strained to make out any movement in the field.

Adam raised his index finger and pointed to his right. I followed his direction and squinted. At first, I saw nothing. Nothing but rows and rows and rows of corn stalks. Then I spotted it. Just beyond the ruined house. The corn stalks moved ever so slightly in an unnatural way. I nodded.

Then I heard the rattling breathing of a Rasper.

How had they found us? It was as if they had a damn GPS locator on us. The bastard moved into view. My finger itched on the trigger, but we needed to wait. Our ammo was low and we needed to see how many were out there. We were so dead if it was a horde. Three or four we could handle. Any more than that, we were in trouble. Or, worse yet, if they had weapons.

I stood still while every muscle in my body screamed for me to move.

The Rasper cleared the cover of the crops and left himself completely exposed. The desire to shoot the bastard overwhelmed me. The grip of the gun slipped in my damp hand. The Rasper turned toward the barn and stared. Had he heard us? No, he couldn't have.

Minutes ticked by and the Rasper remained alone. Finally, he took a few steps forward. The moon highlighted his face and I could tell the blood drained from mine.

It was him. The Rasper from the picture. The Rasper from the car. The Rasper who knew my name.

Without warning, he ran toward the barn and slammed into the wooden door, smashing it into pieces.

"Shit." Adam ran to the loft's edge. I followed right behind.

The Rasper stopped when he spotted Megan.

My throat swelled. I reached the wooden railing to the loft just as he looked up, his gaze locking with mine.

"Val." The Rasper held his hands out like he wanted me to rush into his arms for a hug.

Like hell.

"Cover me." Adam shoved his gun in his jeans and climbed over the railing. He leapt from the loft and slammed into the Rasper. I aimed the Glock. No clear shot. Damn it. I couldn't risk hitting Adam. The Rasper landed a punch to Adam's stomach. Adam recovered and grabbed the Rasper by the throat. They rolled and rolled. The darkness made it hard to make out who was who—and who was winning.

I shoved the gun in my jeans and slid down the ladder, the sides ripping my palms raw. I dropped to the ground and pain exploded up my legs. Through watery eyes, I leveled the Glock. Still no clear shot.

I holstered the gun and picked up an iron rod from the ground. I charged at the Rasper, hell-bent on bashing in his head. I was only a few feet away. I lined up the target, closed my eyes, and swung the rod like my dad had taught me to swing a softball bat. The rod connected and I opened my eyes. I expected to see half of his brains oozing from his skull. But no, he must have turned at the last minute. I'd hit his shoulder instead of his head.

The Rasper hit Adam in the jaw and tossed him onto the ground. Adam groaned and struggled to his feet. The Rasper turned to me.

I raised the rod again, swung, and connected with his hand. He yanked the weapon from my grip and threw it at Adam. The rod hit him in his injured arm.

"Aaah." Adam grabbed his arm and dropped back to the ground.

I reached for my gun.

Smack. Bursts of pain burned my cheek. The slap from the Rasper stunned me long enough for him to push me backward. I stumbled and fell. Scrambled for the gun.

"Val. Come. It's time." His hand reached out. The candlelight reflected off the pearly tip of his finger. He was close enough I could smell his rotten breath. I rolled and tried to get away. It was no use. His hand wrapped around my leg and tugged me back. I kicked with my free foot, but his grip was too strong. This was it. Adam couldn't help. Any second now I—

A gunshot rang out. The Rasper's right knee exploded in a shower of blood. Another shot and his left knee was minced. The Rasper crashed to the ground with an unnatural growl.

I looked at Adam. He was clutching his wound, and he was unarmed.

I spun around. Megan stood with the shotgun still aimed at the Rasper, even though it was empty.

"You asshole. You killed my family. I won't let you have my friends." Tears poured down her pale face. "They're all I have left. They can't die, too."

"Megan—" I started to tell her thanks, more than just thanks, but her eyes widened. I turned back to the Rasper. He tried to stand. His busted kneecaps wouldn't let him.

"Quick, grab some rope or something to tie him up." Adam hollered and aimed his gun at the Rasper's head. "Don't move, you son of a bitch."

I sprinted back to my bag and ripped out the rope. "What should I do?"

"Can you tie knots?"

"Not well enough to hold him."

"I can. Uncle John taught me." Megan handed me the shotgun.

She tied the end of the rope around one wrist, and then proceeded to wrap his hands in a complex web of knots and bindings. When she was done, Adam hoisted the Rasper to his feet and pushed the muzzle of his gun into the Rasper's back. The Rasper sniffed the air. What was he doing? He should be in pain, but he was sniffing. Crazy mutant.

"That's the same Rasper from the car roof." I stepped backward.

"Are you sure?"

"Positive. He must be tracking us somehow." Saying the words aloud sent a chill through my lungs, making it hard to catch my breath.

"Well then, all the better we didn't kill him." Adam shoved the gun harder into the Rasper's back and directed him to the old car seat. "Sit here. Megan, can you grab some of the chains?"

She grabbed a length from the wall. She expertly tied the Rasper's feet together then bound him to the seat. He sniffed the whole time. Freaky. I propped two flashlights up on the hay on opposite sides of the floor so the beams highlighted him. His knees were no longer bleeding. Holy hell.

My fear turned to anger. Anger I was so hungry. Anger I had lost my parents. Anger I had lost my way of life. The life I loved. It was time for answers.

"Are you Dr. Kane?" I demanded of the Rasper.

He swiveled his head from side to side and sniffed again.

I pointed the Glock at him. "Look at me."

The Rasper met my gaze and a shiver slithered down my arms. I couldn't look away. "I asked you if you're Dr. Kane."

"The human life form you name has been terminated." The Rasper spoke in a monotone voice. The chills moved from my lungs and snaked down my spine at the way he pronounced each word, as if it were an individual sentence.

"He's dead?" Megan picked up the shotgun and cradled it to her chest.

Another sniff, then the Rasper bobbed his head up and down. "The human data has been retained by the Colony."

"What the hell does that mean?" Adam jabbed the muzzle of his gun into the Rasper's arm.

I held my hand up. "Hang on, Adam."

Adam stepped back, but kept the gun trained on the Rasper.

"Why do some people..." I cleared my throat. "Die right away?"

"Human control vessel primitive. Some balanced. Most imbalanced."

"What does that have to do with anything?" Megan took a step toward him and shifted the gun forward.

The Rasper sniffed again.

"Injection of Colony buds only grow in balanced humans. Injections into imbalanced causes termination."

Holy mother of God. The sting was how it created more. Goose bumps broke out all over my body. Thoughts of silver Bug babies swimming through my blood and lodging in my brain forced me to one knee.

Megan took another step toward him. I caught him shift his bound hands. His index finger twitched. His stinger. His pearl-white stinger was still intact.

"Meg—"

I lunged. Shoved her out of the way. Unloaded two bullets into his hands.

A streak of blue whizzed past the spot where Megan had been and ricocheted into a support beam, leaving a black scorch mark.

"Megan, are you okay?" Adam pulled her behind him.

"Yeah."

"Glad to have you back, by the way." He gave her shoulder a quick squeeze.

I fought the urge to shoot more bullets into the Rasper. Blood dripped from his hands, then stopped, just like his knees. I should have checked his finger. Stupid. Stupid. Stupid. "Damn, Megan, I'm sorry."

They were evolving too fast. This Rasper could shoot his venom. Shit.

The Rasper's face shifted from a mask of pain to a serial-killer smile. "Fresh human."

"He's here for me?" Megan's voice shook and she retreated to the pile of blankets.

Anger roared through my veins and my heart pounded the drumbeat of battle. I aimed the Glock at the Rasper's chest. "Is that why you are following us? To turn us into your zombies?"

The Rasper cackled and a stench of rotten meat spewed from his mouth. "I didn't follow us. I track the life form Val."

An anvil of weight crushed my chest. Adam held my arm to steady me. "Me?"

"You. Are. Val."

I couldn't think. It was crazy. What would the Raspers want

with me? The desire to cry warred with the urge to shoot the Rasper in the head. It was a stalemate. I stood there with my mouth hanging open unable to shut it.

"Why does the Colony, as you called it, want Val?" Adam asked.

"Val. Join us." His gaze locked on mine again. As much as I tried, I couldn't look away.

"Like hell she will." Adam stepped in between the Rasper and me, breaking the crazy eye contact.

"Why me?" I rubbed my palm down the back of my hair. Breathed. In and out.

"Queen commands you join Colony."

Queen? What the hell? Why? How? My mind swirled with unanswered questions. I sank back to my knees. This couldn't be real. I had to be dreaming.

"Where are you from?" Megan asked in a hushed whisper.

"Far away."

"You're an alien?"

"Do not understand."

Aliens? Where did Megan pull that from? But what if he was? No. Aliens weren't real. But...

I pointed the gun at him. Their damn queen knew my name and wanted me. My throat constricted.

I'd reached my limit. I couldn't listen to this crap anymore. I choked down my terror. It was time. Time to fight back. Time to survive. Whoever the guy had been in human form was already dead.

"Adam, Megan, trust me." The irony of my words rang in my ears. "If you can, tell your queen I'm not interested."

I aimed for the Rasper's chest and pulled the trigger.

17

The bullet screamed from the gun and tore through the Rasper.

Megan gasped, her hands quick to cover her eyes.

Adam stood motionless.

I shoved the Glock in its holster, grabbed an old plastic spaghetti jar from the workbench and dumped out the metal parts. Running back to the Rasper, I skidded to a stop in front of him.

Blood soaked his shirt crimson and his eyes had rolled back so only the whites were visible in his yellow skin.

"Why?" Adam wiped his palm across his forehead.

"Watch." I prayed for my theory to work. I prayed I hadn't just done the stupidest thing ever.

Megan's brown eyes peeked out from behind her fingers. The barn was silent. Dead silent. I knew what I had to do. If I missed, we'd all be in jeopardy. The loud crack of the Rasper's jawbone breaking away from his skull exploded through the silence.

"What's happening?" Megan squealed and clutched Adam's arm.

Skin ripped from the Rasper's face and his teeth fell from his mouth like a set of dominoes crashing to the floor. It should happen soon; I just needed to wait for it. I stepped closer, only inches from his body, holding the container in my right hand

and the lid in the left. My heart rate pounded the insides of my rib cage. The Rasper's tongue flopped out of what remained of his lower jaw, bounced off his shirt, hit the right knee, then landed on the floor with a wet thump. Megan made a retching noise, but I couldn't tear my gaze from the Rasper.

With a laceration of the lips, the Bug's legs emerged. The metal creature crept down the face and onto the shoulder of the dead Rasper.

I moved closer.

It brought its front legs together. The metallic song sliced through my eardrums like a cheese grater scraping against a steel box. The Bug crawled down the Rasper's leg and onto the floor. I moved at a speed that surprised even me, scooped the damn thing into the jar, and screwed the lid shut with a vicious twist. My insides matched the movement.

"What is that?" Megan cried.

"A Bug. You heard the Rasper. The human was already dead. I couldn't let the Bug continue to use whoever the guy used to be."

I picked up one of the flashlights and shined the beam into the transparent prison. The Bug scuttled back as far as the jar allowed. Which—to my pleasure—wasn't much. I searched, but couldn't find any eyes. How did it see? Maybe it was like a bat and used that radar echo crap.

I thrust my middle finger at the jar, but was sure the Bug had no idea what my gesture meant. Or even if it saw it. Still, that simple act made me feel better.

"Now what?" Adam's words shattered my thoughts.

"Ah, I probably need to cut some air holes in the lid. Forgot to ask the bastard if they breathed air when they're outside humans." I smiled and a giggle slipped past my lips. "Oops." My words sounded cold and a wee bit crazy. Maybe I was losing it. Maybe this was it. Maybe I had given up my mind to the metal Bug that was most likely growing in my head.

Adam walked to the workbench and searched through the tools until he found a battery-operated drill. "Let's hope the batteries still have a charge." He hit the button and the drill bit spun to life. "Hand me the damn thing."

I gave him my prisoner. He set the jar on the bench, held it steady with one hand, and put the drill to the lid. I pointed the beam of the flashlight on the Bug. A scent similar to burnt toast filled my nostrils as the drill bit penetrated the thin metal. A whisper of fabric came from behind me, then Megan was at my side, twisting the sleeves of her jacket together.

"What are you going to do with it?"

I shrugged. I hadn't thought past catching the damn Bug. "What do you think?"

"Step on it." Megan's voice was a few octaves higher than normal.

There was no way I was stepping on the Bug. It still had the ability to sting in this form. I didn't want to risk a second attack since the first one obviously hadn't worked as planned. What to do with it? I didn't have a damn idea.

"Here." Adam returned the jar. It now sported five air holes in the lid.

I took the bastard from him. "I guess we bring it with us."

Megan's eyes grew wider than I thought possible. "I don't think that's a good idea."

"We'll figure it out later." I reached for my backpack and shoved the container inside. I nestled the jar in a shirt. "Megan?"

She turned to face me.

"I'm glad you're okay. That you're—back. And that you saved us. Thanks."

"It's what fam—friends do." Her eyes glistened and she turned away. "I gotta get out of here. Is it light yet?" Megan walked to the barn door and slid it open.

The first golden rays of the day highlighted the corn stalks in the field. I slung the bag over my shoulders and followed her outside. The fog had dissipated, leaving the day looking bright and promising. Adam fell into step beside us and we walked to the edge of the cornfield. The sound of a bird singing wafted through the air.

"Do you think we should bury the body or something?" Adam cracked his knuckles.

"Oh, God. Can't we just leave it?" Megan whined.

"You know the damn Raspers scarf up every dead body and take it away. Like they can smell the things miles away. I was thinking it might be a calling card to our location." Adam plucked an ear of corn from the stalk.

"There's no way I'm touching the dead body. Let's find some gas and get out of here." Megan shoved her hands into her pockets.

"And why was this one alone?" As I said the words, my mind flashed back to the one I'd shot on my birthday. He'd been alone too. "More importantly, what do they want with me? How do they know my name?"

Adam peeled the corn. "I wish I knew." He snapped the rotten cob in half, then chucked it into the field.

"It doesn't make any sense." We walked back to the buildings.

"The Rasper said the Colony. Call me a nerd, but do you think it works like the old sci-fi show with the aliens who had to assimilate? What was that show called?" Megan pulled her hair back, spun it around her fingers, then let it fall on her shoulders.

"No idea." Adam said.

"Yeah, anyway, the name doesn't matter. My point is, what if what one of them knows, the others know?"

A chill shot through my spine at Megan's words. It was like what Frank and John had said. I swallowed hard and choked out, "You're thinking they're aliens? Aliens can't be real."

"Why not? I believe there's more out there." Adam looked up at the sky. "More than just us."

I looked up, too. Aliens. From another planet. Here for what purpose? To kill humans? I didn't want to focus on the possibility. "Okay, we need to find some gas and get moving. Get to Site R. There have to be more Raspers coming. He was probably a scout or something."

"Let's split up. Five minutes of searching, then we meet in the barn."

"I'll take the destroyed house." Megan said.

"I'll check the silo." Adam took off to the left.

I walked to the building with the ripped roof and opened the huge doors with a shove. There had to be a can of regular gas around somewhere. Large, hulking equipment filled the space. Probably a combine or something, but I really didn't know.

The scent of oil was stronger in here than in the barn. I searched along the inside perimeter of the building. All the while, the Rasper's words played over and over in my mind. *"Queen commands you join Colony."*

They were after me. *Just me.* Adam and Megan would never be safe as long as I was around. Maybe I should leave. I'd survived on my own before. I could do it again. I hated to admit it, but I wanted to stay with them. I liked them. My heart split in two. Part of me wanted to stay, but another part told me to leave. If I was going to do it, I had to do it now. Before anyone else got hurt because of me.

"Hey, Val, where are you?" Adam called out, interrupting my plans.

I wedged myself around the hulking machine. How did people learn to drive these big ass things? The seat was so high up. It gave me an idea.

"Val?"

"By this big ass tractor thingie."

"Did you find anything?" Megan called from somewhere by the front of the building.

"Not yet." I climbed into the seat of the huge metal beast. I was as high as I could get in the building without climbing a massive ladder. I scanned the space for any sign of the precious liquid.

My search came up empty, but in the back corner, I spotted a blue Volkswagen Beetle. My pulse quickened. I scrambled down from the machine and weaved my way through the equipment to the car.

"There's a car back here." I yelled.

I opened the Beetle's door. No keys. No way to tell if it had gasoline in the tank.

"Maybe we can poke the tank open like we did at the repair shop," Adam said.

Megan came up from the other side. "Or we could just use the gas in the containers back here."

"What? You found some?" I wanted to hug her. I knew leaving

now wasn't an option. I would have to wait until Megan and Adam were safe somewhere.

"Over here." She disappeared behind some large piece of machinery I couldn't identify.

Adam and I found her standing over two five-gallon gas containers.

"Are they full?"

"Yep." Megan grinned.

Thank God. We could get away from this damned farm and maybe leave some of this dark despair behind. I knew that wasn't possible, though. There was no escaping the horror that had taken up residence in my life. I should be contemplating homework and the purchase of my first car. But no. I had a queen of the Raspers hot for me to join her colony. A colony of possible aliens. Extra-terrestrials. ETs. It couldn't be true. But... What would they want with me?

"Earth to Val."

"Huh?"

"Can you grab one?" Adam's words pierced my cloud of negativity.

"Sure." I bent down, hoisted the can, and followed him out into the sunshine.

Adam dumped all the fuel into the thirsty truck and tossed the empty cans in the back. "Okay. Ten gallons should at least get us to Ohio."

We jumped into the pickup and I wedged my bag between my feet to keep the Bug upright.

"Val, do you have any food left?"

I didn't have to search my backpack to answer his question. I knew my inventory. "I have two cans of spaghetti rings, three single servings of applesauce, one bottle of water. Oh. And one Bug in a jar." We had depleted the granola bars and the tuna. I thought about the jar of peanut butter left on the counter in the chlorine house and my stomach contracted.

"I have zero interest in eating the Bug, so we have to find someplace to get more supplies or it won't matter about Raspers and Bugs because we'll die of dehydration and starvation." Adam turned the key and the truck roared to life.

"We need to get back on the interstate and find a town."

***

We drove in silence for at least an hour before we reached the interstate. The entire time my thoughts circled around the image of the Rasper's face.

"Holy crap, look at the road." Megan pointed at the windshield.

The road was a torn up mess, riddled with holes and gaps. The earthquakes had done a number on it. A few cars rested, abandoned. A blue minivan had all its doors open and its hood raised, as if it was waving a flag of surrender. Adam dodged the vehicles and swerved to avoid a motorcycle stuck in a crack in the asphalt. A black helmet rested riderless along the berm.

What had happened to the rider? All the death and destruction seemed pointless. Nothing gained, and so many had lost everything. Like my parents. The sting of tears welled in my eyes yet again. I needed to stop crying and focus on what to do with the Bug. Maybe I had been premature in killing the Rasper, but I had been so angry at what he said. There was no conceivable reason the queen would want me. I was a nobody without any special talents. Well, except my shooting skills, and I doubted the Raspers cared about that. What did they want with me? Especially if they were really aliens. The urge to yank the Bug out and run over it with the truck was overwhelming, but I resisted the urge—at least for now.

Fields paraded non-stop past the windows. The only noise was the tires beating a steady drum against the asphalt. My thoughts were like seaweed, all tangled up with no sense of order. Each time I tried to work on one strand, it caught in the others. I didn't know how long we'd traveled, but I needed a break. My head hurt and my throat was dry. I retrieved the last bottle of water out of my bag.

"I need a drink. How about you guys?" I knew I was dehydrated because I couldn't remember the last time I'd gone pee.

"Yes."

I took a small swallow, even though I wanted to drink the whole thing down in one gulp, then passed it to Megan. She took a drink, handed it to Adam. We continued to share the bottle until it was gone. It took all of about thirty seconds and left me still parched.

"Hey, there's a sign for the next exit. Keep your eyes out for one listing restaurants, hotels, and gas stations. The more they have, the better our chances of finding some food," Adam said.

We crested a hill. I spotted a blue sign proclaimed three fast food joints and two hotels at the next exit. Another one touted two gas stations. If only it were as simple as pulling off, getting gas, and going through a drive-thru.

"Get off here. There's a MegaCamping." Megan bounced in the seat as if she was going to Disneyworld.

"A what?"

"MegaCamping. They have everything. Camping, hunting, fishing, sports, *everything.*"

Within minutes, we parked in front of the store. I pulled out the jar with the Bug. He didn't move, so I shoved him back into the darkness of my bag.

"Looks okay. No earthquake damage. Let's go." Adam cut the engine and jumped out.

He ran to the glass doors and smashed them with the butt of the empty shotgun. The glass cracked, then exploded into thousands of tiny shards. We stepped into the store. The only sound was the crunching of glass under our shoes.

The three-story store sent a jolt of—did I dare think—happiness through my system. An enormous display of taxidermy animals drew me closer. Deer, rabbits, birds, even a grizzly bear stared at me with glass eyes. The mountain scene climbed almost to the ceiling, revealing more and more animals artfully posed.

Adam tapped me on the arm. "Think we need to search for Raspers?"

"I don't hear them. I think we're good."

"Hunting section first then?"

"Most definitely." I ripped my gaze from the harmless teeth of the bear and blocked my thoughts of Bethany.

"I'm going to go get water and food. They have ready-meals here. Like the stuff they give soldiers and astronauts." Megan took a shopping cart from the corral. "Meet back here in a fifteen minutes?"

I checked my watch. "Okay."

Adam and I wheeled our carts past the back wall of the store, which was all glass except for the arms-span-wide climbing wall that stretched up the entire three stories. We went into the hunting section.

"Check this out." Adam slammed his palm off the top of the gun display case. He broke into a wide grin and leapt over it. "What model of killing weaponry may I help you with, Miss?"

I tried not to laugh, but couldn't help myself. I cleared my throat. "Well, I would really like to start with ammo for these fine weapons."

"Yes, ma'am."

Our hands touched when we both reached for a box of 9mm. My stomach flip-flopped and my heart beat a tad faster.

Adam met my gaze and laughed in a voice lower than his usual level.

I tried not to focus on how much I enjoyed his slight touch. I cleared my throat and glanced away.

He dumped box after box of 9mm bullets and shotgun shells into my cart, filling it almost half way.

"Kind sir, some new firearms might also be in order."

"Right you are, ma'am." He smashed the top of the glass case and we each reached in and grabbed two guns.

"Okay. Let's go. We need to meet Megan." We pushed the carts, alternating between running behind the carts and riding on them. Dad had showed me this fun sport—much to Mom's disgust—when I'd barely been big enough to see over the handlebar. Megan came into view and for the first time, I smiled at the memory of my parents.

"Wow. You got a lot of food." I pulled my cart to a stop, but rammed into the side of Megan's water and food-filled buggy.

"Check this out." She tugged open a vacuum-sealed bag and the scent of seasoned meat tempted my stomach. "Jerky."

"Mine." Adam dashed around our cart cluster and snagged

the bag. He shoved two strips in his mouth whole. "Good." He managed to sneak in between chews.

Megan shook her head and tossed me a bag. "Here, there's plenty for all of us."

I chewed on the salty and spicy meat. "Clothes." I said my mouth full of jerky and pointed a strip of meat at the second level. Megan was right. This place was heaven. We didn't have one in Alberdine. If we had, Dad probably would have lived there.

We grabbed jeans, tees, sweatshirts, socks, and changed in the dressing rooms. I took in my reflection in the mirror. I looked skinny and tired. Black shadows rimmed the corners of my eyes.

"Guys?" Megan peered over the curtain of her area.

"Yeah?" I tugged a black tee over my head.

"What do you think the Rasper meant by balanced and imbalanced?"

Adam came out from the men's area wearing relaxed-style jeans that hugged his backside, a blue shirt, and a gray hoodie. The gray highlighted the green of his eyes. My heart leapt at the sight of him. "It all sounded hokey to me. Was he referring to mentally balanced? Like if you're not insane, you die right away? 'Cause my mom wasn't crazy."

"And when he said Colony, do you think he meant the black oozy stuff?" Megan gagged and stuck her tongue out.

Even though we were discussing awful terrible horrible things, my mood stayed high. It reminded me of shopping with Sofie and my friends.

Megan came out of the dressing area and punched Adam in the arm then they both burst out laughing. I allowed myself a smile. I wasn't sure when it happened—probably after she shot the Rasper, but I wasn't worried about Megan anymore. I trusted her as much as I trusted Adam. These were my friends now. My close friends. My family. My responsibility. I needed a new Rule Number One. One like...leave no one behind.

"I don't know. I just hope to never see it again." I pushed the curtain aside. "Let's get the truck loaded."

It took about two hours for us to reload the guns, fill the truck with more guns, bullets, knives, food, water, sleeping bags, tents, and a camping-sized propane grill with two extra tanks.

Adam took the empty gas cans from the truck's bed. "Do you think there's gas in the display four-wheelers?"

"We can try."

We filed back into the store to the vehicle section. At least ten different models of ATVs, a dozen kayaks, and two small motorboats took up the area. Boats. The Bugs had come out of the river. No way was I going in a boat. Who knew how many were still out there swimming. I hoped the water rusted their damn metallic shells.

"What do you think? Cut the gas line?" Megan whipped out a wicked hunting knife.

I shrugged and walked to the glass case behind the one motorboat. GPS units. "Hey, guys?"

"Yeah?"

"A GPS should still work if the satellites are still in the sky, right?" I plucked a box from the shelf.

"I would think so. Bring it. Can't hurt." Adam yelled. "There's gas in this one."

I tucked the box into my bag, then hurried back. The four-wheelers had gas, but cutting the lines was messy. It took seven of the ten ATVs to fill our cans and top off the truck.

"I'm going to put these in the truck." Adam lifted the full cans.

Megan twirled the knife in her hand. "We'll do a last sweep for anything else we need."

While Adam stowed the cans, Megan hit the camping section. I climbed the non-working escalator to the top level. We hadn't checked the third floor since golf, other sports, and exercise equipment covered the entire area. I picked up a golf club and hit the treadmills as I walked past.

"Hey, I found a survival manual book. It has info on how to properly siphon gas." Megan called from the second level.

"Grab it. Who knows what other info it might have." I stopped at the glass wall and looked down. The rock wall reminded me of the climb out of the mountain. A shiver danced along the hairs on my arms at the memory. I gazed out the window and it felt like a glacier took up residence in my veins.

"Megan?" My voiced cracked.

"What?"

"Get Adam. Have him grab binoculars, and get the hell up here."

"What's wrong?" Her voice screeched higher.

"Just hurry."

I stared out the window waiting for them. Their footfalls thundered up the escalator.

"What's going on?"

"There's a mall out there." I pointed to the window.

"So?"

The Bug rattled in my backpack.

Adam reached the top with the binoculars dangling from his hands. I ripped them from his grip. With trembling hands, I held them up and adjusted the knobs.

It felt like an elephant leapt onto my chest and all the air rushed out through my mouth. "Oh, God, no."

18

I twisted the knob on the binoculars. The black goo came into clear focus. Too clear. The substance puffed out, then sucked back to the rooftop as if it was inhaling and exhaling. Breathing. Alive.

"They're out there."

A rattling noise erupted from my bag. I opened it and took out the jar. The Bug scuttled back and forth, trying to climb up the sides of the plastic container. He was failing. My stomach clenched at the sight of his struggles. He had to know others were around. He could sense it somehow.

Ribbons of terror tangled in my veins. Oh, no. Were they able to sense him? Had I sealed our fates by bringing a damn homing device for the Raspers? I bit my cheek so hard, I tasted blood in my mouth. Maybe I should kill it. No, they would hear the gunshot.

"Why is it making that noise?"

"I think it knows Raspers are close by." The wavering of my voice emphasized my worry. I brought up the binoculars and zoomed back in at the mall.

"Let me see," Adam said in a stern voice I hadn't heard him use before.

"Hang on." Something moved at the entrance. I adjusted the

focus. Figures. People. Raspers. Yellow-skinned, sunglass-wearing Raspers. I dropped the binoculars to the floor. "We gotta go. They're coming."

I shoved the Bug back in my bag and took off for the escalator.

"Val, wait," Adam said.

I stopped and turned. "What?"

"How many are there?"

Megan picked up the binoculars and looked out the window. "I see two. We can shoot them easy enough."

"That will draw out more. Remember how many came out at the seminary? We need a plan." Adam pulled out his gun.

The Bug squealed louder.

"Shut up." Adam yelled, but it didn't stop.

Megan shrugged. "I can stay here and be a look out if you guys want to go out with guns blazing."

"Maybe. But—"

"What the hell are we going to do? They're getting closer." Megan's voice climbed higher and higher.

I snapped my fingers. "We need a diversion."

"Like what?"

"I don't know, maybe—" My bag jumped and thumped like it was full of popcorn.

A shadow passed over the store's skylight. "God, what was that?" Megan's eyes widened further.

We all looked up, but there wasn't anything there. Goose bumps marred my skin. "Hopefully a bird and not more Bugs."

"We need to see what's happening out front." Adam took out his radio. "Does yours still work?"

I snatched Megan's from my screeching bag and turned it on. Static squawked. "Yes."

"Megan, take mine. Let us know if more come out." Adam tossed her the radio.

Megan nodded and bit her bottom lip. "Okay."

Adam and I ran down the escalator turned stairs to the first floor.

"What about a remote control vehicle or something? We could send it out and the Raspers would go after it," Adam said.

"Even if there's a remote control car in here, the battery wouldn't be charged."

"Good point. What else could we use?" Adam turned to the vehicle section. "The ATVs. We left gas in three of them. We could rig one up with a mannequin and send it out the back door. Then we race out the front and escape in the truck."

I peeked out the front window. Nothing. "It might work." I radioed Megan and told her the plan while Adam used a boat tow-rope to strap a mannequin dressed in camouflage to a four-wheeler.

"How's it going to go?"

"I strapped a weight to the gas pedal. Once we turn it on, it will take off. At least that's the plan."

"Hope it works."

"Me too, because once we open the door, our fly is down."

"Nice analogy."

Adam grinned, his dimples framing his mouth. "Thanks."

We pushed the ATV to the store's back door. "What's happening outside?" I asked Megan on the radio.

"The original two are on the street, lurking around. I haven't seen any more—wait, hang on, there's more. Damn. I don't know where they came from. There has to be at least twenty."

"Okay, get down here. We're all set."

The Bug squealed louder. The damn thing knew the Raspers were out there. We positioned the ATV right by the loading dock door.

My radio squawked. "Guys, go ahead, send it out. There are more Raspers coming. I'll be right there."

"Hurry." My throat tightened. "I hope this works." I didn't want to think about the alternative.

Adam grabbed the door's chain. "Once the door's high enough, turn the key, and it should go."

"Got it." I had my right hand on the key and my left clutched my Glock.

Adam yanked on the chain and it began to open. I held my breath. The door creaked and groaned as it ascended. Almost there. I turned the key. The engine roared to life and the four-wheeler jumped forward, then stopped. Crap. The Bug's song sliced into my head. I jammed the weight down. Nothing happened. "Move, you bastard."

I pushed with every ounce of strength I possessed. That did it. The ATV lurched out under the door. The Raspers swarmed around the vehicle. One came toward the door. I fired. She fell.

"It's clear. Let the door go!" I yelled. The dummy flew into the parking lot and bowled over a Rasper.

Adam released the chain and the *clack clack clack* of the door dropping grated down my vertebrae. "Let's go."

I gave one last look back. A red-haired Rasper slid under the door. I squeezed off another shot, blasting her in the leg. The Bug screeched and squealed.

Thwunk.

The door slammed down on the Rasper and blood squirted, spraying the floor in an abstract image.

"Come on." Adam clutched my hand and ripped me from the gory display.

"Megan, where are you?" I yelled as we ran toward the front entrance.

"Coming," she hollered.

I glanced up to see her grab hold of one of the climbing wall's safety harness ropes and swing down like she was zip lining. She landed behind us, binoculars dangling around her neck, blonde hair flying out behind her. "What the hell was that?"

"Fastest way down. Did the dummy work?" Megan's breaths came fast and her cheeks turned a dark shade of pink.

"Yeah, but it won't matter if we don't get out of here."

We stopped at the front, readied our weapons, then after a three count, shoved open the door and ran to the truck. The Bug's squeal hit a shattering pitch.

"Raspers!" Megan screamed, fired, and shot one in the head.

Adam hit another one in the chest.

I aimed at a white-haired female Rasper who darted around the corner. "Get the truck started. I'll cover."

Megan and Adam jumped into the truck. I fired at a Rasper wearing a business suit. The Bug went berserk, banging and bumping my back. Pain serrated my eardrums.

"Come on, Val," Adam yelled from his open window.

Five more Raspers surged toward the truck. I hit one and jumped inside. Megan reached across me and slammed the door shut. Adam gunned the engine and rammed into two Raspers. The tires rolled over their bodies with a wet thunk. I fired two more rounds out the window, but didn't see if any were direct hits.

Megan spun around in her seat. "They're still coming."

I reloaded the Glock while she fired out the open back window. The Bug continued its horrid song.

"Holy hell! There's a car coming!" Megan yelled.

"What?" Adam swerved the truck hard to the right, then the left, just missing a huge hole in the road.

"How many inside?"

"At least two. Maybe three."

I grabbed the shotgun from behind the seat, setting it next to me. "What do you think the range is on this?"

Zzzurmp.

"What the frick was that?" Adam cut the wheel hard to the left again. I smashed into Megan.

"They're armed. They're shooting at us!" Megan shrieked. "Duck!"

The Bug's noise made it almost impossible to communicate.

"Shut that damn thing up."

"If they want the damn Bug, then give it to them. Throw it out the window."

"No." I couldn't do that. "I have an idea. Cover me." I holstered the Glock and climbed out the small back window into the bed of the truck.

"What are you doing?"

"Get down." I shouted at Megan. Another bullet ripped into the cab of the truck. "Shoot out of the passenger window when I tell you to."

I pushed aside the sleeping bags and clamped my hand down on the propane tanks.

"Val, look out."

I dropped down and slammed my forehead off a case of water. Adam turned to the right. A box shifted and fell onto my ankle. Pain soared through my lower leg. Another bullet lodged into the side panel of the truck. I needed to hurry. Their aim was improving.

I clutched one tank with both hands and hurled it at the car. The tank bounced on the road and rolled toward the car.

"Shoot the tanks!" I yelled to Megan, and launched the second one.

Gunshots exploded. Megan shooting, the Raspers shooting. A spray of bullets tore through the boxes in front of me. Then a burst of heat and a whoosh rocked the truck. The propane tanks exploded. I fell backward and scraped my back on something.

An orange and purple fireball consumed the car, but it kept coming, looking like a demon car roaring out of hell. I sat up and fired my entire clip. It still kept coming.

Megan wedged the shotgun out the window. "Move over."

I tried to make myself as small as possible and covered my ears.

Boom.

The Rasper's car exploded in a burst of white flames. It lifted off the ground, flipped over, and hit the ground with a groan of crumpling metal. The wave of heat knocked me back on my ass.

Adam hit the brakes with a screech of tires, and the truck stopped.

Megan wedged herself out the back window. "Val? Val? Val? Are you okay?" Her words were muffled.

I sat up and rubbed the back of my head. I had a lump the size of a lemon. "Yeah. Nice shooting." I reached up to give her a high-five. "Adam, nice driving."

"Let's get out of here before any more catch up with us. God, they can drive now. Shit. We're doomed."

***

The only things that changed during the next few hours were the clock, the trees, and the gas gauge. We had enough food and water to last us until we reached Site R. The gas was another story.

I turned on the truck's radio and searched through every FM and AM station. I only found static.

Adam shot me a quick look. "Did you expect something to have changed?"

"No."

Megan shifted for a more comfortable position. "Do you think we're going to make it?"

The spinning of the tires on the pavement was the only sound until I broke the tension.

I swallowed. "Yes I do." I sounded a lot more confident than I felt.

I glanced down at the Bug. Thankfully, it had quieted down after the explosion. I had kept it out of the bag as an alarm. After it settled, it hadn't moved except to shift its legs once. I picked up the jar and leaned back in my seat. The Bug still didn't move. I tapped the glass. No response.

"Can't you put that damn thing away?" Megan narrowed her eyes at the jar.

"No. It freaks out if Raspers are near. We need it."

"We can hear it just fine if it's in your bag." She crossed her arms with an attitude and gave me her back.

"How much gas do we have left?" I tore my gaze from the jar.

"Half a tank."

I snarled at the Bug, then put the jar in my backpack. "Okay. Okay." I put it away.

She spun around. "Good. I never want to see it again. Why do you keep staring at it?"

Because it knows my name. Because it said its queen wants me. Because it might be an alien. But I didn't say any of that aloud. She was upset enough as it was, I didn't need to remind her of my issues. Raspers had killed her family, maybe mine too, but the Rasper colony hadn't taken a sick interest in *her* joining them. Just me.

I shrugged in response to her question. I thought it would be a better option than spouting the truth.

"Lord, help me, if you pull the jar out again, I'll throw it out the window." Megan contorted her delicate face into a grotesque shape.

"I wasn't going to. But we can't just throw it out the window."

"Val's right. We can't toss it." Adam said.

Megan made a harrumph sound, and then crossed her arms across her chest.

"We need to kill it." Adam added, bringing a smile to Megan's face.

"Not yet." I wanted nothing more than to kill it, but if I was going to get any answers, I needed the damn mutant.

"Why not? It can't tell us anything more since you killed its host," Adam shot back.

"Excuse me. I thought it would be better than getting stung." My voice rose at least ten decibels.

"We already have been!" Adam's cheeks flamed red, then blanched white.

Megan's mouth dropped open and she grabbed the dashboard in a death grip.

19

"What? Are you shitting me?" Megan's voice shrilled. "Holy hell. You two are Raspers?"

She twisted and made it halfway over the seat before Adam grabbed her leg. He let go of the wheel and yanked. The truck veered to the side.

"Adam, watch out," I yelled as we headed toward a ditch.

He spun the wheel and straightened the truck. "No, damn it. Now sit your ass back down before you get us killed."

"For God's sake, will you tell me what's going on? You've obviously been keeping secrets."

"It's true, Val and I were stung by Raspers, but we seem to be immune to the toxin." Adam held up his hand. "And before you ask, no, we don't know how or why we aren't affected."

We *were* affected, but not how everyone else was. We had heightened senses and greater physical ability. Was it doing anything else to us? The look on Adam's face told me he was thinking the same thing.

"When were you going to tell me?" Megan wiped away a tear.

"I'm sorry. It never seemed like a good time." I never intended to tell her. A headache nagged at my skull. This wasn't going well. We *should* have told her before now.

"You lied to me." More tears dropped from her brown eyes.

"No, not on purpose. We didn't want to scare you." Adam went to touch her arm, but she jerked it out of his reach.

"You didn't want to scare me? Didn't want to scare me!" Megan's voice turned into a shriek. "And telling me now while I'm locked in a truck between you both, with the damn Bug in a jar at Val's feet doesn't scare me? I want out."

Neither Adam nor I said anything. What could we say to make her feel better? When she spelled it out that way, we seemed like jerks.

"Now!" Megan slammed her palm on the dashboard.

"No. I'm not letting you out." Adam said in a low voice that rumbled down my spine.

"What? Are you keeping me hostage? Going to lock me up in a jar like your precious Bug?" Her eyes grew wide. "Or maybe have the Bug sting me so I can be like you freaks?"

Adam turned to Megan then back to the road. "No. None of that. I won't let you out because if I do, you'll die. Maybe not from a Rasper or Bug attack, but from exposure or dehydration. We're stronger together. We're your friends and friends don't leave each other to die."

"Friends don't lie either."

Her words knifed me in the heart.

"Meg, look, we're sorry. Please believe me, we never intended to lie to you. Or hurt you. I wish we'd never been stung, but we can't change that." I exhaled and rubbed my temples, trying to will away the headache stabbing the back of my eyes. "I know the Bug creeps you out, but it knew my name. And it said the queen wanted me. I'm more than a little freaked myself." I didn't add that for some crazy reason, I felt like having the Bug might keep us safe if we encountered more Raspers.

Megan crossed her arms and shot my bag a nasty look. "Hmm."

I glanced at my bag too, but not for the same reasons. Could he hear us? Understand us? "Hold on." Adam yelled as the truck bounced.

The road had fallen apart. Tire-sized potholes dotted the pavement. Vehicles were scattered across the road, many smashed into one another.

"Shit." Adam jammed down the brakes.

We were going too fast to stop in time. We were on a bridge, but the bridge was partly gone. Nothing connected it to the other side. An eighteen-wheeler hung off the edge.

"Stop!" Megan screamed.

Adam practically stood on the brake while he jerked the wheel to the left. The tires screeched as if they were being tortured. The big rig kept coming. Closer, closer. I grabbed a hold of the handle above the window and Megan clutched my arm. We shifted hard to the right and I slammed into the passenger side door, my face pushed against the window. We barreled closer and closer to the eighteen-wheeler. Adam tried to stop us. With every inch we gained on the hunk of metal on wheels, the tighter my chest constricted.

I calculated our options. If we hit the semi, we'd die. Flip over—die. If we flew over the railing into the lake, die. All of the scenarios ended the same. We die. I couldn't die this way. Not after everything I had survived.

Our truck jerked to a stop, but the back of the bed hit the eighteen-wheeler. A metallic groan roared. "It's going down! Drive!" I yelled.

Adam turned the wheel more and hit the gas. We shot back down the bridge, tracing the way we had come. I spun around. The semi ground against the metal of the bridge and fell into the lake with enough force to splash water all over our vehicle, and our supplies.

Once we were safely back on solid ground, Adam stopped the truck and rested his forehead against the steering wheel.

Megan covered her face with her hands and bent over.

"You guys okay?" I focused on my breathing. In and out. Slow and steady. My heartbeat began to return to normal.

"That was messed up. I thought we were going to..."

"Me too."

"We could die at any time." Megan moaned through her fingers. "I don't want to die alone."

"Me either. I'm so sorry we didn't tell you." I touched her arm.

Megan flinched, but didn't pull away. "Just don't leave me alone."

I gave her arm a squeeze. "We won't. We'll stay together."

***

Adam found another road and we kept going. We kept the lake on our left and farms covered the right. A couple looked like they had been animal farms. Large hunks of brown that had once been cows filled one field. A few had swarms of flies around them. Here and there, a lone skeleton rested among the grass.

"Don't open the windows. It will stink something horrid out there," Adam said.

I didn't need to open the window to smell it. The stench permeated the air filter of the truck. Megan tucked her nose in her shirt and I thought about doing the same, but settled for covering my face with my hand.

Finally, the farms gave way to trees. Lots and lots of trees.

I plugged in the GPS I'd swiped from MegaCamping. It took forever to boot up, but it found zero satellites. "Damn it."

"Here's a map I found at the store." Megan handed me a road atlas.

I tried to pinpoint our location on the map. I knew we were on the border to Ohio, but that was it, since the map didn't give small road detail.

Nothing seemed out of the ordinary here. Just a two-lane road running through the trees. When the sun started to drop to the horizon, Adam said, "We need to find a place to stay for the night."

We were still on back roads and currently the only thing around us was another large lake and plenty of woods. "Wonder what lake that is."

"Don't know. Check that out." Adam pointed out his window.

The edge of the lake ended in a large dam. The road ran past it and I caught a large overflow sluice shooting water into a river that snaked next to the road.

The trees gave way to a house here and there. Then civilization sprang up along the road. Restaurants, hotels, big-box retailers, all in a state of collapse. Some buildings were missing roofs, and a few stores had sunk into the ground so only their roofs showed. Every car I spotted had no glass in the windows. Some buildings had been reduced to a pile of rubble, undistinguishable from what they used to be.

Two burnt gas stations flanked the street on opposite sides—no hope of getting gas from them. The few cars in the parking lot were shells of twisted and charred metal.

"This is depressing." Adam checked out the gas stations. "See anything promising?"

"No."

We continued to drive. The other side of town was the polar opposite. It hardly looked damaged. It was as if people had just disappeared. Cars stood empty in the road and parking lots, while stores and restaurants sat ready for their next customers.

"Wow. This is weird." Adam glanced out his window.

"I know. Feels freaky to me." I rubbed my hands on my arms, trying to ward off a chill.

Megan didn't say anything. She just stared out the window.

Adam weaved through the maze of vehicles and pulled into the parking lot of a home improvement store.

The store had a few broken windows, but otherwise seemed unscathed. A small restaurant and a tire shop sat next to the store.

Adam parked the truck next to a Jeep and we all got out. I pulled on my bag, but the strap was caught on something under the seat. I bent down to check it out and…

A rumble filled the air.

"What's that?" I pulled out my gun. Nausea crept up my throat like an unwelcome visitor.

Adam scanned the area. "I don't know."

The ground shifted violently. I lost my balance, scraped my knee on the pavement, and lost the Glock.

"It's another earthquake!" Adam grabbed the Jeep, but couldn't hold on and dropped to the ground.

My gun slid toward a gap in the asphalt. I couldn't lose it. It was my lifeline. My protection. My only connection to my father. I got back to my feet, ignoring the hole in the knee of my jeans and the pain that went with it. I scrambled after my gun.

My fingers closed around the grip just before the gun dropped into the expanding fissure.

"Val, come on!"

I jumped up and spun back to face Adam. He stumbled to the truck.

Another bone-tingling shake dropped me to the ground. My bag. I had to get it. A second crack grew at an alarming rate, headed right for me. I shoved the gun in its holster and dove to the side, scraping my cheek across the ground. Gravel bit into my skin and pain shot through my face. I wiped my hand across my cheek. I had to get to the bag. It had everything. The gap widened at my feet and my boot slipped inside. I scrambled to the other side of the crack.

A loud crash and a thunderous groan echoed off the buildings.

"What's happening?" Megan screamed.

The ground settled, but the roar grew louder and louder. I stumbled to my feet. Adam held onto the passenger side mirror of the pickup.

The roar turned into an explosive crescendo. The ground stayed still while the noise built and built and built.

"We need to go," Adam called.

The noise shifted into a sound I recognized. Goose bumps covered my arms.

Adam's head swiveled toward the direction we had come from. "Holy—"

A mass of water drowned out his words. It crashed through the buildings and churned right at us. Oh, God. The earthquake had broken the dam. I ran for the truck.

The water crashed into everything in its path, sweeping cars into its fury.

"Val!" Adam yelled. He raced to the driver's side. He wasn't going to make it in time. The wall of water slammed into the back of the truck, knocking it forward.

As if stuck in a slow motion scene, I watched in horror, my heart pounding against my throat. Megan bounced off the side of the truck and went under. The water knocked Adam from his feet and swept him away.

I tried to scream, but the cry caught in my throat. The tide slammed into the back of my knees. I flailed and fought to stand. The water knocked me around as if I weighed nothing. My right arm smacked into something and pain shot through my system. My body twisted in the swirling water and I found myself face to face with the grill of a car caught in the wave's path. It was going to hit me.

The wall crested and I went under. Water filled my ears and I couldn't tell which way was up. I struggled to stand, but it was too deep. I kicked out and touched nothing. Water spun me around like I was caught in a whirlpool, and my lungs threatened to explode. My back hit something to the right. I reached out and grabbed at it. Missed.

Air. I needed air. Needed it now.

I kicked and thrashed my arms. My head broke through the swirl and I gulped oxygen. I spiraled, helpless in the wave of destruction. A minivan loomed ahead of me. I tried to move out of the way, but I couldn't control my body. I collided with the cold hard metal.

Everything went black.

20

I came to, gasping for breath. Every part of me seemed beaten and bruised. I was sprawled across a flat, rough surface filled with pipes and water. It looked like—what the hell—a roof. I sat up and my muscles screamed in objection. Water lapped at my legs. Where was I?

My head pounded and my stomach rolled. I leaned over and threw up a bunch of water, then wiped my mouth with the back of my hand. My clothes were soaking wet and my body shook from the cold wind. I reached for my holster and exhaled when my fingers closed around the gun.

"Adam. Megan." My voice was gruff and sounded more like an old woman. I glanced around. They were nowhere in sight.

I stood and everything spun. My legs crumpled and I grabbed the only thing I could—a pipe jutting through the roof, and clung to it as tightly as I could.

I touched my head and my fingers came away dotted with blood. Another head wound. That might explain why I felt like I was stuck on the teacup ride at an amusement park. I reached for my bag to get a Band-Aid, but I didn't have it. My bag was gone. My life locked in nylon. The link to who I had been before. Besides my gun, it was all I had left. Could it still be stuck under the seat of the truck?

Tears slipped down my cheeks. I pictured the photo of my parents I kept in the inside pocket; it was the only thing I had to remember what they looked like. Even if I found the bag, the picture would be ruined.

My food and supplies and, oh God, the Bug. Was it still in the bag?

When the wave of dizziness passed, I tried standing again. This time I stayed vertical.

Holy crap. I was on top of a roof and the water was high enough it spilled over the gutter's edge. A few feet away, part of the roof had collapsed and left a hole the size of a washing machine. I made my way over, one step at a time. My steadiness increased with each step. Once there, I knelt down and stared into the hole. Water swirled around the red and yellow old-style booths of a McDonalds. Ronald McDonald had saved me.

"Adam. Megan. Can you hear me?" I yelled. Thankfully, my voice had returned to normal. And my head had stopped its relentless pounding.

No one answered. Staying on the roof wasn't an option. That left only one way. "Okay. Here I go."

I slid off the roof and splashed into the icy water with a gasp. Shivers sent my body trembling. I swam away from the fast food joint.

I needed to find the others, the truck, my bag. And get out of the water, but it was everywhere. No edge or end in sight. I swam for a distance until the water dropped to waist-height. Numbness spread through my arms and legs. I pushed on. I couldn't tell which way I had come from or how far I traveled. The home improvement store wasn't anywhere. Crap.

I shuffled through the water, searching for my friends. The truck. My bag.

Ahead, two cars, one a police car, were nose to nose and debris was backed up between them. A log raced to the pile.

I climbed on the hood of the police car and searched for the store. Megan and Adam had to be there. Had to be. I jumped onto the roof, stepped over the light bar, and looked around for something—anything—that might tell me the right direction. I didn't recognize a thing. Megan and Adam could be anywhere.

The truck and my bag could be anywhere. I didn't want to think about the Bug. If it got loose, it could be hiding in the water.

I turned and caught a flash of metal. The pickup rested against a store, dented and missing the front bumper. I scrambled off the car and slogged through the water, which now reached my knees.

I reached the truck and jerked open the door. Empty. No Megan. No Adam. I raced to the other side. Nothing. The panel on the passenger side was crumpled against a now-flat tire. The truck was toast.

And all our supplies had washed away, except for a handful of water bottles lining the edges of the truck bed. I jumped in to get them. Even the gas cans were gone. I slammed my palms against the roof of the truck.

Another piece of my heart broke. Everything was gone. My friends. The food. Transportation. Everything. Again.

I needed to be strong. To act, not react. To keep going. First things first. I had to find my bag. I went back to the cab. It was still wedged under the seat. I reached for it, but it wouldn't budge. I struggled, but still it refused.

I patted my legs. I blew out a quick ball of air when my fingers closed on the handle of my knife. I unhooked it and stretched, reaching under the seat, until I balanced on the tips of my toes. I hacked at the strap holding my bag prisoner. The blade sliced through the nylon with a rip.

I wanted to open it, but I had to get out of the water first. I'd lost all feeling in my feet. I cradled the backpack and knife in my arms, searching for a way out of the frigid river. It took me a few moments to spot higher ground. I waded through the water, trying not to twist my ankle on objects lurking in the murkiness.

I scrambled up the embankment. My hands and knees were covered in mud. I set the bag on the ground and unzipped it. The jar was still there. I pulled it out and brought it close to my face. The Bug sat still in a puddle of water. I tapped the plastic. It didn't move. Was it dead? Maybe it had drowned. I tipped the container sideways and drained the water out of the air holes.

Everything in my bag was wet and the strap was broken. But at least I'd found it. I could use the clothes if I got them dry.

I stuck the knife back in its sheath, stood, and wrung the water out of my shirt the best I could. I would have to deal with drying my stuff out later. Right now, I needed to find Adam and Megan. I called for them over and over until my voice went hoarse. I walked up and down the water's edge, looking for any sign of them or of the home improvement store.

Night crept into the sky. I needed to find cover. I couldn't stay here or out at night. I walked on, clutching my bag by its good strap.

The stench of fish overwhelmed any other smell. The scent grew with every step I took. Then I spotted them—tons of fish, floating in the water, sprawled on the dry ground, caught in trees. Dead.

The fish had obviously flowed out with the water when the dam broke, but I had no idea why they were all dead. My seafood aversion wasn't strong enough for me not to contemplate trying to cook one. It was the fact I couldn't figure out why they died. That and my lack of filleting skills, a pan, a fire. I exhaled and tried to block out the stench.

The sky turned a smoky gray and dark clouds zoomed by as if they were racing against the dark. I had to find shelter.

About twenty minutes later, I finally found the home improvement store. It seemed to be in okay shape structurally, with just a few windows broken. I walked in. The water only reached the tops of my boots. I called for Adam and Megan. No answer. They had to be here. Where else could they have gone? I refused to listen to the little voice that whispered they might have drowned. That wasn't a possibility I'd consider. I had to find them.

Armed with my flashlight, I searched the store. They weren't anywhere. I went to the checkout counters and pulled everything out of my bag. I set the jar with the Bug on the metal bagging area. It didn't move. Maybe it *was* dead.

I found a roll of paper towels under the one register, and with water-withered fingers, I dried my extra flashlights, all my weapons, the radio. Was it waterproof? I turned it on. To my surprise, it clicked to life. "Adam? Megan? Can you hear me?"

No response. I tried again. Still nothing. Did Megan even have hers? I shut the radio off and sighed. There wasn't a lot of battery left.

I hung my extra clothes over the display shelves and laid the food out on the counter. The couple of cans I had left were good. I spread out the rest of my supplies. The newspaper was wet, but I set it aside. The water had soaked all my Band-Aids and wipes. I chucked them into the corner.

I opened the interior zipper pocket and fished out the picture of my parents. Ruined. Water had smeared their images beyond recognition. I crumpled the photo into a ball and tears slipped down my cheeks.

"Why?" I yelled to the empty store. I threw the destroyed photo against the wall and collapsed onto the tile floor. I ripped off my dead watch and tossed it after the picture.

My entire body shook. Sobs racked my body as I released it all. All the pain. All the terror. All the guilt.

All the hope.

Life wasn't supposed to be this way. Anger at the Raspers, the Bugs, and the environment spun through my stomach. Why had I survived? I wasn't special. And just when I started to have a hint of possibly having some normalcy again, it was stolen.

I wasn't sure how long I wallowed in misery, but my tears eventually dried. I didn't know what I would do when the sun came up tomorrow. I was now living hour by hour, instead of day by day. And right now I had to get out of my wet clothes before I froze.

My only chance of finding clothes in a home improvement store was the employee break room. After searching a dozen or so lockers, I struck gold. Well, as close to gold as I was going to get: an XXL long-sleeve Harley Davidson T-shirt. I gave it a quick sniff, stripped off my wet jeans as well as the rest of my clothes. The shirt hung to my knees. It wasn't great, but it would do until my clothes dried. I stuck my feet back in my wet boots. They were cold and squishy, but it was better than going barefoot.

I gathered supplies from the store. Candles, lighters, flashlights, batteries. I pulled the softest rug from the display racks and found a patio bench in the clearance area. I dragged both to the front of the store and set the bench against the register counter. I stuck the rug over the metal bench then went to the curtain aisle. I opened the package for a brown suede curtain and wrapped it around my still chilled body. Back at the bench, I put batteries in the lantern-style light.

Setting my wet boots on the counter, I picked up the jar and sat on my makeshift bed. I held the container in my left hand and tucked my feet under the curtain. I stared at the Bug for a long time. It didn't move. Was it really an alien? It wasn't green. Or gray with big eyes. It didn't fit what the movies made me think extra-terrestrials should look like.

"Where did you come from and what do you want with me?" My voice broke at the end of my question. The Bug didn't move. For the briefest of seconds, I contemplated opening the jar, but I didn't have the nerve. I shook the container. Nothing. No movement at all.

"Stupid thing." I wanted to throw the jar against the wall like I had with the picture, but set it back down. The jar wobbled, and I reached out to steady it. I'd set the container on the edge of the counter and it almost lost its balance and fell.

Balance. The word rang through my head. The Rasper had said *balanced mind.* What did he mean? Did he mean metaphorically or literally? Balanced mind. Like using both sides equally? Like someone who could use both their right and left hands? I had read once that left-handed people used both sides of their brains more than righties. Was that it? Left-handedness? I had no idea.

I tried to reach Adam and Megan again on the radio. Still no answer. I clicked it off and set it next to the Bug. My mind spun with a cyclone of worries and my pulse accelerated with each minute. I hoped they were together, alive and safe. I'd promised Megan she wouldn't be alone.

When my eyes grew heavy, I did my best to get comfy. I set my gun on the counter right behind my head and closed my eyes.

I woke to darkness and gagged on the overwhelming fish stink. It was like being at the beach times a thousand.

Something moved outside the store. I swiped the gun and pointed at the window. It was too dark to see what was out there. Raspers? Bugs? Both? Adam and Megan? No, it wouldn't be them. They knew better than to prowl around at night.

That meant it was bad news and I wasn't dressed for a fight. More like a biker chick slumber party. Crap. I'd been an idiot to change. Shoulda left the wet stuff on. I yanked my boots off the counter and slipped my feet into the dampness.

I focused on the movement. Tried to figure out how many there were. I couldn't turn on the flashlight. If they didn't know I was here, I wouldn't put myself in the spotlight.

Splash. Splash. Splash.

I lowered my feet to the floor and slipped through the water to the windows. I leaned against the damp glass and tried to see what was outside lurking, stalking, hunting. I couldn't shake the picture of the once-scientist-turned-Rasper-now-dead-guy's face. The Bug hadn't made any noise. Maybe it wasn't Raspers. Then again, the Bug might be dead.

A shadow moved in front of the window. My breath caught. What was it? Something splashed in the water. What the hell? A growl sliced through the quiet. An animal? Had to be.

With precise and hopefully noiseless steps, I went back to the bench. I kept my boots on and pulled my legs up, huddling under the curtain with my head on my knees, gun in my hand. Ready to fire.

Splash. Rip. Crunch.

I tightened my grip on the Glock. Then I figured it out. The fish. Animals had come to eat the dead fish. The band of fear belted around my chest loosened. I was safe, at least until the fish ran out.

I stayed on the bench and waited. For the animals to leave, for Raspers to come, for daylight.

Eventually, the sun began its climb up the morning sky. It was time. I ran my hands through my hair and touched the cut on my forehead. No blood. No scab. Completely healed. Whoa. I still felt a little wonky, but my muscles didn't hurt anymore. I was healing faster than I should. Like Adam's bullet wound.

I tossed the curtain aside and grabbed my underwear from the display shelf. Thank goodness, it was dry. I got dressed and repacked my stuff in the still slightly damp backpack, then shook the lifeless Bug once more before shoving it in the bag. How had the water killed it? The Bugs had been crawling out of the river by the thousands when Adam had saved my ass with the dirt bike. Adam. I pictured his hair and how it brushed the tops of his shoulders. I sighed. I needed to get it together. I would find him—and Megan. I strapped on my gun, downed a bottle of water, stuck my bag on my shoulder, and turned on the radio.

"Adam? Megan?"

Nothing.

My heart said to keep the radio on in case they responded. My brain argued to shut it off to save the batteries since the store didn't have the type the radio needed. I groaned, shut it off, and clipped it on my belt. I turned back to the window, didn't see anything. Getting closer meant any remaining animals might see me. I needed to go higher. I made my way to the back of the store, found the roof access ladder, and climbed.

Once on the roof, I looked around. The sun glistened off the blood-filled water. Fish carcasses were everywhere—in the water, on the dry spots. It looked like a scene from a movie showing the end of days prophecies from the Book of Revelations. Birds swooped in and flew away with dead fish pieces in their beaks. A lone animal, maybe a fox, feasted on the edge of the water. I searched the landscape for other animals, but didn't spot any.

I tried to reach Adam and Megan on the radio. Again, silence answered me.

I gripped the Glock harder than I needed to. I could fire a shot. If I fired the gun, Adam and Megan might hear me. Then again, if I fired the gun, everything else would too. Animals. Bugs. Raspers. I rolled my bottom lip between my teeth as I weighed my options.

Oh, hell. I pointed the gun in front of me. Aimed high. Pulled the trigger.

The bang scared the fox and the birds as it echoed off the nearby buildings. I clicked the radio. "Can you hear me?"

Nothing.

"Adam. Megan. Are you out there?"

Still nothing. I slumped to the rooftop and buried my head in my knees. I felt like giving up.

The radio squealed and then, "Val?"

I jumped. My heart beat double time. "Adam?"

"Thank God."

"Is Megan okay?"

"She hit her head, but she's doing good."

"Where are you?"

"In a house. Where are you?"

"On the roof of the home improvement store. Surrounded by water and dead fish."

"According to the sun, we're east of where the store was. We're on Poplar Street. Number 413. It was the first water free place. I'd guess it's about a mile away. I can come get you."

"No, stay there. I'll find you. I have to get away from the water."

He was alive. The coil squeezing my heart loosened an inch. I got off the roof, exited the store, and ran, leaving the freezing river behind. The water that covered the pavement reminded me of how it used to look after a hard rain. I kept going, passing streets all named after trees.

Sycamore. Pine. Oak. Poplar.

I jogged down the suburban street that was oddly lacking in trees. When I came to 413, I raced to the door, but pulled up short. It might not have been Adam on the radio. The Raspers knew my name. It had sounded like him though. I drew the Glock, just in case, and knocked.

The curtain covering the side window shifted, then Adam opened the door. His skin was the same. No yellow. "Val!"

All the air rushed from my lungs. "Thank God. You're okay."

"I thought you were..." Adam stepped closer to me and held his arms out.

I went to him, heart rate skyrocketing. The heat from his skin penetrated my still-cold senses. He gave me a long hug. I glanced up at him. He leaned down. Closer and closer. My lips parted. He kissed the tip of my nose, then pulled back, and let go. My stomach tightened. I'd thought...*wrong*. I glanced away. "Where's Megan?"

"She's asleep upstairs. What happened? Where did you go? We searched until dark for you."

I put my gun away. Adam walked into the family room and sank onto one of the beige microfiber couches.

I set down my bag, sat on the other couch, and took in the room's shades of brown, beige, and white. A very plain room that reminded me of my house.

I rubbed my hands across my face and pushed back a few wayward strands of hair. "The water knocked me down and I almost drowned. And then I woke up sprawled across the roof of a McDonalds." I took a breath. "I called for you guys. I found the truck. Everything was gone. I searched until it got dark then I hid in the store. There were dead fish everywhere and animals came in the night..."

I looked at the wall.

"The water beat me down too," Adam said. "I was able to hang onto the truck and was propelled with it. After the truck smacked into a building, I struggled to find Megan. She was hysterical and bleeding. I think I might have banged my head too, because I was so disoriented. I didn't know what direction we had come from. We stumbled out of the water and kept going until we found this house." He licked his lips. "I'm sorry."

"For what?"

"For not trying harder to find you. It made me sick not knowing where you were."

He got up and sat next to me. The heat in my chest expanded as Adam laid his hand on top of mine and rubbed small circles over my knuckles. "I couldn't sleep at all last night. I was so worried something bad had happened to you." He leaned forward again. I licked my lips, then held my breath.

"Val!" Megan ran into the room, skidding to a stop when she noticed how close Adam and I were.

I jumped up. She wrapped her arms around me, pulled me back down to the couch. Her hands hit my bag. "Oh."

Both Adam and Megan stared at the bag. "Yeah, it's still in there." I answered their unspoken question. "But, it hasn't moved. I think it might be dead."

21

We raided the place, came away with a few supplies, and walked from house to house searching for a car with keys. We had to bust the windows in some homes to get in, while the glass was already broken in others, and a few were unlocked. We found zero car and key matches. Why didn't anyone keep their keys on a peg by the door instead of in their purse or pockets? Would have made my life a lot simpler.

The next house we came upon stood by itself and was remarkably intact.

"What about that place? Maybe they have a car. We'll never get to Site R without a working vehicle." Adam walked up the driveway.

A sense of...something I couldn't quite identify came over me. I tried to shake it off. "I don't know."

"Why?"

My head felt heavy and my legs a little weak. "I can't explain it. Let's skip this one."

As I turned to leave, I noticed a fine white powder scattered along the cement walkway to the front door. "Hey, hold on. What's this stuff?"

I bent down and scooped up a few of the white granules. I

lifted them up and a familiar scent, while faint, wrinkled my nose. I dropped the powder and blew the excess off my palms.

"What is it? It's everywhere around the house." Megan pointed to a trail of the white substance.

"Chlorine."

"Again? What's with that?" Adam sniffed his own handful.

"It was—" My backpack shifted. I pushed it back up, but it moved again. What the—? I set the bag on the ground and pulled out the jar.

The Bug was awake and alive. It smacked into the sides of the container.

"What the hell is it doing?" Adam dropped the chlorine and held out his hands.

I handed him the Bug.

When he clutched the plastic container, the Bug went berserk. It rubbed its legs together creating a nerve-pinching metallic squeal. It then alternated between launching itself off the sides to more teeth-grinding sounds. "What the hell is wrong with it? I thought you said it was dead?"

"Obviously, I was wrong." I drew my gun and scanned the area for Raspers. They must be close.

"It's the chlorine." Megan stepped closer.

"What?"

"Chlorine. I'm guessing the Bugs don't like chlorine. Let's see." She picked up a bit of the chemical and dropped a few tiny granules into the jar.

The Bug released a sound so deafening, I was sure my eardrums burst. The Bug slammed itself against the jar hard enough Adam lost his grip. The container hit the ground, bounced once, then rolled across the driveway, coming to a stop at the grass. The Bug squealed even louder.

"Make it stop." Adam clasped his hands over his ears.

I swore I could feel blood trickling out of mine, but when I touched them, my hands came away clean. Megan seemed much less affected than Adam or I. I shoved my gun back in its holster, raced to the jar, and picked it up.

More pain and pressure built in my ears. I had to get the chlorine out. I flipped the container over and the Bug fell to the top. I shook the jar until the granules came out and landed on my boot. The wailing of the Bug stopped. I exhaled and sat on the grass, slowly turning the jar upright. Pain snaked from my eardrums to the top of my head.

"Told you." Megan said, hands on her hips.

"Are my ears bleeding?" Adam leaned toward her.

"I don't see anything."

"I feel the same way." I tugged on my earlobes. Opened and closed my jaw. Tried to stop the pain.

"Must be part of your crazy ass connection, because my ears are fine." Megan's voice sounded smug.

The pressure in my head released and my ears popped. The pain disappeared. Freaky shit. I didn't want to analyze the similarities in my reaction and the Bug's.

"I say we pour all the chlorine we can find in the damn Bug's jar." Megan bent down to scoop some.

Adam grabbed her wrist. "Meg, no. As good as that would make you feel, we can't."

"And why the hell not? They killed my family. All of our families! Why are you protecting it?" She yanked her arm out of his grip. "Are you protecting it because you're both really Raspers, waiting to join their army?"

"Knock that crap off." Adam said in a low voice that made the hairs on my arms stand up. "We already told you we aren't."

"Fine." Megan crossed her arms and kicked the ground with her sneaker.

I tucked the jar back in my bag. "Why chlorine?"

Megan shrugged. "Don't know. Don't care. Let's just keep going."

But I cared. It might be our only major weapon.

After a few miles, Adam stopped. "I've been thinking—"

"About what?"

"That maybe we should go back."

Megan rolled her lips into her mouth as if she was trying to keep herself from talking.

"What do you mean?" My chest tightened and I clutched the lone good strap of my bag.

"Who knows how long the houses go on for and if there are

any cars with keys. I think maybe we should go back to where the water is and find one there. There are more stores for supplies and there's probably a better chance of finding a vehicle. We need to get to Site R." Adam ran his hand through his hair, flipping it out of his eyes.

"We've walked for *miles* in this direction. There might be a shopping center around the next corner. Then again, maybe there won't. If we turn back now, it will be dark before we get there." I took out one of my last two bottles of water, drank a third, and passed it around.

"Which is why we need to decide..." Adam smacked the empty plastic bottle off his thigh. "What should we do?"

"Go back to sleep and hopefully wake up from this horrible nightmare I'm having?" Megan said.

Oh, how I wished this was a nightmare. I wished the throbbing pain that had taken up residence in my head was a nightmare. Then I could wake up to my mom making me pancakes on Saturday morning. Finish my plans to go job hunting to pay for car insurance. Keep eating pizza with Sofie at Romeo's. I blinked a few times in hope, but nothing changed. I was still stuck in the middle of broken down suburbia with a metal Bug trapped in a jar in my backpack. Super.

"Realistic ideas?"

"The known or unknown." I held my hands out, palms up, as if I was weighing the decision. "As much as this kills me and my feet, I think we should go back."

"No." Megan shouted. "We've spent too much damn time going back. Forward. We need to keep moving forward."

"Okay, forward then."

And the walking and checking of cars continued. When the sun started shifting lower in the sky, we were no closer to a car with keys than we had been before. Going forward might not have been our best decision.

"Holy—"

"Watch out." Megan's arm clotheslined me across the stomach.

We stood about five feet away from a gaping hole in the ground. It expanded in front of us like a divider line, stretching farther than I could see. It was at least the length of an eighteen-wheeled truck.

"Well, hell." Megan balled her fingers into a fist.

"It goes out in both directions. How are we going to get across?" I heard the whine in my voice and cringed. No whining. Mom always told me not to whine. I should have made it the fourth rule.

"We'll have to go around it," Adam said.

"Let's go this way. We know what's back the other way. Maybe it will get thinner and we can jump over." Megan turned to the right and started walking parallel to the ominous gap. Adam and I followed.

We walked. And walked. And walked.

"I think the gap looks smaller." Megan craned her neck and stared into the rift.

"Yeah, you're right. Down by the tree." I pointed at a sagging oak tree.

We sprinted to the tree, Adam and I reaching it first, Megan lagging behind.

The gap had shrunk to about twenty feet wide. "There's still no way we can jump over."

"Then we keep going." Megan stomped ahead.

We had walked about another half-hour past ruined houses and fallen trees when the chasm ran parallel to the road again.

"That truck has a ladder." Adam ran to a beat up truck covered in rust and hauling painting supplies. "Help me get it down."

"For what?"

"It should be long enough for us to get across the gap." He hopped onto the truck and slid the ladder down.

"You want us to cross the gap with this rickety old ladder? I think I'd rather stay on this side of the chasm." Megan crossed her arms.

"But there are Raspers for sure on this side. They might not be able to cross it. Forward, remember." I took one end of the ladder and Adam lifted the other.

"We don't even know how long the gap is. It could end in another fifty feet." Megan trailed behind us.

"And it might go on for fifty miles." Adam said.

"Fine." Megan uncrossed her arms, but her body language still telegraphed disagreement. "Who's going over first?"

"I will." I didn't want to, but I was lighter than Adam, and I wanted him to hold the one end.

We stretched the ladder out as long as it would go and dropped it across the gap. The ladder just spanned the distance with only a foot on each side to spare. Crap. The other side wouldn't be sturdy without someone holding it.

"Ready?" Adam squatted and clutched the ladder's ends in his hands.

No. I blew out a breath and tightened the single strap on my bag. Maybe Megan was right and we should stay on this side. Thoughts of the bridge incident in the mountain made my hands slick. I wiped them on my jeans. "Let's do this."

I crouched and slid past Adam's chest as he let go of one side. I tried not to think about my butt being in front of his face or how my backpack could slip and knock me off balance. I tried not to think about how far down the chasm went. I tried and failed.

My cheeks flamed at the thought of him staring at my butt. *Again.* My back muscles twitched and the bag slipped an inch. The scent of dirt and metal drifted around the ladder. The chasm dropped at least three stories into the dank earth.

Right hand and knee forward. Then the left. Right again. I focused on the movements of my body and not the slight sway of the ladder. The ladder was the only thing separating me from certain death.

Don't look down. Don't look down.

I looked down.

The sight threw off my balance and my knee slipped to the side a fraction too far. I clutched the sides of the ladder with all my strength as my body slammed forward and my chest crashed into the supports. I struggled to recover my position.

"Val, are you okay?" Megan's voice screeched.

I didn't move.

"Val?"

"I'm all right. Gimme a sec—" I moved slowly and deliberately until I was back on all fours. I licked my lips and continued my crawl across the abyss of darkness. When I was about six feet away from the edge, the ladder shifted again.

"Hold on. I have it!" Adam yelled. I pictured him straining to keep the ladder in place. This time I was thankful he'd been stung and had a little extra strength.

He steadied the ladder. "Go ahead."

A few more rungs and then I was the rest of the way across. Once on solid ground, I took off my bag and flopped onto my back, staring at the darkening sky. My chest rose and fell in rapid succession. I needed to calm down. I'd done it. I'd made it.

"Sorry. It slipped." Adam said.

"It's okay." I stood and gripped the edge of the ladder, holding it tight. "Megan, come on."

Megan looked like a cat, crossing the gap with perfect balance. Within a few minutes, she was safe next to me.

"Nice."

Megan blew out a breath of air. "Thanks. Those eight years of gymnastics finally paid off."

Adam's progress across the ladder was slow and deliberate. Eight feet to go. Six feet. He was almost there when the other end shifted and slipped from the edge of the ground.

"Son of—"

"Adam, Hurry up." Megan dropped to her knees and helped me keep the ladder steady.

His hands reached my end. The ladder swayed to the right and he lost his grip.

I clamped my hands down on his wrists.

"Oh my God." Megan fought to keep her hold on the shifting metal.

"Hang on." I tightened my grip, but my boots scooted forward. I couldn't hold him. "Megan, forget the ladder. Grab my ankles."

She released the makeshift bridge. It completed its final sway and then dropped away. Adam slammed against the dirt edge of the ravine.

"Shit." He struggled to pull himself up.

Megan yanked on my ankles. I kept slipping forward. We were losing. I called on any extra strength the sting had given me and pulled. Hard. Fast.

"Come on. Come on." I wasn't sure if I said the words aloud or chanted them in my head.

Adam tightened his grip and almost ripped my shoulders from their sockets.

At an agonizingly slow rate, Adam inched closer. Sweat moistened every crevice of my body, but there was no way I was letting him go. One final yank and his chest reached solid ground. He scurried past the edge and collapsed on the dirt. Megan and I released our grips and doubled over, gasping for breath.

"Thanks." Adam panted. "It looked easier in my mind."

"No problem."

"That blew." Megan stood and offered me her hand. I took it, picked up my bag, and we both helped Adam to his feet.

"Hopefully, the chasm spans across the world and cuts us off from the Raspers." *And the Bug in my bag is the only one on this side.*

"That'd be awesome, but I doubt it." Megan's voice sounded dark and depressed.

Adam looked at the sky. "It's going to be night soon. I think we should start looking for a place to hide."

"Preferably one with food." Megan ran her hand across her stomach.

The only sound we heard during the next hour of walking on the cracked asphalt was the birds, twittering an off-tune song. The country road turned into four lanes littered with cars. They all had keys, but no gas. Just our dumb luck.

Megan pointed. "What's that?"

A group of vehicles decked out in camouflage sat in a precise line on the road and screamed military convoy. A flipped-over tour bus rested half-on, half-off the pavement.

Adam stopped walking.

I drew the Glock. "What is it?"

He didn't answer me and his face clouded over with an expression I couldn't read.

"Hey, you okay?"

He didn't respond.

I glanced at Megan. She shrugged her shoulders and pulled her gun from her waist pouch.

"Adam?" she whispered.

He started walking again. I pointed for Megan to take his left side and I came up on his right. I had no idea what he was doing. I didn't hear anything, and no smells beside nature's normal perfume reached my nose. Whatever he saw or sensed, it couldn't be good.

We reached the line of military vehicles. Army vehicles carried extra gas, didn't they? I zeroed in on the Humvee in the middle of the pack. Adam kept walking toward the bus. I tilted my head and Megan followed him.

A rumbling noise tore through the bird song. "What's that?" I tightened my grip on the gun.

"Vehicles." Megan whispered.

"Shit. We need to hide." I ran, grabbed her arm, and moved toward the bus. "Adam, come on. We can duck in here." I let go of Megan and pulled Adam by the hand.

A few of the bus's windows were broken, but most were still in place. I pried at the door and managed to jimmy it open. The roar of the engines grew louder and louder.

"Faster. Get in." Megan pushed on my back.

I dropped into the sideways bus and hit the driver's seat, climbed over it and out of the way. Adam and Megan scrambled in and walked over the glass windows, working their way over the seats. I moved back to the door and pushed the close lever. It wouldn't budge.

The engines got closer and closer. We had to get the door shut.

"Help me pull it back." Adam and I managed to tug it closed. We crawled over the fabric seats and peeked out the half-shattered windshield. A cloud of dirt rolled down the road. Oh, God. We aimed our guns out the busted window.

"What do you think it is?" Megan said, just loud enough for us to hear.

"Ssh." Adam tilted his head. "It's got to be a lot of cars. Maybe they're here to rescue us."

"Not with our luck," I mumbled, and wiped my upper lip on my sleeve.

"Get ready. Here they come." Adam's back stiffened and he leaned closer to the window.

The engine noise grew to a deafening level. Then the trucks drove past. Twelve black courier-type trucks. Twelve trucks driven by twelve yellow-skinned Raspers.

22

"Did you see—"

"I think—" I stopped whispering when the Bug made a hushed version of its song. I wasn't sure if the Bug was being quiet or if the backpack muffled it. Either way, the Raspers might hear.

Megan pushed over a stack of pillows and blankets from the next seat. "Cover it."

I buried the bag at the bottom of the pile, but I could still hear it.

"Shit." Adam gave the pile a quick glance, his gaze full of anger and worry.

The last truck in the convoy stopped. The Rasper left the engine idling and climbed from the driver's seat.

Megan gasped. Her hand flew to cover her mouth.

The Rasper had a rifle in his hand. Not only did they have vehicles, they had weapons too. The rest of the vehicles screeched to a stop and the Raspers got out. Twelve total. The armed Raspers walked like trained soldiers and formed a semi-circle on the bus's side.

We were toast.

The closest Rasper made a few head bobbing motions that made me think he was sniffing the air. Smelling for the Bug. For us. Crap.

The Raspers all turned together, like a choreographed dance move, and sniffed.

My heart thumped and I swore I could hear Adam's and Megan's pounding. I rubbed the smooth trigger of the Glock. I longed to pull it, but we were outnumbered. Outgunned.

The Raspers looked right at the bus. This was it. They had caught our scent or heard the Bug. Maybe I should have killed it when Megan wanted me to. One of the Raspers took a step closer.

I shifted to the right an inch to keep him in my gun sight. "Leave. Leave. Leave." I meant to say the words in my head, but I whispered them instead. Stupid.

The Rasper that stepped forward suddenly moved back into the formation. All the Raspers turned in unison and looked right, then left. Seconds passed with no movement, then they all got back into their trucks and drove away.

No way. I let out a breath of air that sounded five times louder than it was.

"That was close." Megan put her gun on her thigh.

The Bug gave a long, loud squeal.

Then it went silent, the thudding in my chest the only thing I heard. Rivulets of sweat rolled down my back and into the waistband of my jeans. I pulled my shirt away from my skin and a chill replaced the sweat. A chill that had nothing to do with the rising temperature in the bus.

I uncovered my bag and pulled out the jar.

"Give that to me. I'm going to shoot it. They heard it. We almost died because of the damned thing." Megan tapped the muzzle of her gun on her jeans.

"No."

"Val's right. We can't shoot it. No extra noise." Adam slumped down in the sideways seat. "We should just stay here tonight."

Megan looked on the verge of tears. "What if they come back? More of them will be out when it's dark."

"I say we stay." Adam lifted one of his fingers. "First, it's almost night and we have no idea where the next shelter will be." He lifted another. "Second, I don't think they'll be back. At least, not tonight."

"How the hell do you know that?" Megan's voice shrilled.

We needed to calm her down or the Raspers might hear. "If they knew we were here, they would have attacked. I think Adam's right. We're safe tonight. I vote we stay here."

"Fine." Megan grabbed a blanket and pillow from the one seat and curled into another seat toward the back of the bus. "Sorry. I'm just so scared."

I crawled into the seat next to her. "Me too. Me too."

Adam dropped a blanket and pillow on me, and sat on Megan's other side.

I clicked on my flashlight. "You were awfully quiet before the trucks came."

He didn't look at me. "They were attacked."

"Who was? What do you mean?"

"The bus was transporting families of important people to a safe place. They were escorted by the military." Adam said in the voice he used when he told me about his mother. "And they were attacked and killed by a band of Raspers. Maybe even the ones we just saw."

"How can you know that?" Megan frowned and her eyebrows almost touched each other.

"Because it's the exact same scene as the one I ran away from before I found Val."

The air rushed from my lungs and my entire body broke out in goose bumps. He hadn't told me he was part of a military convoy. Who was he?

"Why were you part of an armed military escort?" I whispered.

"Because of my dad's job as a scientist for Pearan Chemicals. They were funded by the government. About a month before they announced they'd found the oil, my dad started getting weird. I asked him what was going on and he told me, 'There's something wrong. They won't listen. All they care about is making money.' He put in long hours and one night mumbled something about the data being crazy. How it was too thick. More like tar than oil. Within hours of the Great Discovery announcement, he called my mom and told her he had been right. They had lost the oil platform in the middle of the Gulf. He then had my mom and me pack a bag with food and supplies.

He put us on a bus for families of 'important' people. We were supposed to..." He trailed off and seemed to get lost in his memories.

Anger spiraled around in my stomach churning up the burning acid. "How do the Raspers and Bugs fit in? Aliens and oil? It makes no sense." I stomped my foot like a child, so tired of this whole thing.

"I don't know how or where the Raspers and Bugs came from—"

"Do you think these convoys were specifically targeted by the Raspers?" Megan turned to Adam.

He just stared at the seats rubbing his wrist, so I answered her. "I don't know. It seemed they went for anybody they could get. I don't think they targeted anyone in particular."

Except me. They targeted me. Heaviness pushed down on my chest with the weight of an elephant.

"There's something else." Adam said, his gaze now fixed on the dark window.

"What?" I barely said the word.

"They marked me."

"Who marked you? The Raspers? How?" I balled my fist. What was he talking about? Had they put a tracking device on him somehow? Maybe that was how they kept finding us.

"No. Not the Raspers. The military."

I had no idea if that was better or worse.

"What?" Megan yelled.

"Not so loud." I shot her a look and she narrowed her eyes in return. The jar was quiet in my bag, but we didn't need her yelling and the Raspers returning.

"My wrist. They inserted something in my wrist before we left. They did it to everyone who got on the bus. It hurt for days. Now there's barely a mark."

"Do you think that's why you didn't react to the Rasper sting?" Megan pulled the blanket up to her chin even though it had to be eighty degrees in the bus.

"No, I mean, everyone else died. My mom turned into a Rasper, for God's sake." He ran his hand through his hair.

"I don't have anything implanted in my wrist." I touched my rules. They were barely there now.

"I think it was something for when we reached the safe place." Adam's voice sounded distant.

Scenes from old movies ran through my head. "I bet they did it to be able to identify those who could enter the safe center. If you don't have the tag or whatever it is, you can't get in."

"To get inside Site R, we might need your wrist." Megan said.

"I'm sure they wouldn't leave kids outside fighting for their lives while they were safe inside." At least I didn't think they would. That would be—cruel.

Megan shivered despite the heat. "Creepy ass shit. Can you feel whatever it is?"

Adam ran his hand across his wrist. "No. That part freaks me out. I mean is it an ID tag or a vaccine that obviously didn't work?"

Something he said pulled at me, but I couldn't figure out what it was. "Why didn't you tell us before?"

"Would you have trusted me if I told you my dad might have been partially responsible for what happened?"

I picked at my ripped and dirty nails. "Good point. The thing in your wrist? Want me to try to cut it out?"

He turned with a look of horror across his face. "No, thanks, even though you did a great job bandaging my bullet wound."

"You were shot? Who shot you?" Megan's eyes grew wide and round.

Adam made a noise that was a cross between a snort and a laugh. "Val."

Megan's mouth dropped open. "No way, really?"

Adam nodded and I shrugged.

"You'll have to tell me the story later. Why do you think you two weren't affected by the sting?"

We *were* affected. "I don't know."

"You know, my dad acted funny and was super excited when you guys showed up." Megan said.

"What do you mean?"

"Remember I said he was really interested in you two being left-handed?"

"Think that's the link? That we're both lefties?" I tried not to laugh. The thought had wedged itself in my head back at the home improvement store. "The hand we write with can't be what kept us from turning into Raspers."

Megan shrugged. "What else do you have in common?"

"We like the same music," Adam said.

"We're both sixteen."

"Age. Music. Left-handedness. Probably isn't music and I'm the same age—"

"Hang on." I scrambled back to my bag and dragged it over. "What?"

"Gimme a sec—" I pulled out a sweatshirt, set the jar aside, and dug out the paper from the bag. It was still damp, but—maybe. I held it to the flashlight's beam. The picture of the professor—turned Rasper—who had stalked me. He held a glass in his left hand. "Adam, was your mom right or left-handed?"

"Left. Why?"

"He was left-handed too." I tossed the paper at Megan. Adam leaned over the seat and squinted at the picture.

"I can't look at him." Megan crumbled the paper into a ball and tossed it at the back door of the bus.

"Were any other Raspers lefties?"

I tried to remember. I hadn't paid any attention. "Yes. Maybe. I don't know. I don't remember."

Megan dropped the blanket. "Wait a minute. Wait a minute. Dad taught a course one semester about the psychology of the brain. He said that left-handed people tend to use both sides of their brain more equally than righties—"

"Balanced mind." I smacked my palm off the fabric seats. Maybe my theory back at the home improvement store hadn't been so far off.

"You're right. The Rasper said balanced mind. That must be it. Lefties become Raspers and righties die..." Megan's face twisted in a look of horror like a twenty-pound spider sat in front of her. "Oh, God. That means I'll die..."

My nails dug into my palms so hard they left crescent moon indentations. "Nobody's dying. But if left-handed people become Raspers, why didn't we change?"

***

I barely slept; I was too wired. Visions of becoming a Rasper played over and over in my head. What was it about Adam and me? There had to be something different about us. What? I went through everything. We were born in different states, weren't related, we'd gone to different schools, never had any strange illnesses. Besides the left-handedness, what we had in common was normal teenage crap. Food. Music. Sports. Movies. Adam had a love of driving video games. I wasn't a gamer. Nothing useful. But something linked us. Something was keeping us human.

At least for now.

When the dark turned to light, we left the bus and I bee-lined toward the Hummer in the middle of the convoy. It had keys in the ignition, but it wouldn't turn on. No gas. I checked the back. Three full gas cans and a metal box rested in the cargo space. I flipped the latch of the box and gave a low whistle at the sight of three rifles snuggled together and ammo belts strapped to the lid. I took a belt and slung it over my hips. I switched the bag to my right side and hoisted the rifle over my left. Look out, Raspers. I was armed and dangerous.

"Very G.I. Jane," Megan said after I came around the side of the vehicle. "It suits you."

"I know, right? What's he doing?" I nodded toward Adam, who stood staring at the over-turned bus.

"Your guess is as good as mine. Are there more?"

"In the box in the back of the Hummer."

I turned toward Adam. "Hey, we're ready to roll. Are you?"

Megan came back, tugging on the strap of one of the two rifles she wore.

"Yeah, I'm good." Adam shook his head, ran his hand through his hair, then walked over to where we stood by the Hummer.

"You okay to drive?" I prayed he would say yes.

"Man, you two look like you're going to war. Where did you get the weapons?"

"In the vehicles, but I don't think they normally pack these." Megan took off the guns and hopped in the back seat.

Adam filled the gas tank.

I climbed in the passenger seat with the Bug while Adam settled into the driver's side. I pulled out the GPS again and plugged it in the power socket. The device searched for a satellite. I prayed it would find one this time. Finally, it located us. "Yes."

"Type in Waynesboro, Pennsylvania." Adam drummed his fingers on the steering wheel. "My dad said that Site R was designed as a backup for the Pentagon if there was ever nuclear war."

"I remember Uncle John saying something about it. Isn't it connected to the place where the President vacationed?" Megan yawned.

"Camp David?" Adam gave Megan a quick glance.

"I have no idea. I never heard of the place before Adam mentioned it." I typed in the city.

We drove all day, stopping once to refill the gas tank. My butt and legs ached from being in the same position so long.

The roads were destroyed in some places and perfectly fine in others. The same with the towns we passed. Some were burnt-down shells of their former glory, while other towns looked like people simply ceased to exist. When the sun started its slow descent into the horizon, we were somewhere outside of Pittsburgh, Pennsylvania.

"Should we stop somewhere or keep going?" Adam needed a break and I guessed I could drive the big beast.

Megan yawned again. "Let's find someplace to spend the night."

"I could drive for a little while," I offered.

"I'm not sure driving at night would be a good idea," Adam said.

"Why not? We're in a damn bullet-proof, military-issued Hummer." I hit the door. "Solid."

"But the roads are crap. We could end up in a canyon if we drive in the dark."

"We have the headlights. I say we keep going. I'll drive." I wanted to get to Site R. Needed to end the running and the hiding. I really wanted hot food, a shower, and a worry-free sleep.

Adam yawned. "Fine." He stopped the Humvee and we switched positions. It took a few minutes and a few too many stomps on the brakes until I got comfortable driving the mammoth vehicle. The GPS directed me, but couldn't warn me when the road would fall apart or when a car or truck would suddenly appear dead in my path. Adam leaned against the window, sleeping. Megan snored softly from the back.

Again, my thoughts turned to the possibility I was housing a Bug in my brain. This was all wrong. I wanted to be back in school worrying about my grades and what college I was going to go to. Not worrying that any minute I might turn into a yellow-skinned mutant.

The GPS said we had about thirty more miles until we got to Site R. Thirty miles until safety.

A faint buzzing sound penetrated my eardrums. I glanced at Adam and checked Megan in the rearview mirror. They were still asleep. The Bug was in my bag next to my seat, but the noise wasn't coming from the jar. It was outside. I lowered the window a crack and the sound grew louder.

I opened the window the whole way, stopped the Hummer, and shut off the headlights. The buzzing grew to a roar.

"Guys, wake up." I tapped Adam on the arm.

Adam straightened and seemed wide-awake. "What is it?"

"Why are we stopped?" Megan asked, yawning.

I held up my hand. "Listen."

"I don't hear anything." Megan leaned closer to the front.

"It's an engine." Adam pulled out his gun.

Shit. An engine. Had the trucks found us or was it a different group? Or something else? Something worse?

Megan grabbed her rifles.

I tucked the shotgun next to the door.

"Okay, now I hear it." Megan tightened her grip on the gun. "Should we keep driving?"

"I don't know."

The engine grew in intensity and proximity.

"Maybe it doesn't have anything to do with us. Turn the Hummer back on so I can open my window."

As soon as he had the window lowered, I shut the motor back off.

"Do you think we should—" The engine's roar drowned my words. Where was it? I leaned out the window and a bright light blinded me.

"What the hell?" Adam yelled. More light mixed with the first.

"Exit the vehicle." A voice boomed over a loudspeaker.

"Don't do it!" Megan shouted.

I didn't plan to get out, but a red laser shined into the windshield and painted Adam's chest crimson.

"Lasers. Do it. Get out. Now." Adam shouted over the engine noise.

We climbed from the Hummer, all of us clutching our weapons. The bright lights came from an object hovering in front and above us. More noises joined the first engine. These more distinct. More recognizable. Helicopters. They circled, their searchlights blazing down on the Hummer, the road, and us.

The red laser marked Adam's chest again. Then one on Megan's.

I looked down and my breath caught at the scarlet line trained on my heart.

23

"Drop your weapons," the voice commanded from one of the chopper's loudspeakers.

"We're here for protection." I held up my right hand and the rifle, but kept the Glock low in my left.

"You have five seconds to drop your weapons or we will fire."

Shadowed figures rappelled from the chopper. Soldiers clad in black swarmed around. Three more laser beams joined the one already trained on my chest. The four beams swirled together between my breasts in a space about the size of a quarter. Well, shit.

I looked at Adam and Megan. Adam gave an almost indistinguishable nod. We laid our guns on the ground. A piece of my heart ripped apart when my hand left the Glock. These bastards were forcing me to give up the one constant in my life. At least I still had the knives and the extra guns in my bag.

A tall, bald guy came toward us, a black wand in his one hand, and a pistol in the other. I scanned the skin of the others. No yellow anywhere. The man reached down and picked up my gun. My heart dropped into my stomach when he tucked the gun in a pocket of his black vest.

Two other men stepped from the darkness and collected the

rest of our weapons. The wand guy ran the device over Megan. Nothing happened.

What was the device? A metal detector? He turned the wand to me. It went crazy with a combination of red lights and strange whirring noises.

"Put down your bag," he ordered.

I didn't want to give it up, but I had no choice. I set it next to my foot. He stepped in and kicked my bag to another guy who picked it up. When the short stocky man threw the bag onto his shoulder, the air rushed out of my lungs.

The tall guy waved the wand over me again. It went nuts again. "Hold her."

Two large soldiers pinned my arms to my back and something metallic clamped over my hands. Handcuffs? What the hell?

"Hold on. We came here for help. Now let her go." Adam tried to sound fierce and I appreciated his effort. The tall dude laughed.

"Shut up, boy." He then brought the wand to Adam and it went berserk. "Guard him too."

Two more soldiers took hold of Adam and yanked his arms behind his back. A click clamped his hands like mine.

"What are you doing?" Megan cried.

"You, be quiet." He aimed his gun at her and she snapped her mouth shut.

One soldier tapped his ear and spoke into an unseen microphone. "Bring two of the birds down."

The wind kicked to tornado proportions and two choppers landed. Two men dragged Megan to the one on the right while the other soldiers pulled Adam and me toward the other one.

"No. We stay together." I ground my heels in and tried to stand firm, but the men were much stronger. "Let me go." They hoisted me into the chopper, kicking and cursing.

They dumped me into the back and shoved Adam into the seat next to me. Two of the soldiers climbed in front of us. One guy slapped headphones over our ears, then the helicopter lifted off.

I tried to watch the chopper carrying Megan, but I lost track of it when our flying tin can merged with the other five helicopters.

"Where are you taking us?" I yelled. No one answered my question.

The helicopter bounced up and down and my stomach matched its movements. Who were these guys? They weren't Raspers, but they weren't good guys either. If they were, they wouldn't treat survivors this way.

The helicopter banked to the right and my stomach lurched toward my throat. I swallowed and wished I had the use of my hands.

All these choppers took gas. Where did they get it? Site R? My head spun faster than the blades of the flying prison cell. Before we landed, I had to get my hands free. I couldn't do a damn thing with my hands bound. I pulled and tugged at the bindings, but only managed to rip skin from my wrists.

The helicopter bobbed and landed. One of the guys ripped the headphones from my head and shoved us out.

Megan got out of her helicopter. "You okay?"

"No talking," one soldier said, waving his gun.

Megan narrowed her eyes at the asshole, but kept her mouth shut.

We had to get out of here. I glanced around. Lights from the aircraft lit the entire area. The spot we stood in was charred black, as if a fire had ripped through everything. A large—and that was an understatement—hole opened up in the blackened mountain. A massive door, big enough to drive a tank through, barred the entrance.

Rocks surrounded the door, held back by a chain link fence. Beige cement blocks formed the rounded shape that cut into the mountain. From my vantage point, it looked like someone could stand on the ledge overlooking the entrance. A satellite dish, a hundred times the size of the one on my house, pointed at the sky from across the road. A little ways down, I spotted a rounded building, which looked like it might house vehicles. I half expected an army of armed SUVs to come zooming out.

A panel sat inside the rock wall and a green light blinked from the right corner. Electricity. They had power here. What I wouldn't do for a hot meal and shower. But I was pretty sure neither would be happening.

The tallest soldier pushed a series of buttons on the electrical panel and sirens erupted around us. If my hands weren't pinned behind my back, I would have covered my ears to shield them from the howling alarm. The massive door barring the tunnel opened with a clunk and a whoosh. The sirens stopped.

Another soldier drove up in a black golf-cart-on-steroids. A smaller golf cart whizzed up behind the first.

"Take her inside." The guy in charge pointed at Megan.

A soldier guided Megan to the smaller golf cart. "Get in."

"No, I'm staying with my friends." Megan stomped her foot and crossed her arms.

The soldier with the wand directed his gun at Megan again. "You'll do as you're told. Now go."

Megan caught my eye. I gave a small nod. If she didn't go, I was sure they'd shoot her. She didn't have a choice. She climbed in the front seat of the four-person cart and a soldier sat behind her. The driver hit the gas and they zipped away down the dark tunnel.

"Take these two to the containment center." Tall dude waved his wand at us.

"What? No. I demand you release us, now." I tried to rip my arms away from the soldiers holding me, but their grips were tight as iron shackles. So much for my extra strength. There was no way I was letting them take me to some containment center. "We came here for help. Not to be treated like criminals."

I brought up my foot and slammed my boot into the one soldier's kneecap. He groaned and let go. The other one grabbed for my arm, but I spun too quickly for him. I tried to free my locked hands.

"Val, no," Adam yelled.

I turned in time to see the soldier in charge hold a weird device up to my neck.

Zzaapp.

***

I woke with a fuzzy recollection of moving from the golf cart to a transport like the one we rode to get to Magic Kingdom at

Disneyworld when I was younger. I remembered nothing after that. I couldn't remember how I got to wherever it was they left me. I sat up and checked out my surroundings.

I was wearing scrubs like doctors wore, but they were white and long sleeved. Zip ties shackled my wrists in front of me. They were stronger than the standard plastic ones, probably some military grade material. I pulled and twisted but the bindings held.

The room gave off a sterile vibe. Medical type equipment I had no hope of identifying filled the glass-and-mirror walled room. I sat on a padded table draped with a white sheet. I jumped off and landed on the white tile floor. My socks slipped and I grabbed the table. Shoes. I needed shoes. Where was my bag? Where were my clothes? My knives? My guns? The bastards had taken everything.

Then a chill slithered down my spine. Somebody had changed my clothes. A combination of fear and panic slammed into me. I yanked on the elastic waistband of the pants. Thank God. I still had my pink underwear. I released a long breath of air, brought my bound hands to my face, and tried to wipe away the tears. I dropped my head in my hands.

This was a nightmare. It had to be. Adam's safe house was a prison. Had he tricked me? What had they done with him, and what about Megan?

I lifted my head and tried to wiggle my hands out of the plastic ties again. It still didn't work, but when I shifted, I felt something on the inside of my left elbow. I shoved the sleeve back and saw a cotton ball taped down to my skin. They had either taken blood from me or given me a shot. This was so wrong.

I sniffed, stood, and caught my reflection in the mirrored wall. Purple bags colored the skin under my eyes and my hair stuck out from its ponytail. I looked like a sleep-deprived, malnourished zombie. I turned away from the reflection and walked to the cell's glass wall. The image I saw through the glass burned into my retinas.

Adam lay on a white-sheeted table, dressed in the same

scrubs as me. He had a tube running from his arm to a machine, sort of like an IV in a hospital.

I brought my hands to the glass and lightly rapped my knuckles on it. Adam stirred, but didn't get up. I banged a little harder. His head moved, but he appeared to be sound asleep—or drugged.

I had to get my hands free. I dashed to the many drawers and cabinets lining the one wall next to the table. There had to be scissors in here somewhere. They did medical stuff in here.

Nothing. No sharp object whatsoever. Just bandages and towels and sheets. I tugged on a large locked cabinet. It didn't budge. Damn. That was probably where they kept the good stuff. I shoved a pile of expensive equipment onto the floor. The stuff hit the tile hard and shattered into pieces. I sank down on the floor and pulled my knees to my chest, burying my head between them.

How had everything gone so wrong? This was supposed to be a safe place, not a torture chamber. Everything kept getting worse and worse. Maybe it would have been better if I hadn't survived. It would have been easier, but...I wanted to live. Just not like this. I wanted it like it used to be.

My tears dried and a new resolve took their place. It was time to get the hell out of here. I jumped up and banged on the glass again. Adam didn't respond.

I moved to the mirrored wall, ignored my hideous reflection, and slammed my palms on the mirror. "Let me out of here. You have no right to treat us this way." I pounded again, this time with my knuckles. "I want out of here." I banged until my fingers were red and bloody. Still no one answered.

My throat closed when I thought of myself trapped in a glass cell. Like the Bug. God, did they think I was a Rasper? They could just listen to my breathing to know for sure. Or look at my skin. The resolve I had moments ago disappeared. I slid down the wall and curled into a ball on the floor. Minutes—maybe even hours—passed.

Movement in Adam's cell caught my attention. I slid to the glass. A woman in a white lab coat removed the tube from his arm, made a note on a clipboard, then left the room through a door that blended into the wall.

Energy surged through me. I searched for the door in my room. Once I knew what to look for, it was easy to spot. I raced to it and banged on it with all my force. "Hey, help me." Maybe the woman would answer a cry for help.

The door remained shut. Bitch.

A pounding sound thudded behind me. I turned and Adam stopped banging. He gave a small wave with his bound hands. I sprinted to the glass.

"Can you hear me?" I said, louder than normal.

"Yes, can you hear me?"

I nodded. I didn't know if our better-than-average hearing helped. Nor did I really care. We could hear each other and that's what mattered. "Where's Megan? Where are we? Why are we tied up? What's going on?" I fired the questions at him.

"The last I saw Megan was when they drove her away in the other golf cart. After the dude tased you, we were put in the other cart then moved to an underground train thing. It took us through the mountain. When it stopped, they jabbed something into my neck. Next thing I remember is waking up here."

"There was a woman in a lab coat just in your cell. She removed a tube from your arm." I held my palms flat against the glass. The ties bit into my wrists.

Adam brought his hands up to mine and mimicked my gesture. We'd be holding hands if the glass wall dividing us weren't there.

"Val..." Adam bit his lip. "I'm sorry. I was sure this place was safe." He leaned his forehead against the glass.

I did too. When I pulled back Adam had already moved, and I thought I caught the glistening of tears in his green eyes, but when I blinked, it was gone. "We need to get out of here. Look in your cabinets. See if there's scissors or something. I couldn't find anything sharp."

He nodded then searched all the drawers and cabinets he could open. He returned to the glass frowning and shaking his head.

A click rang out through my room. I spun around. Three black-clad armed soldiers filed into my cell.

"Come with us." The tallest guy gestured with his rifle.

I glanced back and caught sight of more soldiers in Adam's room. I made a quick calculation. Outside of the room was better than locked in, so I followed them.

Two soldiers flanked my sides and the other stayed behind me, his rifle tapping me in the back as I walked down a corridor lit by bare bulbs on a string. It reminded me of Megan's underground bunker.

I tried to figure out where I was, but they marched me down a cement tunnel with no markers or any identifying features. When we reached a black door, the soldier to my left typed a code into a gray box on the wall. A shield designed to keep prying eyes away dashed my hope of seeing the combination.

The door hissed and slid back into the wall. If I wasn't ready to pee my pants in fear, I might have found the place cool. We walked down another corridor. The coldness of the ground seeped through my socks. I so wanted my boots.

As we walked, I tried to find anything that could help me, but the walls, floor, and ceiling were rock. My only weapon could be a busted light bulb and that wouldn't do me much good against gun-toting soldiers trained to kill.

We passed through another door and the décor changed. Rows and rows of equipment covered worktables. People sat in chairs and fiddled with the knobs and dials. Some wore headsets while others didn't. Three massive screens covered the far wall, currently displaying what looked like weather patterns.

We entered what I would call a conference room. A large black table covered with computers and phones took up most of the space. Twelve high-backed leather chairs surrounded the table. A man dressed in a uniform occupied one. A woman and man, each wearing a white lab coat, filled two other chairs. The woman was the one who had been in Adam's room.

A large screen sucked up all the open wall space on my left. The screen displayed a map of the North America covered with red and green lights. The soldiers escorted me to the far wall where two metal folding chairs sat empty.

They deposited me in one chair and then took position behind me. I wanted to shout something—anything—but decided it was best to keep my mouth shut. For now. The faint scent of sweat permeated my nostrils.

I stared at the faces of the three people assembled at the table. I didn't recognize any of them. Not the President or Vice President. I wondered if they were still alive. Were these people in charge of the government—if one even still existed?

The hawk-eyed scrutiny they appraised me with made my skin crawl. I was about to ask what the hell they wanted when the door opened and the soldiers led in Adam.

His face seemed sunken and his skin pasty in the harsh light of the room. When he caught my eye, his green eyes flashed his anger. They shoved him into the chair beside me with much more force than the soldiers had used on me. His trio of guards lined up next to mine. I almost laughed aloud at the ludicrousness of it all. Six armed soldiers guarding Adam and me. What did they think we were going to do? They'd taken all our weapons.

The man wearing the medal-laden uniform stood at the head of the table. "What are your names?"

"Adam and Val." Adam raised his chin a little higher when he spoke.

"Why are we handcuffed and being treated like prisoners?" I made to stand, but a firm hand pushed me back down. I glared at the soldier. He focused his gaze on the dude with the fancy uniform.

"I am General DeCarlo. I am in charge here. What do you want from us?"

I couldn't help myself. "Uh, a safe place to stay. What do you think?"

Glances flew between the man and woman seated at the table.

"Look, I was alone for months while others died, the world went to shit, and creatures appeared out of nowhere. We're just trying to find Site R, the safe place Adam's father told him about."

I caught Adam wince out of the corner of my eye. I probably shouldn't have mentioned his dad.

KATHLEEN GROGER

"You've found Site R." General DeCarlo turned his attention to Adam. "Who is your father?"

"Was."

"Pardon me?" The general's eyebrows arched into a unibrow.

"My father was Dr. Solomon. *Was*. He's dead."

"Dr. Solomon?" The general snapped his fingers and the woman leapt to her feet, her lab coat billowing behind her. She pulled a black device that looked like a calculator out of her pocket and walked to Adam.

She grabbed his right wrist and waved the device over the spot he had been rubbing earlier. Her machine beeped and she made no facial expression as she read the tiny screen. She pushed a strand of hair behind her ear and handed the device to the general.

"You are dead, Adam Solomon."

"Really? I don't feel dead. Maybe your little machine is broken," Adam said just a little too sharply.

The general narrowed his eyes at Adam. "Listen, I don't need lip from some punk ass kid. You were declared dead months ago along with the rest of your group."

"I survived the attack."

"Attack?" General DeCarlo dropped the device on the table.

"You know, from the Raspers." I made another move to stand. Once again, the soldier's hand came down on my shoulder.

"What are you calling a Rasper?" This came from the bald man whose red nose betrayed his long-term allergy suffering—or possibly a drinking problem.

"The yellow-skinned, shallow-breathing, night-walkers that are out to kill us."

"Quite an accurate description. I like it," the man said.

Great. Someone else liked my name for the damn things, but he'd probably be disappointed in my unimaginative naming of the Bugs.

"That's not the point right now, Doctor." General DeCarlo shot the man a look, and the doctor shrank in his seat.

The general seemed more feared than revered around here. Good to know.

"Young lady, tell me about the specimen you had in your bag."

"We caught it."

"Where?"

I wanted the answers to my questions, not to answer this dude. I sat up straighter in the hard chair. "Tell us why you're treating us like this. And where is Megan?"

"You are not in any position to be demanding answers." The general folded his arms across his medaled chest. "I expect you to answer me."

His arrogance fueled my anger. It had started out as a slow smolder. Now it reached inferno proportions. "If you don't have the human decency to uncuff two kids, we have nothing to say."

Adam's fingers lightly brushed my leg. I gave him a small smile as I shook on the inside.

"Do you have any idea who you're dealing with?" General DeCarlo charged like a bull toward my seat.

My body screamed for me to pull back, but I fought every flight instinct slamming through my brain.

"Enlighten us."

He stopped right before my chair. If I could have smacked him across his wide cheek, I would have. I sat up straighter. The man and woman in the chairs tightened their posture, but made no move to intervene.

"Let us go!" I shouted and jumped up before the guard could force me down. The soldiers made to grab me. General DeCarlo waved them back.

"There's no way I'm letting you go."

I balled my fists and tried to fight the tears welling in my eyes. "Why not?" I hated that the words crackled as I spoke them.

"Because you register as infected."

24

The word pierced my skull like a dagger. Infected.

We weren't infected. Just stung. Did their tests mean I was turning into a Rasper? I glanced at Adam, then at my hands. Our skin was still normal.

"They can change at any time. Move them to Corridor XC where we can keep them contained. I need more information, doctors." General DeCarlo stormed from the room.

I tried to protest, but my heart hammered faster than a scared rabbit and my voice failed. I glanced at Adam, his gaze locked on the now-empty doorway.

When the soldiers started to move, the lady doctor stood and held up her hand. "A minute, gentlemen?" Our armed guard hesitated, then fell back into position.

"You know something." Adam directed his statement to the woman in the lab coat, who seemed to be in charge in the general's absence.

Her shoulder length dark hair was perfectly styled and her clothes under the coat screamed designer. She made me feel like a troll.

"I'm not sure what I know anymore. These last four months proved we all still have a lot to learn." She walked toward us stopping just outside our reach.

Probably in case we jumped her. Smart.

"My name is Dr. Morgenstern and this is Dr. Collins."

"Can you help us?" Adam gestured to me with his cuffed hands.

Dr. Collins walked forward. "We can't answer that honestly until we complete more tests." He took glasses out of his pocket, wiped them on his lab coat, then held them up to the light to inspect them before putting them on.

"What tests have you done already?" I pictured the gauze taped to my arm.

"Standard blood screens. I do apologize for doing that without your consent. I had my orders." Dr. Morgenstern held her hands out, palms up.

I bet she did—straight from General Asshole.

"We would like to run more advanced tests. We need to find out why you register as infected, yet show none of the normal symptoms."

"Yes, find out whatever you can," Adam said automatically.

"Miss?" The doctor turned to me.

While I had no desire to become a human pincushion, I wanted—needed—answers the good general didn't seem ready to offer. "Okay."

Dr. Morgenstern rubbed her hands together. "Excellent. I am sorry for your situation. If I get answers, maybe General DeCarlo will allow your restraints to be removed."

The soldiers took up position on our sides and escorted us from the room. Once in the corridor, we turned right and walked in a different direction. The place was a maze. We went down another cement tunnel and through a series of electronically locked doors.

If I called the first place a cell, this was the slum of cells. A soldier, who had the body type of a professional wrestler, punched a code into the digital display and two doors swung open. Another soldier shoved Adam into one room while the barrel of a rifle guided me into my own private hellhole.

A thin mattress sat in the corner of the room. My feet slipped on the concrete floor. The ceiling and three of the walls were made from cold cement block. I shivered and noticed the barred wall with the door had a small slot at the bottom. It was truly a prison cell. This couldn't be happening. My head throbbed and I felt like I was going to be sick.

"Hold out your hands," the wrestler guard said.

I tried to catch his eye, but he avoided making contact. How could he believe locking a kid in a cell like this was right?

"I'll unbind your wrists. If you try anything, my partner will shoot you." He nodded to the rifle-jabbing soldier.

I held my arms out while trying not to vomit on his combat boots. He whipped out a pair of cutters and in one swift snip, the plastic cuffs fell from my wrists and into his gloved grip. The soldiers then backed out of the cell and shut the door.

The lock clicked into place, announcing the door was secure. No hope of escape.

"Val, can you hear me?" Adam's low voice carried on the damp, stale air.

I leaned into the bars and stuck my arms through like I had seen prisoners do on TV. "Yeah."

"Do you think we're on camera right now?"

I hadn't thought about being watched 24/7. "Probably. I mean they have electricity coming out their ears."

"This really sucks."

I laughed. "That's an understatement."

Another door to our own private Alcatraz hell whooshed open and Dr. Morgenstern walked toward us, accompanied by three soldiers. I might have a chance against one, but three and the doctor weren't good odds.

"My, this is depressing." She gave the room a look and wrinkled her nose as if she smelled dog poop. "Okay, let's see if I can find out anything, shall we?"

She nodded to the first soldier, who unlocked my cell. From this angle, there was no way I could see the code. Dr. Morgenstern entered while one soldier took a position in the door and the other two flanked the barred wall.

She set a plastic container on the floor and gave the room a once over. "Hmm, this would be easier with a chair."

"I agree. We should go somewhere else," I said in a calm, authoritative voice.

"No. Unfortunately, I'm just here for some more blood. The general wants a medical guarantee you won't change. Maybe soon."

I pushed my sleeve up past the bandage.

"Let's do the other arm. That way your arm won't be as sore." Dr. Morgenstern prepared her syringe and whatever else she needed.

I checked out her container. Besides the needle she held and another one presumably for Adam, I didn't see anything I could use as a weapon.

"Where's Megan?" I said it loud enough to make sure Adam heard.

"Who?" Dr. Morgenstern frowned and lines crinkled around her eyes.

"The girl we came here with."

"I'm sorry, dear. I don't know anything about another girl. Just you two."

What the hell? Where was she? Hadn't they at least tested her blood to make sure she was clean? They wouldn't have sent her somewhere else. Would they?

"What about the Bug?" I looked away before she inserted the needle.

"Are you referring to the specimen you had in the jar?"

Well, at least she knew something. "Yes. Where is it?"

"I've been studying the vile thing." She switched vials and filled another tube.

"What kind of doctor are you?"

She placed the vials filled with my blood in a holder, then put a gauze piece and tape over the spot on my arm. "I specialize in infectious diseases. I work for Zigotgen. The government asked for my help in containing the situation."

She pulled another thicker needle from her pocket and held my right wrist. She injected me with something.

"What was that?"

"Standard security identification. Everyone here has one." She capped the needle and slid in back into her pocket.

Now I had one of the things in my wrist. Wonderful.

"Did a disease make people into Raspers?" I tugged my sleeve down. I hoped Adam was paying attention.

Dr. Morgenstern picked up her container. "Not like I've ever seen. And it's not communicable. If it was, there would be no way you wouldn't be quarantined."

I felt like I was quarantined. Being isolated and alone might be better than this cell. "Then what is it?"

"That, my dear, is what I intend to find out. Will you cooperate with the general for information?"

I nodded. She signaled the guard and left.

The soldier reengaged the lock and they moved to Adam. He tried to find out more about Megan, but the doctor wouldn't budge. She insisted she knew nothing about her.

After the group left the corridor, a wave of exhaustion slammed into me. It had been forever since I had been able to truly relax. My head pounded and my vision blurred. I turned to the nasty mattress. It was disgusting with its stains and a scent of stale body odor wafted off it. There was no way I was laying on it.

I sat on the floor, my back to the wall, tucked my knees to my chest, and rested my head on them. Images of the last four months blended together. The voices in my head fell silent.

The corridor whooshed open. My head shot up, my heart pounding into overdrive. I reached for the gun I no longer had.

A group of soldiers filed down the hall. One of them pushed a cart that emitted delicious smells. My stomach prayed they were bringing us food.

One man shoved a covered tray through the opening at the bottom of the bars.

I waited until I heard the click of the soldiers leaving before I took off the lid. The scent of chicken and potatoes made me almost cry. I stared at the paper plate filled with a breaded chicken breast, small red potatoes, carrots, and a roll. A bottle of water rested on its side next to the plate. There was only a plastic spoon for silverware. I didn't care. I devoured the food. An honest-to-goodness hot meal. Besides the soup we made at Megan's, I hadn't had a hot meal since before the Great Discovery. Maybe staying in here for a few days might be worth it, if they fed us this way three times a day. Maybe I'd get some muscle and strength back.

"That was so good," Adam said.

"I think I ate too fast." I rubbed my belly. I thought about licking the plate, but stopped myself.

Moments later, the corridor opened again and the same group of soldiers wheeled their cart back down the hall. After they took my tray, one of them stuffed two blankets and a pillow in the slot.

I clutched them to my chest. "Thanks."

He didn't respond. Even with the blankets, the thought of using the mattress was revolting. I spread one blanket on the floor and huddled under the other one.

I slept, but nightmares of Bugs crawling over my skin plagued my sleep.

Morning brought eggs and toast for breakfast with a cup of coffee. Hope that life would go back to normal disappeared with the last sip of coffee. My life was at its lowest point since the Great Discovery, but my stomach was at its highest. Go figure.

I finger combed my hair and pulled it back into a tight ponytail. If they let me shower, I might cease my plans for escape.

Soldiers came to get us and they rebound our wrists. They directed us to a room like the conference one, but without the big table. A number of cushioned chairs and end tables filled the space dominated by a blank video screen.

"Sit." The command was brisk and gruff.

When General DeCarlo entered the room, all but two guards left. Dr. Collins and Dr. Morgenstern stepped in behind him.

"Val, Adam. Dr. Morgenstern has informed me of your willingness to cooperate, so I would like to offer an information exchange."

I glanced at Adam and he raised his eyebrows ever so slightly. I was sure the general never did anything that didn't ensure his victory. We had nothing to lose. We both nodded.

"Very well." General DeCarlo held his hands out, palms up. "What is it that you would like to know?"

"Where's Megan?" The words sprang from my mouth faster than my brain processed.

"Yes. Your friend." He stepped up on a small platform that made him taller than before. "She's fine and being well cared for."

"Is she locked up too? We want to see her."

The general stroked his chin a moment before answering. "I don't know if that would be a good idea. Let's see how this exchange goes. Then I will decide."

What a horse's ass. My hatred for him grew stronger every time he opened his mouth.

"What happened to the world, to everyone, and what was the Great Discovery?" I blurted it out so I wouldn't piss him off until he gave us something.

"Good questions. Four months ago Pearan Chemicals located what they thought was a large natural deposit of oil in the Gulf of Mexico." The screen lit up and he pointed to a spot on the large map behind him. "Enough to end our dependence on foreign oil." He looked at Adam, who just glared back. "I believe your father was one of the team leaders on the project.

"Calculations showed this deposit expanded deeper into the earth crust than any discovered previously. When drilling began, Pearan soon hit what appeared to be a hard outer shell. Your father ran the test on the substance and determined it was not of this earth. He concluded it to be an asteroid that crashed around the time the Mayans were in power. Your father tried to convince Pearan to stop drilling, but there was too much money committed to the project to cease. It's unfortunate no one listened to him."

"An asteroid? Like what wiped out the dinosaurs?" My voice held a note of disbelief. This was getting crazier by the second.

"Yes."

"How did they live that long? Why didn't they die?" I hugged my bound wrists to my chest.

"Dr. Morgenstern believes they go dormant after so long in the water."

Tingling spread across my chest. When I had thought the Bug

was dead, it had only been asleep. And it could have stayed that way for thousands of years.

Adam shifted in his chair. "That would explain my dad's change in attitude."

"I guess. Well, the damn pencil pushers decided they needed a big show to inject enthusiasm into their Zigotgen investors."

Dr. Morgenstern half-coughed, half-laughed. The general gave her a quick glance.

"They announced to the world the date and time they would break through the crust to access the oil. They got more than they bargained for." He laughed, a dry psychopath-worthy laugh. "When they broke through the crust, instead of finding oil, they found these goddamned aliens."

He sighed and pinched the bridge of his nose. "The creatures overwhelmed the drilling platform instantly. Within fifteen minutes, there were reports of them showing up on beaches and river inlets all along the Gulf Coast. We've been battling them ever since."

I pictured the Bugs swarming out of the river and on top of the bridge back when Adam saved me. I swallowed against the dryness clinging to the inside my mouth.

Adam glanced from me to the general. "Did my dad figure out where the creatures came from?"

The general shook his head. "I don't think so. He only determined that they weren't of our planet."

The room fell silent.

Aliens. We were *really* dealing with aliens. No. Not possible. My mind refused to accept it. I had wrapped myself in a cloak of denial since Megan had first said the word.

"What happened to my mom, my family?" Adam sounded very calm, but pain seeped through his tough exterior.

"The alien life forms started killing people by injecting them with a toxin, which allowed a new creature to grow and attach to the brain of the human. The aliens took over large portions of our surviving population at an alarmingly fast rate." General DeCarlo's eyebrows lowered and pinched together.

"What do you mean by *surviving population*?" I was finally able to get a few shallow words out of my dry throat.

General DeCarlo waved his hand at Dr. Morgenstern.

She stood and paced the room. She made eye contact with Adam first, then me. "Earthquakes and other natural disasters killed the majority of the population. It appears the aliens occupied the asteroid and helped give it its shape, much like air does in a balloon. When the air is released, the balloon collapses. We believe the collapsing asteroid caused a worldwide shift in our tectonic plates, resulting in our severe weather, earthquakes, and global eruptions." Her voice came across like a teacher's, or a mom's, would.

I slumped further into the chair. Aliens were responsible for it all. All the quakes and crazy weather. All the screams and sounds and then the silence while I'd been in the basement. How everyone I knew died. I wanted to kill every last creature. Wipe them from existence. I wanted revenge. A burning sensation spread across my chest.

Dr. Morgenstern leaned against the wall. "During this time, the number of aliens continued to grow. I am working on trying to isolate what makes some people able to be hosts while the majority die. The only outcome to the toxin was either becoming a host or dying. Until now. Were you two stung by the bug-looking creatures or human hosts?"

This kept getting worse. My skin tingled as if small spiders walked over it. An alien had injected me with a poison. Oh, God. Was I an alien mutation and for some reason just hadn't turned fully yet? The room spun and I clutched the chair to keep from passing out. If I had a damn Bug in my head, I would rather die than live as a Rasper.

"Hosts. So, you're saying there were a certain number of the alien creatures in the asteroid and they increased their numbers by injecting something to make another alien grow inside a person's brain?" Adam sounded as shocked as I felt.

"In essence, yes. The creature injects its—for the lack of a better term—reproductive fluid—into a person and the alien grows on the brain and controls its host."

"What happens if the host dies?" I asked, my voice scratchy and not my own.

"It appears if sufficient time has passed since gestation, the alien can exit the host and start reproducing."

Pain exploded through my skull. I couldn't have a Bug attached to my brain. Couldn't. I pushed the heels of my bound hands against my forehead.

Dr. Morgenstern continued, "We believe the alien compresses the vocal cords of its host, causing their raspy breathing."

"And the yellow skin?" Adam asked. His own skin looked tinged with green.

"I haven't figured that out yet. Might just be the body trying to fight off the parasitic invader. Possibly something similar to jaundice."

"What do they do with the dead? And what about the black tar-like substance? We saw Raspers come out of it. Are they making more? Or reviving the dead bodies somehow?"

She shook her head. "All excellent questions we don't have the answers to yet. Believe me, I wish we did know."

General DeCarlo steepled his fingers. "Now it's you turn. What we want to know from you is what communication you have had with the extra-terrestrials."

Adam told them everything. About me shooting the Rasper and seeing the Bug for the first time. About being stung. About them chasing us. About the dome on the seminary and mall. About how they seem to work as a group. Thankfully, he didn't mention the part about our left-handed theory or them wanting me to join their collective.

I thought he said too much. He should have held something back to bargain our release with, but he was too trusting. I didn't trust the general, or the doctors, and I was starting to doubt I could even trust myself.

"The specimen you kept in the jar. Have you learned anything from it?" Dr. Morgenstern started pacing again.

"When it got wet, I thought it was dead. But from what you said, I guess it was asleep or something." I rolled my shoulders.

"Anything else?"

Adam nodded. "It doesn't like chlorine."

"Chlorine?" Dr. Morgenstern stopped. "What do you mean?"

After he told her about the Bug's reaction to the chlorine,

she rubbed her hands together and a slight smile played at the corners of her mouth. "Excuse me, I have work to do." She ran out the door.

"General, is it possible for the kids to be moved to regular rooms?" Dr. Collins asked.

"Not until the test results come back. They need to be secured in case they change."

I jumped up. "What about Megan? We want to see her."

The general's mouth formed a thin line and his eyes narrowed. "I'll consider it."

Asshole.

＊

Soldiers took us back to our cells and gave us grilled cheese sandwiches with French fries. For the few minutes it took me to eat, I thought I was in heaven. Then reality crashed down. I wrapped the blanket around my back and slid onto the cement floor.

Aliens. Bugs. Raspers. Me.

Was I one of them? I needed to stop thinking about it. "Adam?"

"Yeah?"

"Talk to me. Please."

The hours ticked by as Adam and I talked about our childhoods. We found out we had the same dislike of math. The same love of cheesy comedy movies. When he told me he'd often been the new kid in school since his father's job moved them around, I wished I could see his face and hug him.

At one point, I pushed back my sleeve and caught the faded words that made up the rules. I hadn't retouched them since I walked out of the house and left Adam. I rubbed my hand across Number One. *Trust no one.* I had violated that one to the point I was starting to think if the situation was different, I might want to date Adam. The way he smiled made my insides melt.

I yanked my sleeve back down and ran my hands across my face.

"What's your favorite—" Adam stopped talking when the corridor door slid open.

A lone soldier, dressed somewhat like the stereotypical ninja, walked down the hall. I leaned into the bars as far as I could. Adrenaline pumped through my veins. They had never sent just one soldier before.

The guard stopped part way down the hall and threw a black cloth over—now that I noticed it—what looked like a video camera dome mounted on the wall.

25

When Megan reached my cell, she held a gloved finger to her lips. I nodded at her. She entered the code to unlock my door and grabbed my hand, pulling me from the cell. Megan then repeated the same procedure with Adam. She then pulled white fabric from under her shirt and put on a lab coat over her uniform.

She led us out of the corridor, down another one, and right to another guard.

"What are you doing?" His voice was gruff and bored.

Megan laughed deeper than I imagined she could. "Dr. Morgenstern asked for them. If I don't get them to her STAT, she'll be pissed. Do you want to deal with her?"

"No. You're good. Go ahead." The soldier shrugged and let us pass.

Megan took us down another passageway, then shoved us inside a room, ripped off the lab coat, and stuffed her blonde hair into a black beanie hat.

"Okay, we need to move fast. I have uniforms and boots for you. Adam, I had to guess at your shoe size. I hope these fit."

"They'll be fine."

"What's going on? How did you do this? Where were they

keeping you?" I shot the questions out in rapid fire as I threw the uniform over my scrub top.

"They pretty much forgot about me once they determined I was normal. Nothing interesting like you two or the Bug."

The room didn't possess a private changing area and I was beyond caring. I turned around and switched pants.

"How did you get the codes for the doors?" I stuffed my feet into the boots and laced them. I was never taking shoes for granted again.

"If you're dressed the part, no one really notices if you're somewhere you're not supposed to be. And having a photographic memory doesn't hurt."

That was new information. "Well, thank you. You're amazing." I gave Megan a quick hug that from the look on her face shocked her.

"Don't thank me yet. We still have to get out of here. I tried to get some weapons, but unlike clothes, they lock up their guns."

"Hopefully we can find some somewhere." Being outside and weaponless was not a good idea. I adjusted my hat. "Ready?"

"Do you know the way?" Adam flexed his fingers.

"For the most part, but not one-hundred percent."

"Well, that's good enough for me." He grabbed one of my hands and one of Megan's. "Guys, I'm so sorry I brought us here. This was a mistake and it's all my fault."

"It's not your fault, so stop apologizing." Megan gave his hand a squeeze then let go, which left Adam and I awkwardly holding hands.

We each let go at the same time. Heat rushed to my face.

"Are you guys ready?" Megan bounced on the balls of her feet.

"Yes, but we have to tell you something."

Megan turned to face me. "What?"

"The Raspers and Bugs are aliens like you thought. Extra-terrestrials. ETs."

Her mouth dropped open. "Seriously?"

"That's what they told us."

"Well, I was right. We gotta go. You can tell me the rest later." She peeked out the door, then motioned for us to follow.

We went down the hallways, walking as if we had a purpose.

Like we belonged. We ducked into a rocky alcove. Megan held up her hand. "Okay, here's where it gets tricky."

Adam glanced left and right. "What do you mean?"

"There are four ways out of here. They call them Portals Alpha, Bravo, Charlie, and Delta. I overheard some of the soldiers mentioning patrols only go out of two of them, but he never said which ones. I would think the two that have patrols would be easier to get through. We can say we're heading out on a mission. The problem is which two."

"What portals are we closest to?"

"A and B."

"Then we should take one of those." Adam said.

"Which one?" Megan glanced from him to me.

Adam shrugged, so I said, "A."

"Here's the other part. It's a good few miles out of here. They brought us in on golf carts and that tram thing. I don't think we can risk the noise, so we'll have to hoof it. And they can notice the blacked out camera anytime." Megan glanced over her shoulder as if she expected soldiers to appear behind her.

"Lead the way." I pointed in a sweeping motion.

We crept along the wall to keep out of sight as much as possible. The tunnel—or Portal as they called it—went on forever. Fluorescent lights, sporadically placed, cast just enough light to see, but nothing extra.

"There it is." Megan whispered.

The large door—our last obstacle to freedom—loomed ahead.

"Do you have the code to open it?" Adam pointed to the electronic key pad.

I glanced around. "There's no guard. I think this is the wrong door."

"Shit."

"Should we go back and try another one?"

"It would take too long."

"We should be able to get out before any soldiers get here."

Megan stared at the panel. "I don't know. This door is different. It might trigger an alarm if the code's wrong." She backed away from the door.

"You're the best chance we have. We can't stay here. Right?"

Megan and I nodded.

"Punch it in." Adam said.

Megan exhaled, bit her lip, then started pressing buttons.

I heard a number of faint clicks. Thank God. Then I realized it wasn't the door unlocking. Someone was loading a gun.

A deep voice rang out, "Freeze or I'll shoot."

Crap. I spun around. Soldiers, wearing uniforms like us, fanned out from all sides and pinned us to the door.

"Put your hands in the air."

"We're just kids. You can't keep us like this." Megan's voice rose.

"Put your hands up or die. Those are your only options. You have five seconds before the choice will no longer be yours." A brief pause. "Five."

Damn it, I wasn't going back.

"Four."

With Adam's and my speed, we might be able to take them.

"Three."

But there was no place to take cover.

"Two."

And Megan has normal speed and would be slaughtered.

"One."

"Okay." I held up both my hands. Adam and Megan followed my lead.

"Rollins, cuff 'em." The guy—who acted as if he was in charge—spoke to the bald and muscular man to his right; the same one who had used the wand when we'd first arrived. He shackled us in the plastic cuffs.

My hope for escape disappeared as the plastic bit into my skin.

"Got them secured, sir." The leader spoke into a radio, then pressed his gloved hand to his ear. "Roger, that. We'll get them to Sector Five."

Rollins shoved us into golf carts and we sped back into the mountain.

Sector Five was deeper in the bunker than we had been before. At the entrance to what looked like another communication center, we got out of the golf carts. The soldiers opened a rounded door at least three feet thick. Not a good sign.

The massive door closed behind us with a resounding thud. The locks clinked into place. We weren't getting out that way any time soon. The soldiers pushed us forward, then took up positions along the rock-walled circular space.

I focused on the room. It was about twice the size of my parents' garage. A raised platform held a glass chamber about the same dimension of the average bathroom, minus the fixtures. A lone plastic chair sat in the enclosure. Cameras pointed at the empty box and my mind scrambled to figure out what its purpose might be. A row of monitors and keyboards stood next to the chamber. Dr. Morgenstern sat on a stool at the largest monitor. Her eyes met mine and gave me a sad, odd look I couldn't decipher. I glanced away and focused on another monitor showing a map of North America covered in red.

"Well, well, well." General DeCarlo strutted through another door.

I kept my head high and tried to stare him down while my insides twisted in knots.

"I suppose I have you to blame for their botched escape attempt." He towered over Megan, but she refused to back down. "What's your name?"

"Megan."

"Ah, yes, the Megan they begged me for information about." He smiled an out of place, tooth-filled grin. "I thought you were a smart girl. Not a criminal aiding the enemy."

"They aren't the enemy. They're my friends." Megan raised her eyes to meet the general's gaze. "My family."

General DeCarlo tapped his chest. "That's touching. But they're mutants. Look at this screen." He pointed at the monitor with the map of North America. "Red means the creatures have taken over there. These two have the aliens inside their heads. Do you know that the only reason they're not breathing funny is a fluke?" He stared down at Megan.

Her nose wrinkled and she snapped back, "At least their breath doesn't reek like yours."

Oh, no.

He grabbed Megan by the arm.

"Let her go," Adam yelled.

General DeCarlo pushed Megan aside. She stumbled, but stayed on her feet. The general closed the distance between him and Adam. "Do not tell me what to do, punk."

"Screw you."

The general snapped his fingers. A soldier stepped forward and swung his gun. The smack of the gun's butt on Adam's flesh reverberated through the small room. Adam dropped to the ground, blood dripping from his nose, and his cheek flared an angry crimson.

My insides burned and anger built to a boiling point. I dashed to Adam. He sat up and tipped his head back, pinching his nose to stop the bleeding.

"Anderson, we need to teach this kid who's in charge." General DeCarlo told the soldier who hit Adam.

"Help him." I directed my words to Anderson. He backed into his spot against the wall.

"Put *him* in the chamber." The general pointed to Adam.

"Sir?"

"Do it, Anderson, or you'll take his place."

"He's just a kid."

"Oh, for God's sake, he's not just a kid. He's one of them. Now step aside, you pansy ass. Jones, Rollins, do it."

"Yes, sir."

What? No way in hell. I looked around for a way out. The two ape-like guards clamped down on Adam's arms.

Thwack.

General DeCarlo smacked his palm against his thigh. "This is what you kids need to understand. I am in charge here. The government you knew has ceased to exist. The President is alive, but in hiding. No one cares what I do here as long as I figure out how to kill the aliens. And you're going to help me. Right here. Right now."

The anvil weight crushed down on my chest. Again.

"I need to test Dr. Morgenstern's theory. Since Adam volunteered when he mouthed off, I wouldn't want to deprive him of the opportunity to help his country."

The soldiers pushed Adam forward. Blood drops fell to the floor in a polka dotted line. "Go into the chamber."

"No." I couldn't let Adam do this. I had a suspicion of what the general had in mind.

"You can't do this." Adam slumped between the guards.

General DeCarlo snapped his fingers and the wrestler soldier pointed a gun at my head.

This man was a psycho. My fingers itched for my Glock.

"Or he can blow her brains out and we can all see the alien in her head." The soldier stepped next to me and pushed the muzzle into my hair. I sank to my knees. He pulled the gun back, but kept it pointed in my direction.

I had to be the one who went into the chamber. It had to be me. The aliens weren't calling for Adam. They wanted me. Me, not him. Not Megan. And Megan wouldn't be here if the Raspers hadn't tracked us to her family's hideout. They'd still be alive. Bethany would still be alive. I had to be the one to pay the price.

"Let me go." Adam twisted to shrug off the soldiers' grips. Blood flew from his face and hit the glass wall of the chamber.

"Adam, don't. I'll do it. I..."

He faced me. I stood and walked closer.

The soldiers restraining Adam loosened their hold just a tad. "Val, no."

Megan sobbed.

"Ah, young love. How sweet." General DeCarlo sneered.

When I hesitated, Adam took another step toward the glass case. That propelled me forward. I reached out to touch him, but the soldiers yanked him back.

"You have until the count of three for one of you, I don't care which, to get in there or Nelson shoots your pretty little friend." The general held up his index finger. "One."

Not another countdown. I turned and locked my gaze on Megan. The soldier, Nelson, pointed his gun at her chest. Tears streamed down her face.

I licked my lips. I couldn't let her die. I had to do this.

I spun and marched to the chamber. The closest soldier gave me a slight shove. I stumbled and fell, banging my knees on the cement floor. He hoisted me up by my bound wrists, pushed me in the chair, and secured my ankles to the chairs legs with more zip ties.

"Doctor, the specimen." The general slipped his hands into fireproof-looking black rubber gloves.

I hoped he would get stung.

Dr. Morgenstern gave me a look filled with guilt, unlocked a cabinet, pulled the jar out from under a cloth, and handed the Bug to the general. He twisted the lid open and tossed the Bug into the chamber with me, then locked the door.

"No!" I tried to get loose. Tears blurred my vision.

The Bug scuttled and righted itself.

I had to get free. Get out. The ceiling, the walls, the floor were all thick glass. I struggled to break the restraints, but they bit deeper into my flesh, slicing it open. If I had more time, I might be able to free myself, but time was running out.

The Bug twitched its legs and inched closer.

I choked on the stale air. My head felt heavy and I was sure I was about to pass out. I tore my gaze from the Bug and locked it on Megan and Adam. Megan's face was red and swollen from crying. Adam was on his knees and the wrestler soldier had a gun aimed at his head.

Fear clawed at my insides.

The Bug scuttled closer to me and stopped inches from my boot. If I could get my legs free, I could stomp on it. I yanked with all my strength. The plastic loosened a bit. Blood seeped from the wounds and a droplet landed on the floor inches from the Bug.

It brought its front legs together and sawed. The screech filleted my eardrums. Pain twirled through my brain and exploded behind my eyes in bursts of colored shapes.

I was done. I was going to die.

I tried to think of something happy. My parents...my dog...Adam.

This slow agonizing torture shredded what was left of my willpower. Tears rolled down my face. I didn't want to die. I wanted the pain to stop. Fogginess crushed down on my brain. I was on the edge of unconsciousness.

It was time. Time to finally surrender. Time to accept my fate.

The Bug's song ceased. The pain ebbed and I snapped back to reality. I sniffed back the remaining tears and stared at the damn creature.

It stepped forward and onto my boot.

Oh, God. Oh, God. Oh, God.

With precise movements, the Bug crawled up my leg. My stomach soured. Six steel legs ticked up over my knee and onto my thigh. My skin felt like it would slip from my bones. Chills slithered through my system, but sweat dripped from my temples.

Logic screamed for me to react, but I was paralyzed. Trapped. I couldn't move. Couldn't breathe. Couldn't lift my hands to flick the Bug away. All my muscles had turned to stone.

The Bug inched up my leg toward my hands. It tapped my left fingers with its spindly legs. Shivers rippled through my nerves. When I didn't move, the Bug tapped again. What the hell?

The Bug gave my fingers three short taps then it inched into the back of my hand.

My chest heaved. I braced for the sting. I couldn't watch. I shut my eyes.

Waited.

26

Time stood still. Why didn't the Bug sting me and get it over with? The air in the glass chamber pushed down on my lungs, forcing me to take deep breaths. A burning sensation spread across my chest. Don't panic. Don't think. Just do.

The Bug clicked forward. I couldn't take it anymore. I wanted to scream. Wanted to run. Wanted to cry.

I stared at the *alien*.

"Come on already." I gritted my teeth and balled my right hand into a fist.

The Bug shifted its legs. More tingles zipped through my nerve endings. Where was its stinger? One of its legs?

Anxiety slid through every one of my cells. Hopefully, my death would be painless. If I didn't die, the alternative meant becoming a Rasper. I couldn't do that. Wouldn't do that. Maybe...if I ended it myself, it would all be over. But I couldn't leave Adam and Megan. If I became a Rasper, I would kill General DeCarlo.

I liked that idea. A lot. But I didn't want to be a Rasper. The Bug inched closer.

"No. Please don't."

The Bug stopped. Raised its front legs and brought them to my bound wrists. I closed my eyes so tight my cheeks ached.

The cool metal legs brushed against my skin. All the hairs on my arm stood at attention. My lungs refused to work. The Bug slipped its leg under the plastic tie and sliced upward. What the hell? I opened my eyes. The binding fell from my wrists. The Bug turned so it was facing the general.

My ears buzzed. A thought formed in the back of my mind, but it was too fuzzy, too disjointed for me to see clearly.

The Bug sat on my leg. It didn't move. I stared at it. "Please don't move." I whispered the words to myself.

The Bug remained still and silent. I spun my wrists and wiggled my fingers to get the feeling back.

Dr. Morgenstern, wearing a hard plastic, biocontainment-type suit and thick black gloves, walked toward the chamber. She unlatched the door, scooped the Bug into a container, and backed out of the cell, leaving the door ajar. She locked the jar back in the cabinet.

The general leaned forward, his mouth hanging open like a dog begging for scraps. Megan continued to cry and her face was a puffy red mess. The soldier still had a gun trained on Adam. He looked up, met my gaze, and smiled.

General DeCarlo balled his hands into tight fists. "Doctor, explain what the hell just happened."

Dr. Morgenstern took her hood and suit off, then looked from Adam's smiling face to the general. "Sir, I—"

"I can explain it." Dr. Collins walked into the room, accompanied by a soldier.

"Then you better get to it, Dr. Collins." I expected General DeCarlo to froth at the mouth.

"She's immune to the sting."

"What?"

"It appears the toxin had no effect when she was stung. The alien race failed to grow inside her system. She carries the serum, but her body will not allow the creature to grow. The Bug thinks the girl, and the boy, are already one of them. It has no desire to sting them."

Shock and disbelief made it seem as if my body defied gravity. I was immune?

"How is that possible?" General DeCarlo' eyes widened and

he ran a hand across his face. "Can an antidote be created from their blood or DNA or something?"

"This is where it gets interesting. The answer to your question is no. They are only immune because they already carried the antibodies of the alien toxin. I just got the test results." The doctor flapped a few sheets of paper.

What?

A soldier cut the remaining straps and dragged me from the chamber. I fell to my knees. The room refused to stay still. Megan raced to my side and bear-hugged me. Hard.

"How did they get the antibodies? Can we get more?" The general's tone came across angry and impatient.

Dr. Collins shook his head. "This goes back twelve years or so, when Sheri, um Dr. Morgenstern, and I worked on the team at Zigotgen. The team's goal was to find a cure for the common cold."

Dr. Collins glanced at Dr. Morgenstern. She gave him a slight nod.

"Back when these two were kids, they received vaccinations against all the basic diseases kids need to go to school. Our project had three hundred randomized subjects who received our test vaccine for the common cold hidden inside the chicken pox vaccine. The vaccine testing was halted after a number of kids became violently ill and one died, but a lot of children received the vaccine with no effects. And most of them rarely, if ever, got sick."

Test vaccines? My parents couldn't have agreed to let me be a research subject. Maybe they didn't know. It wasn't possible. But...but I tried to remember the last time I had a cold. And couldn't.

Dr. Collins helped Megan and me to our feet. "After checking their backgrounds, I determined they were part of the vaccine trial. The team, we..." He waved his hand at Dr. Morgenstern. "I was only an assistant. But we only ever knew the subjects by number. After finding out their names and some background information, I was able to determine Val's subject number's XA115 and Adam's XH254."

The general's face got redder and redder. "What was in the

vaccine? Can we reproduce the antibody and vaccinate everyone else?"

"The vaccine was uh...experimental."

"Damn it, you're the doctor. Whip up another batch." General DeCarlo's voice went deeper, lower, scarier.

The doctor shook his head. "It's not that simple. We need the correct serum. It took years to create it."

I swallowed. "Why was it experimental?"

Dr. Collins couldn't meet my gaze. "Uh...we created the vaccine by using the alien toxin. This isn't the first time these creatures have surfaced."

Alien toxin? Not the first time? Nerve-rattling disbelief blossomed at my temples. Shoots of white and gray colored my vision. I blinked hard and tightened my grip on Megan.

"How did you vaccinate them? And did they know?"

Dr. Collins turned to Dr. Morgenstern. "This is more Sheri's area than mine. As I said, I was only an assistant."

She pursed her lips. "The biotech industry is highly competitive, with payouts in the billions. We focused on the common cold. Can you imagine a vaccine that keeps you from ever catching a cold? Can you imagine the profits?" Her face took on a dreamlike look, then she focused on the soldier aiming his gun at Adam.

"The serum was discovered after Zigotgen acquired the remains from an archeological find in Tikal, the ancient Mayan city. How the serum was found, I don't know. We were the researchers. We studied the composition of the fluids given to us. The fluids carried antibodies for many diseases. We were able to recreate the serum in the lab. But we need to work from the original source. Sort of like stem cells."

She cleared her throat and took on a teacher-like tone. "The fluid held promise for curing other diseases as well. If we succeeded with curing the common cold, we were prepared to move to trials with our cancer vaccine. And we tracked the vaccines, but the subjects didn't know they were testing them."

Illegal vaccines? The Mayans? Cancer vaccine? My stomach clenched. There was no way all this was real. I had to be trapped in a nightmare. The problem was, I didn't know when the

262

nightmare started. When I was a kid? Four months ago? A few days ago? Today?

"I was able to pierce the metallic shell of this bug creature, and its fluids hold the same signature. Same antibodies as the original sample. But much weaker. The original sample was so much stronger. Like it came from a considerably stronger creature. At this lower strength, the sample would not be able to survive the processing required to create a new line."

General DeCarlo stared at the Bug. "But you can make it?"

Dr. Collins answered this time. "In theory. The cell-line from the Seed Plot Project is stored in a secure vault at Zigotgen."

Seed Plot Project? 300 Seed Plot. John and Frank thought it meant the seminary. But it didn't. Three hundred test subjects. And I had been number 115. Dizziness made me sway me into Megan.

"So, she—" General DeCarlo yanked my arm pulling me away from Megan. "She is basically one of them?"

"Yes. And it seems the aliens work with a hive-like mind mentality." Dr. Morgenstern pointed at the jar. "We've received reports from other zones. Drone crafts were able to record the synchronized movements of the Raspers. Dr. Leventhall's team at another facility caught one and is in the process of a detailed autopsy."

The general's hand tightened on my arm to the point where I would have a nasty bruise. I twisted to pull away. He increased the pressure. "Explain what you mean."

"It's almost like what one host knows, the rest learn. As if they suck all the memories and information from the hosts' brains and send it back to their colony. Our study of this behavior leads us to believe there is some type of a queen in the collective, similar to bee hives."

I would have collapsed if the general didn't have such a tight grip.

It was true. I hadn't wanted to believe it before.

Collective. The Rasper had said they wanted me to join the collective. They knew my name. They *did* work as a unit. It was all starting to make sense. The way the horde of Bugs lined up in the street. The way the Raspers seemed to get smarter and now came out in the daylight wearing sunglasses. The way they kept finding us. Their coordinated movements. We were so screwed if we left this rock dungeon. Hell, we were screwed staying here.

But what didn't make sense was why they wanted *me*. That question nagged at the back of my mind.

"So, if you kill this queen thing, the rest of the damn things die?" General DeCarlo pointed at Dr. Morgenstern.

She nodded. Her sleek hair bobbed, then went back into place perfectly. "That is our current theory. And when I contacted Zigotgen, they set in motion a protocol to test chlorine's toxicity on the aliens."

I pulled and twisted. The general gripped my arm tighter.

"Let her go." Adam stood. The soldier kept the gun trained on him. My heart beat faster at his words, but they were useless.

"Hold him." The general ordered. Soldiers clamped down on Adam's arms, forcing him back. The general was about to say something else when an alarm screamed through the room and the ceiling lit up in blazing crimson.

"What's happening?" Alarms and lights never meant anything good.

A soldier burst into the room. "Sir, we're under attack."

"By whom?"

"The aliens."

General DeCarlo released my arm. "How did they get so close without us knowing it?"

"Sir, they're our soldiers. Or were our soldiers. They knew—know—our codes, procedures, everything. And they're making demands."

"What do they want?"

The soldier focused on me and pointed at my chest. "They want her."

No. This couldn't be happening. The Raspers were attacking. Demanding me. Why?

"Soldiers, come with me. Doctors, guard them. Do not release them until I come back." General DeCarlo swept from the room. The soldiers exited and the lock clicked place.

Locking us in.

Adam leaned into me and brushed his shoulder against mine.

Dr. Morgenstern and Dr. Collins stared at the door, ignoring us.

I took a risk and smashed an empty container to the ground. Using a shard of broken glass, I cut Adam and Megan's ties. Dr. Morgenstern didn't react. Dr. Collins gave a one-shouldered shrug.

They were after me. *Me.* I leaned against the wall, then slid to the floor. There was no reason they would want me, specifically. My body shook and I wrapped my arms around my knees. I had been unknowingly vaccinated. I had been followed and tracked by a company that might have killed me.

I glanced at the map. The red-lit areas, or the Rasper infested areas, covered more of the map by the second. The green areas were clustered north by the Canadian border. And there were tiny green dots throughout the Midwest. But the entire east and west coasts were almost solid red.

Dr. Morgenstern broke the stillness and walked to the map. "It doesn't make sense. How are they spreading so far, so fast? What is it that makes some people become Raspers?"

"We came up with a theory." I stood and glanced at Adam and Megan.

Dr. Morgenstern turned to face me and frowned.

Adam shook his head. I tried to smile at him, but I think my expression came across as pain-filled. She could help us get out of here. We needed to give her something. "We think that only left-handed people turn into Raspers and righties die when injected."

"What? Why do you think that?" Dr. Collins walked to Dr. Morgenstern's side.

"Before I killed the Rasper who carried that Bug, he said humans have to be balanced to become Raspers. And left-handed people tend to use a balanced amount of both sides of their brains."

"All three of you are left-handed?" Dr. Collins asked.

Megan shook her head. "No. Just the two of them."

Dr. Morgenstern seemed to have slipped into deep thought. She absently tapped her nails on the table.

I debated about asking her what she was thinking, but before I spoke, the door lock clicked open. General DeCarlo walked into the room accompanied by a group of soldiers. "Doctors."

Dr. Morgenstern gave a tight-lipped head bob, then she and Dr. Collins scurried to the back corner of the room. General DeCarlo's hair was sticking out on the side and his uniform was torn. His disheveled appearance pleased me.

He didn't seem to notice that we were all untied.

"Goddammit. We've held them off for now, but we can't keep battling them head to head. Ten percent of my men became Raspers and turned on the rest." He smacked his fist onto the table, cracking its fake wooden top. "They got close because they transformed our own damn men who went out on patrol. They led the bastards right back to us. We're not only battling the enemy, but ourselves. We need to stop the damn things. Doctors!"

Dr. Collins and Dr. Morgenstern jumped as the general shouted the last word.

"I need answers. Now."

I ran my hands across my forehead and down my cheeks. Exhaled. My throat burned.

Dr. Collins shoved his hands in his lab coat pockets. "Sir—"

General DeCarlo's eyes narrowed into lizard-like slits. He turned to me. "The aliens and their hosts found our little hideout, thanks to you. Seems they know all about you, Val. Had a real hard on to find you. They demanded you before we killed them." He laughed, a maniacal, twisted laugh.

The man was seriously messed up. I refused to play his game and kept my mouth shut.

"It seems they want you to join them. And it gave me an idea. Doctor, the key." He held out his hand.

Dr. Morgenstern walked forward. Placed the silver key in the general's palm.

He removed the jar from the cabinet, set it on the table, and closed the distance between us. He leaned down to my level and breathed stale coffee breath into my face. I wanted to pull away and gag, but I held my ground. He wasn't going to bully me.

"Since they already think you are one of them and specifically asked for you, I think you should go to them."

"No!" Adam yelled and pulled me back behind him.

"Oh, how touching." The general laughed in a way that sounded more like a cackle.

"We're..." Adam didn't say anything else.

"No matter. You'll be joining her."

"What are you talking about?" I stepped out from behind Adam. He didn't need to protect me.

"You two will go with a group of my men to a 'hive' we believe is in Washington, DC. We are going to test the doctor's theory first-hand. There, you, with the help of my men, will kill the damn queen thing. With luck, it will destroy the rest of the Colony."

"No, she'll be killed." Adam said.

"I don't care if they kill her as long as you two kill the queen first."

A lump the size of a golf ball filled my throat. I wanted to rip the gun from the closest soldier's side and put a bullet through his head.

As if he knew what I was thinking, Adam reached for my hand and squeezed. "No. We won't do it."

"Well, then. It seems you need to be persuaded." General DeCarlo stepped away from us and moved to the table. He picked up the jar and in a flash was at Megan's side. He pulled her in front of him, hostage-style.

"No. Leave her alone." I stepped toward him. Adam yanked me back when the general set the Bug down and withdrew his pistol.

"You will either do as I order, or your pretty friend here dies. By Bug or gun. Your call."

He was bluffing. He had to be. He wouldn't turn the Bug on Megan—but he had on me.

"Let her go," Adam said in a deep, low voice.

Another peal of laughter rang through the room. "You know what? I have a better idea." The general waved his hand at the red and green map that was turning more red than green each second.

"You two." He pointed at two soldiers. "Take this one to Sector 12."

The men each grabbed one of Megan's arms. And they dragged her from the room, kicking and cursing.

"No," I screamed. Icy chills made me shiver, but sweat dripped down my back.

General DeCarlo faced me. "And so we are clear, she will die if you don't leave within the hour."

I caught Dr. Collins's eyes and pleaded silently for him to help. He looked away, took off his glasses and started to polish them. Dr. Morgenstern refused to meet my gaze. She was focused on the five remaining soldiers. She tapped on the table with one finger.

"If you are human, like you claim to be, you'll help us in eradicating the aliens from our planet, and she'll live. If you refuse, she'll die."

"You sadistic bastard." I spit the words at him.

"One life is nothing compared to the lives of the rest of us. The President has authorized me to use any means necessary to exterminate the alien threat. What's it going to be?"

I wanted to kill him. I rubbed a hand across my rules. Trust no one. I trusted Adam and Megan *now*, but sure as hell didn't trust the general.

"On certain conditions." I took a step closer to him, but Dr. Morgenstern stepped up behind the general and jerked her head to the right. I retreated to the side.

"You're in no position to make demands," the general snarled.

Dr. Morgenstern reached in her lab jacket pocket and pulled out a gun. "Neither are you." She raised her left hand and aimed at the back of General DeCarlo's head.

And fired.

27

Blood, brains, and blowback flew everywhere. Splattering the walls, the floor, me. The general's body dropped to the ground.

Two of the soldiers shot the other three, their bodies collapsing in a sick mosaic of arms and legs.

Holy shit. What was going on? She just shot the general. He was dead. Dead. Blood was everywhere. It was on me. The room spun and I struggled not to collapse.

Dr. Morgenstern put the gun back in her pocket and pulled her brown hair back from her face. "Now that we have the unpleasantness out of the way, we have lots to do. Albert?" She turned and stared at Dr. Collins.

His face was pasty and he looked on the verge of being sick. He pushed his glasses up on his nose. "Coming." He stepped around the bodies without looking at them.

She didn't wait for an answer before she spoke to the remaining soldiers. "I will have to inform the President of how bravely General DeCarlo fought the aliens. Shame they killed him."

She then turned to us. "It was the general's dying wish that you two come with me and Dr. Collins to Zigotgen. Rollins and Jones will accompany us. Put them in metal handcuffs. I don't trust those plastic ones. We leave now. Get the blood off her or people will ask questions."

Leave now? Go to Zigotgen? Metal handcuffs? This was worse than the general's plan. Zigotgen was probably surrounded by red on the map. I'd thought Dr. Morgenstern was on our side. The reality stung more than the clink of the cuffs around my wrists.

Jones used a small towel to wipe my hands and clothes. "Good enough."

Dr. Morgenstern scooped up the Bug jar and walked out the door. Dr. Collins stayed a few steps behind, like a loyal dog. With my hands cuffed in front of me, Rollins grabbed my right elbow and made me walk with him. Jones did the same with Adam. The doctors led us through the underground labyrinth.

I kept searching for any way to escape or anyone who could help us, but the complex resembled a ghost town. No weapons or people.

"Where is everyone?" Dr. Collins asked Dr. Morgenstern in a whisper.

"Hiding from the aliens." Rollins said under his breath. I wasn't sure if anyone but me heard him.

We walked and walked through corridor after corridor. Red strobing lights bounced off the walls, giving the tunnels a disorienting effect. I thought I saw blackness climbing the wall in one side tunnel. Oh, no. If the black slime was covering the building...

My heart beat faster and I increased my pace. We had to go faster. I pulled ahead of Rollins and he let me. But he tightened his grip on my arm and tugged me back when we turned the next corner. Two soldiers, armed and angry looking, blocked a regular sized metal door.

"Doctors, what are you doing?" the taller of the guards asked.

Rollins pulled me forward. "General DeCarlo was killed in the attack. His last request was that these two and the docs be taken to the alternative containment center." Rollins used his do-not-question-me voice.

"Of course, sir." The other soldier stepped over to an

electronic panel. He typed in a long code and the door rattled open. "There are two transports at the ready."

"Thank you. Carry on." Rollins led us through the door into a darker and colder tunnel.

He deposited me into the passenger side of a black golf cart and took the wheel. Dr. Morgenstern climbed in the back. Jones drove Adam and Dr. Collins in the other. The lights in this tunnel were spaced far apart, but close enough we never plunged into absolute darkness.

I turned to look back at the other cart. The doctor pulled a larger-than-normal-cell phone out of her pocket. She pushed in a sequence of numbers. "This is Morgenstern. I need an immediate extraction at 39.6483°N, 77.4650°W. Six total. Two are EDTS. Yes, sir, what we've been searching for."

"EDTS?" My existence had been reduced to numbers and letter codes.

She clicked the phone off. "Extremely dangerous test subject."

"Adam and I are extremely dangerous? That's funny. Why are you taking us to Zigotgen?"

She ran her index finger over her perfectly arched eyebrow. "Because we need you."

"For what?"

She folded her hands in her lap and ignored the question.

I changed my tactic. "Why did you let me uncuff Adam and Megan before, if you were just going to put me in these?" I shook my hands and the metal jangled.

Dr. Morgenstern tucked her hair behind her ears. "I wanted to gain your trust so you would tell me what you knew about the Raspers. Besides, it was only a matter of time before you figured out, that with your elevated strength, you were stronger than those plastic things."

I wanted—needed—to believe she would take us to safety, not to Zigotgen, wherever it was. But the metallic handcuffs digging into my skin said otherwise.

It seemed like we drove forever. In reality, it probably only totaled a distance of ten or fifteen miles until the tunnel ended and we faced another metal door, this one guard-free.

Rollins pulled me from the cart and dragged me to the electronic key pad. He typed in a code, then put his eye to the small scanner. It registered his identity and with a loud click, the door slid open.

He shoved me through the door and waited for everyone to join us in what appeared to be a storage room. Metal filing cabinets topped with papers lined one wall. Random furniture filled the rest of the room. The table closest to me held more stacks of papers.

Nothing I could use as a weapon. No scissors, screwdrivers, or even a pen among the colored file folders and paper filling every available space. Damn it, there had to be something—anything. I was about to give up when I spied one item I could use. I had to do it now or I'd miss the chance.

I pretended to stumble and stuck my hands on top of the papers on the table for support. My fingers slid across the small metal paperclip. I yanked it free and palmed it before Rollins pulled me back.

"Single file up the stairs. Val, you're behind me. Don't try anything or the good doc might shoot you with her gun."

"You know if you insult me, I can revoke my offer of vaccinating you." Dr. Morgenstern's voice was honey laced with poison.

I whipped around to look at her. "You have more of the vaccine?"

She didn't answer me. I tried to make eye contact with Adam, but Jones stood in front of him.

Rollins spun me back. "Move out."

Anger at the doctors, Rollins, the entire situation burned and boiled the acid in my stomach.

We followed him up the wooden stairs. My eyes bored into the middle of his back. Why wouldn't she answer me? Did they have more or not? Rollins shifted, breaking my wandering thoughts. I contemplated grabbing the gun he had holstered at his lower back. Could I get it with the handcuffs on before he drew the other gun he had on his hip, or the rifle slung across his chest? Probably not.

But the longer I stared at the gun, the more familiar it looked.

It had a tiny notch out of the handle grip. I knew that gun. It was Dad's. Mine.

Chills and excitement coiled together and rolled around in my stomach. Rollins must have been the one who took it from me back when the helicopters picked us up. Yes. He had been the one with the wand. My hate for him reached new levels. I had to figure out how to get it back.

We reached the top of the steps and went through another metal, keypad-secured door into a large bowling alley. Where were we? Rollins led us down a long hallway past some closed doors, and out a door into black and charred grounds. The sky had turned dark, and gray storm clouds made it look and feel like a scene from a horror movie.

"Welcome to Camp David, the President's vacation compound. It looked better before the general had everything burned to block the aliens. Like that did any good." Rollins hurried us across the ash toward a gray, wooden-looking garage.

Adam glanced around. "Shouldn't there be guards?"

The burnt grounds were eerily quiet. No noise whatsoever. The scent of smoke hung in the air. A cold breeze played with my hair, making me shiver. The sensation of being watched slithered over my skin. We needed to find cover.

Rollins paused for less than a second and gave a quick scan of the area. "Not anymore."

Against the dark sky and torched ground, Dr. Morgenstern's white jacket stuck out like a target. Dr. Collins had removed his at some point.

A thumping noise broke the hushed silence. We all looked up. A black helicopter with a white Z on the side and a small picture of an anchor hanging off the end of the letter landed in the open space to our right. The blades swirled ash into the air. The thumping pounded in my chest.

"Let's go," Dr. Morgenstern mouthed and raced to the chopper.

The rest of us ran behind her.

A tingling started in my head and worked its way down my nerves. I glanced over my shoulder. Adam gave me a questioning look.

"What?" Rollins pulled the rifle into his hands.

Screeching from the Bug, audible over the helicopter's noise, made Dr. Collins almost drop the jar.

Dr. Morgenstern yelled something that looked like "now" and yanked me by the arm, pulling me into the helicopter next to her in the three forward facing seats. Dr. Collins pushed ahead of Adam to secure the spot next to Dr. Morgenstern and closest to the window. The Bug slammed against the jar and the metallic squeal pierced my eardrums as if it was a nail being hammered into my brain.

"Go. Now!" Dr. Morgenstern yelled at the pilot.

The pilot turned to stare at the doctor. "Ma'am? The others?"

"I don't care about them. Leave now or else!" She aimed her gun at him.

He turned back to the controls, pushed buttons, and flipped levers.

The Bug got louder. So did the chopper's engines.

Jones dragged Adam into the helicopter and pushed him onto one of the two seats across from the doctors and me. Rollins jumped in right as the chopper lifted from the ground.

"Thanks for waiting." Rollins narrowed his eyes at Dr. Morgenstern and clung to the handle by the open door.

The doctors focused on something out the other window. I glanced over and saw them.

At least ten Raspers. Some wearing dark suits and armed with guns.

Rollins sighted his rifle and fired. Jones left his seat and fired at the Raspers too.

Thwonk. Thwonk.

"We're taking fire." Rollins and Jones pulled back, but kept shooting out the open door.

"Shut the damn door." Dr. Morgenstern tried for bossy and bitchy, but her words came across shaky and scared.

This was my chance. I twisted open the paperclip I had snagged from the table and jammed it into the handcuff lock. Almost had it. Almost... The helicopter jerked and the paperclip fell from my grasp.

The small piece of metal, the small piece of hope, hit the floor of the chopper.

I bent over and tried to feel for it. Where? There. When my finger touched the clip, the helicopter jerked again and it slid out of reach. I dropped to the floor pretending the jolt had knocked from the seat. I leaned and grabbed the clip.

"Get in your seat." Rollins yanked me by the arm and shoved me.

"Leave her alone," Adam yelled.

"Shut the hell up." Jones slammed the rifle butt toward Adam.

Adam reacted a millisecond too late and the weapon slammed into his skull. He slumped back into his seat.

"Adam." I reached for him.

"Sit down and shut up." Jones hollered.

Dr. Morgenstern grabbed my elbow and pulled me back into the seat.

I leaned back and stared at Adam's lifeless body. I searched for the rise and fall of his chest. Didn't see it.

More bullets hit the side of the chopper. Jones shifted and stood in front of Adam.

"Get us out of here!" Dr. Morgenstern screamed.

I slid the clip back into the lock. I never thought I'd use the trick Mom had used to win Dad's heart. She had claimed it sometimes paid to bend the rules. I almost smiled at the memory.

I got my hands free and pocketed the paperclip.

Rollins pulled back to reload. I jumped into the seat next to Adam to give him room. I touched Adam's wrist, feeling for his pulse. It took a second, but I caught a weak thumping.

I needed my gun. Needed to save Adam. Needed to get away from the crazy doctors.

I glanced from them, to the Raspers, to the distance to the ground. Ten feet. Twenty. Twenty-five. It was now or never.

I scooted to the edge of the seat.

It was time.

With everything I had, I lunged at Jones.

I slammed into him so hard, he fell to the floor of the chopper, blocking the doctors.

Using my extra speed, I grabbed Adam and dragged him to the door.

Took a deep breath.

And jumped.

28

I swore I heard Dr. Morgenstern scream, but the helicopter kept rising.

Adam and I fell through the air. Water slammed into my body. I lost my grip on Adam. Spun around. Lost which way was up. The cold from the water pulled me deeper. I forced myself to swim. Air. I needed air. I kicked harder and harder, broke the surface, and gasped for air.

Adam. I had to find him. I sucked in as much air as I could and dove under the surface. I reached out.

Nothing. Empty water.

I needed to go back up for more air. Then I collided with something solid. I grasped hold and used my extra strength to swim to the surface.

I pulled Adam's lifeless form on top of me and held him with my right arm under his chin, clutching his shoulder.

I kicked and pulled forward with my left arm. The shoreline seemed so far away. I pushed myself harder. The cold from the water made my teeth chatter and my muscles scream.

A little farther. Kick. Pull. Kick.

My feet touched bottom. I shifted so I was standing in the shoulder-depth water. I dragged Adam until I reached land. I pulled him out of the water and dropped to my knees next to him.

"Adam." I checked his neck. No pulse. "No. No. No. You can't be dead. Come on!" I pounded on his chest. "Damn you! You can't leave me. Not now. Not after everything we've been through." I pounded again.

No response.

I tilted his head back and to the side. Pushed hard on his chest. He coughed and groaned.

He was alive. I rocked back on my heels.

Adam sputtered and sat up and rubbed the side of his head where Jones had hit him. His handcuffs clanked together. I checked my pocket. I'd lost the paper clip and couldn't free him.

"What happened?" His voice was scratchy. He glanced around. "Where are we? Why am I wet?"

I pushed strands of his hair from his forehead. "We—"

Water splashed. I whipped around. Rollins broke the surface. Shit.

I glanced up. The chopper was long gone.

Then I remembered the Raspers. I jumped to my feet and yanked Adam with me. "We gotta go."

Rollins crawled onto the land. He coughed and hung his head. I had one chance.

I let go of Adam and ran to Rollins, and yanked my gun from his back before he noticed I was there. I hoped wet guns still fired.

Rollins struggled to stand and spit out a mouthful of water. "Damn doctor bitch pushed me out of the chopper right after you jumped. I knew I shouldn't have trusted her lying ass. How did you know you'd hit the lake?"

"I didn't." I let the words hang in the air. I hadn't aimed for water. Hell, I didn't even know there was a lake. I'd just thought my enhanced abilities would give us a better chance for surviving than if we stayed in the chopper with the doctors.

Rollins stared at me. "Well, hell."

The familiar feeling of extra eyes watching me crept across the back of my neck. I broke eye contact with Rollins. Spun around, searching for the Raspers.

"Val." Adam's voice cut across my nerves. I turned. The Raspers came out of the surrounding trees.

"Shit." Rollins grabbed a gun from his ankle holster. "Some of them were Secret Service."

The Raspers swarmed forward. Adam raced to my side. Rollins stepped closer to me.

We were outnumbered. Out of options.

Rollins fired and dropped one Rasper. They aimed their guns at us. Didn't fire back. Rollins took out another one.

I aimed the gun, but didn't pull the trigger. Dizziness made me sway. I blinked and focused on a dark suited Rasper.

Buzzing zinged through my head.

The thought that had been out of reach before finally became clear. Shivers darted across my skin.

I tapped Rollins on the shoulder. "Stop shooting."

He fired again.

"Stop."

He turned and the look in his eyes was beyond fear.

"Trust me. Stop shooting."

If I was wrong, we were all going to die. Hell, Rollins might be dead either way. He was right handed.

"Guys, stand behind me." I held the Glock loosely in my left hand.

I turned, faced the Raspers, and held up my right hand. "Stop."

"Val? What are you doing?" Adam's voice went high and squeaky.

Rollins shook his head at me. "That's not a good idea." He aimed his gun at the closest Rasper.

The Raspers all stopped and cocked their heads to the side.

"What's happening?" Rollins's gun shook in his hand.

Adam glanced between the Raspers and me. "Val?"

The buzzing increased.

Two Raspers with guns stood about ten feet from Rollins. His eyes were wide and a tendon on his neck throbbed. He was going to start shooting as if he was a one-man army. I needed to do this.

I took a deep breath. "Back away. All of you."

The Raspers all turned to focus on me. And at the same time, they all took a step back.

"What's happening?" Adam shifted closer to me.

My heartbeat launched into hyper-speed. The buzzing grew louder. A band of pressure tightened across my chest. This was it. My only chance. If I was wrong, we were dead.

"I need to send a message to whoever is in charge." My voice was full of authority and power I didn't possess.

Adam's body went rigid. He gave me a quick glance before staring at the Raspers.

A Rasper, dressed in a dark suit and holding a gun, stepped forward. The rest stood still and focused on me. I walked toward him and stopped when I was about a foot away from him. His yellow and cracked skin highlighted all the lines across his face.

I took a deep breath to center myself, but sucked in the sulfury scent of rotten eggs spewing from his mouth.

"I will not join your collective. If your leader wants to talk to me, she needs to come to me. I don't follow her orders. Do you understand my message?"

The suited Rasper nodded his head. "I do." His voice rattled with each word.

"You will not harm me, or these two men. Leave here and go tell her. All of you. Leave." I waved my gun at the group in a dismissive gesture.

The Rasper leaned forward and licked the air. He cocked his head and a look of confusion flickered across his face. He turned to face the others. They shifted to the left and right, leaving a path in front of him clear. He walked between the two groups.

The buzzing grew louder and louder. A loud zapping noise replaced the buzzing.

All the Raspers turned in perfect synchronicity and followed the Rasper who spoke to me. Within seconds they had run from the area.

The noises stopped. My heart rate slowed and the weight pressing on my lungs released.

Rollins's mouth hung open.

Adam turned to me with an expression of shock. Slowly his

face relaxed and his shoulders rounded. "You told them what to do. And they listened."

"What just happened?" Rollins relaxed his grip on his gun.

"I still have no clue why their 'queen' wants me, but I realized she must have ordered them not to kill me. Remember the one on top of the car who let go?" I searched Adam's face.

"Yeah. But—"

"And all the other ones. They weren't trying to kill me. They wanted me to go with them."

"If that's the case, I'll bet your message is going to piss off whoever's in charge." Rollins holstered his gun.

"I know. We don't have much time. And who knows if they'll listen to me again." I caught Rollins's gaze. "Which way is the camp? We need get back to the bunker and free Megan."

"She's not there." Rollins ran a hand across his bald head.

"What? Where is she?"

"General DeCarlo sent her to another bunker up north. He left orders for her to be executed if you two didn't help him. And before she pushed me out, Dr. Morgenstern ordered Zigotgen to recover your body."

My mouth went dry. "What's Megan's timeline?"

"I'm not sure."

My dad had always drilled into me that family came first. Megan had started out as my enemy. Then became my competition. She slowly became my friend. But after shooting the Rasper, freeing us from the cells, and risking her life for ours, I knew what she was. Megan was family. I faced Rollins. "We have to find her. Will you help us?"

Adam frowned and rubbed the bruised spot on his head. "Val, are you sure you want to trust him?"

"You heard him, Dr. Morgenstern pushed him out of the helicopter. He wants his revenge. The Raspers won't stop. And it looks like Zigotgen is hunting us too. We'll need him to find Megan."

"Honey, you told the aliens what to do and they listened. You're my new best friend. I'll go wherever you want. Here." He dug in his pocket and tossed keys at me.

I caught them and unlocked Adam's handcuffs.

"I need to figure out where we are. Stay here. I need to recon the area." Rollins walked away from the lake.

Adam stepped closer to me. So close.

"Val, we can get out of here. Run away somewhere." He clasped my hand and brought it to his chest. "We can leave him."

His heartbeat thumped hard and fast. I couldn't breathe. It was as if a knife stabbed me in the windpipe. I couldn't think. I wanted to fall into him and say yes to what he suggested, but Megan's face flashed before my eyes.

I glanced up at him and almost lost myself. "We can't. Megan. She's our family. Our responsibility. We can't fail her."

Adam ran his index finger down my cheek. "I know. It's just that...I didn't find you by accident. It was like I followed a beacon and it led me to you." He slid his fingers into my hair.

A shiver raced from the roots of my hair to my toes.

He leaned down and pulled me closer to him. Heat radiated off his body and wrapped around me. When his lips found mine, I forgot how to breathe. He slid his tongue across mine. My heartbeat pounded in my ears.

I forgot all about the Bugs, the Raspers, the doctors. About anything but his lips and the tingling sensation sizzling across my mouth.

Adam pulled back. "Val, trusting Rollins goes against your rules."

I laughed. "You know, I gave up on my rules the day I shot you." I glanced down at my arm and pushed my sleeve back. The words had faded to a gray outline.

He leaned down and brushed my his lips over mine. Another tingle shot through my body. I couldn't believe he was kissing me. *Again*. I didn't want the feeling to end.

He grabbed my hand. "Then we do this together."

"Together. And we can make new rules for a new beginning."

Adam squeezed my hand.

I squeezed back. My insides twisted and plunged as if I was falling into a dark abyss. Two kids and one soldier were going to fight a war against aliens, the military, and possibly more freak doctors at Zigotgen.

We had no hope of winning.

But first, we had to find Megan.

I tucked the Glock in my waistband. "Okay, let's do this. New Rule Number One, always fight for your family. It doesn't matter how much the world collapses, family is why we love, family is why we live, family is forever. Let's go get ours back together."

ACKNOWLEDGEMENTS

I first want to thank you, dear reader, for reading the beginning of Val's journey.

Writing is hard work. Sometimes, lonely hard work. Writers spend hours in their heads with only their pets and keyboards to talk to. But creating a book takes teamwork. I want to thank my team for helping me create this book.

I want to send a huge thank you to Kendall Grey. You were the first person, outside of my family, to read one of my manuscripts. Thank you for being kind and encouraging me back then when my story obviously needed so much help. Rock on, woman!

To my Readerlicious ladies: Brinda Berry, Kelly Crawley, Christina Delay, Susan McCauley, Abbie Roads, Jennifer Savalli, Carol Michell Storey, N.K. Whitaker, Jenn Windrow, and Sandy Wright. You are my friends and my go-to for daily advice and my sounding board. Thank you for being there for me.

To Randi Jo Flynn and Sarah Zettler, thank you for prioritizing your schedules so we could meet every other week. I love and cherish our meeting times. Thank you for all your words of wisdom, critiques, laughs, and for pushing me toward my dreams.

Jen Crane, I'm grateful for your beta-reads, your insights, your advice, and for being my friend.

My writing wouldn't be at the level it is without Margie Lawson. Margie, your teaching elevated my words and gave me the tools to push myself harder and harder.

Thank you to all those who have helped guide my words:

Jenna Grinstead, Suzanne M. Sabol, Eva Siedler, Sandy Williams. I treasure your insight.

Dad, Jo, Chuck Sr, Judy, Donna, Ernie, and Brenden: thank you for everything. For being my personal cheerleaders, and believing in me. I appreciate all the time you spent reading my words and giving me feedback. And I can't pay you back for all the help you provided so I could write or research or attend a workshop or conference.

Alex and Zack: You two are the shining stars in my life. You have both grown into young men I am proud to call my sons. Thank you for putting up with my moods and pizza for dinner when I was working hard. I love you!

And to Chuck: my soulmate, my best friend, my other half, my idea man, my echo editor, my unpaid assistant, I love you so much. Thank you for supporting my dreams and me.

ABOUT THE AUTHOR

Kathleen wrote her first story in elementary school about a pegasus named Sir Lancelot. It had no plot or conflict, but it sparked a dream. After serving a fifteen-year sentence in retail management, the bulk in big box bookstores, she turned her love of reading into a full-time career writing dark and haunting characters and stories.

She lives by the mantra that a day is not complete without tea. Lots of tea. Kathleen lives in Ohio with her husband, two boys, and two attention-demanding dogs. When not writing or editing or revising, you can find her reading, cooking, spending time with her family, or photographing abandoned buildings.

Follow Kathleen into the abyss.
www.kathleengroger.com
Facebook: Kathleen Groger Author
Twitter: @KathleenGroger
Instagram: kathleengrogerauthor
Pinterest: Kathleen Groger
www.Readerlicious.com

53353620R00183

Made in the USA
San Bernardino, CA
14 September 2017